Unwelcome

Books by Michael Griffo

UNNATURAL

UNWELCOME

Published by Kensington Publishing Corp.

Unwelcome

AN ARCHANGEL ACADEMY NOVEL

michael griffo

KENSINGTON PUBLISHING CORP.

www.kensingtonbooks.com

K TEEN BOOKS are published by

Kensington Publishing Corp.
119 West 40th Street
New York, NY 10018

ISBN-13: 978-0-7582-5339-2
ISBN-10: 0-7582-5339-7

First Kensington Trade Paperback Printing: September 2011
10 9 8 7 6 5 4 3 2

Printed in the United States of America

For Linda

Acknowledgments

Once again I have to express enormous gratitude to my agent, Evan Marshall, and my editor, John Scognamiglio, for their continued guidance and encouragement and their belief that my work was worthy of a sequel. And heartfelt thanks to my family and friends who are now my most enthusiastic fans.

one drop
two drops
three drops
four

water is mixed
with blood once more

shadows and light
on a crimson stain

will the sun prevail?
or will darkness reign?

prologue

Outside, the earth was cold.

The New Year brought with it an early frost, burying the past, at least temporarily, beneath a thick layer of snow. Archangel Academy was practically empty, most of the students spending their holiday break with family, so the campus was a sea of white, an enormous unsoiled blanket with only a few patches of brownish-green grass, bruised yet resilient, peeking out every hundred yards or so as a reminder of what was and what will be again. Tomorrow when classes resume, the sprawling blank canvas will be tarnished with footsteps, the imprints of students making their claims on the land, their own private piece of the world. Looking out from his dorm room window at the wintry landscape, a landscape that would soon be altered, Michael was once again amazed at how quickly everything can change.

Only a few months ago he was looking out of a different window at an entirely different landscape, wondering when his life would begin, when it would change. And now here he was, half a world away, his life transformed in more ways than he could ever have imagined or even thought possible. Sometimes he didn't know what was more incredible: the fact that he was a vampire or that he had a boyfriend. He looked over at Ronan sleeping in the bed that they shared, the moonlight making his skin look almost translucent, his thick black hair tousled like a little boy's, a faint smile on his full red lips, and Michael's breath caught in his chest for he was fully aware that Ronan and everything else that had happened to him since he left Weeping Water were the answers to his dreams. It was just that everything had happened so quickly.

He didn't hear the sound until a few seconds after it began, a sound like teeth, sharp and strong, clicking, chattering. It had started to rain and the raindrops, more ice than water, were hitting the window, striking it, as a welcome, a warning. That's why Michael loved the rain; it could be so many things. It could cleanse, destroy, interrupt, change. The first time he saw Ronan, it had rained. The memory of rainwater riding down Ronan's cheeks, clinging to his lips, still stirred feelings within the pit of Michael's stomach, still made him feel nervous and excited and passionate, still made him feel incredibly alive, even though technically he wasn't.

He watched two drops of rainwater travel down the window. One moved swiftly in a straight course from the top to the bottom, never slowing down, never hesitating, bubbling at the bottom of the window until it could no longer hold its shape, then bursting into the air to continue its journey elsewhere, maybe fall into the snow-covered earth below and wait for the rest of the world around it to melt. Or perhaps become something completely new, a glade of ice, hard, silver, and sleek.

The other drop of rain moved with caution, traipsing slowly to the left, then the right, pausing a moment almost as if to ask Michael toward which direction it should travel. But Michael had no advice, so the raindrop was forced to make its own decision. Slowly it continued to move down the window on a slight angle, hugging desperately to the glass so it wouldn't fall, so it wouldn't stray too far and too quickly from what it knew, moving in its own time. Finally, it reached the base of the window, long after the other raindrop had disappeared, and made the decision to stay, content in its travel, content to allow life to continue to move around it as it stayed unchanged, a simple drop of rain, nothing more, nothing less. For a moment Michael felt regret, just for a moment, but the presence of the emotion, no matter how fleeting, was profound because he was beginning to realize that nothing in his life would ever be simple again. Not even his reflection.

In the window, through the crisscrossing currents of rain, among the grayish-black shadows of the moonlight, he was reminded once again that his image was forever changed. Changed by a drop of red, one tiny drop of red blood that clung to his lip.

Before he came here to Double A, before he met Ronan, he would have thought a spot of blood would spoil his image, ruin it, but now he knew that it enhanced his reflection and gave him strength and courage and power that he had yet to fully comprehend and employ. He flicked the dash of red, the stubborn blood drop, with his tongue and savored the taste, the taste that reminded him of a feeding earlier in the day, the taste that reminded him of Ronan and of himself. And he couldn't help but smile. Michael thought how fascinating it was that something like the bitter taste of blood, someone else's blood, that a few months ago would have been repulsive is now a vital aspect of his life. And it was all because of Ronan.

Before Michael could turn to look at Ronan, a thunder-clap roared somewhere far above him, somewhere out of reach but somehow right next to him, and his gaze remained with the rain, with the cold, with his grotesque face. Because the rain, falling with more intensity now, had altered his reflection. He saw that he wasn't the Michael he remembered, the Michael he was still trying to hold on to, he was something different, something much, much different from who he was when he began his journey to this new place.

It was as if each drop of rain latched on to the window, sliding in a multitude of directions to create dark, watery veins that sprawled across Michael's face like sins as they begin to etch into a soul. His image, torn and dissected, heightened and distorted, looked back at him as if to announce, This is who I am now; that other Michael is no more. But strangely he wasn't afraid. He didn't know exactly how he felt, but he knew that this harsh truth didn't frighten him. Maybe it was because he was stronger now or because he was learning to accept the unacceptable. Or maybe it was simply because he knew he was no longer alone.

There was no more time to ponder his misshapen reflection or how his present was so vastly different from his past, because he heard his name. Ronan's husky whisper never failed to arouse Michael, never failed to remind him how lucky he was, how grateful that he was exactly where he was born to be.

"Michael," Ronan said, his eyes still half closed with sleep. "Where are you?" Michael didn't move, but he smiled. *His first thought is about me, the first word he speaks is my name.* It filled Michael with joy, and yes, pride. "Michael!"

"I'm right here."

The two boys stared at each other, Michael framed by the

first determined rays of the sun that demanded to be seen through the dark gray rain clouds, and Ronan sitting up in bed, his bared flesh almost as white as the rumpled sheets, his black hair a stark contrast. Reaching out his hand to Michael, he said, "Come back to bed." And Michael did because he missed Ronan's touch just as much as Ronan missed his.

Silently, the boys melded together as one, Ronan behind Michael, his strong, powerful arm wrapped around him, their hands finding one another, their fingers intertwining. A soft kiss on Michael's neck, a shiver down his spine, bodies moving even closer together, then Ronan's even breathing, a gentle rush of air every few seconds passing by Michael's ear, reminding him that he wasn't alone and that he won't be, not for the rest of eternity. A comforting feeling and one that Michael had begged for but never imagined would come. But it had come so quickly that sometimes, like now, his mind was filled with thoughts and emotions so powerful and conflicting that it was hard to fall asleep. So instead of sleeping peacefully, he simply held Ronan tighter around him and listened to him breathe.

chapter 1

After the Ending

Michael was being watched. He liked how it felt and so he kept his eyes closed even though he wasn't sleeping, hadn't been sleeping since he crawled back into bed a few hours before. He could feel the sunlight on his face, not strong, but enough to remind him it was morning and he could smell the fresh chill of rain that lingered in the air. January was colder than the locals had predicted, snow had already made several appearances, so Michael, like most sixteen-year-olds, preferred to stay in bed on a Monday morning rather than be up and about, getting ready for class. Especially since he had an audience.

Ronan loved watching Michael. It didn't matter if he was talking to friends, swimming, reading a book, or as he was now, pretending to be asleep, he cherished the view. And even though Michael's attempt to get a few more moments under the covers would result in his being annoyed when he'd ultimately have to scramble to get dressed and get to class on time, Ronan smiled at the boyish trick. He then decided one boyish game deserved another.

Leaning over Michael, Ronan let his tie dangle an inch over his boyfriend's face, swaying in the air like a benign pendulum, casting a thin horizontal shadow across Michael's cheek. Michael lay still. He could feel Ronan's presence, he knew what was coming, but he didn't move, because that would ruin the game.

Bending over even further, Ronan's tie scraped the tip of Michael's nose, but Michael still didn't respond. He didn't move until the endpoint of the tie brushed against his lips, then he smiled. He felt the silky material glide over his lips, his chin, his cheek, as if to say hello, good morning, it's time to get up. Then the tie began to fold and bunch up as Ronan lowered himself and brought his face closer to Michael's. Both boys were smiling mischievously now, knowing how their game would end, but Michael kept his eyes closed; he knew the rules.

"Who's there?" Michael said, purposefully adding a nervous tremor to his question.

Ronan lowered his voice as low as he could and growled, "It's the big bad vampire."

Michael opened his eyes and feigned a look of fear, but forced himself not to laugh. "Oh no, not again."

In one fluid movement, Ronan whipped off the blanket and sheets and jumped on top of Michael, his naked body now practically hidden by Ronan's larger frame. Then he did his best Dracula impersonation, "I've come to suck your blood." Instead of inciting fear in Michael, Ronan's imitation of the legendary icon made him laugh out loud, which it always did, and so Ronan continued to speak the way the count was portrayed in all the old movies. "You are not afraid of me? You do not fear my power?"

Ronan was many things, Michael thought, but a mimic was not one of them. "Not when your accent sounds more Jewish than Transylvanian."

It was Ronan's turn to laugh, hearty and buoyant, and he kept laughing while kissing Michael, wishing they could stay in bed all day exploring and enjoying each other's bodies, but they had to get to class, couldn't start the new semester off by being late for first period. Before he could drag Michael out of bed and make him get ready, however, he noticed something in his eyes, resistance perhaps. Could it be sadness, disappointment? "You're not still upset about your father, are you?" Ronan asked quietly.

Michael looked surprised and shook his head before he spoke. "No. I didn't expect him to call on Christmas, not after I told him I didn't want to spend the holidays with him in Tokyo." As usual, Michael's father changed their plans at the last minute and informed him a few days before Christmas that he had to go out of town on a business trip to oversee yet another crisis at one of his factories. Far from being upset, Michael was relieved. He was not looking forward to spending his break with Vaughan, not after the endless series of arguments and disagreements they'd been having lately. He was much happier spending every moment with Ronan. But Michael was bothered by something and he found it curious that he was actually still a bit disappointed by his grandfather's inaction. "You know, I kind of convinced myself that he would call either on Christmas or New Year's Eve," Michael confessed. "I am the only family he has left."

"Age doesn't make people wiser, Michael," Ronan said, brushing the smooth side of his tie against Michael's cheek. "Just makes them older."

Luckily, age was not something Michael and Ronan were

going to have to worry about. And for that matter, Michael thought, neither should education. "Hey, why don't we go see Germany today instead of hearing a lecture about it? Or what the hell, why not Tokyo?" Michael suggested. "I'm sure it's really exciting even if, you know, my father's there."

Oh, I can't wait to travel the globe with you, Ronan thought, *country by country, but those kinds of adventures will have to wait.* "We have forever for me to show you the world," Ronan said. "First we have to learn about it."

Underneath Ronan, Michael sunk deeper into his pillow, one hand pressing into the back of Ronan's neck, the other into the small of his waist. "That's 'cause you have a crush on Old Man Willows."

Taking the bait, Ronan pushed his body closer into Michael's, making the mattress bend even further under their weight. "No, but McLaren's bloody hot."

"I knew it!" Michael cried out in mock jealousy, slapping Ronan on the shoulder. "That's the only reason you like to read!"

"And if you want to read past a tenth-grade level, you need to get up now and get dressed," Ronan declared. "You've world history in fifteen minutes."

Thanks to his preternatural speed, a minute or two later, Michael was completely dressed, his clothes a bit unkempt yet presentable, and ready to leave, but still he was without his usual enthusiasm for education. "Seriously, Ronan, why do I need to go to school anymore?" Michael moaned.

The question surprised Ronan. "I thought you loved school."

"I did, but that was, you know, before, and, well, now . . ." Michael stuttered, then announced, "I'm a vampire."

"Um, so am I, mate."

"And you're also a student, which just doesn't make any sense."

Tucking Michael's shirttail into his pants, Ronan looked knowingly at his boyfriend. He understood his questions, his desire to be an active part of the world and not just read about it in a textbook, but he also understood that outside of Archangel Academy the world was different, it wasn't as safe, it wasn't as receptive to their kind and so, for now, this is where they needed to remain, to learn and prepare themselves for the world beyond the academy's borders. "We may be immortal, Michael, but we're not infallible," Ronan said, aware that his tone was dangerously close to patronizing. "If we want to prosper and lead, we can't be ignorant prats; we have to study, learn everything we can."

"You can teach me everything I need to know," Michael said.

Ronan blushed and thought how wonderful it was to have someone need him so much, someone who revered him, but no, he was forced to acknowledge that even he had limitations. "About being a vampire, yes, but Double A will teach you how to become educated." Michael couldn't stop his eyes from rolling. "And trust me," Ronan whispered, his lips a breath away from Michael's, "there is nothing sexier than an educated vampire."

Sitting in world history, listening to Professor Willows drone on about some military skirmish that lasted for a couple weeks over a century ago, Michael thought he would risk being the most unsexy vampire who ever walked the earth if it meant he could escape having to hear another one of his monotonous lectures ever again. Now that he was equipped with the armor of immortality, he shouldn't have to act as if he was like everyone else, like he had to follow rules. Oh, but maybe Ronan was right. *He has been a water vamp longer than me, but still, Willows's voice is just so grating, especially when he asks a question.*

"The Serbo-Bulgarian War, Mr. Howard," Professor Willows said. "Which side emerged victorious?"

Michael had no idea, but luckily he didn't have to know everything when he possessed other skills. Because of his inhuman dexterity, no one saw him flip through his history book and in less than a second find the answer. "That would be Bulgaria, sir, winning on November 28, 1885," Michael replied. "In just under two weeks, or, um, a fortnight."

If the professor was impressed that his student, who he felt certain was daydreaming, answered his question immediately, correctly, and with added information, he kept all thoughts of surprise to himself. His expression was as unexpressive as his speaking voice. "Hmm, yes, quite right." Just as Willows opened his mouth to continue his oratory, the bell rang signaling the end of class and mercifully, Michael thought, the end of his pain. Shoving his books into his backpack, Michael smirked. How thankful he was to have his vampire skills; it would have been a lot more painful if he failed to answer Willows's question correctly. His smirk grew as he silently remarked, *You may think I'm ignorant, Ronan, but I'm not stupid.*

"What do I think?"

Startled, Michael turned around to see Ronan standing behind him. "What are *you* doing here?"

Not exactly the greeting Ronan was hoping for. "I thought I'd walk you to your next class," he explained. "But what were you saying? I never said you were stupid."

Damn that telepathic connection. Michael would have to be more careful if he wanted to keep his private thoughts private. Smiling the way one boyfriend should smile at the other, Michael said, "I didn't say that." He kept smiling as he tried to think of a plausible explanation for his words, but couldn't, so he flirted. "If you're going to eavesdrop, sir, please do it right."

Whatever Ronan thought Michael had said no longer mattered, not while his beautiful green eyes were sparkling, not while it was clear that Michael really was happy to see him. "Well, sir," Ronan replied, "next time I'll be sure to try harder."

On their way across campus, Michael continued to smile, in part because he was walking alongside Ronan and in part because he was getting a little bit smarter every day.

Someone else who boasted a nontraditional kind of intelligence was Fritz. He may not be aware that creatures other than humans also called Double A their home, but when it came to social networking and interaction, knowledge acquired outside of the classroom, he was the smartest kid on campus. Running through the parade of students, Fritz finally reached Ronan and Michael and wedged himself in between the couple, pausing a moment to pant from his sprint. When he finally spoke, tufts of cold air emerged like crowns above each word, which was appropriate since his words were a proclamation: "At tomorrow's assembly they're going to unveil the new headmaster to replace Hawksbry," he announced.

"Really?" Michael asked. "So it's official, then; he isn't coming back?"

"Nope, just up and left town, the old sod. Not a bleedin' word to anybody."

Ronan knew that wasn't the truth, but he wasn't about to share the information. Let them believe that Alistair was simply irresponsible and grew bored with being sequestered in the countryside, or could no longer take the stress of being in charge of so many young lives so he left unannounced and without explanation. Better that than the truth, that he was either killed or, worse, transformed into one of Them, one of Brania's people. Ronan hoped it was the former, though based on one of the last conversations he had with the Headmaster, where he alluded to the fact that he knew the truth about Ronan and was disgusted by his presence, Ronan was led to believe that he had been turned into their kind. No need to mention any of that. He would keep those beliefs to himself and instead offer a new suggestion. "Maybe he finally found a totty and ran off to Las Vegas to get married."

Michael appeared confused. "Totty is, um, British for girl, right?"

"You're starting to catch on," Ronan said, happy that Michael could make him smile no matter what he was thinking.

"But you're not, mate," Fritz said. "Hawksbry's a pouf, you know that. We caught him red-handed with his hands all over that chauffeur bloke."

An image of Alistair and Jeremiah walking arm in arm down an alleyway in Eden pierced Michael's memory. "That's right, Ro, we did."

"If he ran off anywhere to get married, he and the chauffeur would've driven to Canada, which is like Vegas for you people!" Fritz laughed so hard at his own joke that his whole body shook and he slipped on a piece of ice on the walkway in front of St. Joshua's. If it weren't for Michael grabbing his arm and steadying him, he would've fallen flat on his back. "Quick reflexes, Nebraska," Fritz said. "I owe ya one."

Another change. Michael noted to himself that Fritz was becoming a real friend. Ever since Penry's death, they had been getting closer. And the closer they got, the more Michael realized his loud, abrasive exterior hid a loyal, thoughtful guy. He wasn't as innately kind or amiable as Penry was—very few of the students he met were—but he was proving to have worthwhile qualities all his own, the most obvious one being the ability to make Michael laugh. But unfortunately, thinking about Penry inevitably made

Michael think about his girlfriend, Imogene, which wasn't a laughing matter. "So, do you have any news about Imogene?"

Fritz shook his head, his smile gone, in its place a look of concern and apprehension, his dark bronze complexion growing pale. "Looks like she really did run away." Once again, Ronan remained silent while Michael and Fritz discussed how out of character that seemed. Imogene was not the type of girl to run from something. Whether it be a problem or an opportunity, she ran toward things. Even still, the police investigated the situation and concluded that that's what had happened; Imogene ran away from the trauma center either because it was something she had always planned on doing or as a result of Penry's death. It didn't make sense to either boy, but since the only other alternative—that Imogene could also be dead—was too painful to consider, both Michael and Fritz chose to believe the police department's official statement.

Let them believe in their own hypotheses, Ronan thought. *Sometimes ignorance is preferable.* It wasn't a luxury he could embrace, but he had learned to hide darker secrets; one or two more wouldn't matter. And what did he really know anyway? Only that Alistair was definitely not on his honeymoon, and Imogene wasn't a runaway. Ronan shrugged. "We may never know where either one of them is."

How did we get to talking about such unpleasant things? Fritz thought. *Isn't the first day back to school unpleasant enough? Must change the subject and must change it now; luckily, I always save the best piece of information for last.* "True, but I do know where one of our friends has been spending all of his time lately," Fritz declared proudly. "And the new and much older boyfriend he's been spending all of his time with."

*   *   *

What was that horrible smell? For a terrible moment, Nakano thought it was coming from him. He'd dressed quickly this morning, but he did remember to use deodorant, didn't he? Yes, of course he did; he wouldn't forget, not when he had an early morning date. Could the odor be clinging to his clothes? No, he just had his whole uniform washed; he felt like making a good impression for the first day of class. Oh, that was such a lie. He couldn't care less about his classes, about Archangel Academy even. The only reason he remained enrolled was because Brania told him that her father revered education and rewarded those who demonstrated academic excellence. No, the only reason he washed his clothes was to impress his boyfriend. And despite whatever that offensive smell was, he seemed to be doing just that.

Nakano thought Jean-Paul Germaine was, without a doubt, the most attractive man he had ever met. And what made him so incredibly attractive was that he was a man, not a boy, not a teenager, but an adult, twenty-one years old in fact. And of course absurdly handsome and French and, as of three weeks ago, his boyfriend. He never would have thought someone like Jean-Paul would be interested in dating someone like him, but as they snuggled in the backseat of his car, kissing quickly and impatiently, while his fellow students raced to their next class, there was no doubt, his boyfriend was very interested in him.

"I weesh you had a free period every morning," Jean-Paul said, his words sounding like the perfect lyrics to accompany the violin music that floated throughout the car.

"Me too," Nakano said. His words sounded harsher, more like gasps, sharp intakes of breath. *But that's okay,* he thought, *I'm still sort of new at this; I'll learn; I'll learn to be just as perfect as Jean-Paul.* The day's lesson, however, was over because just then Jean-Paul's cell phone rang, the dramatic, sweeping music of the *Nessun dorma* overtaking the soft violins and reminding Jean-Paul that while he was a boyfriend, he was also an employee.

"That's zee boss's ring," he said, with a resigned shrug.

"That's okay, I have to get to math anyway," Nakano said, trying to sound excited, as if he were expecting Father Fazio to unveil new and exciting revelations about geometry. From Jean-Paul's response, it sounded as if it worked. "Cool, math was my favorite subject." Straightening his clothes, Nakano decided he would really pay attention in class today; maybe the priest would provide him with some useful information after all.

As Jean-Paul focused on listening to his boss's instructions, all Nakano could concentrate on was that smell that was still lingering in the air. It wasn't Jean-Paul, that was for sure. He smelled like a man, simple and clean, like a just unwrapped bar of soap. This odor was sort of spicy and reminded him of that stupid American holiday, Thanksgiving, that he loathed because it was simply an excuse to eat all day long, and who cared about that? He sniffed deeply and it finally came to him: cinnamon! That was the smell. So foul, so pungent, so boringly human. He would have to remember to get Jean-Paul a new air freshener since he planned to spend a lot more time in the backseat of his car.

"I'll be there in fifteen minutes, sir." Jean-Paul snapped his cell phone shut and looked at Nakano intently for a moment before speaking, "I have to get to zee airport. Will I see you later?"

"I have swim team practice 'til six."

A smile appeared on Jean-Paul's face, lopsided, the right side higher than the left, and slowly his lips parted to reveal his tongue lazily brushing against his sparkling white teeth. "I'd love to see you in nothing but your swimsuit."

"Okay." Nakano heard himself say that one word and even though he knew it was a stupid, completely unromantic response, he couldn't think of anything else to add, so he kept quiet and hoped that the image of him wearing just his Speedo would occupy Jean-Paul's thoughts and not Nakano's inability to flirt.

They both got out of the car and walked toward the driver's side in silence, the only sound the soft crunch of snow under their feet. By the time Nakano got around the car, Jean-Paul was wearing his chauffeur cap, his straight, dark brown hair tucked neatly behind his ears, looking very important, like a man with a career. Nakano looked up until his eyes met Jean-Paul's and reminded himself not to slouch, to stand as straight as possible. Taller might make him look older, he thought, and even though Jean-Paul never commented on his age, never said anything except that a five-year age difference wasn't a big deal, Nakano couldn't help but feel like an imposter in his presence. As if he were the one part of this couple who didn't belong. But he was, he was part of a couple, he was Jean-Paul's boyfriend, and the way Jean-Paul kissed him good-bye was proof of that.

A frigid wind blew across Nakano's body, making his white shirt ripple, his tie fly past his shoulder, but he didn't feel the cold; he could feel only the heat that lingered from Jean-Paul's lips. Filled with energy, both nervous and unbridled, Nakano rubbed the back of his head briskly, hardly noticing the feel of the strong bone underneath, the coarse bristles of his crew cut flicking through his fingers, and watched Jean-Paul in the driver's seat, looking relaxed and professional.

"See you later," Nakano said, not even aware that his hand was still massaging his scalp.

"Yes, you will," Jean-Paul replied. He started to turn the car around and then suddenly stopped. "Have you ever thought about letting your hair grow out? I bet it would look très chic."

As Nakano watched his boyfriend drive away underneath the iron Archangel Academy front gate, he realized he had yet one more thing to think about.

The only thing Michael was thinking about was how happy he was that the first day of classes of the new semester was officially over. Now the fun could really begin, starting with swim team practice. The excitement of being part of a team still hadn't lost its novelty and for good reason. For the first part of his life, Michael was a loner, spending his time either by himself in his bedroom reading, thinking, dreaming, or at school acting as if it was his preference to stay on the outside looking in, to pretend that he didn't want to belong to any of the school's cliques. It was a lie. It was not at all what he wanted, but he felt that it was better to let everyone think he was independent and chose to be alone, instead of the truth, that his solitude was forced upon him. There were a few times in grammar school and at Two W, his old high school, when he tried to break through the wall that the other students had built around him, tried to make contact with someone, just one other person who might want to be his friend. But for whatever reason, he was never successful. He never found anyone who wanted to call him their friend, until he came here.

Here he was a starter on the swim team; he had attempted something and he had succeeded. Nothing like that had ever happened to him before and he was sure that Mr. Alfano, his old gym teacher, would be proud. He knew exactly what he would say to him—"Better late than never, Howard"—in a voice filled with more respect than surprise. Then Michael wondered what Mauro would have to say. How surprised would he be that Michael was an athlete now—correction, a star athlete. But wait, no, Mauro couldn't say anything because Mauro was dead.

On the other side of the gym, Michael saw Nakano dragging Mauro Dorigo's nearly lifeless body across the ground, the Weeping Water track in the background, the smell of blood in the air, and he had to shut his eyes tight to wipe out the memory. *It wasn't my fault,* he told himself. *I let him go; I was going to let him live no matter the consequences. It was him, Nakano. He killed Mauro. I wouldn't even feed off his blood. I couldn't, even though I hated, hated, hated him, I couldn't do that to him.* "Are you all right?"

The memory was gone and Michael was back in St. Sebastian's Gym, standing next to Ciaran. "You look, pardon the expression, a bit queer," his former dorm mate said.

Grateful for the diversion, Michael exhaled, unaware that he had been holding his breath. Forcing a smile, he replied, "Oh yeah, just a bit nervous, I guess, about getting back into practice."

Because Ciaran was both very perceptive and fully aware of Michael's history, he knew he was lying, but because he was also his friend and now an honorary member of his extended family, he didn't press the issue. "You'll be fine. Ronan tells me the two of you got in some practice over the break."

"A little," Michael admitted. "It was kind of fun, just the two of us here while everyone was away." It was Michael's turn to be sensitive. He didn't rattle on about how enjoyable it was to spend a few weeks alone with his boyfriend when he knew that Ciaran had to spend most of that time in Devil's Bridge, a small town in Wales with his stepmother and her relatives. Michael had been informed that this step-family was a bizarre clan who practiced alternative medicine and ran their own church and who, in Ronan's opinion, made water vamps look completely normal in comparison. Michael thought he would get to see Ciaran on Christmas at Edwige's flat in London, but Ciaran had decided to stay in

Wales since his stepmother, though hardly loving and affectionate, was slightly more maternal toward him than Edwige. Since she had spent most of the day lamenting how much she hated the pagan holiday, Michael thought Ciaran made the right decision. Still, he hadn't realized how much he missed his friend until just now. "But I'm glad everybody's back." Michael said. "I'm looking forward to a fun semester."

Ciaran glanced over at Ronan, who was chatting with Nakano. "One can only hope. If one happens to be the hopeful type."

Michael also saw his boyfriend talking to his ex-boyfriend and was happy to note that he could hardly feel the pangs of jealousy any longer. He had to be honest: They were there, but just barely. "Well, you know me, Ciaran. I'm Mister Hopeful."

Yes, you are, Ciaran thought, *hopeful and eager and filled with little optimistic rays of sunshine.* Ciaran stopped his sarcastic stream of unconsciousness. He liked Michael, he really did, but sometimes it was hard to like the guy who always gets everything he wants. "Well, it looks like all your dreams have come true," Ciaran said. "So why shouldn't you expect more of the same?"

That's right, Michael told himself, *so much good stuff has happened to me so far, in such a short period of time, why shouldn't I expect my lucky streak to continue? Because all good things must come to an end,* he reminded himself. *Nothing lasts forever.* Michael laughed out loud at his last silent and foolish remark. Not only some things but also some people last forever. Fortunately, Mr. Blakeley blew his whistle at the same time Michael laughed, so he didn't look like a total fool in front of Ciaran. Not that he had much time to worry about his reaction; within seconds, Blakeley had the starting team lined up for the first practice heat of the new season.

Ronan, Michael, Nakano, and Fritz each took their positions on top of their swim blocks, goggles on, bodies bent, heads down, arms stretched out behind them, no one daring to move a muscle until the loud blast of Blakeley's gun was heard. But Michael couldn't help himself; he was too close to Ronan, the magnetic pull between them too strong for him not to shift his eyes the tiniest bit to the left to get a glimpse of him before they were all underwater. He was glad he took the risk. In his arched position, Ronan's body was like sculpted white marble, his calves a solid curve, his thighs strong and thick, his right arm a series of rolling muscles. When Michael looked up to see Ronan's perfect profile, he was thrilled to see Ronan smiling back at him. He was trying to get one last eyeful of Michael as well.

While the echo of Blakeley's gun still reverberated off the walls and windows of the gym, the boys were already in the pool, stroking, stroking, stroking, left arm, right arm, deep breath, kick, kick, kick, each trying to win, each trying to claim the first victory of the season. Michael felt the cold water rush past him, envelop him, and he imagined he was swimming in the Atlantic Ocean off Inishtrahull Island toward The Well. He tried to swim toward the finish line with the same abandon and the same purpose. If he did, maybe he could get there first.

But Ronan was a formidable opponent. He had more experience and knew better than anyone on the team how to move with unabashed freedom in the water. And even though he loved Michael and wanted him to achieve every one of his goals, Ronan also hated to lose. Out of the corner of his eye he saw Michael had a slight advantage over him, less than half a stroke but a definite advantage, and Ronan was duly impressed. Not impressed enough to admit defeat prematurely, however. Using all his natural and preternatural skills, Ronan surged his body forward to pull ahead of Mi-

chael to come in first, which everyone, including Ronan, expected would happen anyway. No one, however, expected
Michael to come in second.

"Kano, you're slipping!" Blakeley called out. "You let
Howard beat you by two full strokes!" Before he could continue berating Nakano in front of the whole team, his cell
phone rang. Looking at the number displayed on his phone,
Blakeley grimaced and started walking toward the locker
room. Just before he disappeared from view, he hurled one
more barb over his shoulder. "B team, get ready so you can
show Mr. Kai how to swim like a loser."

Michael spit out some pool water he laughed so hard.
"Looks like I'm beating you in everything these days!"

Lifting the yellow goggles off his eyes and onto his forehead, Nakano stared at the pool water for a moment. There
were still little waves rising and falling all around him from
the race. He was confused by Michael's comment. Not by the
words; he knew they had nothing to do with swimming and
everything to do with Ronan, but by the tone. It was arrogant and smug. Nakano had been spending so much time
with Jean-Paul that he hadn't thought that much about
Ronan and less about Michael, and he thought everyone had
moved past all that, grown up a bit. Guess not. "Like I care,"
Nakano finally replied, in a quieter voice than Michael had
used. "I found someone a lot better than any of the boys here
at school."

Still feeling the power of the swim and obviously feeling
the pangs of jealousy more strongly than he originally
thought, Michael tried to keep his mouth shut, but couldn't.
Climbing out of the pool, Michael felt adrenaline pump
through his veins, he felt the water race down his face, his
chest, his legs, and the late afternoon sun penetrate the gym
windows and warm his body. He knew how he looked, like a
glistening young god, and he knew looking down at Nakano,

who was still half submerged in the pool, that he would think he looked like a god too. He took advantage of his superior position and hurled another insult at his nemesis. "Yeah, you had to go find some old man because nobody here wants you!"

Even if Ronan spoke out loud, he wouldn't have been heard, not with the roar of laughter that sprang from the crowd, but he knew Michael had heard him telepathically. Since Ronan created Michael and together they had offered their souls to The Well, they were linked; symbolically, they were one. However, they could also exercise free will and choose to sever that connection forever or for a moment, as Michael did now. He didn't want to hear Ronan's unspoken warning to back off from Nakano because he's stronger; he was strong too, didn't Ronan know that? He was stronger than ever before. And to prove his point, he pushed Nakano back into the pool just as he was on the top step of the ladder.

Although Ciaran couldn't eavesdrop on Ronan and Michael's telepathic conversation, he knew Ronan well enough to know what he would say. He also knew his words would not help Michael change his mind or his actions, so Ciaran grabbed Ronan by the arm just as Michael dove into the water after Nakano. "No," Ciaran advised. "He's got to learn on his own."

Propelled by a desire Michael didn't completely understand but couldn't resist, he grabbed Nakano by the ankle and, just as Kano's head broke through the surface of the water, pulled him back down. Caught by surprise, Nakano had time only to take a quick breath, hardly enough to fill up his lungs, but he wasn't concerned about that. He really wanted to know why he was being attacked. Motives would have to wait because Michael wasn't showing any mercy.

Nakano felt Michael's grip around his ankle tighten and in

the next second he was being hurled sideways with such force that when the back of his head hit the bottom of the pool, he thought he was going to black out. This wasn't just a game; this was a fight and one that Nakano was losing.

Michael couldn't believe he was winning; he really had the upper hand. After all those years being bullied, being afraid and weak, he was finally the stronger one, the one with the power, the one who could push people around, and he was happy to admit that it felt good. At least for a while anyway.

The third time Nakano kicked his leg, he was able to break free from Michael's hold and when he did, the force of the movement made Michael stumble back a bit and lose his footing, his arms rotating furiously to create two little whirlpools on either side of him. He placed his foot on the bottom of the pool to regain control and was about to push off to hurl his body into Nakano's, but what he saw made him stop. Nakano had decided to change the rules and not fight like two teenagers. He wanted to fight like what they were, two vampires who didn't particularly like each other.

Fangs hanging over his lips, eyes black as hate, Nakano lunged forward, and before Michael could swim out of the way, he felt two powerful hands around his neck. Immediately he was hurtled back in time, back to that other place that had caused him so much pain, back to being the victim, and he felt his body and spirit grow weak. He saw foul things in Nakano's eyes, things he didn't ever want to see again, things he didn't think a person would willingly latch on to, and he knew a bit too late that even though he had more power than he ever had in his life, there were still people, things, more powerful than he.

Somewhere in the distance he heard screaming voices, chanting, gruff and persistent. He wanted to hold on to those voices, use them to pull him up and out and away from this fiend who was attempting to kill him, attempting to finish what he had foolishly started, before it was too late. He felt Nakano's thumbs press harder onto his throat, push into his larynx, and he felt pain. He was a vampire. He wasn't supposed to feel physical pain, he wasn't supposed to be able to die—or could he? He had no idea; he wasn't sure of anything anymore except that he had to fight back and he had to fight back now.

He managed to wedge some fingers in between his throat and Kano's thumbs and instantly the pain was relieved; it wasn't gone, but it gave Michael a chance to regroup and regain his strength. Pushing upward, Michael was able to lift himself so both he and Kano were now vertical instead of horizontal. He looked right into the eyes of his opponent, the black lifeless eyes, and he saw his image. It was clear and strong and it wasn't alone. Ronan was right beside him.

Underwater, Michael turned his head to the left and then the right, but Ronan was nowhere to be found, except he was everywhere. "Use me, Michael," he heard Ronan tell him. "My power is within you." He then realized the image wasn't literal, Ronan wasn't physically present but a part of him, emotionally and spiritually. It was all the strength he needed. Using the force that Nakano was exerting to work against him, Michael released his grip just slightly so Kano, caught off guard, perched forward, giving Michael the mere second he needed to swing both his legs up and push them into Kano's stomach. Michael didn't wait to see where Nakano landed, he sprang up out of the water and let the air race back into his body. It was over. His first fight was over and he had won. Yes, he had some help, but he still won and that's all that mattered. Nakano, however, was not ready to concede defeat.

Climbing the ladder, Michael was about to step onto the gym floor when he felt a hand grab at his bathing suit and toss him back into the pool. He was so startled that he didn't hear Blakeley's whistle blow or the splash he made when he jumped into the pool to prevent Nakano from coming after Michael. It was due either to exhaustion or to fear of retaliation that Kano didn't fight back against Blakeley. He still wanted to teach Michael a lesson, but he knew if he let himself go and used his full strength against his teacher, he would suffer the consequences at the hands of Brania and the others. He was furious, but he was trying not to be stupid.

"I turn my back for one second and this is what happens!" Blakeley shouted. "You act like a bloody animal!"

Just as Michael emerged from the water, he saw Nakano pointing a finger at him. "He started it!"

The American? Blakeley found that hard to believe, it wasn't like him; he was, oh, what was the right word? Bookish, refined, whatever the word, he wasn't a bully and he didn't pick fights. Nakano on the other hand did. "Apologize."

Nakano was dumbfounded. "What?!"

It was Blakeley's turn to point a finger. "You know the rules in my pool! You start a row, you apologize."

"I told you I didn't start it!"

"Tell it to somebody who bloody well cares! Apologize right now or you're off the team!"

Glaring at Michael, Nakano wasn't able to conceal his hatred. It could be felt and Michael knew there was no way Nakano was going to apologize, so he had to make a choice: He could let Blakeley continue to think Nakano was the initiator or he could admit the truth. It was an easier decision than he thought. "I started the fight."

Oh, how Blakeley hated to be contradicted. "What?!"

"I'm sorry," Michael said. "It was me, I started it." Michael couldn't see Ronan, but he knew he was proud. "Nakano, I . . . I'm sorry."

That isn't good enough, Nakano thought. "What about you?" he asked Coach Blakeley.

The gym teacher wasn't sure he heard Nakano correctly, so he thought he'd give him a chance to rephrase his question. "Would you mind repeatin' that?"

I don't need this anymore, Nakano thought. *It's like I always suspected; they're all jealous and I am way too good and way too mature for this.* "You know something? I quit! I'm done playing with the boys!"

First everyone was speechless and then Fritz broke the silence the only way he knew how, with his trademark laugh. Nakano had barely fled for the locker room before, one by one, the rest of the students joined in and the gym was filled with laughter instead of shouting. Blakeley made a feeble attempt to quiet everyone down, but even he knew it was pointless, the students needed this release after such a tense situation, so being more practical than professional, he joined in. And when the laughter finally subsided, he announced the new revised team rosters. "Ciaran!" Blakeley shouted. "You're taking Nakano's place on Team A." Ciaran tried to act indifferent but wasn't entirely successful, gladly accepting the whoops of congratulations from his friends, and when Ronan grabbed him by the shoulder, he didn't pull away.

"Welcome to the big time, brother," Ronan said.

"Thank you," Ciaran said. "Or I guess I should really thank Michael."

Michael wasn't at all sure that he deserved thanks. In fact, at the moment he wasn't sure what he deserved. Blakeley was sure of one thing, though; he needed another swimmer. He studied his clipboard and then cried out, "Bhattacharjee!"

A slight Indian boy with a thick mop of black hair and reddish skin the color of sun-faded brick stepped forward from the crowd. "Yes, coach?"

"Amir Bhattacharjee, you're the newest member of Team

B," he announced. "This is your chance to make something of yourself. Don't screw it up!"

The cheering continued, and since he and Ronan were of different species, Amir thought it was safe to whisper to himself, but he was wrong. Ronan heard his words as clearly as if they were shouted. "Don't worry, Nakano, I'll make our people proud." Ronan didn't make the same mistake and silently remarked to himself, *Oh, well, one vamp out, another vamp in.*

"I don't know what happened to me." Showered and dressed, Michael needed to get away from the continued chatter and was staring out the ice-covered windows that encased the far wall of the gym, gazing at what could be seen of The Forest. When he thought about how dumb he acted, how reckless, he was embarrassed and confused and could hardly look at Ronan.

"You got a little carried away, it happens," Ronan said, knowing full well the temptation to want to use one's power, show it off, especially when it's new. "But you have to be careful."

Michael understood, he got it. He just didn't want to hear it at the moment, so he cut Ronan off. "I know."

Ronan allowed the silence to continue for a while; he knew Michael was upset with himself and he wanted to choose his words carefully. "C'mon, let's go home."

Just as Michael turned, he finally realized what the windows reminded him of. They were covered with large patches of ice that made them look as if they were being encased, protected, until the time was right for them to rejoin the world. Just like a cocoon that was about to burst open and unleash a new life. Michael knew exactly what that felt like.

chapter 2

From inside, it appeared as if the sun was winning. Despite the frigid temperature and the dark gray clouds that hovered over the grounds of Double A, one ray of light after another pierced the locker room windows to create a long row of sunshine. Dr. Lochlan MacCleery, sitting on one of the narrow wooden benches, his back facing the light, felt the warmth penetrate his tweed jacket and spread out across his hunched shoulders, down his back, up toward the nape of his neck. But despite the sunlight's heat, he still felt the chill. It wasn't the outside cold that made him shiver, it was Alistair's note.

Evil walks among the angels. The children must be protected. It must have been the fiftieth time he read it and he still couldn't imagine what the words meant. He had known the former headmaster for many years, the entire time he worked at Archangel Academy, and not once had he spoken so cryptically, so fantastically. No, Alistair was a logical man. *Like me,* he thought, *someone whose mind had a firm grasp on reality.* But could it be possible that Alistair discovered that their reality had changed, shifted in some horrific way?

"How can I protect the children if I don't know what I'm protecting them from?" Lochlan muttered to himself. He had started that habit about a month ago when it became clear that Alistair wasn't returning to his post, that he had decided to seek out a new life or was being held captive somewhere against his will or something equally preposterous, and he would have to ponder this mystery alone. Many times he wanted to reach out to someone for help, share this unwanted information in the hopes that perhaps a more fanciful mind might be able to uncover its meaning. But who could he possibly turn to?

He was tempted to confide in one of his colleagues even though he usually kept personal matters private, but he couldn't think of anyone he could fully trust. And he knew it would serve no good to turn the note over to the police, they would simply file it away as proof that Alistair was delusional, at best formally deem the abandonment of his post as the action of an academic in the throes of a midlife crisis, either way forever ruin his reputation. Lochlan knew that's what most people already believed, a dozen rumors were circulating among the students and the faculty, but gossip isn't as concrete as evidence, and for some reason the doctor felt that he needed to protect his friend's reputation. Because the more he dwelt on it, the more he was convinced Alistair would not willingly desert his students. "But what the hell happened to you?"

"Practicing your speech, MacCleery?"

The voice startled Lochlan so much that he sprang up from the bench with such force, he would have knocked it over if it wasn't bolted into the floor. "Whoa there," Blakeley said, raising his two hands in front of him as if Lochlan were a horse that needed taming. "If public speaking makes you this nervous, why'd you demand that you be the one to give the speech?"

Because I need to clear my friend's name, he thought. "Because I felt like it," he replied, trying to look and sound disgruntled and not panicky.

"Well, you hardly look like you fancy talking in front of a bunch of out-of-control kids," Blakeley observed. "Go out wearing that face and those juvies will make you wish you were back in med school slicing open cadavers." Lochlan never liked the gym teacher; he found him crass and loudmouthed. Now he disliked him for a new reason; he was also perceptive. Try as he might to put forth an earnest façade, an enthusiastic expression, he was clearly unsuccessful and couldn't fake that he was not only terrified to speak in front of such a large group of students but highly uncomfortable speaking about things he didn't fully understand.

"Don't waste your time worrying about me," the doctor hissed. "Try to figure out how to make something out of that miserable soccer team of yours." Now it was Blakeley's turn to look unnerved. A good insult always made the doctor feel better, so when he walked out onto the gym floor, he felt more confident than he had in days. But then he made the mistake of looking up into the bleachers and he felt the familiar chill slither down his spine. Every student of both Archangel Academy and its sister school, St. Anne's, was seated in the stands, looking directly at him, waiting for him to speak, daring him to say something important and profound. Before he got to the microphone, he cursed Alistair under his breath. "You better have a damn good reason for putting me in this position."

Michael leaned over to Ronan and whispered, "I didn't know this was going to be a health seminar."

Ronan smiled, thankful that Michael was in a better mood than yesterday. "It isn't supposed to be."

"Then what's MacCleery doing headlining the event?"

"I don't know," Ronan replied. "I think this is the first time I've ever seen him out of his office." Ronan was just as confused as Michael and because he never trusted anything the doctor said or did, he was also suspicious.

As Lochlan stood before the podium, adjusting the microphone so it was closer to his mouth, Michael surmised, "I guess we're about to find out why."

"Hello." Lochlan's voice echoed loudly throughout the gymnasium, followed by a shrill screech.

"Nice reverb, doc!" one of the rowdier students shouted, causing ripples of laughter to emerge from various spots among the crowd.

"Sorry," Lochlan mumbled. He glanced at the notes he had prepared, the words he had written about his friend that he wanted to share with the students so they could understand their former headmaster better, but when he looked down at the paper, he didn't see his handwriting. All he saw was the phrase that had been playing in a loop in his brain for the past several weeks: *Evil walks among the angels. The children must be protected.* He couldn't very well shout that into the microphone, so he remained quiet, which only caused the students to fill in the silence.

"What's up, doc?" Fritz cried out, causing Phaedra, who was sitting between him and Michael, to slap him on his knee. Fritz enjoyed hearing his schoolmates laugh at his outburst, but he was happier that Phaedra was getting more comfortable with him. Her touch felt deliberate and pronounced, not so light and airy as before.

"One of these days that mouth of yours is going to get you into trouble," she whispered.

"Too late for that!" he replied, not quite as softly.

Lochlan cleared his throat into the microphone to try and get the students to quiet down, but it only resulted in their imitating the doctor by coughing into their fists. Not used to such open defiance and blatant disrespect, Lochlan froze, he forgot about the note, he forgot about Alistair, and all he could think about was Blakeley's comment. Yes, right at this very moment, he would have preferred to be performing an autopsy on a badly decomposed corpse, preferably one of the students, than trying to form coherent sentences in front of a hostile group of teenagers. *To hell with protecting the children, Alistair. I'm the one who needs protection!* Which is just what he got and from a very unlikely source.

"All right! Put a bung in it!" Blakeley shouted into the microphone. "Or you'll all be back here this afternoon to run laps for detention!" Standing to the side of the bleachers, Sister Mary Elizabeth, headmistress of St. Anne's, backed up Blakeley's rebuke in the best way she knew how, with silent prayer. The combination worked and after a few moments the coughing stopped. Blakeley cupped his hand over the microphone and told Lochlan, "Now would you mind getting on with it? You're making my soccer team look like bloody national champs."

This time Lochlan didn't look up. He didn't risk it; he looked down at his notes, pushed all thoughts of angels and evil out of his mind, and read the words he had scribbled down last night. "Alistair Hawksbry was a good man," he began. "As headmaster he was fair and supportive and he worked tirelessly to make this school one of the best in the country." Feeling a bit braver, Lochlan looked out into the faces of the students but was again annoyed to see that many of them were talking to each other, laughing. A few were even taking catnaps. *Why, you ungrateful good-for-nothings! Don't you know how hard he worked for you?* he wanted to shout, *how desperately he wanted to enhance each one of your lives?* "He lived and breathed this school and he lived and breathed for every one of you!"

This time when Lochlan's voice bounced off the gym walls, the students didn't mock him; they were too stunned by his tone. Michael turned to see if Ronan was as shocked by the doctor's outburst as he was and he could tell by the way his jaw was clenched, how the little wrinkles had formed between his thick eyebrows, that he too was surprised. But Ronan wasn't surprised because of what Lochlan said or how he spoke, no, he understood the doctor completely, and that's what disturbed him. This was all the confirmation he needed, Ronan was certain, the headmaster was dead and the reason the doctor was leading the assembly was because that is what he suspected as well. "And just because he can no longer be with us doesn't mean he cares for you any less," he continued. "For as long as this school stands, Alistair Hawksbry will be a memorable part of it!"

The thunderous applause he imagined would follow never came. True, a few kids clapped, but weakly and without enthusiasm, and one kid did shout, "Hawksbry, we hardly knew ya," but for the most part the gym was silent. *Fine,* Lochlan thought, *if you don't care about your headmaster, then protect yourselves.*

Angrily he gathered his notes, shuffled them into a crumbled pile, and started to leave the podium but abruptly stopped when he heard Blakeley cough loudly into his fist. At first, he thought the gym teacher was mocking his previous attempt to quiet the crowd, but then he realized he was once again trying to help him, remind him of the reason they were having the assembly in the first place, the reason he was at the podium, to introduce Hawksbry's replacement. Grabbing

the side of the lectern tightly, Lochlan barked into the microphone, "Here's your new headmaster, David Zachary."

Once again, there was no wild applause after Lochlan
spoke, but something did happen. The sun that had been so
strong all morning, illuminating St. Sebastian's Gym with a
glow, golden and alive, was suddenly overtaken by the
clouds. In its place a gray pall crept into the room, the result
of the shadows that fell from the ice-covered windows and
sprayed out like cobwebs, splintered and dark, along the
gym floor. An eerie calm seemed to descend from the ceiling,
cloaking the students, rendering them speechless, and the
only sound that could be heard was the click, click, click of
footsteps coming from the locker room. With each step the
sound was getting closer, and with each step the anticipation
was growing. Lochlan surveyed the faces of the kids and his
anger grew, now they were attentive, only now were they interested. Gone were the apathetic expressions, the restless
body language; in their places were the faces of children
eager and hopeful, waiting to see what was walking toward
them, what would walk among them.

When Lochlan saw David Zachary enter the gym, he involuntarily clutched Alistair's note that he had shoved into
his jacket pocket. He felt the words throb in his hand as if
they were lifting off the page and burning into his palm, as if
his friend were using every ounce of strength he had to reach
out to him, connect with him from wherever he was. *This is
the reason I wrote the note; this is why the children need to
be protected.* The message ripped through Lochlan's mind
like a bullet obliterating every other thought that he had,
leaving only one meaning, only one belief, that this man who
was walking toward him was dangerous. And before the
doctor knew it, the man was standing before him.

The new headmaster was easily five inches taller than
Lochlan, but height wasn't the only reason he seemed to

dwarf the doctor, he was a strapping man, maybe thirty-five, maybe forty, but possessing a muscularity that couldn't be contained beneath the fine woven wool of his navy blue suit. His chest threatened to tear the soft cotton material of his white shirt and his tie—a collection of cream-colored flowers springing from delicate brown branches against a background of sky blue silk, the same color and texture as his eyes—floated, then fell with each breath. David held his chin level and smiled down at the doctor as he reached his hand out to greet him, but Lochlan was reluctant to let go of the note; he felt that if he did, he would lose the connection to Alistair, lose the meaning of what he needed to do. Unfortunately, he had no choice. And when he felt David's hand engulf his, it was as if he was being enveloped by something completely foreign and yet completely familiar. He felt as excited and defenseless as a child.

"Thank you, Lochlan, for that lovely introduction." The doctor didn't think he saw David's lips move, but he must have; he heard every word he said. His voice was smooth, soft, but compelling, and seemed to float in the air like a breeze that had no beginning and no end. Despite his immediate reaction, despite feeling that Alistair's words were trying to warn him about this stranger, Lochlan, like every other person in the room, was entranced by David Zachary's presence.

"He is, like, way hotter than Hawksbry ever was," Michael sighed. He couldn't believe he'd just admitted that to Phaedra, but it felt good to express such thoughts, the kind that he usually kept to himself and, anyway, it was the truth. The new headmaster looked like the pictures of those Norse gods he saw in books about classical mythology, fiery and imposing, with close-cropped red hair and a thin beard that didn't soften but accentuated his sharp cheekbones and square jaw. Phaedra didn't respond to Michael's comment, not because she didn't agree with him, but because she couldn't take her eyes off the man who now stood in front of the microphone, his two large hands placed on either side of the podium as if resting on the arms of a throne. Gazing out at the crowd, at his subjects, David didn't say a word, he merely smiled and nodded his head, only slightly, welcoming the students into his world instead of the other way around.

Amir was the first to applaud, loudly and without embarrassment, he didn't care if he was alone in his zeal. But he wasn't. Nakano, sitting next to him, quickly followed his lead, a bit miffed that he hadn't thought to start applauding first, so he made sure he was the first one to stand. Then one student after the other, followed by members of the faculty, all joined in until everyone in the gym was standing and cheering the appearance of the man who would signal a new era at Archangel Academy. Everyone except Dr. MacCleery and Ronan. MacCleery could not believe the reception this stranger was receiving, and Ronan couldn't believe he was staring at a face from his past.

David basked in the applause until he was certain that it would continue for as long as he would allow it. He raised his hand, and the cheering halted; a few seconds later he bent his arm until his palm was once again resting on the side of the podium, and everyone sat down, waiting, waiting, waiting, for him to speak. "Welcome to the family." The words landed on each student's ears as if they were a private message, hushed and secret, and each student leaned in to hear more. "These are the words my headmaster spoke to me when I was a student here many years ago and these are the words I speak to you now. Archangel Academy is more than a school, it is more than a place to learn, to grow, to be challenged. It is home." David smiled as he saw his words caress each face, wrap around each throat, burrow into each heart. "And now it is once again my home and I am thrilled and proud to return here, this time not as a student but as your headmaster." And then he noticed that his words had failed to penetrate one student, Ronan, who did not stare at him in admiration or awe. Ah well, that was what he had expected. What he didn't expect to see, out of the corner of his eye, was that MacCleery noticed it as well. But that was all right; the doctor could be handled. "With your support I will lead our home into the future and make it stronger than ever before. But the future can only be prosperous, it can only conquer, if there is a strong foundation and an unbreakable connection to the past."

Softly, David began to sing. The students recognized the words, but it was as if they were hearing them for the first time. *O feathered wings that soar above this land that we call home.* The school's alma mater never sounded so honest, so heartfelt, so perfectly fitting. *Immortal creatures filled with love protect us as we roam.* First Amir and Nakano and then a handful of others began to mouth the words along with David, eager to proclaim their unity, their solidarity with their school and their school's new leader. *Throughout this earth and back again over land and sea, guide us so we may return where we were born to be.* And now most of the students began to sing along, sincere and sober, without a trace of ridicule in their voices, without a hint that the words they were singing were not words that they completely believed in. MacCleery was stunned. The kids hated this song; they wrote parody lyrics to it, they mocked it the way kids are supposed to mock an ancient, outdated verse. What the hell was going on? *This hallowed ground, our resting place, Archangel Academy.*

When the singing stopped and the kids began to clap and cheer, Lochlan looked around at the faculty members, trying to gauge from their expressions if they were as alarmed as he was. Most of them were applauding along with the students, visibly impressed by David's ability to command authority, tame an otherwise unruly crowd. But not all of them. Blakeley looked skeptical, or was he just jealous that David had accomplished with a soft voice and well-chosen words what he could achieve only with shouting and threats? He glanced over at Sister Mary Elizabeth, her lips moving frantically. Was she praying? Did she too see through to this man's soul?

"Archangel Academy," David said, his voice breaking through the clamor. "May she live strong and may she live forever."

The pride that Michael had felt when he first walked through the iron entrance gate and stepped foot on Double A soil came rushing back to him, flooding him with an almost overwhelming sense of joy. But unlike before, when he wasn't sure why he was experiencing such euphoria, the thrill was accompanied with the knowledge that he was someplace special, somewhere that he belonged. He couldn't be happier or more grateful. And Ronan couldn't be more distressed. *He's buying this,* Ronan thought, *like every other gullible prat in the room.*

All around him, kids were shouting their approval, the memory of Hawksbry forgotten, ravaged with calculated ease, and replaced with something new, something better, something that Ronan knew couldn't be trusted. Perplexed, he turned to scour the crowd to find someone, anyone, who shared his concern, but it was useless. And then his concern grew to fear when he saw Brania sitting in the bleachers, dressed in a St. Anne's uniform.

She waved at Ronan like the schoolgirl she wasn't, wide-eyed and openmouthed, and shrugged her shoulders at the chanting that was taking place around her. She shook her head and spoke so that only Ronan could hear her, "Can you believe all the commotion?" Actually, Ronan couldn't. He turned to look at David, who was once again holding up his hand as both recognition of the glory bestowed upon him and reprimand that such glory was inappropriate, and when Ronan turned back to look at Brania, she was gone. His eyes flitted about the bleachers, but she was nowhere to be found, she was just someone else playing a game.

"Thank you," David said, his audience immediately quieting so as not to miss any of his words. "On behalf of Archangel Academy, it will be my pleasure to serve each and every one of you. And I know you, in kind, will welcome each and every opportunity to serve her." *You mean to serve you,* Ronan thought. When he saw Michael applauding with the rest of the students, he felt cold. He needed to speak with him, tell him that he was being manipulated, but he knew that nothing he said now would register, nothing would breach the bond David had so successfully and so quickly created. For now, Ronan stood alone, just like Dr. Mac-Cleery.

All around Lochlan, teachers, visiting priests, even his own nurse, were swarming David, trying to shake his hand, have a brief yet personal audience with the man, while the doctor stood back, his right hand once again shoved into his jacket pocket, clutching Alistair's note. "Bloody amazing, don't ya think?" Blakeley asked. Lochlan didn't know how to respond, so he just shrugged his shoulders. "I hate to admit it, doc, but I think we can learn something from this bloke."

"I already have," the doctor muttered.

As the students started filing out of the gym, the sun seemed to take back some control. Shadows were replaced with streaks of sunlight that brushed at the darkness, pushing it to the side, not completely disposing of it but making it less apparent, less compelling. Ronan fell into the crowd behind Michael and Phaedra, giving his boyfriend time to talk to his friend while he looked around to see if he could catch another glimpse of Brania. Usually, he went out of his way to ignore the girl, but today he thought she could provide him with some answers, make him understand what was going on here. However, he figured any conversation he had with Brania would only create more questions, because the problem with girls, as Ronan had come to realize, was that you never really knew what they were talking about.

"I'm glad you decided to stick around," Michael said.

Phaedra tugged at a curl that had escaped the hair clip she was wearing in an attempt to smooth out her otherwise wavy hair. "My work here isn't done yet."

Really, Michael thought, *what else could you possibly do for me?* Phaedra had come to Double A at the request of Michael's dying mother, to protect him, to make sure that he became what he was born to be. Phaedra had seen to that, she had done her job, Michael was now like Ronan, an immortal hybrid, a member of a rare species. What reason could she have to stay? Not that Michael wanted her to leave. Phaedra had become a good friend, one of the few people who knew him utterly, and one of the few people around with whom he could be himself, without any pretense. But didn't she already grant his mother's wish? Didn't she already prevent anyone from standing in the way of his destiny? Then he saw Fritz and it all made sense.

"Oh, now I get it," Michael remarked. "But I didn't think efemeras cared about guys."

Blotches of pink began to form on Phaedra's cheeks and she tilted her head so it almost touched Michael's. "Neither did I."

So Phaedra was now working for herself instead of him. That was fine with Michael. He found the man of his dreams, why not her? "He really is cute," Michael said. "You know, in that cocky, European sort of way."

"I know," she agreed. "It's like he thinks everything he says is brilliant just because he's got this accent."

Michael clutched Phaedra's hand and shook it. "Absolutey! Ronan's got the same thing going on inside his head." He glanced around quickly to make sure his boyfriend was out of earshot. "Makes me a little crazy sometimes." Then it was Michael's turn to blush. "But, you know, it doesn't make me love him any less."

Love? Is that what she felt for Fritz? She didn't know because she had never felt love before. She of course knew it existed, but from a purely intellectual viewpoint, she really didn't understand its meaning on an intimate level. Giggling to hide her anxiety, Phaedra realized that she had no idea what she was doing, she had no clue if she should be entertaining romantic thoughts about Fritz or about any other boy for that matter, but then she realized most teenage girls had no idea what they were doing either, so she should lighten up. *But you're not a teenage girl,* she reminded herself. Trouble was she didn't know what she was any longer.

"Well, you deserve it," Michael said. "After everything you've done for me and my mother, after everything you've given us, you ought to have some happiness of your own."

"I'm still here for you, Michael," Phaedra said. "Don't ever doubt that."

Michael was a little surprised to hear that, since he could have used her help yesterday to defeat Nakano, but even without her aid, it all worked out okay, thanks to Ronan. "The most important thing is this," Michael beamed. "If you like Fritz, you should go for it."

How could she possibly make him understand? He might be immortal now, above the laws of nature, but he was still a boy, still so young and inexperienced, he had no idea that there are rules that govern every aspect of the universe, every creature that inhabits it. Nothing is created without a limitation. "I guess," Phaedra replied. "It's just a bit confusing."

"First relationships usually are," Michael said, feeling like an authority on the subject. "But they can also be extremely liberating." *Look at me,* he thought. *I have no boundaries. My relationship with Ronan has freed me from a life filled with restrictions.* "Plus I have a feeling that Fritz can be a whole lot of fun."

Finally, something she could agree to wholeheartedly. "That is probably the understatement of the year." A statement that was about to be tested.

"Ulrich." The name pierced through the noise, interrupting their conversation, and making Fritz and all those around him stop and turn. When Fritz saw who had called out his name, his dark complexion turned white.

"Crikey," Fritz groaned. "Am I in trouble already?"

David walked, unhurried, toward the young student and was impressed with what he saw. Fritz stood taller than most, and although he was exotic-looking, he still exhibited that wonderful, youthful vigor David revered so highly. He was a perfect specimen, a good candidate, someone who might one day, if necessary, prove useful. *How opportune that today I shall reward him,* David thought. "No, you're not in trouble, son; on the contrary, I have a gift for you."

"A gift?" Fritz questioned. He wasn't the only one surprised. Michael, Phaedra, Ronan, MacCleery, even Sister Mary Elizabeth were surprised to hear that Fritz, one of the more unpredictable and cheeky students at Double A, someone who usually received detention, was being given a gift.

"There's a package waiting for you in my office," the new headmaster announced. "Plainly wrapped, but a gift nonetheless."

Looking around at the crowd, Fritz saw everyone staring at him. Some like Michael and Phaedra were happy for him, others of course were stunned, and then there were those who looked at him with more than a hint of jealousy, and oh how he liked seeing their expressions. How nice for a change to see people envious of his position, wishing they could trade places with him. Most of the times when he was singled out by an authority figure, it was because he had done something wrong, taken a joke too far, and was on the brink of getting publicly admonished, but this time was different. He was being rewarded with some sort of package, a present. Why, he had no idea, but he didn't care.

Until he found out where the present had come from.

"It's a gift from one of our fallen students," David said. "From your friend Penry."

The mention of that name was like rainfall on a flame. It silenced every flicker of light, every hope for warmth, and returned the world back to the cold, to the dark. Fritz stared at David, sure that he had heard what he said but unable to comprehend its meaning. Phaedra touched his arm gently to let him know that he wasn't alone in his surprise, his sadness, and Fritz, though he couldn't respond, was thankful.

"Forgive me," David said, not only to Fritz but also to the crowd that appeared just as speechless. "I didn't mean to cause you any pain, any of you. On the contrary, I thought it would gladden you to know that your friend, one of our own, lives on even though he is no longer among us."

No, because he doesn't live on, you stupid fool, Fritz thought. *He's dead.* Michael felt the same way except that he knew Penry wasn't merely dead, he had been murdered. He sought out Ronan, the only other person who could understand his grief, the only other face that could offer solace, but Ronan was focused on David. Why was he staring at him so intensely? Why did he look as if he were standing before The Well and about to transform? And why was Fritz running out of the gym?

Phaedra started to follow him, but David called after her, "Miss Antonides, I don't think that's wise." Had she not been so concerned about Fritz, she might have caught something interesting flash across David's face, something unnatural, but her thoughts were elsewhere. "The gift is for Fritz alone. And besides, I believe the rest of you have classes to attend."

For a moment no one moved until Blakeley shouted for everyone to file out. "Assembly's over!"

Using only his mind, Ronan told Michael that he had a free period and was going to the library. They agreed to meet later at St. Martha's during lunch period, but before Ronan could leave the gym, Lochlan grabbed his arm.

"Can I help you, doctor?"

"I think you can," Lochlan replied, his eyes involuntarily darting in David's direction. "Come back to my office so we can talk."

It was clear that the doctor distrusted David just as much as Ronan did, for entirely different reasons of course, but Ronan wasn't ready to enter into an alliance. "And why in the world should I do that?"

"Because I saw the way you looked at him," Lochlan hissed. "And you can trust me."

Ronan almost laughed in the doctor's face. "Since when?" Not waiting for a response and unwilling to be cornered any longer, Ronan walked away, leaving Lochlan to be swallowed up by the crowd exiting the gym. Just as Ronan was about to leave, he saw Brania once again sitting by herself in the bleachers, dressed like she belonged, waving. But this time she wasn't waving to Ronan, she was saying hello to her father. Without hesitation or concern, David waved back.

chapter 3

Luckily, Ronan had practice concealing his thoughts. It was one of the perks of being a vampire, but when he used the power, it didn't always make him feel like a good person because all he was doing, really, was hiding the truth. Like he had done all day with Michael.

There are certain things Michael doesn't need to know just yet, Ronan kept reminding himself, *certain things that he needs to be shielded from.* And since he created Michael, brought him into his world, Ronan could choose what he wanted to reveal to him, how much information, how much of his mind, he wanted to share. In The Well, their souls were joined together as equals; outside Ronan had the upper hand.

Watching Michael sleep, the angles of his face softened by the shade of the moon, his vibrant flaxen hair and the rosy color of his cheeks replaced with the black-and-white shadows of the night, Ronan thought he looked like a memory. So young, so innocent, so unprepared. "I have to protect him," Ronan heard himself say out loud. Then he remembered what he told Michael just the other day, that knowledge gives us power, and a part of him wanted to wake him up and tell him everything he knew about David Zachary. But what good would that do? Michael wouldn't fully understand or believe that David was anything more than a charismatic and passionate headmaster, a man who had come to Archangel Academy with no other purpose than to steer the students toward a more promising future. He wouldn't accept the truth, not just yet. David had made sure of that by using his immense power to dazzle his audience. No, he needed advice on how to handle the situation, and there was only one person Ronan could think of, only one person Ronan knew who would understand the situation. He gave Michael a soft kiss on his forehead and then left to see his mother.

Edwige was one of the few people Ronan couldn't hide anything from. He didn't understand her control over him, but he assumed it was simply the maternal connection between a mother and child, heightened because they were both vampires. She didn't transform Ronan, but in a very similar sense her blood ran through his veins, and that somehow bestowed with Edwige power over her son, it somehow allowed her to know what he was thinking when he was in her presence or even sometimes when they were separated. She didn't always care what her son thought—the thoughts of most people, in fact, typically bored her—but it was a wonderful tool to possess because Edwige always preferred to be in control.

"Do you think this painting would look better in a smaller room, my bedroom perhaps?" Edwige asked. "Then I could feel as if I were in the ocean as I drifted off to sleep; that would be comforting." Ignoring her son's presence, Edwige gazed at her prized painting and imagined how the cool salt water, a blend of deep, rich blues, must feel as it wrapped itself around the naked bodies of the two men. Actually, she didn't have to imagine. She knew exactly how the ocean water felt against a naked body; she had made the glorious journey to The Well of Atlantis each month for over a decade. And although for the most part she had made the journey alone, there was a time when she had a male companion. *It's been far too long since I've swum with someone by my side,* Edwige noted. *I think the time has come for a change.*

"Everything's changed, Mother," Ronan proclaimed.

Did he say something? "What? No, I think I'll keep the painting right here," Edwige announced. "It needs room to breathe." And Edwige didn't need to be reminded of loneliness each night as she drifted off to sleep. She did, however, need to be reminded that she wasn't alone.

"Are you even listening to me?"

"I have heard every word you've said," Edwige replied, without taking her eyes off the two male figures, the couple whose skin touched barely but permanently, in her painting. "There's a new teacher at your school, hardly earth-shattering, and hardly a reason to leave that beautiful boyfriend of yours alone in your bed." If Ronan could read his mother's mind he would have heard her final remark, that beds were meant to be shared, but since Ronan was having a hard enough time maintaining a verbal conversation with Edwige, it really was better that her private thoughts remained unshared.

"Not just a teacher," Ronan corrected. "The new headmaster."

Pressing her fingers to her temples, Edwige felt the onset of a headache. She dug underneath her close-cropped bangs, careful not to scratch herself with her newly manicured fingernails, and massaged her skin. The pressure felt good. It didn't alleviate the pain, not at all, but did add a layer of pleasure. And lately that's all she had been craving, pleasure, enjoyment, escape, but her craving went unfulfilled and instead she was presented with a child who, although the reasons were still foreign to her, had a problem. "Well, someone had to replace that other one who left."

"Hawksbry didn't leave, Mum, he was killed and you know it!" Ronan charged. "You've always known it!"

"Will you stop yelling?!" Edwige demanded more than requested, clutching her forehead. When she spoke again, her voice was softer, but unmistakably filled with disgust and impatience. "Turned into one of Them or killed by Their hand, what does it matter? Either way it's eternal damnation." Finally she turned to her son, hoping her action coupled with her words would be perceived as a dismissal. "Now, if that's all the news you have to dispatch, I think it's time you left. It is, as you children say, a school night."

Sometimes you really do have to talk to her like she's the child, Ronan thought. "Brania's father is the new headmaster," he announced.

Imperceptibly, Edwige's expression changed. "Why didn't you say so?" Turning her back on Ronan, she walked across the room to the small glass and steel minibar. She lifted a stout pitcher, clear except for delicate etchings of fish that randomly adorned the circumference, and poured herself a glass of water. It was the one liquid her kind could drink, and even though she wasn't thirsty, she did need time to think. The water tasted clean, fresh, not nearly as intoxicating as blood of course, but it served its purpose, it gave her a moment to make her son think his news hadn't startled her. "You must learn to present the most important piece of information first instead of, pardon the pun, vamping."

Ignoring his mother's jeer, Ronan pressed on. "So you agree that this is important, we're in danger?"

"I would hardly say we're in danger," Edwige replied, the glass making a louder clank than expected when she placed it back onto the surface of the bar. "It means just as you said, Brania's father is your new headmaster."

Why does every conversation with her have to be so frustrating? "And why in the world would he take on that role if he didn't want to hurt us, if he weren't trying to make some sort of statement?" Ronan asked.

Why does every conversation with him have to be a challenge? "David has always acted like a little boy," Edwige said, sitting on the acrylic Ghost chair next to the bar, her fingers absentmindedly stroking the smooth, clear armrest. "So it's quite fitting that he would want to be the leader of an all-boys school."

Ronan started to pace the room. How could he make her understand that this situation wasn't funny; it was potentially lethal. "He's already a leader," Ronan cried. "Of our enemy!"

Edwige pointed a finger at her son, the red lacquered nail aiming at him like a blood-tinged arrow. "They are not our enemy. Are you forgetting the truce?"

"They broke the bloody truce when they killed Penry!"

"That human was not one of ours!" Edwige hated to lose her temper with her son, but she also hated to hear her son talk like an idiot, she had raised him to be so much better than that. *He has such potential,* she thought. *His destiny could be limitless, if only, if only he would end this asinine fascination with the lower classes.* Rising from her chair, looking as statuesque as her petite frame would allow, she softened her voice and approached her son. "I know you are fond of these people; you consort with them and you find them to be useful, entertaining, which I will admit they can be, at times, but you must remember that we are not like them."

"But we used to be," Ronan said, sounding more like a child than he cared to admit.

"Past tense," Edwige stressed, then added with unequivocal authority, "We are unto ourselves."

The space between Ronan and his mother was suddenly drenched in shadows and silence. *Could their differences ever be bridged?* Ronan thought. *Yes, of course, we're different, better in so many ways, but the reason we're better is because we're connected to our past, to our humanity. Has she really lost sight of that? Does she really think we exist, that we could exist, without that link, without being bound to humans?* Staring out the window of Edwige's flat to the world below, Ronan saw some people walking in the darkness, scrambling to get somewhere, to someone, and he thought of Michael sleeping alone in his bed, and he suddenly ached to be alongside him, breathing in his smell, drifting off to sleep, secure, loved. He thought of his friends and his teachers, the people he spent his days with and learned from, and it was so clear to him that a contract was broken when two of those people were murdered. Why couldn't she see that?

"They killed both Penry and Alistair without cause and there was no retribution from either side," Ronan said quietly. "They hate water vamps, and now their leader is in control of Double A. This cannot be good for us."

One minute stupid, the next perceptive. Edwige didn't know if her son was contradictory because he was a child or a man. "David's kind has always hated us; that is nothing new," she allowed. "But the murders of your friend and your former headmaster, while unfortunate and unnecessary, were not declarations of war."

"Just the first steps toward the acceptance of one."

She was not going to win this argument. She was not going to convince her son that there was nothing to worry about, that David was just playing an innocuous game because he woke up one morning and decided that he wanted to do something different. So she chose a new tactic. "You have a point."

"I do?"

"A muted, not entirely substantiated point, but a point nonetheless."

Oddly, Ronan felt ambivalent at hearing Edwige agree with him. That is what he wanted, confirmation that his instincts were correct, but if they were, if he did understand what was going on, what David was trying to orchestrate, it only meant that they were all in serious trouble. "Really? Are you sure?"

He was definitely more of a man. Give a man exactly what he asks for and still he's not satisfied. Honestly, would she ever understand that gender? Would she ever be given the chance again? Edwige caught sight of herself in the oval, frameless mirror that hung over the bar, and inspected her reflection with a bit more intensity than usual. Her hair, still very short and very blond, was flattering, and her unlined face looked youthful without appearing innocent. She knew she was enticing to men, she wondered, however, if she would ever find one man who could entice her and satisfy her needs.

She heard the din of Ronan's voice and knew he was talking, knew he was asking questions, formulating theories, but she couldn't tear herself away from her image or her thoughts. Recently, she imagined that she could have found satisfaction with Michael's father, Vaughan, but she was too late, Brania got to him first and transformed him into one of Them. So even though he was quite handsome, extremely handsome actually, he was, what was the polite word? Contaminated? Yes, and in any case, no longer available. She glanced over to the mahogany box on the table next to the window and realized that whenever she thought about men, she inevitably thought about him. Yes, there had been men in her life other than Saxon, but none of them ever satisfied her the way he did, even if she led them to believe otherwise.

"Oh, David, I have never felt this way with another man before." She remembered speaking the words to Brania's father years ago, before she became financially independent, before it became unnecessary for her to rely on anyone other than herself, and she recalled how surprised she was that he believed her. Men really are daft. They really only hear words, not subtext, intent, falsehoods. But Edwige had been speaking a kind of truth—she had never felt as repulsed or demoralized than when she lay embraced in David's arms— so she shouldn't be too harsh on the man. He accepted what she said; he just never suspected her words had a less flattering meaning.

In the mirror, she saw Ronan behind her, staring at her imploringly, and she suddenly realized that she needed to be challenged as a woman and not just as a mother. She loved her son, but it was time she made him leave. "I don't believe there is cause for alarm," Edwige said, turning to face Ronan. "But I do believe there is reason to be careful."

"So what should I do?"

"You should go home and get into bed next to Michael before he wakes up and notices that you're gone," Edwige instructed, then she answered his next question before it was asked, "And no, do not tell Michael who David is. Sharing that knowledge at this point will serve no purpose."

Ronan understood what his mother was saying. He agreed with her, but in spite of that, he felt uneasy. *That's because you're going to lie to your boyfriend,* Ronan reminded himself. *Not lie, just protect. Oh, stop it!* He didn't want to contemplate his decision any further, he didn't want to argue with himself, he just wanted to know what his next action should be.

"But what about David, what should I do about him?"

"Nothing," Edwige instructed. "You treat him as if he is simply what he says he is, Archangel Academy's newest ruler, and I will keep an eye on him."

For the first time since the assembly, he felt more calm than anxious. No matter how frustrating, how infuriating his mother could be, she really never let him down. He might not understand or agree with how she treated others, but he could always trust that she would help him.

"And by the way, his name's not David O'Keefe anymore," Ronan said. "Now he's going by David Zachary."

Edwige laughed. "Of course he is."

David examined his reflection in the mirror and was pleased. The centuries had been kind. He had seen firsthand that immortality did not always guarantee physical resplendence, so he was grateful that he looked as he did when he first converted, even better if he dared say, and why shouldn't he? There were very few around to contradict him. And even if one of the old-timers, if one of those who knew him from that period disagreed with his current assessment, they wouldn't risk contradicting him. They knew what the consequences would be.

He was equally delighted with his office's décor. The furniture was of the old-world, thick, substantial, built by craftsmen who knew their trade, quietly ornate but supremely functional. Things should be beautiful, but they should also have purpose. He especially loved the anteroom to the office. The forest green walls were the perfect counterpoint to his red hair, and standing now in the center of the room, he was reminded of the holiday season that had just passed. "I am like Father Christmas," he said, laughing along with his re-flection. "Revered, immortal, and the giver of so many gifts." He laughed harder, making his reflection distort even more than usual. In the mirror, his blue eyes were a ghastly shade of charcoal, his formidable frame hunched and lop-sided, his creamy complexion stained and, in some areas, burnt. "What is reality and what is perception?" he asked himself. The only response that came was another laugh, this time sinister and without any suggestion of a light heart. "And how have you angels survived without me for all these years?"

David's eyes traveled around the mirror's elaborate, carved oak frame, from archangel to archangel. He was filled with a glut of emotions, not all of them good, and one by one he surveyed the spiritual creatures, casting his eyes upon their likenesses as if they were long-lost relatives. David glared at the figure of Gabriel, his lips forming a sneer to ex-press his rejection of the archangel whom he condemned as loud and ostentatious. His eyes then fell upon Uriel and Ramiel, whom he thought of as more resourceful angels since they used fire and thunder as their weapons, and Raphael, whom David viewed as weak, but allowed his eyes to linger long enough to admire fully the splendid curvature of his muscled arms.

Next he focused on Sariel, whom he appreciated for pro-tecting the dead but acknowledged that he was nothing more than a collector of bones that were the spoils of someone else's victories and, therefore, a disappointment. And then he stared at the one he truly loathed, the thing known as Michael. So much glory, so much recognition, and why? Be-cause Michael was a narcissist, God's pet, a minor player who demanded praise for one questionable conquest. The fact that Michael had outshone them all for eons in the courtroom of public opinion enraged David, but all that anger, all that resentment was forgotten when his eyes landed upon Zachariel. His reflection softened and for once appeared vaguely human as he looked at the carving of the deity who was, according to David, the true sovereign of the archangels.

He was astounded. Even while resting against a wooden replica of the sun, that magical orb, Zachariel's face shone brighter than the others. He exuded warmth, wisdom, and incomparable power. Power that was given to him by the great sun itself. His upturned chin, sharp eyes, and unsmiling mouth were a welcome to those who were worthy and a warning to those who were not, a notice that their time had come to an end. "I am the embodiment of you," David said with reverence. "And I have taken your name out of honor and in sacrifice."

David traced the outline of the sun that framed Zachariel's face, gently, cautiously, afraid the wood might disintegrate from his touch. But he was unable to resist. He commanded his courage to rise and he let his fingers fall across Zachariel's hair, his cheek, his eyes, the eyes that had witnessed more beauty, invoked more fear, than David could ever hope to. "I have returned here to uphold your commandments, your principles," David whispered into the one small wooden ear that was visible, and then abruptly pulled back from the sculpture and closed his eyes. When he opened them again, the beautiful blue irises were gone; so too was any indication of white. All that covered both surfaces of his eyes was black.

As David stared into the wooden eyes of his namesake, it was unclear whose were more lifeless but obvious whose were more consumed with vengeance. "And I will not rest until I rid our land of those who do not belong, those who have tarnished our legacy," David seethed. He closed his eyes and when he reopened them this time, they had resumed their color. Once again they were sparkling blue, as if reborn. Tenderly he kissed Zachariel's lips, feeling not wood but the breath of eternal life. "Oh, Father," he sighed. "It is so good to be home."

When he heard the joyful singing fill the air and invade his private ceremony, David believed it was confirmation, a message to him from Zachariel that he approved of his plan. He could not have been more pleased.

And Michael could not have been more disturbed.

"Ronan?" Michael wasn't completely awake, but one quick look around the room and he knew he was alone. He glanced at the alarm clock on the nightstand and saw that it was a little after two A.M. Where could Ronan be? And what was that sound? He had heard the singing in his dream. He and Ronan were resting on the beach, Ronan sitting against a dune, Michael leaning into him, their eyes closed, not thinking, only feeling, feeling the beautiful music. Now awake, he heard those notes again, soft, lilting, and, most of all, familiar. "Is that you?"

Michael lifted open the window and peered out, ignoring the bitter cold breeze, and scoured the trees in search of the music's origin. Could it be? Could it possibly be the meadowlark that traveled with him from Nebraska? The same lark he heard from his bedroom window back home? Who witnessed Michael and Ronan emerge from the ocean after offering their souls to The Well? He hadn't heard his beautiful melody since that day and it brought him such delight to know his friend, his companion, had returned.

Throwing on some clothes and sneakers, Michael left his room and ran downstairs. He couldn't resist; he had to get closer to the music and see if he was right. But when he walked outside, he forgot about his mission; he was overwhelmed. He felt as if he had stepped inside peace. Overhead a full moon shone brilliantly, its grayish-white light luminous, making the night sky look like an immense sheet of black velvet in contrast. Michael couldn't believe how luxurious it looked, he wanted to wrap himself in the night, let the texture of the unknown embrace him. Just when he didn't think it could get any more perfect, the sky changed. Speckles of light appeared in the darkness like tiny silent firecrackers, and Michael thought the stars had come out of hiding, but it wasn't stars. It was snow.

Slowly, Michael watched pieces of white fall from the darkness, floating without care, without concern, their only ambition to touch the earth. He looked up and smiled as the first snowflakes landed on his cheeks, his nose, moist and cold. He didn't mean to impede their journey, but he was compelled to make contact, so he stuck out his tongue and savored the fresh taste of winter, laughing at how childish he was acting, but loving every second of it.

And then he heard a noise.

The sound took away his youth and immediately he remembered who and what he was and the kind of danger that existed in the world in which he now lived. Then in the next moment, he remembered what kind of protection also existed in his new world and, calmer, yet still heedful, he waited for the fog to come, to encase him and separate him from whatever was out there in the darkness. But nothing happened. The fog didn't appear. The darkness wasn't joined by mist. He was still alone. And now even the music had stopped.

The noise, however, was getting closer.

Standing near St. Joshua's, David could no longer hear the music. He had followed the sound for as long as he could, drawn to its notes, its melancholy, but as abruptly as it began, it ended, replaced by the silence only nature could produce. David stood motionless in the snow, his arms outstretched like a forgotten scarecrow in an abandoned field, and accepted the chill as it penetrated his skin, the white flakes as they fell freely all around him, and he listened to the quiet.

Until it was interrupted.

He stared into the night, through it, using his preternatural vision like a beam of light to illuminate the dark. With no movement of his head, his eyes darted left, then right. Nothing. Although he was certain the sound came from the direction he was facing, he quickly turned around and scoured the area behind him. Still he could see nothing, alive or dead, nearby.

And yet he heard the sound again, this time even closer.

Phaedra, I need you! Michael didn't speak the words but shouted them inside his mind. He had never called out to Phaedra before, never asked for her help because he never had to, whenever he was in danger, she appeared. But now, just like the other day in the swimming pool, she was nowhere to be found. Why was she abandoning him? He had no idea if she could hear him, but he called out to her again, and still no response. Didn't she just tell him she would continue to protect him? Was she somewhere with Fritz right now, preoccupied, concerned with her own pleasure and not his safety? Michael didn't want to prevent Phaedra and Fritz from starting a relationship, but seriously, wasn't this the reason efemeras existed in the first place, Michael thought, to respond to the silent pleas of those in need? Then again, perhaps there was no danger; perhaps he was just overreacting. When he heard the growl, he knew his first impression was correct.

Involuntarily, he felt his fangs descend and his eyes narrow. He watched his fingers elongate and the space in between them turn into webbing; he felt the leather of his sneakers stretch and he knew the same change was happening to his feet. The beating of his heart quickened as his body prepared for battle even while his mind prayed a fight would never come. He hated feeling this way, apprehensive, no, that wasn't being completely honest, he was afraid. Still afraid like the boy he used to be. *What's the use of being immortal if I'm afraid to defend myself? If I'm afraid of being defeated? If I'm just the way I always was?*

His fear was short-lived, however, and replaced by the will to survive when he was struck from behind.

Breathing deeply, David recognized the scent, it was one of his own. Pungent and thick, it quashed the more appealing aroma of the snow-filled air and, for a moment, David was greatly annoyed. He hated wanton intrusion. But one of his children was restless or possibly in trouble and like every good father, he had a duty to come to the aid of his child, to offer comfort and, of course, punishment if that was deemed necessary.

When he got to a clearing and saw what was happening, saw that Michael was being attacked from behind, he knew there would be no need for punishment or reward, but merely intervention.

Michael felt his fangs cut into his lower lip as his face crashed into the snow, small droplets of red tarnishing the otherwise white landscape. What was happening? Who was on top of him? Of course, it had to be Nakano! He knew that he wasn't going to allow Michael to get away with embarrassing him in front of his classmates, forcing him to quit the swim team. He wanted revenge, and Michael stupidly gave him the perfect opportunity by wandering outside alone.

He felt Nakano's hand grab the back of his head and he knew that if he didn't escape, if he didn't get out of this position, his head was going to be bashed into the ground until his skull shattered. The anger he felt breathing down his neck was that potent. Michael had no choice, so he allowed his instinct to take over. Instead of fighting against the fear, he let it fill him, he let it consume his mind and his heart so he could take action. Reaching back, his hand over his head, he grabbed ahold of Nakano and pulled at his hair until he heard him cry out in pain. Michael pulled with all his strength and he could feel the strands of hair stretch, forcing with it Nakano's scalp. He had to keep pulling until Nakano couldn't take the pain any longer and fell off of him so he could be free. But wait, no, something wasn't right. Nakano's head was practically shaved; he didn't have hair long enough to pull.

Someone else was on top of Michael, someone else who just wouldn't give up. Until that someone was ordered to.

David admired loyalty, but this action was premature, he did not want death to mar his homecoming. And it was not well planned. Death, like life, should have purpose. Just as David gave the command to release Michael, he heard the roar. He had to admit that it was a touching sight, Ronan coming to the aid of his young companion, but he felt a greater sense of relief watching his devoted subject scamper away, on all fours close to the ground, like a wild animal. "Good, you were unseen, which means you cannot be prevented from trying again," David said. "When, of course, the time becomes right."

"Did you see who it was?" Michael asked, his breathing beginning to return to normal.

Ronan shook his head. "What are you doing out here?"

What *was* he doing outside? He tried to remember, but he

felt as if he was in a trance. "Music." Yes, that was it. "I heard music and I thought it was . . . so I came out here to find out . . . I . . . I couldn't find you. . . . Where were you?"

Ronan felt the tears sting his eyes. *If I'd returned just a few seconds later, you might not be alive; if I hadn't gone out at all, you would never have been in danger.* "I wasn't where I was supposed to be," Ronan cried.

David turned away, not interested in watching the two boys embrace, one comforting the other, and started to walk back to his office when something else just as irritating caught his eye. "Those damned roses," he hissed. "Will they never die?"

Along the outside of St. Joshua's Library, as always, was a row of white roses in full bloom, their petals soft and shimmering despite being sprinkled with snowdrops. David yanked one out of the hardened ground, its roots dangling between his fingers, and slowly crushed it in his hand, smiling cruelly like an angry child clutching a fly in its tiny fist.

Michael looked into Ronan's eyes and knew that he should be angry with him for leaving him alone, but he couldn't. He saw in his expression such tenderness, such gratefulness that Michael was safe and unharmed, that all he could feel was the love that had been in his heart from the moment he laid eyes on Ronan. Kissing his boyfriend under the moonlight, the snow tumbling around them, Michael felt like both a man and a child, aware of the passion burning inside of him and relieved to be held by someone stronger, someone he could always trust.

Opening his fist, David stared in disbelief as he watched the crumbled rose spring back to life, reclaiming its robust form. *Some things just cannot be trusted to stay dead!* It was then that he felt her presence. Startled, he looked around and, for the first time in decades, no, more like centuries, his confidence waned. He couldn't see her, but that didn't matter, he knew she was there.

He wasn't the only one who had returned home.

chapter 4

Phaedra stared at Michael. Michael stared at his food. Neither of them spoke a word.

It just won't work, Michael silently complained. He was attempting yet again to make his shepherd's pie disappear from his plate, master a vampire trick that would fool others into thinking he was eating when all he was doing was making his food evaporate by using his preternatural vision as a sort of laser beam. It was a handy trick that Ronan had been trying to teach him, that Ronan could execute with the skill of a bored magician, but Michael just couldn't do it. He knew it was a necessary alternative for times like now, when he was sitting at a crowded cafeteria table in St. Martha's and it wasn't possible to use his incredible speed to toss his food to the side, but no matter how hard he tried, his uneaten meal remained on his plate for all to see. Aggravated, he glanced at Phaedra sitting across from him and thought he should ask her for help. She was, after all, the expert at transforming solid matter into thin air, but then he realized she was the real problem. How could he focus on dematerializing his lunch when all he could think of was how much he wanted to confront her?

"Why didn't you answer me last night?" Michael blurted.

Phaedra didn't understand the question. Maybe she didn't hear him properly; the lunch room noise was quite loud. "What?"

"I called for you. I really needed your protection, Phaedra, but you never showed up," Michael explained. He then pushed his plate aside, abandoning all pretense of trying to make it look as if he were eating and leaned in closer to his friend to whisper, "This is the second time you abandoned me."

Looking into Michael's eyes, Phaedra could tell he wasn't being dramatic or exaggerating. Looking into her heart, she knew he was telling the truth. As much as she didn't want to admit it, something was happening to her, something unforeseen, and it was preventing her from helping him. "What do you mean, the second time?"

Michael recounted his fight with Nakano in the swimming pool the first day of the winter semester and then last night's encounter. He emphasized that both times Ronan came to his rescue so there was no real harm done, but he couldn't stop himself from reminding her of what she told him. "You said you were still here for me."

"I am!" Phaedra cried, sounding as if she were trying to convince herself even more than Michael. "I'm sure if there was any real danger, I would have heard you."

"Well, I didn't realize I was in any real danger until, you know, my head was being bashed into the ground," Michael said with a heavy dose of sarcasm. "And by then I figured it would just be better to take my chances and fight back instead of waiting for the cavalry."

Stunned, Phaedra could barely respond. "I'm sorry, Michael," she stammered. "I had no idea."

Now that Michael had said what he wanted to say, albeit with a lot more aggression than he had expected, he felt bad seeing Phaedra so upset, truth was she had helped him survive many other perilous situations. "Clearly our communication skills suck," Michael said, trying to lighten the tone of the conversation. "Why don't we come up with a code word? Something super specific that's just between the two of us so there's no way you won't know it's me." Michael thought for a moment and then exclaimed, "Something like Mykonos, where you said you were born!"

Phaedra was only half listening to what Michael was saying, she was too busy hearing her own voice berate her, call her things like selfish, embarrassing, dishonorable. The only reason she existed was to protect, and if she couldn't do that properly, well, then maybe she should leave, return. But no, she didn't want to think about that; she was definitely enjoying her time here on earth. She had forgotten how many exciting adventures this planet had to offer and she had never inhabited the body of a teenage girl before. It was a good fit. No, she wanted this to work. "That sounds like an excellent plan," she said finally. "Our own private code word. I'm sure that will solve everything."

"Perfect," Michael said, glad that Phaedra was so agreeable and that his harsh words didn't put a permanent kink into their friendship. And then again, not so perfect. Doubt breached his confidence. If Phaedra couldn't hear his panicked pleas, what made him think she would hear some lame code word? He knew that made sense, but maybe all she needed was a reminder, make her remember that the main reason she was here was to keep him safe. Even if it was very clear that she had other things on her mind. "So, um, how are things between you and Fritz?" Michael asked.

From one controversial topic to another. Despite that, Phaedra couldn't hide her smile. "Things between us are okay."

Not exactly the exciting bit of gossip Michael was hoping to hear. "Just okay?"

"Well, you know *boys,*" Phaedra joked, stretching the word into three syllables. "It's sometimes hard to know what they're thinking."

Michael knew all about that. He had spent the first sixteen years of his life keeping his thoughts to himself. Yes, boys could be a mystery, even boys who seemed pretty easy to read, like Fritz. "You know, I haven't known Fritz very long, but I have noticed a change in him lately," he said. "I think it's all because of you."

Phaedra hoped so, but hoped for what exactly? What could she possibly expect to hope would happen, that she and Fritz would become a couple and live happily ever after? There were no guarantees in her world. No matter how badly she wanted to stay, the decision wasn't up to her. At any time she could be called to return to the Holding Place to await someone else's prayers. *But no, until then I'm here.* Pushing away all disagreeable thoughts, she ran her hand through a clump of curls and confessed, "I was hoping to get to see him today, though. It's not every day that I get to have lunch here, you know, on the boys side of town."

During the winter months, the restrictions about commingling were loosened. If a St. Anne's student had a class near St. Martha's before or after her lunch period, she could eat here instead of walking all the way over to St. Leo's, the girls cafeteria on the far end of campus. Sister Mary Elizabeth made the change a few years ago when she realized, despite the long-standing rule separating the sexes, most of her students were sneaking into St. Martha's anyway. "I hear the food over at St. Leo's isn't nearly as good as over here," Michael commented, then caught a glimpse of his abandoned, yet full, plate. "Not that I would really know the difference anymore."

Giggling, Phaedra nodded. "I don't think Leo would either; he was a big proponent of fasting."

"Was that before or after he sampled the cuisine?" Michael asked.

While laughing at his own joke, Michael tried to inconspicuously look around the room and then at his watch. He thought for sure that Fritz would be somewhere in the cafeteria; this was his lunch period too. But then again, maybe he got another detention. "Maybe he's avoiding me," Phaedra suggested.

"Avoiding you? That's ridiculous," Michael countered. "Have you seen the way he looks at you?"

"Well, yes," Phaedra admitted, but she was still unsure. "I know I don't have a lot of experience, but things seem to be moving a bit slowly."

Slowly? Michael couldn't imagine Fritz moving slowly, taking his time getting to know Phaedra. He thought for sure he'd be trying to get as close to her as quickly as possible. Then again, his mother did once tell him that things and people aren't always what they seem. Maybe Fritz was really shy when it came to girls. That would be ironic. "Maybe that's for the best," Michael declared. "It'll give you time to get used to the whole boy-meets-girl thing, especially since in your case it's really boy-meets-girl-who's-really-an-efemera sort of thing."

No wonder Ronan fell in love with him so completely, she thought; *he finds joy in the most unexpected places.* And most unexpectedly, Phaedra saw something that brought her joy as well. "Let's keep that efemera thing under wraps for now," she whispered. "Fritz and company at two o'clock."

When he reached the table, Phaedra saw that Fritz's expression was not really what could be described as joyful. In contrast, Ciaran, sliding onto the bench next to Michael, wore a smile that was a marked improvement over his typical serious countenance. "Behold a gift from beyond the grave," Ciaran announced theatrically, his hands unfurling to gesture the small box Fritz was holding.

"I told you that isn't funny, you twit!" Fritz barked.

It also didn't sound like Ciaran, Michael thought. He guessed that making first string on the swim team had turned Ciaran the Serious into Ciaran the Cheerful.

Whatever reason for the change, he held his ground. "You, Mr. Ulrich, need to lighten up and accept the fact that inside that box is something quite wonderful."

Dropping the box on the table, Fritz looked quite the opposite, as if it contained hideous secrets that could harm mankind if they were unleashed on the world. Grunting something unintelligible, he plopped down next to Phaedra, forcing her to scoot over quickly or risk being used as a seat cushion. *This is what I was hoping for,* Phaedra thought, *to share some time with a grouchy boy?* "Fritz," Phaedra started, "is there, um, anything wrong?"

Fritz heard her, but his eyes didn't move from the box. "No."

Phaedra and Michael looked at Ciaran, who obviously knew what was in the box and therefore the cause of Fritz's funk and tried to get him to tell them what was going on without actually asking him. After a moment, it was clear that Ciaran's communication skills also sucked. "Ciaran!" Michael said. "Are you going to tell us?"

"Tell you what?" he innocently responded.

"Why this one's face is scraping the floor," Phaedra declared, pointing her thumb in Fritz's direction.

"Do you mind, mate?" Ciaran asked. In response, Fritz barely shrugged his shoulders, which Ciaran took as a yes. When he spoke, it was once again as if he were standing center stage. "This ordinary box that you see before you contains none other than a gift from the other side, from Penry." Finally, communication was no longer a problem. They both understood why Fritz was looking so dour. He was upset thinking about his friend. Reaching into the box, Ciaran took out what looked like a stack of magazines and handed one to each of them. "Gather round, folks, and take a look. I give you comic books, from the creative team of Poltke and Ulrich."

Fascinated, Michael examined the cover of the handmade comic book he was holding, a colorful and fairly accurate depiction of Archangel Academy. The twisted metal of the front gate seemed almost lifelike, the dimensions of the headmaster's office slightly more askew, and the selection of colors, orangey reds and purple-blues, definitely personal choices and not meant to be natural depictions. And right there in the bottom right corner of the page was Penry's name. Dear Penry. Even though he was no longer with them, he still made Michael smile. Just seeing his familiar curvy handwriting delighted him because this was something about Penry he never knew before. He wrote a comic book, and according to Ciaran, he wrote it with Fritz, though he had to take his friend's word for it because the signature that appeared about an inch lower than Penry's was barely legible.

"I see your penmanship hasn't improved," Phaedra commented.

For the first time since he sat down, Fritz looked away from the box and into Phaedra's eyes. "Penry was the artist. I just came up with the jokes," Fritz informed them. "And the title."

Tales of the Double A, Phaedra said, reading from the issue she was holding. "What a cute title!" *Oh, come on, Phaedra, what teenage boy wants to be cute?* "It's, you know, really great," she corrected. "And, um, very mysterious."

"Intrigued me enough to read every issue," Ciaran announced. "And you all know how much I hate to read anything other than a science textbook."

"So when did you two do all this?" Michael asked.

Fritz explained that it was something they created for an assignment in art class as freshmen. They enjoyed working together and of course making fun of their fellow students and teachers in the name of art, so they had continued, spending most of last summer whipping out one issue after the other. "Penry's twin sister, Ruby, sent them to me," Fritz said, his voice suddenly much more subdued. "She thought I should have them."

"That was very thoughtful of her," Phaedra said. "It's a wonderful gift."

"You know what would be even more wonderful?" Michael asked rhetorically. "If you write more issues, you know, to maintain Penry's legacy." Silence was the first reaction to Michael's suggestion and then one by one they all agreed. Ciaran thought it would be a proper memorial, Phaedra thought it would be a lovely way to keep Penry's spirit alive, Fritz was just impressed. "Once again, Nebraska, I owe ya one."

The next few minutes were spent discussing some possible story lines for the new issues. Fritz's suggestions of a zombie infestation, werewolf attacks, and an alien invasion made Michael and Phaedra feel quite normal. Ciaran's idea to make Penry a superhero to swoop in to save Double A from certain destruction was met with enthusiastic cheers, and Fritz immediately came up with his superhero name. "I'll call him The Double P!" It was a silly name, but Penry Poltke knew the importance of being silly, so they all thought it was an ideal moniker.

Fritz admitted that he wasn't as good an artist as Penry, but luckily he was taking another art class this semester, so he would have a chance to work on his technique. The text wouldn't be a problem, though, since Fritz was, in his own words, a bloody amazing storyteller. "So much for humility," Phaedra joked. Fritz blushed and was now staring at Phaedra with the same intensity he had formerly reserved for the box. Michael sensed it was time to give the couple some privacy.

"Ow!" Ciaran squealed. "Why'd you kick me?"

Seriously, Michael thought, Ciaran might be a borderline genius, but when it came to social skills, he was definitely coasting along at a remedial level. "We need to clock in some study time in the library."

"Study?" Ciaran asked. "For what? The semester just started, you can't possibly be behind in your homework already."

Make that pre-remedial. "Will you just come with me," Michael snapped, stuffing the comic book into his backpack. "Fritz, I'll give this back to you when I'm finished."

Although Ciaran missed the reason for their hasty exit, Fritz and Phaedra understood what Michael was doing and were both appreciative. Now they could be alone. Sure, they were in a crowded lunchroom and there was activity all around them, but still, just sitting next to each other felt incredibly intimate. *No wonder girls like to fall in love,* Phaedra thought. *It really is a wonderful experience.*

"So, uh, how do you like your new classes?" Fritz asked, his fingers tracing the tight waves in his hair.

"They're good," Phaedra replied quickly, her fingers pulling at her own curls, making them longer, straighter. "Religion is interesting. Sister Mary Elizabeth has a crazy sense of humor."

"Really?" Fritz said, tossing one of Michael's leftover French fries into his mouth. "Would never have expected that."

And a few months ago, Phaedra would never have expected to be sitting across from a boy, entranced by how he chewed his food. His lips pressed together, moving rapidly, his throat bulging, rising, then becoming calm once again. She wished she could say the same thing about her heart. "I'm finding that high school is bursting at the seams with the unexpected."

Phaedra didn't see Fritz's lips part and form a huge smile. She had lost the courage to look at him and was focused on the plate of food. Suddenly, taking it slowly made total sense to her; it was much more fulfilling and much easier on her heart than some quick, messy physical connection.

Nakano, however, would disagree.

Nakano loved kissing Jean-Paul. He loved how the razor stubble on his older boyfriend's chin grazed against his face, roughing it up a bit. He loved how he could run his fingers through Jean-Paul's hair, watch the long, shiny brown locks extend, separate into smaller strands like the strings of a harp, then fall, quietly, gracefully, back against his cheek. And he really loved how Jean-Paul's lips tasted, eager, hungry, the bitter taste of blood alive in every kiss. Ronan's kisses hardly ever tasted like blood, only if they snogged right after he made a visit to that bloody Well of his. Who wanted to be a vampire if you could only feed once a month? Didn't make any sense. Now this, this made sense, this felt right, Jean-Paul's soft, lean body on top of him and the hard, concrete basement floor underneath.

"I'm glad you could sneak away," Jean-Paul said, his mouth nuzzling against Nakano's throat.

That tickled, but he forced himself not to laugh. "I didn't sneak out so we could talk."

Jean-Paul paused for a moment. His dark eyes glistened, contemplated like a snake's, and he smiled at Nakano, a smile that was much more like a leer, and suddenly Nakano looked a lot older than sixteen. "Then why don't you make me shut up."

Feeling as if he had hit the jackpot and couldn't spend his money fast enough, Nakano clutched the back of Jean-Paul's head and pulled it close to him. Their mouths embraced, their tongues flickered passionately, nervously, and Nakano relaxed enough to allow his body to respond to Jean-Paul's grinding movement. How in the world did he ever get so lucky? And why in the world did it have to end?

"Hello, boys."

Nakano pushed Jean-Paul off of him so harshly that when he fell onto the floor, a small thud echoed throughout the hideout. Across the room, Brania was standing, visually eavesdropping on their private moment but feeling more like a guardian than a voyeur. "Oh, please don't stop on my account."

"Could you maybe knock next time?" Nakano asked, his cheeks flushed.

The clicking of Brania's heels reverberated throughout the dank room, little pieces of metal stabbing the concrete floor, as she walked toward the one table in the room and tossed several envelopes of mail onto its cold, smooth surface. "Come now, Kano, you know I hate to announce myself," she reminded him. "I prefer simply to arrive."

She really thinks she can do whatever she wants! "Well, in the future, could you arrive when we're not here?"

Jean-Paul had tucked his shirt back into his trousers and smoothed the loose strands of his hair behind his ears, so he looked, once again, as crisp and clean as if he were standing next to his car, ready for duty. He touched Nakano's shoulder as a way to silence him, but it didn't work. "I don't know what kind of crazy stuff you get into, but Jean-Paul and I prefer it to be just the two of us!"

How the times had changed. When Brania was a teenager, in years and not merely looks, rebellion was unheard of. She listened, she obeyed, and she hoped that her actions were deemed favorable, hoped that she had pleased and impressed her elders. Today, sadly, it was just the opposite. She watched Jean-Paul caress Nakano's back, his slender fingers sliding up and down the space between his shoulder blades. She imagined his touch was soft but insistent as he tried to remind Nakano that he was in the presence of such an elder. That helped. At least someone in the room, someone other than herself, understood that she was more than what she appeared to be.

"Apologies, Brania," Jean-Paul said. "You caught us, how do you say? Weeth our pants down."

Two out of the three people in the room laughed. Remaining silent, Nakano rolled his eyes. *No, our pants were not down; we were just kissing, just trying to feel some warmth during a free period so when I go back to that prison everybody likes to call a school, I won't feel so miserable. But you two wouldn't understand that,* he thought. *You two get to do pretty much whatever you want. Your lives aren't controlled by school bells and class schedules and writing reports on subjects that have absolutely nothing to do with real life.* Panting, Nakano didn't notice that the laughter in the room had subsided. His mind, like his breathing, just kept racing, stopping only when he heard Brania speak. "I would never stand in the way of true love, or whatever is taking place between the two of you," she said. "But a word of advice: My father is not as understanding. So please practice caution if not restraint."

Turning to go, the only thing that prevented her from leaving was the music. And the only thing that prevented Jean-Paul from answering his cell phone was the glaring look she gave him when he was about to flip it open. *Small pleasures, that's all I ask for,* Brania reasoned. Swaying to the music, her fingers played with the hem of her black wool miniskirt and raised the material an extra inch. She closed her eyes and soon she was far away from this place, the concrete floor replaced with sand, the ceiling lifted to reveal an uninterrupted ribbon of blue, and each breeze that floated through her hair carried with it the most exquisite melody. Along with the harshest scream.

"Jean-Paul!" Vaughan shouted. "How dare you not answer my call!"

When Jean-Paul saw that his boss, impatient and unused to such blatant insubordination, had entered the hideout in search of his unresponsive employee, he remained calm, unruffled. It was Brania who became livid by the interruption and shouted back, her voice quite a few decibels higher, "How dare you screech over Puccini!"

Despite her interference, despite being the obvious reason his driver wasn't doing his job, Vaughan couldn't take his eyes off of Brania. *She really is a voluptuous creature, not like Edwige, not at all like Edwige.* Now why the bloody hell was he thinking of that one when Brania was standing right in front of him? These women were going to drive him round the bend, he just knew it. "Vaughan," Brania purred. "What a pleasant surprise." And he was right.

Stab, stab, stab, one metal heel jabbed into the ground after the other as Brania walked toward Vaughan, the music silent now except for the tune that continued to play in her mind. She stopped only when she was a few inches away from him, closer than he expected, and she saw his shoulders stiffen in response. She knew what she had to do. "Why don't we take advantage of the moment," she proposed, "and go up to dead Jeremiah's apartment to play?"

Completely ignoring the fact that the last time they were together, Brania rebuffed his advances, and the fact that he had pertinent business to attend to, Vaughan felt his head nod in agreement and his legs start walking toward the staircase that led upstairs. Just before she closed the door behind her, Brania called out, "Have fun, boys, but do remember my warning."

Finally alone, Nakano felt tense instead of relieved. He looked at his watch and realized he had about three minutes to get to geometry, another free period wasted. When Jean-Paul tried to kiss him good-bye, he brushed past him and gathered up his books, now more preoccupied than passionate. "Are you afraid of Him?" Nakano asked, trying to sound nonchalant.

"Of Brania's father?" Jean-Paul replied. "No. When you respect and trust someone, there's no need for fear."

That's a roundabout answer if ever Nakano heard one. "What do you think he'd do if he found out about us?"

Jean-Paul looked down at Nakano and smiled, his hair falling from behind his ear, creating a shadow across his face, "*Mon cher,* don't you think he already knows?"

Sitting in the chair a foot away from where Jeremiah had died, Brania recalled a memory. She was once again in this room, watching a man undress, the multiple layers of her long, pale blue silk skirt keeping her body warm despite the chill that clung to her heart, to the fragments of her soul that she still believed existed. He took off his waistcoat and tossed it onto the floor, undid the ruffled ascot that was wrapped skillfully around his neck. Thick curls of black hair peeked out from the top of his tunic, and Brania felt the chill inside her turn icy. She knew how those curls would feel against her naked skin, harsh, oppressive, necessary, and it made her want to flee this place, but she couldn't. In the corner of the room, unseen by the man, her father was watching, making sure that she did what needed to be done.

"Brania, my darling," David had told her, "we need a place we can call home. This man is offering to rent us these accommodations and he wants so little in exchange. You."

She closed her eyes; a new memory took shape. Another man stood before her, darker, his chest hairier than the last, his stomach plump. He rolled his shoulders so the suspenders fell against his wide hips, undid the buttons of his full, pleated pants, and Brania watched as they collapsed onto the floor. Involuntarily, she crossed her legs, but the shimmery beaded cloth of her dress raced up her thigh and exposed too much flesh. She shivered, her hair bouncing slightly. She loathed this haircut. She felt like a boy wearing a short bob and remembered how beautiful her hair used to be, but this look was all the rage so she had no choice if she wanted to fit in. She brushed a piece of hair that had gotten caught within the crease of her mouth and pulled it sharply in an effort to stop her body from shaking. Behind the man, her father nodded approvingly. He thought she was playing the game perfectly.

"Brania, sweetheart," she remembered her father saying to her, "this man is giving us the deed to this land so we can own this piece of earth forever. In return, he asks so little to secure the deal."

"I'm not sure that I feel comfortable doing this."

Pulled from the past, it took Brania a few seconds to address the comment. "We're both adults, Vaughan. There's no reason why we can't find comfort in one another."

Rebuttoning his shirt, Vaughan continued, "But he isn't, that kid downstairs with my driver. It just doesn't feel right."

Why are men so close-minded when it comes to everyone else's desires except their own? "Seriously, Vaughan, you need to get over this problem you have with boys who like boys."

Searching for his shoes, which he kicked off moments before, Vaughan protested, "No, it isn't that! Though personally I have to admit I don't understand that tendency. What bothers me is the age difference." One shoe found, where's the other? "Nakano's just a kid and Jean-Paul, I'm sure you've noticed, isn't."

Grabbing the shoe out of his hand, Brania flung it over her shoulder. "Do you have any idea how much older I am than you?" This man was wasting her precious time. She had work to do.

"Brania, angel," David had cooed, "Vaughan's factory is a godsend to us. I would prefer that he continue to help us willingly and not seek out a new partnership elsewhere. He is getting rather chummy with Edwige. So do what you do best and make your father happy."

Ripping Vaughan's shirt open, she was thankful that men today at least waxed their chests. Unable to resist her force or her kisses, Vaughan succumbed. Brania pushed him onto the bed and straddled him. She leaned over, her long, luxuriant hair falling around her face, concealing the dead look in her eyes. Not that Vaughan would have noticed; he wasn't looking at her face.

She bit his earlobe, the sharp pressure of her teeth making Vaughan writhe underneath her, simultaneously lost in his own thoughts and physically connected to her. He thought he would feel her fangs pierce the fragile flesh of his neck, take some of his blood, but instead she needed to plant a seed. "Don't underestimate the next generation," she whispered. "You should reach out to your son."

Looking up, Brania saw her father in the corner of the room, his mouth, once again, in the shape of a satisfied smile. He nodded his approval and then disappeared so his daughter could complete her task.

chapter 5

With each step, the earth crunched under Ronan's feet. Dirt underneath grass hidden by snow covered by ice, each element bowed when it felt the presence of the young man. Nature understood power. And, in turn, Ronan understood the power of nature.

The rain that fell was more like hail, some particles large, some quite small, bouncing off of Ronan's body, hardly painful, quite refreshing actually, as he walked steadfastly across campus to his dorm, to Michael. Moving in long, purposeful strides, he felt like a king returning home after a long journey to meet his prince. He heard his own voice mock him, sometimes Ronan you really do let those books you read decorate your thoughts. Rubbish, what's the harm in a little embellishment, he thought, when his real world was just as fantastic as any piece of fiction.

"Where the hell have you been?!" Michael yelled before Ronan could even close the door behind him.

So much for romanticizing his reality. "Just running an errand," Ronan replied calmly, rivulets of icy rain traveling down the sides of his face.

"What kind of errand could possibly take all day?" Michael asked. "And you do know that you're getting water all over the place, right?"

"Yes, Michael, I do know that. I'm the one who just came in from the rain."

Yanking a towel off of a hook that hung behind the bathroom door, Michael started to blot up the mess, mumbling something about Ronan being inconsiderate while furiously rubbing the floor until it was bone dry. What was going on here, Ronan questioned, a minute ago he felt like the king of his own castle and now he was being treated like a guest who had long overstayed his welcome.

"Michael, what's wrong with you?"

"Me?" Michael snapped. "So this is my fault?"

Ronan knew that Michael liked things tidy, but he couldn't possibly be this upset just because he got the floor a little wet. "I'm sorry if I tracked some ice in here. I'll clean it up."

Ronan tried to take the towel from Michael, but angrily he brushed his hand away. Well, more like swiped. Were those tears in his eyes? Ronan wasn't sure, but he knew that something was definitely wrong. And somehow, unwittingly, Ronan was the cause.

"I woke up from our nap and again you weren't here!" Michael cried. "I looked all over for you. . . . It was dark . . . and I was alone!" He hurled the towel at Ronan and spat, "Why do you keep leaving me?!"

Ronan felt short of breath. He was right, he was the cause. He had done it again, made the person he loved feel afraid, abandoned. It was a terrible thing to do. He knew how it felt and he didn't think he could be so cruel, so thoughtless, but he had. "No, no, I'd never leave you." Ronan tried to embrace Michael, hold him close, but Michael was too angry for that. He didn't want to be held, he only wanted to be told the truth. "I went out to get you this."

Ronan reached inside his jacket pocket and took out a brown paper bag, stained by a few drops of rain, and pulled out a book. "I wanted to get to the bookstore before it closed," Ronan said sheepishly. At the time it felt like a romantic thing to do, a sweet gesture, to sneak out while Michael was still asleep and then present him with a gift when he woke up. "It's a collection of Oscar Wilde short stories that I thought you'd like to read instead of another dull textbook."

Wiping the tears from his eyes, Michael took the book from Ronan. On the cover was a drawing of a handsome young man. Could have been Dorian Gray, could've been another character the writer created. Michael didn't know his work that well so he couldn't be sure, but he knew why Ronan chose this anthology. "He reminded me of you," Ronan said quietly. "Forever beautiful . . ."

"Forever mine," Michael said, finishing their phrase. It was a thoughtful thing to do, Michael acknowledged. *And how did I respond? By attacking him, thinking the worst of him. Is this what it's like to be in a relationship? One minute the world couldn't be more perfect, and the next it's on the verge of complete ruin?*

Ronan and Michael spoke at the same time. "I'm sorry."

"No," Michael protested, holding the book close to his chest. "It's me, I overreacted. Lately I guess I've been . . ." What exactly was the word? What exactly was the feeling? Michael really didn't know. All he knew was that he was confused and more than a little embarrassed. Shaking his head, he continued, "No, Ronan, you have nothing to be sorry about."

"Yes, I do." Taking his boyfriend's hand, Ronan led him to their bed so they could sit and talk truthfully. "It's been quite some time since I've had a boyfriend."

Great, let's start the heart-to-heart conversation with a lie. "Nakano wasn't really that long ago," Michael corrected.

"He wasn't a boyfriend, not in the real sense of the word." Softly, Ronan traced the lines of Michael's palm with his finger, so many different etchings, intertwined, overlapping, just like the two of them, at least just like how the two of them should be. "I guess I've forgotten what it's like to be in a relationship, to be linked to someone and have to consider their feelings and not just my own. I now have someone I need to answer to."

Michael pulled his hand away. "Look, the last thing I want is for you to feel obligated to me."

"But I am," Ronan replied. "In the most wonderful way you can imagine." He had to make Michael understand. "My people believe we are not complete until we are partnered, and not just with anyone but with our soul mate. I know that sounds like tommyrot. What do you Americans call it? Malarkey? But it's the truth. You are my soul mate, Michael." Ronan wrapped his leg behind Michael and pulled him closer so they could embrace, so their bodies could intertwine just like their souls were doing at this very moment within the depths of The Well. "But . . ." Ronan hesitated.

"After all that, there's a 'but'?!" Michael replied, unconcerned that his voice rose higher than Phaedra's.

Michael's eyes grew so wide and his expression turned so comical, Ronan couldn't stop himself from kissing him. "But I'm a bit rusty is all."

Better rusty than inexperienced. "I get it," Michael said.

"Well, I kind of get it, some of it anyway." He took a deep breath so he wouldn't continue to rattle on incoherently. "I've been trying to avoid it, been trying to convince myself I know a lot more than I do, but the truth is I'm brand new at this relationship thing, so I'm bound to make a lot of mistakes." He took in another deep breath, this time smelling the rain that still clung to Ronan's skin. "Like yell at you because you didn't tell me you were leaving."

"I crocked up, Michael, I'm sorry."

"That means you screwed up, right?"

Ronan nodded. "I'd like to say it won't happen again, but we both know it will."

It was Michael's turn to kiss his boyfriend. "That's okay, as long as you keep bringing me gifts."

"That I can promise," Ronan said confidently. "Mum's quite wealthy and I have access to her bank account."

Kissing while laughing was definitely one of the most pleasant sensations Michael ever experienced. "Excellent, let's always shower each other with presents," Michael said. "And let's always be honest with each other."

Keep kissing him, Ronan, don't give him any reason to suspect. "I promise," Ronan mumbled, knowing full well that he was lying. For a second he thought the truth was going to tumble out, that he was going to tell Michael that David was Brania's father, but he remembered what his mother said. Blimey! Why was he listening to her and not to his heart? Why was he deliberately concealing the truth when he just promised to be honest? Maybe he was rustier at this relationship thing than he thought. Or maybe he just wanted to allow Michael to remain innocent until it was no longer possible. He had plunged him into this new world so quickly, even harshly; why not let him become comfortable, more at ease in his new environment, before changing the rules yet again?

Shaking off a chill, Ronan wanted nothing more than to hold Michael, hold him close, feel his warmth, but for the moment he needed to get away. "I could use a hot shower." Entering the bathroom, he realized his comment could be interpreted as an invitation, which normally he would have welcomed but at the moment would have interfered with his need for privacy, so he suggested Michael start reading. "The story of the young king made me think of you."

It was the night before the day fixed for his coronation. Michael smiled and shook his head at the same time. *Ronan really does like to imagine that I live on a pedestal,* he thought, *like I really am something special.* Gently, he stroked his neck and remembered the first time Ronan touched him there with his hands, his mouth, his fangs. Abruptly, he pulled his hand away. It could also be precarious living up there on a pedestal. *The lad—for he was only a lad, being but sixteen years of age.* Hmm, becoming a king at sixteen must be intimidating, scary, kind of like becoming immortal. *Lying there, wild-eyed and openmouthed, like a brown woodland Faun, or some young animal of the forest newly snared by the hunters.* Sounds like this Oscar Wilde knew what it felt like to be transformed into a vampire. Or more likely that he knew what it was like to fall deeply, unflinchingly in love.

When Michael finished the last line of the short story, he was reminded of why he loved Ronan so much. *And the young King came down from the high altar, and passed home through the midst of the people. But no man dared look upon his face, for it was like the face of an angel.* The words passed through Michael like waves of emotion, pure and resonant, clinging to his heart and convincing Michael that experienced or not, being in a relationship with Ronan was where he belonged. Being beside this beautiful person who considered him an angel. If that was true, then why was he in one room and Ronan in another?

Ronan didn't hear Michael enter the bathroom. The shower water was running and he was singing, slightly off-key, some folk song about The First and The Other that his father used to sing to him. He only knew someone was there when the shower curtain was pulled back. "Crikey, Michael!" Ronan cried. "Do you want to give me a heart attack?"

"Vampires can't have heart attacks," Michael said. "Can they?"

"No, love, they can't," Ronan answered. He then became very self-conscious that he was standing in the shower completely naked except for a few blotches of soapsuds that clung to his body, and Michael was fully clothed. "Is there, um, something I can help you with?"

Michael didn't hear Ronan's question. He was growing envious of the soap and the water as they touched parts of Ronan's body that he believed were exclusively his to explore. Perhaps Ronan thought he looked like an angel, but that didn't mean he always had to act like one. Tossing his halo to the side, Michael entered the shower and kissed Ronan deeply, the hot water soaking his clothes, his clothes holding on to his flesh, his hands caressing his boyfriend's hard, clean body.

Now this kind of surprise is more like it, Ronan thought. He no longer wanted to be alone, he no longer wanted to think. All he wanted to do, all either boy wanted to do, was feel.

The next morning, Michael's feelings were still as strong. However, they weren't good ones. Staring at the text message on his cell phone, the exquisite sensations he felt during his impromptu shower with Ronan were replaced with the unpleasant rumblings he felt in his stomach when he looked at the five short words that were displayed on his phone's screen—*Have dinner with me tonight*. His father didn't call him for weeks and then he texted him an order? Unbelievable! No, scratch that, completely believable because he considered him an employee, someone who didn't have any say in their relationship, someone who had to accept him for the jerk that he was. "Can you believe this?!"

Ronan wasn't sure if he could take another surprise. He was the one who always rose first and had to coax Michael to wake up, not the other way around. Opening one eye, he saw that it was only six A.M. Grumbling, he pulled the covers closer to his chin. "No, Michael, I can't believe this."

"Look at this!" Michael shouted, shoving his cell phone in Ronan's face.

Ronan swatted at the air, hoping the cell phone and even Michael would temporarily disappear, just for another hour. "Later."

"Have dinner with me tonight!" Michael shouted, pacing the room in nothing put a pair of Ronan's boxer shorts.

Turning over in a futile attempt to get away from the sound, Ronan had no idea what Michael was carrying on about. "We don't have to feed for another few weeks."

"Not you, my father!"

Now Ronan knew he wasn't going to get any more sleep. Whenever Michael was upset with his father, a very long conversation followed that consisted mainly of Michael ranting and Ronan listening. While Edwige annoyed Ronan, they had a connection that surpassed the typical mother-son relationship. Michael, unfortunately, barely knew his father, and worse still, his father acted as if that was perfectly fine with him. It confused Ronan because before Michael's mother was even buried, Vaughan swooped in to ask Michael to return home with him. But they never even lived together. He immediately shipped Michael off to Double A, and the two hardly saw each other. Maybe now Vaughan finally realized he'd been acting like a world-class git. Sitting up in bed, attentive and as clearheaded as possible for this time in the morning, Ronan was prepared to discuss the situation. "That's nice," Ronan said, trying unsuccessfully to stifle a yawn. "Your dad making an effort." Michael, however, was too furious to have a discussion.

"You call this an effort?! This is just his way of trying to control my life when, you know, it can fit into his schedule." Ronan started to respond, but Michael continued, "He's just feeling guilty because he blew me off at Christmas. He thinks he can make up for it now. Well, guess what." Ronan didn't even attempt to respond this time. "This is January! Christmas is over!"

Ronan watched Michael pace the room a while longer until the adrenaline started to release itself from his system. He completely understood Michael's feelings and felt he was totally justified in thinking his father was only trying to make up for past wrongs, but Vaughan was still his father. Sometimes parents act like children, it happens, and when it does, children can either make matters worse or decide to grow up. "I think you should say yes."

Immediately, Michael stopped pacing. "What?"

"I know your dad's hurt you by acting . . . irresponsibly," Ronan began. "But I would do anything to have another conversation with my father. Maybe you should take this opportunity to have another one with yours."

Michael had to pace the length of the room a few more times to absorb this information. Finally he stopped and knelt on the bed, touching Ronan's foot underneath the covers for no real reason. Well, maybe to connect with something tangible. His relationship with his father was complicated; a part of him wanted it to move forward and yet a part of him wished it had never existed. The more he learned about his father, the more he realized they were drastically different, they didn't share any of the same interests, and now that he was no longer even technically human, what could they possibly have in common? Plus his father made it quite clear that he didn't approve of Michael being gay. "No, I just don't think there's any reason to have dinner with him."

"It'll give you an excuse to practice dematerializing your food," Ronan quipped.

Michael squeezed Ronan's toe, making him squeal and wiggle underneath the covers. "Ow! That hurts!" Ronan shouted while laughing hysterically.

"Yeah, you sound like I'm killing you." He didn't want to talk about his father anymore. He didn't want to talk at all. Michael crawled underneath the covers and snuggled next to Ronan to calm down before the alarm was set to go off. But before Ronan could ask him again, he answered, "I'm going to do exactly what my father always does to me. Ignore him."

Five hours later, Michael, true to his word, still hadn't responded to his father's text. It wasn't that he was just being stubborn, it was simply that every time he thought of responding, he didn't know what to say. Since it was Friday, he couldn't use the excuse that he was prohibited from leaving campus, because the students were able to visit family on the weekend. And every time he thought he was going to cave in and agree to his father's request, he reminded himself that it was going to be a painful evening. Sitting on the sofa in the anteroom of St. Joshua's Library across from Ciaran, Michael was happy not to have to ponder the question any further, until, of course, Ronan plopped down on the couch next to him. "Have you decided about dinner?"

"What's to decide?" Ciaran asked. "You gents don't eat."

"Pack it up, will you," Ronan cried. "Michael's father wants to have dinner with him tonight."

"Do it," Ciaran responded.

It wasn't so much that Michael was surprised by Ciaran's quick response, it was the tone he used, it was so positive and that wasn't like him. It was the same as yesterday at lunch. He had sounded different, not really like himself, more upbeat, optimistic. The weird thing was it appeared to be natural and not like he was trying to hide anything, force himself to be happy in order to cover up something bad that happened. What were he and Phaedra just saying? That boys were a mystery. "You really think I should?"

Rubbing a soft spot on the armchair where the olive green leather had started to fade, turning yellowish, Ciaran thought of his own father. He would love to call him up and invite him to dinner or chat with him about nonsense or tell him how well he was doing in school, but he didn't know where his father was, or if he was even still alive. Ronan shifted uncomfortably in his seat. He picked at a loose thread in the velvet couch and avoided Ciaran's eyes because he knew exactly what Ciaran was thinking. They both knew the reason Ciaran had no relationship with his father was all Edwige's fault. "Michael, I don't usually tell people what to do, but this time I'm going to make an exception," Ciaran stated. "Tell your father you'd be happy to have dinner with him." This time, despite the optimistic message, Ciaran sounded very much like his old self. He acted like his old self too. "Excuse me, I need to get to the lab."

Maybe it was guilt from watching Ciaran scurry out of the library or compassion from watching Michael trying to deal with his dilemma; regardless, Ronan had made a decision. "I'll go with you."

The comment surprised them both. "You will?" Michael asked, and then just to make sure he understood Ronan cor-

rectly, he clarified, "You'll have dinner with me and my father?"

There isn't a thing I wouldn't do for you Michael. "Yes, I
will join you and break bread with my father-in-law." Without
glancing around to see if anyone was looking, Michael leaned
over and kissed Ronan's cheek as thanks. "Or, you know, laser
beam the bread into millions of little pieces."

The decision finally made, Michael sent a text to Vaughan
accepting his invitation, making it clear that Ronan would be
joining them. He might be giving in to his father, but he was
going to do it on his own terms. A few seconds later,
Vaughan responded with his own text, which Michael read
aloud. "He says, 'that's wonderful. My new driver will pick
you up at six tonight.' "

"Then we're all set," Ronan said, trying to sound as if he
found the prospect cheerier than he really did. "I have to go
meet Fritz and work on a theology report. That bloke's got
some interesting thoughts on eternal life, I must say."

"I'm going to stay here and do some studying. I'll see you
at home."

As he walked by, Ronan cupped Michael's chin and gave
him a wink. Eternal life never felt so good. The same could
not be said for studying for a world history exam. He opened
the thick textbook and almost immediately the words on the
page started to blur together. Michael's eyes were drawn
away from his book and toward the towering portrait that
hovered over the fireplace. Brother Dahey stared at him, his
expression at once bemused and condemning, his black eyes
peering directly at him from across the centuries, from beyond the grave, and suddenly Michael felt very tired. Gone
was St. Joshua's, gone was the portrait and the fireplace,
gone were the endless rows of books, and in their place was
only one thing, The Well.

Michael stood at the curved stone that jutted out from the

ocean's floor just as he had done before, naked and willing, filled with a mixture of modesty and a desire to share in The Well's magnificent power. He wanted to be subject and ruler at the same time. But most of all, he didn't want to be alone.

He turned around to look for Ronan, but he wasn't there. This wasn't right. He wasn't supposed to be at The Well by himself; it went against everything his race stood for, unless something had happened to Ronan, something terrible, something unspeakable. No, that couldn't be. Michael refused to believe that he was going to wind up like Edwige, alone, forever separated, forever one half of a coupling that was supposed to last for eternity. When skin touched his arm, he was no longer afraid. Ronan was beside him, where he belonged.

The Well agreed. It began to hum, its sound growing louder, vibrating all around them, and Michael and Ronan felt the energy of their entire race pulse through them. A beautiful white light burst forth from the center of The Well and they prepared themselves for the final transformation. Fangs descended, bodies elongated, fingers, toes, no longer separated but webbed together. They had been re-created in true image of the inhabitants of Atlantis and it felt heavenly, but everything changed when Michael peered over the stone rim to drink The Well's precious fluid. What he saw horrified him.

The clear liquid, usually so smooth and flat, began to ripple without being touched, to form a grotesque and unrecognizable face. The picture, the illusion, the reflection, whatever it was, lasted for only a second, but it was so disturbing that Michael could still see the image in his mind's eye even after the light retreated and darkness took over the cave. "Ronan!" Reaching out, Michael felt nothing but the cold air. He couldn't see a thing. The darkness was thick, oppressive, and Michael truly thought he was going to suffocate from either fear or the blackness. What was happening? This was supposed to be a heavenly place filled with beauty and light. This was supposed to be a place that felt like a dream, not the most dreadful nightmare. "Ronan! Where are you?"

He clutched at the space in front of him, unable to see his hand move, and sought the edge of The Well. Where was it? It couldn't be that far away, he hadn't moved more than a few inches. Michael admonished himself and tried to stop thinking logically, rational thought had no place here. If it did, Ronan would be standing right next to him.

But even though he couldn't see or feel him, Ronan was near. Through the darkness he could hear his voice, his beautiful Irish accent. "Even in the darkness you have the face of an angel." The words were as clear as if Ronan whispered them into his ear, but when Michael flailed his arms all about him, they still touched nothing, only emptiness.

Is this death? Michael thought. *Is this what I have to look forward to?* Frightened and more than a little bit angry, he refused to believe that the last image he would see before leaving this world would be something disgusting, something unworthy of existing within the presence of The Well. And then as quickly as the darkness fell, light returned.

Michael was no longer in a cave in the Atlantic Ocean. He was once again in St. Joshua's. His eyes darted all over the room and nothing had changed; he had just fallen asleep. Why, then, did he feel he had taken a journey into the future? Why, then, did he feel that someone was trying to separate him from Ronan? And why had Brother Dahey's eyes changed? The whites surrounding his pupils were gone and there was not a spot on the surface of either eye that wasn't covered in black.

chapter 6

Night had come early. It was only four P.M., but already the sky was a deep shade of blue. The lights from the windows of several buildings on campus tried their best to penetrate the premature darkness, but they succeeded only in casting a glow here and there, shooting out brief glimmers of hope into the blue-black dusk. Walking swiftly from St. Joshua's, Michael realized he much preferred the sunlight. Odd insight for a vampire, but luckily he was a vampire who wasn't confined to the shadows. Or, he recognized, barred from places of worship.

Every time Michael stood before Archangel Cathedral he stood in awe. No matter how much of a rush he was in, as he was now, he couldn't help but stop and marvel at the beauty and craftsmanship of the church. He wasn't sure what was more impressive: the wood carvings of the seven archangels that framed the arched doorway or the circular yellow stained-glass window that floated almost ethereally above it. Not that it really mattered, one couldn't exist without the other. In fact, each piece of the cathedral's architecture was built to enhance the beauty of the whole structure. Hawksbry had once told Michael that the cathedral was like the school itself. Each component, like each student, wasn't created to stand out as the highlight, wasn't meant to be a focal point, but was brought together to work in harmony. Building a better school would lead to building a better self, he had said. Watching the moonlight bounce off the yellow stained glass and soften the dark sky, Michael wished Hawksbry was still around; he had always been a calming influence. And by the time he got home, Michael was anything but calm.

"No, Ronan," Michael stressed. "It was much more than a dream!"

Ronan knew Michael might be right. He knew that his outlandish claim could be true, but at the moment, he didn't feel like debating the validity of Michael's latest delusion or even wholeheartedly supporting it. He didn't want to talk about *what if*'s or *could be*'s—he just wanted to finish getting dressed. Wearing only a pair of black chinos, Ronan opened one dresser drawer after the other in search of his favorite sweater, the reddish-purple V-neck that his mother had given him for his birthday last year. Luxuriously soft and slightly too large, it was the retail equivalent of comfort food, and tonight Ronan wanted to be as comfortable as possible. "Here you are," Ronan said, elated. He pulled the sweater from underneath a few T-shirts and laid it on the bed, unfolding it and smoothing it out in the hopes that some of the creases would disappear.

"Are you going to ignore me?" Michael asked.

Unable to remain quiet any longer, Ronan finally spoke. "I'm sure it felt real, but face it, Michael, you have been anxious about us lately, thinking that I ran off to heaven knows where the other day. This *dream* was nothing more than a result of that."

A logical boyfriend is more annoying than a silent one. "Well, okay, that kind of makes sense."

"Because it's true."

Scratch that. A boyfriend who thinks he's always right is worst of all. But he wasn't right, Michael couldn't explain it, he just knew it. "Then why did it feel like it was happening? Or like it was definitely going to happen, like it was our future?"

Crossing his arms, Ronan scrutinized Michael. When he spoke, his tone was as harsh as his expression. "Well, which one is it?"

Stunned by his boyfriend's gruff tone, Michael took a few moments before he responded. "I . . . uh . . . I really don't know."

His frustration mounting, Ronan no longer cared if he sounded sarcastic or pompous, he simply wanted to convince Michael that his theory was nonsense. "Well, I do and it wasn't either one," he said. "It wasn't happening at the moment you dreamed it because I wasn't near The Well, I was in St. Joseph's with Fritz and that dumb prat Amir, working on our theology paper." Before Michael could remind him that he could have had a premonition of their future, Ronan exhaled deeply, grabbed Michael by the shoulders, and pressed his forehead against his. "And how many times do I have to tell you that we will be together forever." Ronan concentrated on how cool Michael's skin felt, how delicious he smelled, until an uninvited thought entered his mind and he stepped back. "That is what you want, isn't it?"

Once again Michael was stunned, this time by Ronan's words. How could he think such a thing? How? *Well, maybe,* Michael thought, *because he was constantly suggest-*

ing that they were on the verge of eternal separation. "No!" Michael protested. "I don't want that!" Realizing what he actually said, Michael grabbed Ronan's arm, causing him to pull farther away. "No! I mean I want us, you and me, always, forever."

Michael mumbled a few more words, but Ronan didn't hear them because he was kissing him. That's all he wanted to know, that's all he wanted to believe. He didn't care about Michael's dreams or premonitions or his crazy ideas, none of that mattered; the only thing that mattered was how wonderful Michael's lips tasted. That and the fact that they now had less than an hour to get ready.

Forget about visions of The Well and Brother Dahey's portrait, that damned portrait, Ronan told himself. *Our life is supposed to be filled with moments like this, mundane but real moments filled with jokes and laughter. Michael just has to stop complicating matters.* "I call the bathroom first."

"Don't hog it up like you usually do." Michael laughed.

It worked. "You do want me to look presentable for your father, don't you?"

"That's just the point," Michael cracked. "He's *my* father. I should be the one making sure I look my best."

"Since he's your father, he's going to think you look smashing no matter what you look like."

This gave Michael the biggest laugh he'd had in days. "Seriously?! My father'll be lucky if he recognizes me!"

A quick kiss, one more, and Ronan ran into the bathroom. Of course the second after he closed the bathroom door, he remembered something he wanted to tell Michael. "Hey! Fritz asked if you found 'that stuff' for him!" Ronan shouted.

"What stuff?"

They were truly never going to be dressed and ready by six o'clock. "I don't know, he wouldn't tell me," Ronan said, swinging the door open. "He was acting all mysterious when

I questioned him about it, though. All he would say is that you promised to look for . . ." Ronan dropped his voice an octave lower. "That stuff?"

"Oh, right, that stuff," Michael said, remembering their conversation. "Of course."

First Fritz, now Michael. Was no one going to fill him in? "Oh, come on! What stuff are you talking about?"

His dream a distant memory and dinner still a part of the future, Michael was enjoying teasing Ronan in the present. "Hmm, could be a bunch of stuff," Michael said. "Are you jealous that Fritz and I have a secret?"

Now it was Ronan's turn to laugh, deep, genuine. "Jealous? Of you and Fritz? Absolutely not." As Ronan continued to howl with laughter, Michael wasn't sure to join in or be insulted.

"Fritz is very handsome," Michael protested.

"I guess, but he's also very straight," Ronan pointed out. Looking at the hands of the clock moving ever closer to their time of departure, Ronan decided it was pointless to keep digging and time to act like the mature one in their relationship. "Fine, I don't give a fig about whatever stuff there is between you and Fritz." Turning abruptly, he went back into the bathroom and slammed the door.

Michael stared at the closed door in disbelief and then shouted, "It's about *Tales of the Double A!* I told Fritz I might have some old comic books he could use as inspiration."

Suddenly the door swung open. "I knew that would make you tell me." Before Michael could respond, the door shut again. "Now hurry up and get dressed," Ronan shouted. "We don't have much time."

I'm a vampire, I need about three seconds to get dressed, Michael thought, and even if he weren't, he didn't care about impressing his father. He would probably just throw on jeans and a T-shirt; no need to make it look like he spent time getting ready. He had better things to do, like find those comics for Fritz, if he could only remember where he stashed them.

He stared at the boxes on the top shelf of the closet and wished that he had X-ray vision. That would be cool, he thought, just like Superman, able to peer through solid objects, see if his old comic books were in any of those boxes, see what kind of underwear Professor McLaren wore. Michael blushed at the idea, but then couldn't help but wonder if the handsome British lit professor wore boxers or briefs. No, he couldn't remember putting the comics in the closet, but he did decide that McLaren was more of a boxers kind of guy.

Pushing distracting thoughts of teachers in their underwear from his mind, Michael lay on the floor and looked underneath his bed. Dust, an old pair of Ronan's sneakers, more dust, and yes, there they were, his comic books jutting out from behind a small shoe box. He pulled the box out and then reached in to grab his comics. Once he felt the familiar glossy material, he was transported back to his bedroom in Weeping Water. The refreshing difference was that this time, the memory was a good one.

In between reading schoolbooks and rereading his favorite classic novels, Michael would often sit cross-legged in bed, ignore the loud, angry voices coming from downstairs, forget about whatever embarrassing incident took place that day at Two W, and immerse himself in the adventures of some superhero. He loved to read that a normal boy could become an incredible, invulnerable being overnight armed with amazing powers. He never thought his fantasy would actually come true. "Guess I am sort of like a superhero," Michael muttered. A superhero disguised as a very curious human.

When he pushed the shoe box back underneath the bed, the lid got caught on the metal bed frame and fell off. Grabbing the lid to put it back where it belonged, he saw that the box didn't contain shoes but letters. He hesitated, he knew he shouldn't rummage through things that weren't his, but, well, it's not like he went looking for the box nor did he open it up deliberately, it was just there, right in front of him, opened.

Instinctively, Michael turned around, but the bathroom door was still closed and he could hear the water in the sink running, Ronan must be washing his face or brushing his teeth, whatever he was doing, he had no idea that Michael was snooping through his things. *I'm not snooping,* Michael told himself. *I'm just getting to know my boyfriend better.*

Ignoring the rational side of his brain and the increased beating of his heart, Michael reached into the box and took out one of the letters. The envelope was a shade lighter than the color of bubble gum and Ronan's address at Double A had been written by someone who used a very thick black marker, the writing bold and obvious as if the person were afraid the letter would never reach its recipient. Michael wondered if the person was also afraid that the letter would ever be read by anyone other than the person it was meant for. *Which is not you.* Once again Michael ignored the rational and very interfering voice and pulled out the letter from its envelope.

Dear Ronan. That's not so bad, it's not as if it said *Dearest* or *My dear Ronan*, just plain old *Dear Ronan.* Michael's luck didn't hold out. *Miss you! Can't stand that we have to be separated, it just isn't fair!* Michael knew he should stop reading right then and there. He wanted to, he really did, but now that he had started, now that he had violated Ronan's privacy, there was no way he was putting the letter back without reading every word on the page. *Doesn't everybody know that we're meant to be together? I mean you know it, I know it, why can't the stupid world just let us be together?!*

Promise me that you'll come to see me! You have to, Ronan,
I'll just die if I don't see you soon!

The desperate plea was signed with a huge letter "S."
Michael thought about all the people he knew in Ronan's
life, and the only person whose name started with an "S"
was Saxon, his father. Well, this letter definitely wasn't written by his father, so who could it be? Mentally, Michael
checked off the family and friends he had heard Ronan talk
about and he realized that Ronan didn't talk about that
many people. This "S" could be anyone.

Then things got worse. Michael searched the letter for a
date, but there wasn't one, which meant the letter could have
come last year or last week. Not only didn't he know who
sent the letter, he didn't even know when it was sent. Furious
that Ronan would keep this "S" person a mystery and hide
his or her letters underneath their bed, the bed they both
slept in, he ripped another letter from its envelope and
started reading.

> *It was so good to see you today, Ronan! I was*
> *really careful just like you told me to be and I*
> *know that no one saw us. Today will be our*
> *secret, just between you and me, no one else*
> *will ever have to know.*

Well, guess what, "S." Somebody knows and somebody
isn't happy about it! This time when Michael shoved the letter into the envelope, he noticed there was writing on the
back flap. The writing looked more like scribbling and he
could make out only two words—on the top line was something that looked like *"Saoirse."* Must be the name of whoever sent the letter, though Michael had never seen such a
name before. Underneath was some scrawl he couldn't read,
and on the bottom was written "France," the only word that

he completely understood. So "S" was Saoirse from France, whoever that was.

Michael tried several times to pronounce the name with little success and figured it must be old-world French even though it didn't sound it. Then again, what did he know? He didn't know the language very well, but didn't every word have lots of vowels that weren't even pronounced? The one thing he was certain of was that it was a girl's name. He just knew it. It looked like a girl's name and the penmanship was flowery and the words, the words weren't like the words a guy would use. At least he would never use them. But why in the world would Ronan have a box of letters from a girl? And why would he hide them under the bed?

Michael tried to convince himself that there had to be a logical explanation for this, but unfortunately, the only logical explanation he could think of was that Ronan was lying to him.

"Who's Say-o-ear-see?!" Michael yelled, flinging open the bathroom door.

For the second time in as many days, Michael had surprised Ronan while he was in the bathroom. This time he wasn't in the shower, but at the sink shaving. Vampires didn't age, but their hair grew. Ronan accepted it as another way to feel connected to the human race. Now as he watched a drop of blood bubble, then slowly slide down his chin, he just thought it was a nuisance. "What are you talking about?" Ronan asked, pressing his index finger against his bloody cut.

"I'm talking about these!" Michael shouted, waving a handful of letters at Ronan. "Letters from someone named Say-o-ear-see. Who is she?"

Licking his bloodstained finger dry, Ronan grabbed one of the letters with his free hand and immediately started to laugh.

No way, Michael thought, he wasn't going to get out of this by laughing. But that's all Ronan did, laugh so hard that he dropped his razor in the sink and had to hold on to the vanity to steady himself.

"This isn't funny, Ronan! I thought we weren't going to have any secrets from each other. I thought you were my boyfriend. But these are from some girl!" *No, no, Michael do not cry in front of him, not again; he doesn't deserve to see that.* "I want to know right now—you tell me and do not lie to me—do you have a girlfriend stashed away somewhere in France?"

The shaving cream felt cool against his face. That was Michael's first impression. His second was that Ronan's blood tasted so incredibly sweet. Ronan was kissing him; involuntarily, Michael's tongue glided over Ronan's and the blood from his cut still lingered in his mouth. *How can I be angry at him,* Michael thought, *and love him so much?*

"Is that the kiss from a bloke who's ever had a girlfriend?" Ronan asked.

Michael allowed Ronan to keep his arms wrapped around him, his arms and chest, naked and warm, felt wonderful against his body. He stared into his beautiful blue eyes and he wished that he had never looked into that stupid box, but he had, and no matter how gorgeous Ronan looked, that fact wasn't going to change. "Then who is she?"

"*She* is my sister," Ronan explained.

Incredulous, Michael wasn't sure he believed him. "Another sibling?"

Shrugging his shoulders, Ronan replied, "Humans aren't the only ones with complicated family trees, you know."

A sister? That does explain things. And what girl wouldn't idolize a brother like Ronan. "So where is this Say-or-ear-see?" Michael asked.

"First off, her name is pronounced Seer-sha," Ronan said.

"It's an Irish word for freedom, and darling little Saoirse does a right fine job living up to her name." He went on to explain that Saoirse was his younger sister, just turned fifteen, and living at Ecole des Roches, an exclusive boarding school in Normandy, France. "Fact is, even though she likes to come off as being independent, down deep she misses her big brother."

Grabbing a towel from the vanity, Michael wiped the globs of shaving cream that clung to his chin, his cheeks, noticing a tiny speck of blood on the towel—Ronan's blood. *No, don't get distracted, say what you need to say, say what's on your mind.* "And you never thought to tell me about her before?"

How could Ronan tell Michael about Saoirse when he hardly understood anything about her? She was his sister and even though she was a legend among water vamps, she was more like a stranger to him. "There's a lot you don't know about me, Michael," Ronan said. "And there's a lot I don't know about you too, but ... but we have time, lots of time to discover every detail."

Something wasn't right. Michael could feel it. He pressed the towel against Ronan's chest, using it like a barrier to create some distance. "I don't believe you, Ronan. You're hiding something from me. Something about Saoirse."

He couldn't possibly be reading my mind, could he? No, it's impossible. "The only thing I might be trying to hide is my own embarrassment. I haven't been a very good brother, if you must know." *That's good; a half-truth is always better than an out-and-out lie.* "Saoirse is always begging me to visit and, honestly, Michael, I can't remember the last time I went to see her."

Enough with the interrogation, Michael told himself, it was time to act like a boyfriend, stop accusing Ronan, and start offering him some help. Tugging on the waistband of

Ronan's pants, Michael pulled him closer. "Then maybe you need to take your own advice."

"And what would that be?"

"Reach out to your sister like you told me to reach out to my father," Michael suggested, feeling quite proud and mature, confident that he had solved the situation in record time. What he didn't know and what Ronan didn't want to tell him was that if he did reach out to Saoirse, Edwige would probably disown him or at best treat him with the same kindness she showered upon Ciaran.

"I'll think about it," Ronan said, swallowing hard. "But right now, love, we have to deal with repairing your family's tattered tapestry."

Sadly, it soon became apparent to Michael if not to Ronan that some families were tattered beyond repair. They had gotten to the front gate with four minutes to spare and now it was a quarter past six, but still no sign of Vaughan's driver. The only sound that interfered with Michael's deep intakes of breath was the creaking of the metal Archangel Academy sign as it swayed in the cold January wind. The temperature had dipped several degrees and Michael was sure it was hovering around the freezing point. The cold didn't bother him very much, but his father didn't know that and still he left him waiting outside in the freezing weather without so much as a text to advise him that he was on his way or that he was running late. For all Michael knew, Vaughan had left on another business trip and had forgotten all about their dinner.

"I don't think he forgot," Ronan said.

There was no way Michael was going to cut his father any slack, not after he went against his gut instinct and agreed to this dinner. He had already given in as much as he was capable. "I wouldn't put it past him."

Suddenly the boys were bathed in two beams of light. "I told you he didn't forget," Ronan said.

The muffled sound of the snow-covered gravel being slowly crushed underneath the tires accompanied the vision of the two high beams moving toward them. Vaughan's driver had finally arrived. "It's about time," Michael barked. But when Jean-Paul got out of the car, Michael's foul attitude crumbled. Long-limbed and lanky, he moved with an effortless swagger that immediately reminded Michael of R.J., the gas station attendant back home. Two memories of Nebraska in a row that didn't make him feel miserable had to be a new record.

"You must be Michael," Jean-Paul said, ripping off his black leather glove with one quick tug and extending his hand to him. "I'm Jean-Paul Germaine, your father's new driver."

Alistair, Professor McLaren, the new headmaster, now this one. Michael couldn't believe how attractive he found these older men. All different, but all appealing. His feelings weren't the same as those he had had for other kids his age and they were nothing at all like the intense feelings he had for Ronan; he simply thought these men were really handsome. The most important revelation was that Michael found it liberating to be able to acknowledge that kind of truth and not feel covered in shame, not feel like he was unnatural or wrong. Once again he was surprised by how different a person he was from just a few months ago.

His father, unfortunately, had not changed.

"Again?!"

"He had to fly to Tokyo to secure a business deal that he said required hees immediate attention," Jean-Paul conveyed.

"Tokyo?" Ronan asked.

"Oui, something to do with one of hees factories."

Again with the stupid factories. "Does this incredibly important emergency business deal have anything to do with those contact lenses my father's company makes?"

That's what Vaughan's company manufactures? His curiosity piqued, Ronan wanted to ask some more detailed questions but decided it best to see if Jean-Paul's response would fill in any blanks.

"I do not know; I'm just zee driver."

So much for detail. Before Ronan could attempt to pry more information out of Jean-Paul, Michael spoke. "You sound just like Jeremiah, except, you know, you talk in a French accent," he observed. "Hey, whatever happened to him anyway?

"I was told he got a better job and quit," Jean-Paul replied, taking off his hat, a few strands of hair falling across his face. "Though I can't imagine a better job than working for Howard Industries or for your father."

Preoccupied with trying to figure out how to subtly ask more detailed questions about Vaughan's business, Ronan didn't notice Jean-Paul's agile fingers tuck the loose strands of hair behind his ear, but Michael did. Michael also noticed how erect he stood and how he had maintained eye contact with him ever since he introduced himself, his dark eyes never looking anywhere else except right at him. Michael wished he could be that poised.

"It's a privilege to work for such a good man," Jean-Paul added.

He might be a member of Team Enemy, but his accent was easy to listen to, enticing, and Michael wanted to hear more of it. He was desperately trying to think of something to say when it became so obvious. "Have you ever heard of Ecole des Roches?"

Jean-Paul and Ronan were both surprised by the question, but for different reasons. "Of course," Jean-Paul remarked. "Eet eez a very famous school. Why do you ask?"

Interrupting Michael before he could say Saoirse's name,

Ronan asked, "How did you come to work for Michael's father?"

"A mutual friend introduced us."

Really? Michael wanted to ask who, but he didn't want to appear to be overly interested. But he did want to keep the conversation going. What else? What else can I ask? "Are you from Paris originally? You look like you'd be from Paris, you know, very fashionable." Cringing, Michael felt like a fool. What a stupid thing to say. He's wearing a uniform, a chauffeur's uniform, that isn't fashionable, that's just a job requirement.

"I was born in Lyon," Jean-Paul said, his eyes smiling and reflecting the moonlight. "But I studied in Paris, so I guess that makes me an honorary Parisian."

"If you keep talking, you're going to make us late."

Three heads snapped in the direction of the passenger's side of the sedan. When the tinted mirror fully descended, both Michael and Ronan were shocked to see Nakano sitting in the front seat, looking angry and smug. "Mon cher, we're not going to be late."

Mon cher? Doesn't that translate to mean something like "my love"? Why would this driver, who was definitely older than they were, be using that kind of language to talk to Nakano? Unless . . . no, that was ridiculous, it couldn't be. From Michael's perplexed expression, Nakano knew exactly what he was thinking.

"Yes, Michael, Jean-Paul is my new boyfriend and we're on a date, so he doesn't have time to play twenty questions with you."

If Jean-Paul was embarrassed by Nakano's outburst, he didn't show it. He was, after all, professional. Instead he put on his cap and offered a small bow in Michael's direction. "Please accept my apologies on your father's behalf." Then he turned slowly, almost as if he knew he was being watched, and walked back toward the driver's side of the car.

"Tell my father," Michael started, but when Jean-Paul turned back around to hear the message, Michael couldn't think of anything he wanted to say to his father that he should repeat in public. "Forget it; don't tell him anything."

Another slight tilt of his head and Jean-Paul was gone. Out of view, Michael imagined that he was leaning back against the black leather interior of the car, feeling its warmth, reaching over to touch Nakano's waiting hand, whispering something to him in French, something sweet and provocative.

"That doesn't add up," Ronan said.

"No, it doesn't," Michael agreed. "How did Nakano ever land somebody like that? Jean-Paul's like . . . an adult."

Ronan remained quiet. He didn't contradict Michael and inform him that he wasn't referring to Nakano's latest conquest but to his father's latest contentious action. Once again, Vaughan was unable to follow through with a plan, and that didn't make sense. He seemed so eager to have dinner with Michael, so willing to bridge the gap that was separating them, and then he just up and leaves to fly halfway across the world without even calling his son. And to make matters worse, he sends an employee to apologize. What could be so important with his factories that he couldn't take a moment to call Michael himself? And why did families have to be so complicated?

"I'm sorry," Ronan said. "I guess you were right."

"That my dad's a workaholic and a jerk?" Michael said. "Yeah, well . . . I was hoping I was wrong too."

Ronan kissed Michael gently and slid his hand into his coat pocket. Their fingers interlocked and the soft, fleece lining embraced their hands, making them feel warm and cozy. "And don't think I didn't notice you flirting with the Frenchie."

Caught, Michael tried to escape from Ronan's hold, which only made Ronan hold on to his hand even tighter. "I was not flirting," Michael protested.

Kissing him again, this time a bit rougher, to remind him of the passion they shared, Ronan felt Michael's hand stop resisting. No need to resist because it was exactly where it ought to be. "Yes, you were," Ronan whispered. "But remember, an Irish brogue is a lot sexier than a French accent."

He was right about that. "Let's go home," Michael said.

Walking home with Michael, his arm around his shoulder, Ronan wished everything could be this simple, glitches, bumps in a relationship were expected and should be resolved quickly. But he knew better. He knew that fathers couldn't be relied on to stick around and that sisters would always cause trouble. Family simply couldn't be trusted.

chapter 7

At first the flame only flickered. Like a baby trying to stand for the first time, it was unsure that it could succeed, take root, and flourish, but soon, its confidence building, its strength growing, the flame expanded. Just as the baby's outstretched arms clutched at the air, claiming more territory for its own personal space, the flame devoured more of the haystack, burning the straw until it turned black, then disappeared to be reborn, violently, miraculously, as fire. The man tied to the stake that stood in the center of the haystack didn't see the transformation take place, but when he felt the heat intensify under his feet, he knew what was happening.

"Burn, demon, burn!" the voice cried.

Ronan had never heard such hatred before. He never knew a voice could be capable of such a sound, so harsh, so brutal, so inhuman. His parents' voices were always filled with such kindness, such love, especially his father's, except now his father remained silent as all around him the voices grew louder.

Saxon closed his eyes when the first flames nipped at his feet. He didn't want his son to see fear, he didn't want him to know that his father had spent his last moments on earth frightened, uncertain if God would welcome him or if he would be plunged into a larger pit of fire as the men, the mortals rioting around him, encircling him, murdering him, had predicted. He knew he was going to be destroyed. He didn't want his son to suffer the same fate.

Eyes shut, he focused on a different, much happier, time. He watched himself entering the cave, kneeling before The Well, Edwige by his side, her long black hair cascading down her back, the back he loved to touch, caress, and he could hardly feel the flames devour his feet. He was stronger than these men, they would take his life, but they would not take his spirit. When he opened his eyes, he was confident that he would not make his son afraid, only more powerful. It would be a wonderful final gift.

"Go back to the devil that spawned ya!" the man holding the torch cried.

Ronan was confused. He recognized the man and had thought he was a friend. He often saw him leaning his head close to his mother's, smiling at her, putting his arms around her to make her feel good and happy like Daddy did to him after he fell and scraped his knee or was feeling sad. This man shouldn't be yelling so loudly; he shouldn't be trying to hurt Daddy with the fire, that's not something a friend would do. "Leave my daddy alone!"

His mother's friend reeled around and stared at Ronan, his eyes gleaming bright, illuminated by the sparks. "You want to join your old man?!"

"Ronan, come to me!"

He heard his mother's voice, but he couldn't see her, there were so many people, all of them shouting, jumping up and down, filled with excitement as if they were watching a parade instead of his father. Maybe he was performing some magic trick. Yes, that had to be it! They were all shouting because they were being entertained.

Ronan looked up and saw his father smiling at him like a magician smiling at a spectator just before doing one last spellbinding trick. And what a trick it was. A column of fire surrounded the lower half of his body, red, orange, and yellow flames floating all around him like autumn leaves swirling in a sudden gust of wind. He could hear the flames crackle and there was an odd smell in the air, but his father never stopped smiling, so everything was all right, there couldn't be anything wrong. But why was his mother still shouting?

"Ronan! Come to me!"

Didn't Daddy tell her that he was going to perform a trick for all the people? Didn't she know that everyone had come to see the magic?

The man with the torch spoke a few more words that Ronan didn't understand, but the onlookers must have, because they gave a great cheer when he was finished. This man, who had to be his father's assistant, threw the torch onto what remained of the haystack, turning it into an inferno of heat and vibrant color unlike anything Ronan had ever seen. He stood up on his tiptoes to try and find his father amid all the fire, but he was no longer there, his smile, his whole body, all that he remembered, was gone. That's okay, he thought, he just disappeared, went some place where there wasn't any fire, it was all part of the trick. But if it was, why was his mother crying?

"Ronan!" Edwige was running toward him so swiftly it was as if she were flying. How lucky he was that both his parents had special powers. She scooped him up in her arms and held his body tightly to hers. He could feel her heart racing. Daddy's magic show must have made her as excited as the crowd. She whispered in his ear, repeating the same words over and over again, "I told you to come to me."

Standing outside of St. Florian's, there were no flames, no heat, only the cold night air and the fallen snow. There were no crowds obstructing Ronan's vision, no people at all, no one except Edwige. "Mother," Ronan asked. "What are you doing here?"

Wearing a white fox jacket, a winter white beret that hid almost all of her hair, and wide-cut pants of the same color, Edwige was almost invisible. If it weren't for the slash of red lipstick, she might have receded into the background, become part of the landscape, but Edwige was not one to blend. "I want to know how dinner went with your father-in-law," Edwige said.

A breeze blew past them, lifting some snowflakes from the ground, disturbing their slumber so they could be airborne once again. Ronan crossed his arms and wished that he had put on some more clothes before answering his mother's telepathic command. He wasn't cold of course, but standing in front of his mother, wearing only a T-shirt and boxer shorts, his bare feet pressed firmly into the snowy ground, he felt more submissive than he preferred. He thought it best to make up for his vulnerable appearance with a more insolent tone. "You couldn't have called me tomorrow like a normal person?"

"You know I can be impatient," Edwige replied, waving away his impertinence. "And that I prefer to speak to my son in person." *You mean you prefer to control the situation and you have nothing else better to do but to meddle in my life.* "Such angry, negative thoughts really are unbecoming," Edwige said, reading her son's mind. "You should choose your words and thoughts more carefully, especially when in the center of such serenity."

Ronan wasn't sure if his mother was referring to herself or their surroundings, but either way he could find nothing serene about his current situation or, for that matter, the earlier events of the night. "Michael's father canceled on him."

Was that disappointment that washed over Edwige's face? Why does she even care about Vaughan? "After trying so hard to reestablish a connection with his son?"

"That was my thought exactly," Ronan said. "There's something not right about him. Something's off."

"That's because the man is a vampire."

"What?!"

Edwige looked at her son as if he had just committed the worst social faux pas of the season. "Will you keep your voice down? Do you want to wake up the entire school?"

Walking toward his mother, his bare feet stomped on the ground so hard, little volcanoes of snow erupted with each step. "What the hell do you mean he's a bloody vampire?"

"Vaughan is one of Them, hand-picked by Brania to be one of her disciples." Edwige watched a snowy white owl perched high in an oak tree, camouflaged from the human eye, crane its neck to look at something, prey perhaps, that had made a noise behind it. "She'll lie down with anything, that one."

Still in shock, Ronan was trying to comprehend what his mother had just told him, but the more he thought about it, the more questions he had. "Why couldn't I see it? How did he hide himself from me?"

Walking closer to the tree, Edwige seemed more concerned with getting a better look at the majestic creature than answering her son's questions. "There are ways of concealing oneself," she replied slowly. "Brania may look like a school-girl, but she's an ancient hag with more than one trick up her old-woman sleeves."

Even though her back was to him, she could hear Ronan talking to her, saying that it now all made sense. He under-stood why Vaughan had backed out at the last minute: He was afraid to be in his son's presence since he thought Michael was still human. Then again, maybe he knew that Michael was a water vamp, that could be it too. Edwige watched the owl noiselessly creep along the branch, his eyes sharp with determination and focus, obviously on his way to feed. She knew from experience watching wild animals that nothing was going to get in its way until its craving was sat-isfied, its need relinquished. She strived for that same focus in her own life, but unfortunately, she could sometimes be-come so easily distracted. "What did you say?"

"Vaughan is working with David!" Ronan exclaimed. "Howard Industries makes those contacts they wear. That's where Michael's father had to go, to his factory in Tokyo."

The owl spotted a field mouse, alone, unable to burrow through an ice patch, and it swooped down, disappearing out of view. Before the mouse could prepare itself, it felt talons pierce its skin and just before it lost consciousness, it felt like it was floating, completely free. Sometimes being the victim had its benefits; it brought with it freedom.

Edwige had spent quite some time questioning herself, wondering why she had let herself become interested in Vaughan and how she could have allowed Brania to take away any opportunity she might have had to find peace within his arms. Now she realized she had been tricked, the playing field had been tilted and she had entered the compe-tition at an unfair disadvantage. Brania and Vaughan weren't playing alone or even together, they were part of a much larger team led by David, and no matter what she felt about her former lover, no matter how much she despised him, she had to acknowledge that he was extremely powerful and a formidable opponent. As powerful as she herself was. Against the three of them Edwige really never stood a chance.

So she shouldn't blame herself for losing, for not emerging victorious as she typically did. The only way she should cast blame on herself was if she didn't attempt to seek revenge. And, oh yes, warn her son. "Tell Michael to stay away from his father."

The finality in Edwige's voice made Ronan nervous, "You think he'd hurt him?"

Would a parent ever willingly hurt his own child? Edwige sighed, knowing full well the answer to that question, but she thought it best to keep that to herself. "Vaughan, like most men, cannot be trusted."

Once again Ronan was struck with how similar he and his mother were; their thoughts about men were almost identical.

When he slipped into bed next to Michael a few minutes later, Ronan wondered if he should trust him with the truth. But when he felt Michael stir underneath his touch, he was overcome with the desire to protect him. He just wanted everything to stay the same, endless nights of sleeping next to the most beautiful boy in the world. He knew in his heart, however, that Michael was no longer a boy. He was changing and it had nothing to do with becoming a vampire. He was taking the first steps to becoming a man, and Ronan was delighted to bear witness to the transformation and proud that he had played a role in starting Michael on his journey. Ronan felt just like his father, which filled him equally with pride and with sadness, and he chose to smile in the darkness the same way his father had chosen to smile through the flames. Ronan wrapped his arm around Michael, holding his hand close to his chest, and was comforted, even as his mind searched for peace, by the steady, unwavering beat of his boyfriend's heart.

He spent most of the night praying that the changes occurring around him, the information that he was acquiring, would not damage his relationship with Michael or end the journey they were just beginning. While Ronan spent the night struggling to grasp abstract issues, come morning, Michael had more practical matters to deal with.

Walking out of the locker room at St. Sebastian's, Michael and Ciaran were stopped by the loud blow of Blakeley's whistle. "You two have to miss a couple swim practices next week," he bellowed, almost as loudly.

His ears still ringing, Michael asked, "Why? Isn't our first meet coming up?"

"Don't worry about that," Blakeley replied. "I've scheduled you for some early morning practices."

"That's very thoughtful of you, sir," Ciaran remarked a bit sarcastically, unable to stop himself.

"That's because I'm a very thoughtful bloke!" Blakeley shouted, believing every word he said.

"Of course, but, um, you still haven't told us why we have to miss practice," Michael reminded him.

"Don't you two pay attention to anything other than your schoolwork?" Blakeley asked. "You forgot to sign up for driver's lessons after school. I put your names on the list."

Michael and Ciaran looked at each other with surprise. Between swim practice, studying, and reconnecting with their friends after the semester break, they had forgotten that they had to take driver's education lessons before they could apply for their licenses this summer. They would both turn seventeen in June, Ciaran on the fifteenth and Michael on the twenty-second, and getting their own license was just one more step toward adulthood. "Of course," Michael said. "I'm looking forward to it."

"Well, if you drive as well as you swim, you won't have any problems," Blakeley announced. "And you bloody well better not because I'm your teacher."

When Blakeley was out of earshot, Michael confessed to Ciaran that he couldn't believe he forgot about something so important. "I've wanted my license for as long as I can remember," he mused. "I always imagined myself stealing my grandpa's truck and just driving west to California. Not that it would've made it past Nevada, it was so beat up."

Ciaran shook his head, the look of disbelief on his face apparent. "Do I have to remind you that you don't need a license to travel anywhere in the world? You could be in California quicker than it'll take you to get to your next class if you wanted to."

For a moment, Michael was truly surprised by that comment. "Wow, sometimes I actually forget that I am, you know, what I am."

"Either that or you still want to think that you are what you were," Ciaran corrected. "You can't have it both ways, mate."

Michael wasn't sure if he was unable to concentrate on conducting the experiment correctly because of what Ciaran said or because he simply didn't have any interest in science. He listened to the lectures, he read the books, he followed the carefully laid out instructions, and yet the liquid in his test tube was still yellow and stagnant and not green and bubbling like the rest of the class's. "How can Ciaran possibly find this stuff exciting?" Michael complained. "I can't even make this stupid potion bubble!"

His lab partner agreed, but Fritz's approach to handling a difficult school lesson was to ignore it entirely and talk about personal matters instead. "I've made a decision," Fritz declared. "The first book should be the introduction of The Double P, sort of like Penry's resurrection." Looking a bit like a superhero himself in a gold laboratory smock and plastic goggles, Fritz had to prod Michael for a response. "Nebraska! Isn't that a great idea?"

"Yes, terrific. Penry would love it," Michael said, his eyes glaring at him from behind his own superhero-inspired goggles. "But right now we have to get this liquid to do something or else Professor Chow is never going to pass us."

"Who cares about him?!" Fritz huffed. "I'll just get Ciaran to do it for me later; the chump loves to show off his science skills." Clearing his throat, Fritz decided it was time to segue into the most important subject of all. "Have you, um, noticed anything wrong with Phaedra?" he asked. "I get the feeling that she's been avoiding me."

Probably because she's never been more confused in all her life, which, now that I think about it, has probably lasted for a really, really, really long time. And since Michael was pretty certain that efemeras were as immortal as vampires, he knew that was quite a statement. "Really? I hadn't noticed."

Fritz grabbed the bleaker out of Michael's hands so he wouldn't be distracted by unimportant lab work. "Don't give me that. You two are like kith and kin you're so close. Everybody knows it. So what gives?"

"I don't really have that much experience, you know, with girls."

"Nebraska, cut it out," Fritz demanded. "You might be gay, but you're a guy and we have to be loyal to one another. Does Phaedra want to break up with me?"

So many thoughts swirled inside Michael's head, he felt the way their lab experiment should look. The fact that Fritz was straight and he wasn't didn't make any difference to

Fritz. He still considered Michael a friend. What a refreshing difference from what he was used to. On top of that, he had found out that not only were Fritz and Phaedra getting to know each other, they were officially dating. Phaedra never mentioned that to him. He would have to remember to yell at her for keeping such a big secret from him the next time he saw her, right after he gave her a congratulatory hug, of course. First, however, he had to deal with the object of Phaedra's affection. "I didn't even know you guys were dating."

"Oh," Fritz said, suddenly aware that he may have exposed a secret. "Well, we were trying to keep it quiet until we were sure about each other and, you know, we only had one date, which I guess was more like studying at St. Joshua's, but I thought it was a date, absolutely."

"Sounds like you're very sure about her," Michael said, smiling.

"First time for everything, I guess," Fritz replied. "I'm just not so sure she feels the same way about me anymore."

Michael knew that Phaedra really had no idea how she felt, but he didn't want to alarm Fritz any more than he already was. It was cute to see him so nervous about a girl, yet another unexpected side to his friend revealed. "I'm sure it's nothing, but I will talk to her."

"Thanks, mate."

As if on cue, the yellow liquid finally started to change color, to a not-so-flattering shade of green, like the face of a seasick sailor during a rough storm. Regardless of how unsightly it looked, their experiment seemed to be working and the boys stared at the test tube in amazement. Soon their amazement turned to cheers of joy as the ugly green liquid started to bubble over.

"I should alert the new headmaster," Professor Chow pronounced. "Today is a national holiday, the first time you two ever made an experiment work."

Triumphant, Fritz and Michael high-fived each other. He felt kind of silly, but more than that, Michael felt proud. What an incredible feeling to know that nothing is insurmountable. And what an incredible feeling to know that he had someone to share his achievements with.

Before he went home and told Ronan about his day, he wanted to do something special for him. No matter how many little arguments they might have, Michael still felt Ronan was the most wonderful person he'd ever met and he wanted to make sure that he knew just how special he was. Luckily, he knew the perfect way to get his point across.

He smelled the bouquet of white roses and it was like breathing in summer. It was so fragrant and sweet that he thought the icicles that had formed on the window ledges and the roof of St. Joshua's would melt away. Even though the existence of the roses was a miracle, unexplained and mysterious, they were still taken for granted by many of the students. The roses had grown outside the library for as long as anyone could remember; they had just become a normal part of the terrain regardless of how odd it was to see them flourishing in the winter. Not as odd as seeing Edwige strolling across campus, however.

"Michael, darling," she called out as she approached him. "How lovely to see you."

"Mrs. Glynn . . . I mean, Edwige, hi." Michael was so startled to see Ronan's mother on school grounds that he almost called her by her full name, which was something she hated. As Ronan once explained, Edwige liked to think she's still a woman and not, shudder at the thought, someone's mum. Whatever she was, Michael thought she was intimidating. "What a surprise! What, um, are you doing here?"

"I was doing some business nearby and thought I'd visit Ronan, but he isn't home," she explained. "Or he's hiding from me. Would you happen to know which it is?"

Michael blinked. He wasn't used to being examined so openly. Well, that wasn't entirely true; sometimes Ronan couldn't peel his eyes away from him, but that was different. That was welcome; this was his mother. And it didn't help that she had the same piercing blue eyes as her son. It was nice to see a connection, but it made him uncomfortable. Michael then wondered if Saoirse had the same blue eyes. He was about to ask Edwige about her, but she interrupted him.

"I asked you a question, dear."

"Oh, sorry. He's probably at the gym," he offered. "You know how he loves the water."

Laughing heartily. "Don't we all." As abruptly as it began, her laughing stopped. "What are those?"

"These? Just some roses I picked for Ronan." Saying it out loud made him feel a little embarrassed. Or was it just the way Edwige was staring at the roses?

"They're beautiful," Edwige said in a strained whisper. She really didn't think very much of the roses, they were flowers, nothing more, but she remembered where she had seen them before, in a vase in Vaughan's apartment, and for some reason that memory was disturbing. "Where did you get them?"

"Over by St. Joshua's," Michael said. "You must know about them."

Cute, but presumptuous. "Perhaps I must, but as it turns out, I don't."

"Oh. Well, um, legend has it that they have some magical properties. They can erase the past and create a more appealing future," Michael explained. "Probably just folklore, but I do think it's sweet. And so does Ronan."

So that was it. Vaughan had used common voodoo to trick her, to conceal his vampire blood from her senses. Juvenile, yet effective. She was impressed by his actions, infuriated that she was duped, but grateful, after all, that she had not lost her intuition. She had known there was something peculiar about the man, and now she knew with more certainty than ever that he would have to pay for his duplicity. Even while imagining how she would make Vaughan suffer for making her doubt herself, for making a fool of her, she was still able to compliment his son. "It's a beautifully romantic gesture," she said honestly. "I'm very happy that my son has found a wonderful and worthwhile partner."

"Thank you," Michael replied, his cheeks reddening.

"I think you must know from what Ronan has told you or from what you've already ascertained that I am not the motherly type," Edwige confessed. "However, I would very much like to be your friend."

What an unexpected proposition. He missed his own mother very much. More specifically, he missed the mother that he knew Grace had desperately wanted to become, the woman that she was for brief moments during her lifetime, but that she was never able to maintain. He missed being able to share his joys and doubts and the boring moments of his life with her, he wished he had the chance to tell her that he had found someone special, someone who loved him dearly. He knew Edwige could never take his mother's place—no woman could—but it would be nice to have an older, sophisticated, female friend to confide in, someone who knew about the world and, of course, all about Ronan. "And I would very much like to be yours."

When Michael shook Edwige's hand to cement their new relationship, a shiver ran down his spine. Regrettably, he assumed it was the result of a sudden wind instead of the warning that it was.

chapter 8

Ciaran thought he was alone. He didn't know he had a visitor because he didn't benefit from having a sixth sense, a preternatural ability to be aware of things he couldn't see. But his movements, his demeanor, were all being studied, analyzed, as if he were the specimen he was looking at through his microscope.

His long, slender fingers deftly adjusted the blood sample that was squashed in between the two thin pieces of glass so that it lined up in the center of the lens. With his right hand he scribbled down notes without looking at the yellow lined pad:—*hu* was part of his own made-up code and wouldn't make sense to anyone else, including the person watching him, but Ciaran knew it meant "not human." He wasn't surprised. When he swiped the bloodstained towel from Ronan and Michael's bathroom sink, he expected this would be the result, no other outcome was possible. He was, however, hoping that it would be Michael's blood he extracted from the towel, not a sample that he quickly recognized, not a sample that he had already analyzed several times before. Peering at the red blob through his lens, his scowl apparent even though most of his face was hidden by the microscope, he wrote *R3* on the pad. Brania, with her extraordinary sight, was able to read it, but she didn't understand that it translated to mean the third sample of blood he had acquired from Ronan.

An unexpected wave of jealousy enveloped her and for a brief moment she feared she would drown. He's so studious, she thought. When she was a young girl, study was never considered necessary or appropriate for her sex, the female gender had other skills that had to be honed outside of the classroom. For a moment she wondered how different her life would be had she been allowed to become a student of science and mathematics instead of other subjects. Maybe she could officially enroll at St. Anne's, take on a full schedule of classes, learn all about chemistry, algebra, and all the other more traditional subjects that had eluded her in her expansive lifetime. She did find their uniform to have a certain girlish charm. But no, a detour wasn't realistic. How could she survive being confined to such a rigid schedule after centuries of freedom? And how could she even entertain a thought like this when her father needed her to help carry out his plan? Academics would have to wait. It was time for action.

"Ciaran," Brania said softly from the front door, "do forgive me for interrupting your work."

Startled, Ciaran looked up, his hand instinctively covering his cryptic notes. So she had finally come back. Took her long enough. At the end of last semester, Brania had waltzed into this very same lab with Nakano in tow and told him that her father wished to propose a business partnership. At the time, he had found the invitation enticing, dangerous but, ultimately, not legitimate. Until now. "Forgiveness is unnecessary," Ciaran said, casually turning his pad facedown on the black granite countertop. "My lab is your lab."

Of course, as long as I don't take a peek at your notes. "That will make my father very happy," Brania said. "You do remember Father's proposition, don't you?"

Ciaran felt his chest tighten, he knew it was an alert, his own body warning his mind, but he didn't want to listen to caution any longer. Just where had that gotten him? He had tried to be reckless before, tried to force others to change his life, turn him into something that he was not, but even that didn't work. He had to face the fact that alone he was weak; it was time to find a partner. "It's all I've been thinking about," Ciaran replied. "But I had begun to think that he had forgotten about me."

Leisurely, Brania walked toward Ciaran. She knew she should quicken her pace, speed up this part of their meeting, but she loved the way her heels sounded clicking against the harsh laboratory floor. And Ciaran did look like he was enjoying the view; most heterosexual men did. She didn't speak until she reached the opposite side of the lab from Ciaran. "How in the world could we forget someone as brilliant as you?" Placing her hands on the lab countertop, the white edges of her French-tipped manicure accenting perfectly against the black granite, Brania stared at Ciaran. The only things coming between them were the microscope and Ciaran's anxious breathing. She might not have had a formal education, but she could teach a master class in seduction. "Or someone as handsome."

"A combination blessed by providence."

The melodious voice was familiar, but Ciaran couldn't place it immediately. He saw an imposing figure standing in the doorway, but only when he stepped out of the shadows did he recognize who it was. "He-he-headmaster," Ciaran stuttered. "What a surprise!"

"Why should it be a surprise?" Brania said, hoisting herself up so she could sit on the countertop, her bare legs dangling, swinging several feet from the floor. "Weren't we just talking about my father?"

David extended his right leg, his foot angled slightly, toe pointed outward, and bowed from the waist. His suit, his whole physical appearance, looked to be the epitome of modern-day style, but his gesture, his character, was definitely from an earlier century. "You spoke and I have come," David said, rising, his eyes meeting Ciaran's perplexed gaze. "It's as if your words conjured my presence."

Brania's father is the new headmaster? How could that be? he thought. Why hadn't Ronan told him; why hadn't he told anybody? He had to know about this. He and their mother lived with this man while Ciaran had been banished to one boarding school after the other, banished from Edwige's sight. Obviously, Ronan was back to his old self, thinking that he was superior to everyone and that nobody needed to be privy to his secrets. "I knew there was something special about you, sir."

How refreshing, David thought, to hear a comment spoken with honesty and not dripping in flattery. At his core, Ciaran was a logical boy, which suited David's plans perfectly. Logic was always much easier to control than emotion. "I had the same feeling about you, young man."

Brania watched Ciaran's posture straighten just barely, but enough to realize that her father's words were having their usual, positive effect. If she hadn't so often been the recipient of David's kindness, she would have envied this latest object of his affection even more, but she knew what it felt like to be complimented by this man, to feel his admiration, unexpected but so very appreciated. Even now whenever he praised her, whenever she heard his words of approval, they pierced her heart like his loving fangs had once pierced her neck. What she wasn't used to, however, was being dismissed.

"You should leave us now," David said.

His eyes still focused on Ciaran. It took Brania a moment to understand that her father was speaking to her. Still, unaccustomed to being told what to do, she didn't move. When David spoke again, his eyes, if not his face, turned to address his daughter. "Are your ears not working properly?"

"Yes, but I . . ." The words caught in Brania's throat, which was an entirely new sensation for her, far too unpleasant, far too human for her liking. "I thought it would serve us all best if I stayed to help answer any questions Ciaran may have in response to your request."

"Well, my dear," David said, his lips forming a tight smile, "you thought wrong."

After a few moments of silence, it was clear that her father wasn't going to speak again, and from the tone he had used, the tone that Brania had heard him employ often over the past few centuries while speaking to subjects, victims, those who inhabited the inferior classes, she knew that nothing she could say would appease him, and most likely her rudeness would infuriate him. Or worse, disappoint him. He was giving her an order and regardless how slighted, how upset it made her feel, she had been taught to comply. "As you prefer, Father."

No one spoke as Brania walked toward the front door, allowing the room to be filled, unencumbered, by the sound of her clicking heels, a sound that she now hated, a sound that now accented her defeat. Outside, alone, Brania acknowledged that she did not enjoy feeling like a pawn. It was some comfort, however, knowing that Ciaran would soon feel the same way.

"Women are always trying to belong," David said. "They simply cannot accept that they are not man's equal. Don't you agree?"

Ciaran didn't agree actually. He always thought women were just as smart and as capable as men. And he knew first-hand from watching Edwige in action that women could also be physically stronger than men. But even though he believed in equality of the sexes, he was shocked to hear himself voice a contrasting opinion. "Yes," Ciaran said firmly. "Women must accept their own subservience."

"Well phrased," David said. Leaning in closer to Ciaran, his blue eyes reflecting the silvery speckles within the granite: "Do you mind if I repeat that idiom in my own private conversation? It's such a clever expression; it just begs for a larger audience."

The new headmaster, Brania's father, thinks I'm clever? "Well, sure, by all means."

"Thank you, Ciaran, I appreciate that."

Even if Ciaran had wanted to stop David's next movement, he wouldn't have been able to, so quickly did he grab the microscope, wheel it around, and peer into it to look at the sample of Ronan's blood. The odd thing was, Ciaran didn't want to stop him; he appreciated his interest. No one ever cared about his experiments, no one ever wanted to know more about what interested him, and here was this man, this really great man, taking notice of his work. The simple truth was it made him feel good.

"I must confess, Ciaran, I am not a man of science like you are," David stated. "But I am fascinated by its principles. Whoever deciphers them holds the keys to the universe."

He gets it! He understands why I'm so passionate about my work! "That's my goal, sir," Ciaran explained. "To unlock as many principles as I can, to learn as much about how the world works and about how we function in this world as I possibly can. It's all I think about most days and, well, I don't mean to sound arrogant, but it's what I'm quite good at. I only hope I'll get the opportunity to continue my research."

Such obedience, such willingness. Some children make it so easy. "Objective assessment of one's own strength is hardly arrogance. On the contrary, it's humility."

And all this time I was afraid to say what I honestly felt because I thought everyone would consider me conceited. "Really? That's being humble?"

"Acceptance of the talent and skill God has awarded you is a most humbling act," David replied. "Take me for example. I accept the fact that God has given me the talent to lead. Is that arrogance?" Without waiting for a response, David answered for his student. "I think not, I am merely acknowledging God's work." David felt the spark of inspiration ignite inside his mind. "Come to think of it, isn't that all that science really is, God's work?"

Never have I thought of it that way, but he's right, he's absolutely right. My research, my studying, the hours I've spent in this lab, have all been for the sake of God. "I've never been so proud to be a scientist."

"And I've never been so proud to give a student the chance to fulfill his dreams," David said. "But first I need you to promise me something."

"Of course, anything."

"For the time being, I would like the fact that I am also Brania's father to remain a secret to be shared by only a select few," David explained. "I trust you will agree to be part of that special group?"

They both knew what the answer would be before Ciaran even spoke. "I would be honored."

And if I were subject to God's will, I would be humbled.

"Now let me attempt to speak in the language you most readily understand," David said. "Science."

Captivated, Ciaran listened as David began to describe the help he needed, the help that only he could provide. "I am very interested in what separates species, the genetic differences that make one life-form unique from another."

Ciaran understood and what's more, he shared the same fascination. "You're talking about the deviations in the genetic makeup between vampires and humans, right?"

Close. "Absolutely!" David replied. "Not only are you intelligent but intuitive as well."

He even gets more excited than my science professors, Ciaran thought. *They just nod and mumble questions. David, I mean Headmaster Zachary, wants to get involved, wants to get involved with me.* "Thank you, sir," Ciaran said. He then unlocked the drawer to his left and pulled out a notebook, page after page filled with scribbled notes in his handwritten code, diagrams, calculations, and complex algorithms, none of which were decipherable by anyone but him. "I've actually started doing a few experiments on my own."

David was very pleased. He had known Ciaran would be willing to help; not many could resist his power of persuasion. But he never expected him to be armed with such vast material from the onset. *This boy has been quite industrious.* "Well, well, well, I see someone has been doing much more than schoolwork." For the first time since David walked through the door, Ciaran was nervous. "Don't worry," David said reassuringly. "I wholeheartedly approve of your extracurricular activities."

Relieved, Ciaran went on to explain that the sample of blood in his microscope was actually Ronan's. "Does your half brother know that you're examining his DNA?"

"Well, not exactly," Ciaran confessed. "I was really hoping to get some of Michael's blood, but once I saw it, I knew it was Ronan's. I have some older samples of his blood, and this one is the same as those."

David was very surprised. Usually he lost interest in someone much sooner than this, but the more Ciaran spoke, the more intrigued he was becoming. "Is there any reason why Michael's blood would prove to be more . . . interesting?"

"Since Michael's been a vampire for a much shorter period of time, I thought he might still have some human genetic composition in his blood. Ideally I'd like to track his blood over the course of several months to see if it changes in any way."

"I see," David replied. "Ciaran, I am more convinced than ever that you are the right man for this job. And furthermore, we will make a magnificent team."

Despite the elation Ciaran was feeling, he was starting to get a headache. If he didn't know any better, he would think it was the beginning of a migraine. But he had never had one of those in his life. "That sounds wonderful, Mr. Zachary, I mean Headmaster."

Laughing, David clutched Ciaran's shoulder, causing him to flinch. He wasn't afraid of this man; it was just that his touch was so cold, like the ice that covered the windows. "You have my permission, in private only of course, to call me simply by my first name."

"Thank you, David," Ciaran said proudly.

Without another word, David turned and started to walk toward the door, stopping only when he knew Ciaran was doing nothing more than staring at his back, waiting for him to speak. "Continue with your experiments and report to no one but me," David ordered.

"I'm not sure if I can do that . . . Da . . . sir."

David's eyes turned black, only for a second, not long

enough for Ciaran to notice, but long enough to remind David how much he detested insolence. "Whatever do you mean?"

"In order to conduct more experiments, I need Michael's blood, and I don't know if I can get that without his knowledge."

He wasn't being insolent, just practical, just being a good little scientist, a good little scientist who had nothing to worry about. "You leave the acquisition of Michael's blood to me," David said. "I'll make sure you have more than you need."

The moment David was gone, so too was Ciaran's headache. What lingered, however, for quite some time afterward, was the feeling that he had just had one of the most significant conversations of his young life.

Although his life could hardly be considered young, David felt the same way. This student, this young scientist, would prove immensely helpful in finding out what made those infernal water vamps walk in the sun outside of the hallowed grounds of Eden and why they only needed to feed once a month. It would bring David one step closer to uncovering the origins of The Well, their pagan god, so he could destroy it once and for all. The beauty of his plan, what made him admire it so much even if he alone created it, is that Ciaran would be doing all the work for him and would never know that he was betraying his own family. Pausing for a moment, David had an incredible thought: Maybe this child was fully aware of what he was doing. Born unto that disgraceful Edwige and saddled with that pompous Ronan for a brother, Ciaran would not surprise him at all if he had begun his research in the hopes of destroying his own family.

"If that turns out to be the case, I promise I will reward him properly."

He wasn't speaking to himself but to his namesake, the archangel Zachariel. David looked up to the unsmiling face carved from ancient oak, silhouetted by the sun, and forever etched into the side of the doorway of Archangel Cathedral, and he was filled with a conflicting combination of love and hatred. Every time he passed by the cathedral, he was disgusted to find Zachariel's image not gracing the apex of the archway, where it should be, but relegated to the side, under the lesser angels. One day he would rectify that imperfection, when his full power was restored, when the academy was cleansed of all its impurities. Until then he would close his eyes and imagine things the way they should be. And, of course, talk to Zachariel, who was always willing to listen to his most loyal servant.

"I have put another phase of our plan into motion," David whispered, believing that his voice was lifted by the breeze and taken to the waiting ears of his king. He also believed that when the wind erupted all around him, uplifting the snow from the ground and off of the branches, and his face and his heart were surrounded with an intense, numbing cold that Zachariel was offering his reply.

"Why has it taken you so long?"

David's knees buckled when he heard the harsh voice, and he almost knelt before the face of the angel, the angel that had suddenly grown angry, so confrontational. But David knew better. He knew that above all, Zachariel longed to admire his servants for their strength, not their weakness. "I have chosen a steady path and not a hasty one," David said, willing his voice to stay calm and resolute. "I have learned by your guidance that quick-footed vengeance does not always guarantee victory."

Slowly, the collection of clouds overhead separated, allowing the sun's rays to shine through. David lifted his head and welcomed the warmth of the sun, feeling its mercy grace his face, and he knew that the path he had chosen was the right one. "With the help of the children, I will make this land holy again."

And with the help of his own child, he was about to return to an even happier time, to a time when he was just beginning to make important choices.

Across campus, Brania was walking aimlessly, as she had been ever since she left St. Albert's, ever since she was told to leave by her father. Wandering, wandering, wandering, amid the snow and the trees and the few curious students who passed by her, wondering who she was. I'm no one, she wanted to call out to them, I am no one, and yet I am more than you can possibly imagine. And I am this way because of Him.

The only reason she stopped was because she heard the music. It was soft, glorious in its tone, and enchanting in its melody, she knew she had heard the sound before, but she couldn't place it. Instead of wasting time trying to determine how she remembered the tune, she sat on the trunk of a fallen tree and allowed the music to consume her, take her on its journey, and as is sometimes the case among those who share the same biological and vampiric bloodlines as she and her father did, she did not journey alone.

Watching herself as a young girl of six, perhaps seven, Brania was astounded she had spent so many years looking as she did just now, like a teenager, voluptuous, forever on the brink of womanhood, that she had forgotten she had once been a little girl. The vision was momentous, but heartbreaking.

It was quite the opposite for David. It was gratifying to be able to see in detail a memory from so long ago, a memory of him and his daughter, just as she was starting to comprehend his immense power. He remembered exactly when this memory took place: 1684, in a field in County Clark in Ireland, where he'd met Brania's mother, a weak woman not resilient enough to survive the birth of her only child. Brania's black hair framed her angelic face in a multitude of tendrils, and her lips and cheeks were a healthy pinkish-red color, like baby's blood. As she ran, her tiny feet were hidden by the overgrowing brush, and she seemed to float; the green silk hem of her otherwise cream-colored dress appeared to be an extension of the grass. She looked like an angel, a dark-haired, bloodstained angel gracing the earth with her presence.

To Brania, her younger self just looked frightened. She knew what was coming, she knew what was expected of her, and even though it was not the first time, she knew it would be difficult. Killing had not come as easy as Father had promised.

"See the boy, Brania," David said, kneeling down next to her, making sure he knelt on his black velvet robe so his white breeches wouldn't be stained with grass. "He's the one I would like. Call him over and ask him to play."

Hesitating, but only for a second, Brania shouted over to the boy and watched him run toward her. She recognized him as a boy from one of the poorer families in the village, but she didn't know his name. Better that way, better not to know too much about the children her father wanted her to kill.

As the boy in the memory got closer, the music got louder, as if whoever was singing, whoever was making that beautiful music, knew what was going to happen and was singing louder as a warning. Useless. Nothing could save the boy, not now, not then, not as long as her father wished him to be dead.

The boy saw David nod in Brania's direction, but he never saw the rock strike the side of his head, the rock that the little girl had concealed within the folds of her dress. He never felt his body fall onto the grass, he never felt the stream of blood trickle down the side of his face, and he never felt David's fangs pierce into his neck. Brania was thankful it was dark, grateful there was no sun to illuminate the scene. She didn't want to see her father drink from this boy, she didn't want to see Him take his life away. All she really wanted to do was run, as far away as she could, but she knew then, as she knew now, that there was no escaping Him.

As her father drank hungrily from the boy's limp body, Brania remembered that he had promised her riches in exchange for her help, toys and jewelry when she got older, the most expensive, beautiful clothes, anything that she could ever want or desire. That helped, knowing that her actions were worthy of reward. And recognition. "My child," David told her, "you will always sit on my right side, on the right side of the Father." It's the only place Brania ever wanted to be.

So lost in her memory, so lost in the confused mind of the girl she was all those centuries ago, that when she saw Edwige she didn't follow her. She had done enough traveling for one day and all she wanted to do was sit and listen to the music.

Edwige was surprised that more people hadn't seen her walking across campus. She was afraid these past few weeks that she might be spotted by David or Brania. Such a meeting would have been unfortunate, but luckily that never happened. She also thought she would have been seen by Ronan's friends or some teachers who weren't fond of adults roaming around school grounds without an obvious purpose. She didn't feel threatened by anyone, but she hated having to explain herself. Perhaps she had gone unnoticed because from behind she looked like just another student. That was entirely possible; being petite really did have its advantages.

Exactly three hundred and forty feet into The Forest of No Return, Edwige turned right and walked until she reached the old oak tree that at some point in its history had been split in half by lightning. And then she turned left and walked until she reached the cave. The area was desolate and wild, which was why she chose it; she knew no one would stumble upon it accidentally. She could remain unworried in the knowledge that here her treasure would be safe.

The opening to the cave was so low to the ground that even Edwige needed to bend as low as she could to enter. Once inside, she noticed the smell, but was no longer repulsed by it, by the dank earth, untouched by snow and still reeking of a fertile and powerful odor. The singing, however, still annoyed her. She did not appreciate music; she much preferred visual art. She could, and often did, gaze at a painting for hours and imagine living within its canvas, but when she heard music, all she heard was someone else's voice and she didn't much care about what anyone else had to say.

Hunched over, she walked through the tunnel that connected the entrance of the cave to her final destination, a crypt that was barren except for two items that Edwige herself had brought here: a torch and a coffin.

She added a few twigs and pieces of bark to the torch to keep it lit and shuddered as the fire warmed her face. Turning away from the flames and the unwanted memory of her husband's murder, she faced the coffin. Even shut tight, the music escaped. Well, Edwige thought, there wasn't much she could do about that. There really was only so much she could control.

Slowly, tenderly, Edwige opened the coffin. The girl was

still there as she had been the last time Edwige visited, her eyes closed, her hands crossed on her chest like the corpse that she was. The only discrepancy was that her mouth was moving, singing softly. Edwige supposed that, to some, the sound could be considered soothing, but it needed to stop, the singing needed to come to an end. "Wake up, lazybones," Edwige commanded. "It's time for you to get to work."

Only when she recognized the voice did Imogene open her eyes and become silent.

chapter 9

Up until her untimely and brutal death, Imogene Minx had been a lucky girl. She was healthy, an independent thinker, and a member of a well-to-do family. Everyone who knew her thought she would live a long and interesting life, not only because of her intelligence and self-assured character, but because the surname, Minx, had become synonymous with success.

It was Imogene's great-great-great grandfather, Nikolaj, who jump-started her family's legacy. Early in his career as a furrier he was struggling to survive, living in poverty, until he decided to change his name from Minksoff to the more glamorous, and professionally appropriate, Minx. It proved to be a shrewd decision and soon Nikolaj Minx was the preeminent furrier in all of Imperial Russia, the man every fashionable empress and dowager could not live without. One of those dowagers became so enamored with the charismatic man that she became his wife three months after she became a widow.

While Nikolaj built his business into an empire, his wife, Svetlana, combined her dowry with his profits to create one of the largest arts centers in Russia, the Minx Center for the Performing Arts, which still stands in the heart of St. Petersburg today long after many of its competitors had collapsed. It was there that Imogene made her operatic debut in a production of *La Bohème* at the age of six. Her mother, Katya, sang the role of Mimi, the ill-fated seamstress who dies of consumption, a role that she played to great acclaim and one that would become her signature, while Imogene appeared as one of the children in the second-act street scenes. Even then, her voice was pitch-perfect, a lilting soprano whose clarity could penetrate a chorus of more powerful and better-trained singers. Katya knew that her daughter had the raw talent needed to become an extraordinary singer, that she possessed a voice that could, if used properly, bring her international renown. But Imogene had other ideas.

One night while they were having their usual postperformance meal of cold chicken and blini with red caviar, Imogene, quite prophetically, told her mother that she wanted to be like Mimi when she grew up.

"Maliysh," Katya said, "my baby, why would you say such a thing?"

"Because Mimi gets to die young," Imogene replied. "Before she gets old and ugly."

Unfortunately, Imogene would be granted her wish. She had escaped death twice, once when Nakano tossed her aside, preferring to take Penry's life instead, and once when she accidentally killed Jeremiah before he could kill her. However, when she got caught in a tug-of-war between two powerful women, Brania and Edwige, a third reprieve was not granted, and it was Edwige who unwittingly made a six-year-old girl's wish come true.

When Imogene regained consciousness and noticed no real difference, no drastic physical change, she thought her luck had held out, that she had somehow managed to escape death yet again. Wasn't her soul supposed to be released from her body; wasn't she supposed to embark on a journey to heaven, a journey that would transcend mortal limitations? And shouldn't she be reunited with Penry, her boyfriend, her one and only true love? That's what the nuns had taught her was supposed to happen; that's what she had come to expect of death. It wasn't supposed to be like this. She wasn't supposed to wake up, unable to move but fully aware that she was in a coffin, hear the world around her, hear the rain fall, the birds chirp, and not be able to respond in any way. This just wasn't right.

After some time, she had come to realize that while she was indeed dead, she was also under Edwige's control and being held a prisoner, suspended between the realms of her past life and true death. She was trapped within her own body, she felt like one of those people she had read about who were about to undergo surgery and appeared to be anesthesized, but who were completely awake. Mentally she was alive; physically it was as if she were in a coma.

The only ability she did still have, however, was the ability to sing, which is how she spent much of her time. It didn't show on her face as she sang, but each note made her smile. Maybe it's because Mama always said that when she sang, it was like hearing an angel rejoice. Maybe if she sang loud enough, Mama would hear her and know that her angel was nearby, know that her angel still looked like her daughter, that she was still alive despite looking like this toy corpse. And so she continued to sing until, of course, Edwige told her to stop.

Now, as she stood outside of St. Florian's, she could smell the roses. The scent was sweet, but powerful, and wafted down from the window on the second floor. It was a scent that consumed her with fear, the same aroma that had filled Jeremiah's apartment and she knew that somewhere in Michael and Ronan's dorm room, there was a vase filled with white roses. Had she complete control of her body, Imogene would have turned and run as far away as possible, far from the smell and the violent memory, but Edwige had given her a command, a task, and she was unable to resist.

She told her body to rise and it did, not stopping until she was able to look through the window and see the boys asleep in their bed. Looking down, she saw her feet standing on air, the snow-covered ground two stories below, and she couldn't help but be amazed by her power. *I don't know how I'm doing this,* she thought, *but it's really impressive.*

When she raised her arm, the window opened as if the two were one. Once again she was impressed with her new gifts, but quickly admiration turned to fear. The sweet scent of roses swept passed her, through her, making her relive that terrible night, making her feel Jeremiah's grip, his desire to destroy her. No! She would not give in. She had survived his attempt to kill her and she would survive this. Closing her eyes to defend herself against the fragrance that rushed toward her, Imogene thought of happier times, the night of the Archangel Festival, Penry, kissing Penry, shopping with Phaedra. It was working; she was breathing easier; her thoughts were replacing the harsh memories.

And then she heard the rain.

Opening her eyes, she saw the rain fall all around her. She couldn't feel the drops, but she could smell them. The rain's fresh scent was combating the smell of the roses and she knew that it was no coincidence. The rain had been sent to help her, to help her regain her strength, her sanity, so she could fulfill her duty. When she was inside the room and saw the vase filled with a bouquet of white roses on the end table next to the boys' bed, her body didn't falter, her voice didn't waver, she kept singing, softly but firmly, calling out to Michael, urging him to rise.

There's that song again, Michael thought, still dreaming. *How wonderful, the meadowlark has finally returned.* But when he awoke, when he opened his eyes to greet one old friend, he was amazed to see another. He blinked his eyes several times, thinking that he was still caught in a dream, but she wouldn't go away, the apparition didn't fade. What was Imogene doing at the foot of his bed singing, floating in the air like a marionette connected by invisible strings to some higher power?

"Hello, Michael."

In the midst of this fantastic occurrence the only thought that popped into Michael's head was a practical one: How can she sing and talk at the same time?

"You need to come with me."

What was going on? He wasn't scared by his friend's presence, just really curious. What was Imogene doing here? He turned to look at Ronan, hoping he would have some answers, but saw that he was still asleep, totally unaware that they had a visitor. How could he sleep? How could he not hear that music? The sound was filling up the room.

"Because I've only come for you."

And now she can read my mind? Michael sat up in bed and fought the urge to shake Ronan, to wake him up so he could share in this incredible experience, to let him know that after all this time, Imogene had returned. But even though he didn't understand what was happening, he intuitively understood that this vision was meant only for his eyes.

The singing stopped, but when Imogene spoke again, her lips still did not move. "I have something to show you."

Quietly, Michael got out of bed and followed Imogene as she floated toward the window. She looked the same and yet something wasn't right, something about her made his heart ache. Her hair was still so black that the light from the moon made it shine blue in some places. It still fell just below her chin, her bangs cut straight across her forehead. Her skin looked as unblemished and pale as Michael remembered, her eyes—yes, that was it! Her eyes were still black, but instead of being inquisitive and alert, they were dull, devoid of any life whatsoever. Imogene extended her hand to Michael and when he grabbed it and felt the chill travel from her fingers up his arm, his fears were confirmed. Imogene was dead.

Before he could contemplate how she had died or why she had come back for him, he was thrust through some sort of tunnel, the wind billowing on both sides of him, echoing noisily in his ears, the landscape changing rapidly from rain and snow and trees to sun and sand and ocean. When they stopped moving, it took him only a few seconds to get his bearings and to realize that he was on the beach, the beach he had dreamed about while in Weeping Water.

Feeling slightly more unnerved now that they had landed than while they were traveling, Michael wanted to ask Imogene why they were here, why she had brought him to this place, but it was so calm, so tranquil, he didn't want to interrupt the serenity with words and remained silent. He followed Imogene, but as she walked on top of the calm ocean, he walked into it. He looked down and saw the wave water envelop his feet languidly, without hurry, felt its coolness wash over his feet, his ankles. He was a part of this landscape; Imogene, his guide, was not. He stopped when the water reached his waist, but Imogene kept walking as if to step out of Michael's memory, give him some privacy for what was yet to come. When she finally stopped, quite some distance away, she looked at Michael, her face a mask empty of any expression. Whatever emotions she was feeling would not be conveyed, and without another word of instruction or explanation, she turned her head preferring to watch some seagulls on their endless quest for food than the images about to befall her friend.

Before Michael felt Ronan's touch, he knew he would be there. This was where they had first met, in his dream, before they saw each other in front of Archangel Cathedral, before the real world caught up with their destiny.

"Ronan, what's going on?" Michael asked.

"I don't know," he replied, smiling. "This isn't my journey."

Tracing Michael's lips with his wet finger, Ronan stared tenderly at his boyfriend. "No matter what happens, no matter what you see, remember that nothing can change the present."

For the first time, Michael felt cold, the ocean water that glided from his lips, past his chin, down his neck was like ice. "I don't understand."

"You will," Ronan said, kissing Michael softly. "When you're ready."

They embraced, Ronan pressing his strong body into Michael as if to give him his strength. Holding on to Ronan's muscular back, Michael felt an odd mixture of passion and panic when he saw, over his shoulder, his mother standing on the beach, her hands outstretched and drenched in blood. Without turning around, Ronan told Michael, "This isn't for me to witness." And before Michael could beg him to stay, Ronan plunged into the ocean and disappeared.

"Ronan! Come back!"

His plea was not acknowledged. The only response was the far-off sound of a seagull's cry. And then Grace's breathing.

Even though his mother was over a hundred yards away on the beach, and the waves were beginning to gain speed and power, their sound escalating louder and louder as they crashed onto the shore, Michael could hear his mother's frantic breathing as if she were standing right next to him. It was so forceful, so commanding, it was as if there were no other sound in the world.

Until she screamed.

Frightened, Michael's eyes searched the ocean to find Imogene, hoping that once he did, she could put an end to this nightmare, end the intense emotional pain he was already experiencing seeing his mother so fragile, so wounded. *This is in the past,* Michael thought. *I don't want to see this again!* Finally, he found his dead friend hovering over the horizon. "Imogene! Please, make this stop!"

Imogene heard him, but she, just like Ronan, had no other choice but to ignore him. What else could they do? They weren't the ones in control. All Imogene had been instructed to do was to bring Michael here so he could see the events unfold as they had originally taken place, as he was previously unable to see them. She couldn't stop them, she couldn't alter them in any way, and thankfully she didn't have to watch them with him. She could fix her gaze upon something in the distance, anything, a whale, yes, that would do, a whale spouting a spray of water into the air as it traveled just beneath the ocean's surface. Anything was better than watching Michael's mother fall to the sand on her knees and shriek.

As Grace's cries pierced Michael's ears, he was transported back to another time, back to the dream in which he had his first kiss with the boy who would turn out to be Ronan, back to the dream in which he saw his mother covered with blood, and he couldn't believe he was being forced to relive the experience. He remembered seeing his mother, the blood pouring from her wrists, staining the beach, the accusing stare in her eyes beneath the look of frenzy, the stare that still haunted him. But as he stared at his mother more closely, he realized that something was different. It was just as with Imogene, there was something different about her eyes. They were consumed by the same look that he remembered from his dream, the same look of accusation, but they were not looking at him. Turning around, he found the reason. His mother was looking at someone else. His father.

Vaughan was only a few feet away, standing on top of the waves, displaying the same impossible skills as Imogene, his feet bare, his white pants and shirt dry even though he was less than an inch above the ocean, the ocean that was growing rougher by the second.

"Dad?!" Michael cried out, unaware that the word had never escaped his lips with such ease before. "What's going on?!"

It didn't matter that it was Michael's memory, his trip through time, it was as if he weren't there. All that existed, all that meant anything, was the space between Grace and Vaughan, Michael was simply a spectator. But even though he was their child, he felt oddly disconnected in their presence. This was the first time he had seen his parents together since he was a very young boy, and looking at them now—his mother wild, frenetic, and blood-soaked, his father calm, aloof, immaculate—he couldn't imagine them ever being a couple. And yet something had united them, something that had been just as powerful as what tore them apart.

He thought of how he had felt when he first laid eyes on Ronan and wondered if his parents had ever felt a similar passion, the same kind of need. No, that was impossible. If they did, they would still be together, they would never have separated, nothing and no one in the world could extinguish that kind of love. Michael knew so much more than they did, he understood so much more about life, and yet if that were true, why did he feel like a child, lost, alone, and scared that he was about to witness something he never wanted to see?

"You!" Grace heaved the word into the air with such force that the ocean roared and this time when the waves crashed beneath Vaughan's feet, he was no longer immune to their aftershock; a fan of salt water rose and arched, showering his body. But when the water touched him, it turned to blood.

Startled, Michael stumbled backward and fell underwater. When he came back up, he shook his head, hoping that would correct the image, but it only made things worse. He watched in horror as rivulets of blood raced down Vaughan's cheeks, his shirt, the side of his pants, staining his outfit, turning the white cloth dark pink. For a moment, time stood still while Michael watched transfixed as one bright red drop of blood hung from Vaughan's foot, seemingly determined to cling to the flesh it had sought out, until gravity interfered and it fell into the ocean. Michael wished he could follow and hide, descend lower, lower, lower, underneath the water's surface, far away from his parents, who were now both dripping in blood. But he couldn't. He was compelled to watch, for no matter how painful it was to see these two people in such a raw, private moment, these two people were still his parents.

In spite of that, he began to suffocate. All the anxiety he felt as a little boy in Weeping Water started to push against his chest, his lungs; all the desperation he thought was gone, buried along with the rest of his past, began to resurface. He wanted to shout, scream as loud as he possibly could to block out what was happening, but his mother beat him to it.

"I'm ashamed of you!!"

Once Grace spoke, Michael was rendered speechless. The words were familiar; he had heard them before, but unlike the last time, unlike the last time she spoke those words in his dream, Grace wasn't talking to Michael, she was talking to Vaughan. Confused, Michael looked at his mother, her bloodied hand pointing directly past him, and he realized that she wasn't ashamed of him, she had never been ashamed of him, she was ashamed of his father. But why? What could he have possibly done to make her react so ferociously? Michael didn't know, but he could tell from Vaughan's expression that his mother's accusation was warranted. Vaughan was staring back at Grace with the expression of a man who could not fight the condemnation being hurled at him.

Waving her arms in the air, blood flinging all around her, Grace continue to yell at Vaughan, "This is all because of you! I'm so ashamed of what you've become!"

Michael was aware that his mother was speaking, that she was forming words, but he couldn't hear what she was saying, nothing registered in his mind because he was consumed with his own guilt. He had spent so much time blaming his mother, being angry with her since he thought she was ashamed of him because he was gay, that he now felt incredibly guilty. She had done nothing wrong; she had loved him like a mother should love her son, unconditionally and with a full heart. Her words—her shame—had been directed at his father.

"I'm sorry!" Michael shouted, but Grace couldn't hear him. She was screaming new words at his father, new accusations.

"Why did you do this to me?!"

Grace held out her hands to Vaughan, fresh blood pouring from her slashed wrists, and it was clear to Michael that his mother blamed her suicide on Vaughan. Something that he did forced her to take her own life. But that didn't make any sense. She hardly ever mentioned him, Michael didn't think they were even in contact with each other. Except for a few phone calls during the holidays, they lived separate lives. They both wanted it that way. Or so Michael thought. Was something going on between his parents that he didn't know about? Something horrendous and recent that would have caused Grace to finally succeed where she had failed several times before?

"What did you do to her!?" Even if Vaughan could hear his son, he would have ignored him. All his attention was focused on his ex-wife. He stared at Grace, no longer as a man who was willing to accept a verbal lashing, but defiant. He looked like a guilty man who knew his innocence would never be disproved. His arrogance only seemed to madden Grace even more.

"I told you to leave him alone! I told you that you couldn't have him!"

Even though Grace wasn't looking at Michael, he knew she was talking about him. Was Vaughan planning on taking him away from his mother and Weeping Water even before her death? Was that what got her so upset the last time? Maybe . . . but if that was the truth, wouldn't her suicide just be the fulfillment of Vaughan's wishes? With his mother gone, no one would be able to stop him from taking Michael away from the only home he had ever known.

Suddenly the waves stopped crashing, the ocean rested, and Grace sped from the beach to where Vaughan stood in less than a second. She stood a foot from the man whom she all but announced was her murderer and there was silence until she spoke. "And now he will never be yours."

Slowly disgust took over Vaughan's face as the truth of Grace's words penetrated his mind. After everything he had done, Michael still wasn't really his son and he never would be. Vaughan grabbed Grace's wrist and pulled her close to him, his lips slithering into a smile. Michael lunged forward, but before he could get next to his father, Imogene was standing before him, blocking him from making contact. "No."

"Imogene, please!" Michael screamed. "He's hurting her!"

There was pity in her eyes, but Michael couldn't see it, her eyes remained as blank as a dead girl's. "There's nothing he or anyone can do to hurt her ever again."

But Vaughan didn't want to hurt Grace, far from it, he only wanted to drink her blood. Kneeling on the now stagnant water, Vaughan held Grace's arm over his head and squeezed her wrist. A fountain of blood squirted out and Vaughan drank. The blood started to flow from Grace's arm with more speed and Michael could see his father's throat, grotesquely enlarged, rise and fall, trying to swallow every drop of fluid. After a few moments he gave up and started to laugh, though no one else joined in. He laughed so hard that the blood spilled out from the sides of his mouth and slid down his chin. Finally Michael tore his eyes away from his father and looked up to see his mother staring at him, tears falling from her eyes.

She sees me. Michael gasped. *She's making a connection.* "Mother!"

He felt the cold grasp of Imogene's hand and instantly Michael was back in the present, standing in the middle of The Forest, his parents, their blood, the ocean, all once again a mere memory. He had so many questions, but Imogene had no answers. "That's all I'm allowed to show you for now."

And then she was gone.

Michael turned around. He looked all over, but he couldn't find her, she had disappeared. But was she ever there in the first place? Was this some sort of dream? Did he imagine it all? A rush of wind erupted from the sky and Michael felt a chill. He shivered; his clothes were soaking wet. No, he hadn't been dreaming, he had somehow entered his dream and saw the truth of the past. It had happened; it was as real as the noise he just heard.

"Mom, is that you?" Michael called out, hopefully.

The second time he heard the sound, he realized it was not the kind of sound that a mother would make. He felt his fangs pressing down on his lips. He looked at his hands and saw that small, translucent pieces of flesh had grown in between his fingers, his hands now webbed were ready for the attack that he knew was inevitable. He felt his eyes narrow and he could see deep into the woods, deep into the darkness, and he saw a body press against a huge oak tree in a futile attempt to conceal itself from him. Adrenaline raced through his body. He didn't know who was out there, he didn't know who was trying to attack him, but he was ready.

What he didn't expect, however, was the fog.

Curls of gray mist appeared to form out of the snowy ground until Michael's feet were encircled, and then the mist lengthened, rising like a solid gray panel, circular, impenetrable, and Michael could see someone in the distance moving toward him. Whoever was out there also saw the fog and knew that it was not a natural creation but a defense mechanism. Phaedra hadn't let him down this time, Michael thought, watching the fog rise even higher and then arch, when it was several feet over his head, to completely conceal him from the outside world.

Relieved, Michael felt his fangs retract, his fingers and eyes return to their humanlike state, and he felt his breathing decelerate. He might not be able to count on the past to remain unchanged, he might not be able to count on dead schoolmates to remain buried, but he could count on his friend. Phaedra had told him she was still here to protect him and that's just what she was doing. Sadly, she was not doing her job as well as she had promised.

A cloud of gray fog enveloped Michael from both sides, thrusting him forward. At first he thought Phaedra was repositioning herself, moving him to even safer ground, but when he felt a fist connect with his back, he knew that someone was trying to punch his way through the barrier from the outside.

Reeling around, his fangs once again cutting into his lips, his preternatural vision restored, he could see bits of The Forest through the fog and it was as if he were looking through an opaque curtain—he couldn't see who was out there, who was valiantly trying to assault him—but it was apparent that Phaedra's protection was no longer secure.

The fog shifted from dark gray to silver, dense to practically transparent, like someone was outside turning a light switch on and off. Every time Michael tried to escape from within the faltering vapor, it would solidify before he could break free. He knew that he was much better protected within the fog, but only, only if it could be stabilized. If not, he would be a lot safer outside in the expanse of The Forest than confined to such a small, dark space.

"Come on, Phaedra, I need you!" Michael cried.

As if she were answering his call, the fog enclosed itself all around him, slamming into the ground and over his head with a crash that sounded like a metal fence locking tight, and plunged him into darkness. But when he felt the sharp fangs scrape against his neck, he knew his worst fears had come true. He was securely trapped within the fog, but this time he wasn't alone.

chapter 10

Michael couldn't believe he was in this position yet again: facedown on the ground, a body on top of him, someone whose only purpose was to keep him from getting up. He felt the hand braced against the back of his head push him down even harder. He couldn't see the snow, but he could feel its icy grip spread out across his face and latch on to him, almost as if it were pulling him down deeper, deeper, deeper into the earth to help his attacker. Feeling pieces of snow and ice invade his nostrils, his mouth, he tried to breathe, but felt no air, only fear.

Involuntarily, Michael screamed. No sound was heard, but his mouth opened wide enough to allow more ice to clog his throat. Knowing its victim was panicking, Michael's unseen attacker pushed down even harder until his lips tasted dirt, and then moved his head forward turning him into a human bulldozer so his mouth would collect the stones and twigs that lay just beneath the snow's surface. Finally, Michael closed his mouth, but it was too late, he was beginning to suffocate.

Pressing his forehead and his hands into the ground, he arched his back and slowly started to rise, but the weight on top of him was immense. Finally, his mouth was a few inches above the snow and he coughed, spitting out the pieces of earth that were trying to lodge themselves in his throat. Saliva and ice dripped from his mouth and he was able to catch a few quick breaths before being pushed back down.

In the blackness, he smelled a cloud of sweet breath envelop him and he blinked his eyes when he felt long strands of hair fall on his cheeks, mingle with his eyelashes. He kept his mouth closed and his chin up as the palms of his hands dug into the hard ground, his body pushing back against his assailant. No, he was not going to give in, he was not going to be turned into a coward, a victim. No matter what anyone thought about him, no matter what Nakano thought, what his grandfather thought, or his father, or yes, even Ronan, he was strong and he could defend himself and he was going to prove it. He wanted this person off of him and he wanted this person off of him now!

"GET . . . OFF . . . OF . . . ME!"

Using every ounce of strength in his body, mortal and immortal, Michael threw his arms back and at the same time jumped to his feet, his knees bending awkwardly. Still, he was standing and that was a good start. Blinded by the darkness, Michael swung his arm with all the speed he could muster until it connected with hard flesh, he heard his opponent crash into the ground, followed by the sounds of a bone cracking, maybe two. He had done it, he had fought back, and by the sound of it, he had fought back well. His freedom, though well earned was short-lived. The body, regardless of how badly hurt, was on him once again. But this time was different. This time Michael was ready.

Less than a second after he felt the arm wrap around his throat, his fangs were burrowed within its flesh. Instead of clamping down and sucking out the blood as he usually did with his monthly victims, he dragged his mouth down the length of the arm toward its wrist, his fangs creating two deep gashes in the skin. The resulting cry was both high-pitched and guttural. Michael couldn't tell if it was a man or a woman, but he knew that whoever or whatever it was, it was in agony.

The screams vibrated within the small space, and the sound of their echoes buoyed Michael, made him stronger. Maintaining his grip despite the taste of foul blood that was filling his mouth, he tossed his head from side to side like a wild animal unwilling to allow its prey to escape, flinging his attacker into one side of the fog and then the other. Thud after thud penetrated the darkness as Michael's assailant-turned-victim crashed into the fog that was now as dense as cement, its ear-piercing wails blending with Michael's feral grunts and roars to create a horrific sound, a sound that to Michael was a pronouncement of victory. His celebration was premature, however, as the fog yet again resumed its unpredictable nature.

A blast of moonlight flooded the makeshift fortress as part of the fog's wall disintegrated. Startled by the intrusion, Michael turned toward the light, releasing his fangs from the ravaged flesh. He heard his opponent scamper into the darkness that still covered the far side of their prison, but before he could see its face, the fog flooded back, solidified once again, concealing them from the light of the night sky. Something was definitely wrong with Phaedra. But it didn't matter now, Michael thought; he didn't need her. He could rely on himself.

Lunging forward, Michael's webbed hands grabbed on to something, something odd, smooth yet bumpy. It wasn't clothing, maybe jewelry, yes, that was it. He yanked at the chain or the necklace or whatever it was, but as he did, the person pulled back, making Michael lose his balance, and when he fell, he heard something crack underneath him, something like glass. Then he felt something sharp against his neck. The fangs pricked his skin quickly; they didn't penetrate deeply enough to suck out much blood, but Michael did feel droplets of blood ooze out onto his skin. Immediately, he felt cloth, like a scarf or a napkin, brush against his neck as if wiping away the blood, cleansing the wound. When he opened his eyes, he was momentarily blinded by the light of the moon that was shining in his face.

"Michael, are you all right?"

For a second Michael forgot that he had just been fighting for his life. Ronan looked positively ethereal, what with the moon glowing behind him and the soft wisps of fog uncurling all around his face. But if Ronan was here, he could also be in danger. "Watch out!" Jumping up, Michael positioned himself in front of Ronan in an effort to protect him, but protect him from whom? From what? There was no one else around. "Did you see anybody?!"

"No, when the fog lifted you were alone," Ronan said extending his hand to quell Michael's shaking body.

Michael slapped his hand away. "That can't be! Someone was trapped in the fog with me."

Two pairs of vampire eyes scoured The Forest for a hint of a preternatural presence, an animal, even a human, but couldn't find a trace of anyone or anything. Ronan saw that Michael's clothes were stained and covered in dirt, his beautiful face marred by a few small bruises that ran from his cheek to his jaw. His neck had a slight puncture wound that was already starting to heal, and while he was relieved that he was relatively unharmed, he was furious that he had acted so foolishly and put himself in danger yet again. "Why the hell are you out here in the middle of the night?!" Ronan shouted, his fear and anger making him unable to remain calm. When was he going to learn?

"I had a dream."

And when was he going to stop blaming everything on a dream? "Oh, come on, Michael! Not another bloody dream."

"No, no, it was more than a dream."

"Well, was it a dream or wasn't it a dream?!"

Why is he yelling at me? Doesn't he know what I've just been through? Why doesn't he understand? "It was more like a journey."

Swiping the air with his clenched fists, Ronan started to pace back and forth, pounding the snow with his bare feet. "First a dream, then a journey! Next you're going to tell me that you were visited by the dead and were shown some extraordinary vision!"

He does understand, he does know what I'm going through. "Yes! That's exactly right!"

Stopping in his tracks, Ronan's chest heaved several times, his breath shooting from his lips to form funnels of white smoke. "Michael, I love you." Ronan then took a step closer toward Michael. His mouth formed a word, but he didn't speak. He tried again, but clearly he couldn't find the right word. Leaning into his boyfriend, his index finger poking the air in front of his face repeatedly, violently, he finally managed to find the correct words to convey what was on his mind. "But you're really starting to piss me off!"

This is insane! After everything I've seen, after everything

I've been through, now I have to deal with this? "I'm telling you the truth, Ronan! Imogene came into our room tonight."

That name changed everything. "Imogene?"

"She really is dead," Michael said, his voice cracking slightly at the announcement. "I don't know how, but I could feel it."

Ronan truly felt sorry for the girl. He liked Imogene, and he knew that however she died, it was not pleasant or deserved, but he couldn't focus on her death or her resurrection at the moment, he needed to find out what she showed Michael, what was so important that she had to lure him out into The Forest before the break of dawn. Luckily, Michael needed to explain what had happened to him as badly as Ronan needed to hear it. "She showed me a vision of my parents. I saw my mother and father in the same ocean that I first dreamed about you."

At the mention of Michael's parents, Ronan felt his skin tingle. It was an odd sensation, curious, but Ronan knew that the body often sensed things before the mind could comprehend them. His body was telling him that Michael's dream, vision, journey, whatever, was not a kind, otherworldly gift, but an occurrence that could only have a devastating consequence. "Your parents? Are you sure?"

"Of course I am!" Michael replied. "I'm sorry if you don't want to believe me, but that's what happened!"

Get control of your own fear, Ronan; don't let him sense it. "No, that's not what I meant. Of course I believe you," Ronan said. "I'm just confused." *And incredibly afraid because if a dead girl was compelled to show you a vision of your crazy mother and your father, a man so duplicitous my own mother doesn't even trust him, then there could be no good reason for her motives.* "It doesn't make sense to me, Michael. Why would Imogene show you a vision of your parents?" Ronan asked. "I mean, she didn't even know them."

"I don't know," Michael said quietly. "But I'm glad she did." Slowly, Michael recounted what he'd seen and how it made him feel. "She was never ashamed of me, Ronan." The words carried with them such emotional weight, such a tight hold on his past, Michael could hardly lift his head. He stared at the ground, felt the tears well up in his eyes. "I hated her for so long." Ronan felt all the anger rush out of his body when Michael looked at him, his expression so pleading, so unconcealed, his voice so remorseful. "Why was I so quick to believe she could hate me because I'm gay?"

The need to hear Michael's story was replaced with the need to comfort him. Ronan wrapped his arms around Michael and the embrace was eagerly accepted. Proud that he would allow his tears to fall so easily, so shamelessly onto his shoulder, Ronan whispered softly into Michael's ear, "Because you spent so much time hating yourself."

Michael cried even harder, held on to Ronan tighter. He wished he was wrong, he wished he could push him away and yell at him for saying such a stupid thing, but he couldn't. Michael had found it so easy to hate himself for who he was that it seemed only natural that everyone else, including his mother, could hate him just as easily. Through his tears, he told Ronan the rest of the dream. "But she wasn't talking to me, she was talking to my father."

Ronan felt his skin shiver for the second time. *Your mother was ashamed of your father,* he repeated to himself. *That can't possibly be good.* "Don't worry about that for now," Ronan said, glad that Michael couldn't see his face or his concern clearly. "You don't need them anymore."

"I know, I know that," Michael said, escaping from Ronan's embrace just a little to look him in the face. "I have you and that's all I need." He meant the words, knew they were fact, but there was more, more to confess. "I wish I had them too, though. I wish I had parents who were together and who loved each other and who lived in a dumb little house somewhere so we could visit and I could bring you to meet them." Michael laughed at the image in his mind, he and Ronan standing on a doorstep, nervous, awkward, then his parents, a united, loving couple greeting them with open arms, ushering them into their home, into their lives. Ronan was smiling at him; he understood. "My mother really could be lots of fun when she wasn't, you know, completely out of her mind."

She had to be incredibly special if she was capable of raising someone as wonderful as you, Ronan thought. He held Michael's slender neck between his hands, the neck that he had bitten into, the neck that had given itself to him so willingly so they could be joined forever, and all Ronan wanted to do was lean in and kiss him, but just as he parted his lips, he saw Phaedra.

"Oh God."

Lying on the ground, her limbs twisted in a peculiar way, Phaedra didn't appear to be alive. The only part of her, in fact, that seemed to be moving was her hair. Lifted by the wind, the long curls rose and fell as if they were breathing while the rest of her body remained motionless. Michael and Ronan, shocked to see their friend in such a state, were frozen, in awe of what they were seeing, until Ronan realized action was needed.

"She needs help."

Michael heard Ronan's comment but couldn't respond. His friend was in this position, this lifeless state, because of him. Phaedra had come to his aid and clearly she wasn't up to the challenge; she wasn't as powerful as she had been, and defending Michael had left her vulnerable. He didn't want to admit it, but it looked like it left her on the brink of death. "Ronan," Michael said. "Is she . . . is she breathing?"

Kneeling next to the girl, Ronan bent his head so his ear hovered over her mouth. Nothing. He bent down closer and was relieved to feel a faint exhalation of air brush against his skin, soft but distinct. "Barely."

So too was her flesh. Just like her breath, it was faded, dim, the veins, blue and haphazard, could be seen underneath the skin like an absentminded drawing under tracing paper. Clearly, her life was fading in front of their eyes and Ronan had no choice but to seek human intervention. "We've got to get her to MacCleery."

"Do you think he can help her?" Michael asked, knowing full well that Phaedra's condition was out of the realm of a mortal doctor's range of knowledge.

Looking at the girl, who felt weightless in his arms, Ronan said, "I don't know, love, but I don't know what else to do."

Nodding in agreement, Michael knew they would be taking a risk bringing Phaedra to Dr. MacCleery. Who knew what he would find when he examined her. On the outside she looked like a normal girl, but upon further inspection he could stumble upon the fact that she was anything but. It didn't matter, it was a risk they were going to have to take, for they had to do something, even if it meant putting all their lives in jeopardy. "Let's go."

"No," Ronan corrected. "I should go myself."

"Absolutely not," Michael said. "Whatever happened to Phaedra happened because she was protecting me. I have to be by her side in case . . . in case . . ." Michael couldn't even finish his sentence. He heard the words shout inside his head—*in case she dies*—but he couldn't speak them. He wasn't strong enough to acknowledge the possibility out loud, even in Ronan's presence, that his friend might die because of him. Luckily, Ronan understood.

"She's not going to die, Michael. She can't die, not really," Ronan reminded him. "I just don't want you around Lochlan. I don't trust him."

"But if you don't trust him, why are you going to let him help Phaedra?"

The body he was carrying actually started to feel even lighter. Time was running out. "I don't have time to explain," Ronan said, already walking toward the infirmary. "I trust him as a doctor, but not as a friend of our people."

Michael wasn't sure he understood the distinction, but he was too tired to question Ronan further and too scared to keep Phaedra from the one man who might be able to help her, so he kept his doubts to himself. "Let me know the moment you find out what's going on."

"I will," Ronan replied, then ordered, "Now go straight home and stay there."

Michael nodded as he watched Ronan practically fly out of The Forest and then he started to follow him. He took one step, however, and felt something crunch under his foot.

Looking down, he saw what it was: eyeglasses, the lenses shattered, the frame broken in half but held together by a string of crystal beads. Touching the smooth surface of one of the beads, he knew this is what he felt in the darkness, in the fog. His attacker had been wearing them, but why would a vampire wear glasses? As a disguise maybe? A means of deception to make him look more human? Michael didn't know, but the more he stared at the destroyed glasses, he knew he had seen them before. For the life of him he just couldn't remember who had been wearing them.

"MacCleery!"

Bursting into the doctor's office, Ronan wasn't surprised

to find it empty. It was the middle of the night, but still he had to find the doctor. Holding Phaedra as securely as he could, Ronan kicked open the door to the private examining room, thinking the doctor might be inside conducting some late-night research or even tending to another student. "MacCleery! We need help!"

"What the hell is going on in here?!"

Whipping around, Ronan saw the doctor standing in the doorway. His hair was a mess and he was clutching an unzipped coat close to his body to ward off the chill. He banged his foot against a filing cabinet to get rid of the snow that clung to his slippers, obviously he had dressed in a hurry to get here. "I saw you run in here, from my window," MacCleery said. "Going so fast I thought you were some kind of animal."

Raising the limp body in his arms, Ronan replied, "It's Phaedra, she's been hurt."

Lochlan eyed Ronan suspiciously, but replied, "I could tell she looked half dead from my window." With a disapproving glare, the doctor swept past Ronan and grumbled for him to bring Phaedra into the examination room. Gently he placed her on the examining table and stepped out of the way as the doctor grabbed a few medical instruments off a side table. Ronan watched helplessly as the doctor listened for her pulse, shone a light into her eyes, and turned her head to look at her neck. What was he doing that for? He couldn't possibly suspect—*no, this is not the time to get paranoid, Ronan. This isn't about you,* he reminded himself, *it's about Phaedra.*

Narrowing his eyes, Ronan was able to get a better look at her condition. He thought her complexion looked better, more robust, and he could no longer see the veins through her skin. He tried to get even closer, but was stopped. Without looking up from his patient, MacCleery spoke, "Wait for me outside." Ronan didn't want to leave Phaedra alone with the doctor; he wanted to see what he discovered, but Lochlan's tone made it clear that he didn't want to work before prying eyes. Maybe it was for the best, Ronan thought. Leave the doctor alone to do his job and take care of Phaedra, and use some of the time alone to come up with a story to cover his own tracks just in case the doctor did uncover that she wasn't human.

He could only hope that she had enough strength left in her body to help herself. When he looked on the wall above Nurse Radcliff's desk, he shuddered. Phaedra wasn't the only one who needed help.

There was a mark on the wall where the crucifix used to hang, a shadow of darkness created from faded paint that outlined the space where something previously existed, something that had been there for as long as Ronan could remember. Now, for some reason, it was gone and he felt unsettled, as if he had lost a friend, as if Double A had lost a protector. "Why would you leave us?"

More practical concerns demanded attention when Ronan saw MacCleery emerge from the examination room. "Is Phaedra all right?" It was weird to see the doctor standing there in wet bedroom slippers, wearing a white undershirt and gray sweatpants instead of his usual, slightly more professional outfit. "Will she be okay?"

Wiping the lenses of his glasses with his T-shirt, MacCleery answered him. "Miss Antonides is going to be fine."

"Really?!"

Thrusting the glasses back on his face, the doctor looked at Ronan skeptically. "You're surprised by my diagnosis?"

Making an exaggerated attempt to appear nonchalant, Ronan shrugged his shoulders and tilted his head to the side. "No, no, I'm thrilled." MacCleery remained silent and so Ronan continued to speak. "It's just that when I found her, she looked pretty sick, you know, like she had been hurt."

That's right, the doctor thought, *keep quiet and these kids will always supply you with more information than they'd like to.* "She's dehydrated, physically exhausted, but her vitals are fine. She just needs some fluid and rest." Now that that's out of the way, Lochlan wanted to get on to the real reason he wanted to speak with Ronan, "Now, where did you say you found her?"

"Excuse me, sir?"

"Don't play dumb and don't call me sir," the doctor huffed. "Tell me where you found Phaedra and I won't report you to our new headmaster."

Get control of yourself, Ronan, you're too smart to be caught by some old man's tricks. Give him a simple explanation, nothing more. "I heard a noise outside and went to investigate."

"Where outside?"

"Outside my dorm."

Perfect. This one thinks he's wise; he thinks he can't trip himself up, but with each answer, he makes it more difficult for himself to escape. "So you're saying that you found this girl unconscious outside St. Florian's almost two miles from her own dorm in the middle of the night wearing just a flimsy T-shirt and jeans," the doctor summed up. "Is that what you're saying Glynn-Rowley?"

Fine, you want to play hardball, I'm through with being the nervous, accommodating student. "Yes, that's exactly what I'm saying," Ronan answered. "I have no idea how she got there or why she was there. You might try to ask her yourself . . . sir."

Ah, here he is, here's the Ronan I've grown to mistrust. "I gave her a sedative; she won't be talking for a few more hours." Plopping down into one of the waiting room chairs, the doctor smiled at Ronan. "Why don't you have a seat so we can have a proper conversation or, as I said, I may feel the need to wake up our new headmaster."

That's the second time he's mentioned his name. Hesitating, Ronan tried to maintain eye contact with MacCleery, show him that he wasn't anxious, but he felt his eyes roam the room, for what exactly he wasn't sure. Did he think the doctor had a hidden surprise somewhere, an ally crouched behind a desk, one of David's people waiting just outside the window, or maybe David himself was hiding somewhere. Could that be it? Could he and the doctor be on the same team? "Fine," Ronan said, sitting across from MacCleery. "I don't know what else I can tell you, though."

"You can tell me what you know about David Zachary."

This is a trap. I sensed it from the moment I walked in here. Ronan locked eyes with Lochlan; he didn't dare look anywhere else. He had learned that if you want to outwit your opponent, it was crucial to look into their eyes, where every move began, where every motive could be seen. "And what makes you think I know anything about Archangel's new leader?"

MacCleery inhaled a deep breath through his nose. He didn't like Ronan, he never did, but he knew he could be helpful. He just sensed it. "I know the two of you are connected somehow, in some way," the doctor replied. "I can't explain it, but I can feel it."

And now the student has become the master, Ronan said to himself. Unable to resist showing the doctor a little smirk, nothing too broad, just enough to show him that he was no longer scared, no longer such easy prey. "I thought doctors were taught to rely upon fact and not feelings," Ronan said. "It seems to me that you're going about this exercise counterintuitively."

"Enough games!" MacCleery erupted. "Tell me how you know Zachary!"

Feeling the contempt for this man rise up from his gut and

wrap around his limbs, Ronan could no longer remain seated. Rising up, he walked over to the doctor. He didn't want to threaten him, he didn't want to reveal himself to him, but he wanted him to know that he too had had enough of the game playing. "I don't know what you have against me, doc, but I'm telling you that it ends right now," Ronan seethed. "If you've got something against Headmaster Zachary, I suggest you take it up with him and not me."

"I would, but according to my file, Headmaster Zachary doesn't even exist."

"What do you mean your *file?*"

So I've piqued the young man's curiosity, have I? Mac-Cleery thought. *That's the first step toward gaining his confidence.* "You're right about me. I'm a man of fact, not feelings, so when I felt disturbed by Zachary's presence, by his sudden intrusion at this school, I decided to do some research," the doctor explained, pausing to see if Ronan was growing even more curious.

Ronan sat back down. "Go on."

It was working, the student was beginning to appear quite studious. "I haven't been able to find anything on the man," he continued. "I cannot find a shred of evidence that David Zachary existed before he came to this school."

MacCleery might be a brilliant physician, but he was an incredibly stupid man. "Maybe being a private investigator isn't your thing, doc."

"Could be," he agreed, shrugging his shoulders. He then leaned toward Ronan, resting his forearms on his knees and folding his hands, trying to create a connection with him. "I figured I'd have a problem digging up any dirt, I mean information, about the man's past, but here's the strange part: I can't even find proof that anybody by the name of David Zachary was ever a student here at Double A."

Why is he doing this? Why is he getting involved with this man who could destroy him in an instant and without an ounce of mercy? "People change their names."

"Yes, they do," MacCleery replied, thrilled that Ronan was now participating in the dialogue. "But I checked the records of the years when he would have been a student here, and all the Davids are accounted for. All seventeen of them. I was able to track down each one of them."

You're never going to find out anything about him because he doesn't want you to; don't you get that, you stupid git! "Somebody's been busy."

"Yes, I have because somebody's got to protect the students!"

What? Ronan watched MacCleery's face even more closely. There was something else going on with him. He wasn't just suspicious of David, he was scared. If there was one emotion that Ronan could identify, it was fear. "Protect us from what, Dr. MacCleery?" Ronan quietly asked.

Getting up from his chair, the doctor waved away Ronan's query. "Nothing." But he suddenly felt Alistair's spirit as if his old friend was in the room with him. He reached into the pocket of his sweatpants and felt Alistair's crumpled-up note, the note that he always carried with him, and the words wouldn't remain silent any longer; they could no longer remain his own personal property. They had to be shared. "Because there's evil here. Right in this school, there's evil, and it has something to do with Zachary! I know it, I can feel it, I just can't explain it, goddamit! But you can!" Now Mac-Cleery was pacing the four corners of the room, without direction, only the need to keep moving. He clutched the note harder, his fist striking against his thigh inside his pocket. "I've always known there was something wrong with you, Ronan. I don't know what it is, but I know that you're connected to this man and that you're connected to whatever evil thing he's brought here!"

Fighting the impulse to show the doctor just how evil he

could become, Ronan remained still, and when he spoke, his voice was harsh and foreboding. "You have no idea the danger you're putting yourself into, do you?"

The doctor jumped at him so quickly, with such satisfaction, Ronan flinched. "You do know something you're not telling me!"

There was no more room for pretense, even if the doctor didn't know the truth about who and what Ronan was, he was never going to change his opinion about him, he was never going to think that he was nothing more than trouble, someone who couldn't be trusted, so it didn't matter what he said to the man. However, with his hand on the doorknob, he was compelled to give him a warning before he left. "I suggest you forget all about your bloody investigation and concentrate on your cushy job," Ronan said. "You can't help any of us if you're dead."

"I'm trying to help Alistair!"

"Trust me, Lochlan," a new voice said, "Alistair no longer needs anyone's help."

Seeing Nurse Radcliff standing in the doorway—the snow gently falling behind her, her long hair pulled back in a bun, her little nurse's cap perched on top of her head—should have been a comforting sight, but instead it frightened Ronan. *This night has been out of control,* he thought to himself, *even for me.* "You'll keep an eye on Phaedra?" Ronan asked.

"I won't leave her side," MacCleery declared.

Nodding to the nurse, Ronan left, eager to be out of their company. Now that it was just the two of them, the doctor thought he could relax, but something was wrong. Maybe he was still riled up from his argument with Ronan, or maybe he didn't like being spied on. "Were you listening from the other side of the door?"

Hanging her coat on the hook that jutted out from the

wall, Nurse Radcliff sat behind her desk. "Why on earth would I do that?"

Lochlan shook his head and mumbled something. He was definitely tired, but he wasn't imagining things. He saw her there, when Ronan opened the door, just for an instant and she looked like she had been caught. And he heard her, he heard what she said. "What did you mean, Alistair doesn't need anybody's help?"

Turning on her computer, Radcliff sighed. Clearly she was more interested in getting her desk in order than she was answering the doctor's questions. "Obviously the man wasn't happy here and wanted a new life," she said. "Doesn't take a detective to figure out that he doesn't need help, especially from anyone who reminds him of his past."

Logical, yes, but also disturbing. In fact, so was her presence. "What are you doing here anyway? It's three in the morning."

Glowering, Radcliff consciously softened her expression. "Another bout with insomnia," she said. "I saw the lights on and figured you were having another emergency."

A plausible explanation, but still it left the doctor unsettled. He explained that Ronan had brought in Phaedra and that she was resting comfortably now. "Then I'll stay overnight to watch the girl," the nurse declared. "Sleep will be an elusive friend for me this evening, I'm afraid."

Lochlan couldn't explain it, but he didn't want her here. *Oh, for God's sake,* he thought, *enough with these feelings, these emotions.* They were going to send him to the crazy farm. "I'm going to stay with the girl," he declared. "Stay, go home, do whatever you want." Just as he was about to enter the peace and quiet of the examination room, he thought of something else. "How are you doing any work without your glasses?"

Laughing, Nurse Radcliff tossed a file from one pile to another. "I was wondering when you'd notice. I had LASIK surgery last week. Remember I was out for a few days?"

The doctor didn't remember, but he no longer cared. Everywhere he looked, the whole world was changing. No, that really wasn't the problem, the problem was, he wasn't looking in the right places.

When he closed the door behind him, Nurse Radcliff pulled up the sleeve of her sweater, the marks were still there. She thought they would heal on their own by now, but she was wrong. She tried not to judge herself too harshly, she was new, she was bound to make mistakes, she was bound to not be perfect. She thought for a second and then remembered what David had taught her. David always knew best, that man knew everything. She held her arm closer to her mouth and let her tongue slither out over her lips, past her chin, until it touched her wounded flesh, the flesh that had been disfigured by that disgusting water vamp. She licked the gnarled skin with her long, narrow tongue and allowed her saliva—what did David call it? Yes, her *preternatural* saliva— to accumulate and soak into the gash.

When the whole wound was covered, she raised her head and heard a noise like someone squishing raw, moist meat between their hands. The sound grew louder and she was proud to see her unblemished flesh bubble slightly at its edge and grow, extend, conceal the wound until her arm was once again smooth and unscarred. She had been so eager to prove her worth to Father that she had been a little bit careless. She might be a new disciple, but she understood very clearly the need to rid Archangel Academy of all water vamps. She took out the handkerchief from her purse, the white one with the embroidered lilacs and several stains of Michael's blood. She didn't know why Father had wanted samples of the boy's blood, but it wasn't her place to question His motives. All she needed to do was carry out his requests.

chapter 11

The Ending

Outside, the earth was changing.

Speeding across campus, Michael looked down and saw that the ground was mostly green underneath his feet. The color was hardly vibrant, more like a mixture of moss and dirt, but at least the widespread patches of snow were gone. February had brought with it an unexpected flurry of spring-like temperatures, enough to help Double A thaw out, temporarily, from winter's clutch. No one knew how long it would last, but until the next, inevitable ice storm struck, this reprieve was a welcome change.

As they ran past the Archangel Academy entrance gate, Ronan first, Michael a few strides behind, neither one of them felt the bursts of electricity that were designed to prohibit intruders from entering or willful students from leaving the school grounds. Such deterrents couldn't hold them back, not on a typical morning and especially not on a morning when they needed to feed.

Watching Ronan sprint across the countryside, his broad back becoming a blur, Michael wondered where they would wind up and who would be waiting for them. "I found the perfect location," Ronan had said and so Michael was letting him lead the way, as he always did. Each month was the same: Ronan led and Michael followed; it simply seemed more natural that way. For now at least.

A mile or two outside of Double A the terrain started to become less smooth, more rugged, gone was the flat campus and in its place an untamed countryside. Where was Ronan taking them? They hadn't fed as a couple very often, but usually they went to a house in a poor neighborhood to feast on an elder who was brought home to die or to a hospital where they could choose from an array of patients, all of whom were within minutes, sometimes seconds, of dying. This was different. They seemed to be going away from civilization instead of into its heart. But, Michael reminded himself, Ronan had never let him down before when he was hungry, so there was no reason to suspect he would start now. And he was right.

When they reached a cluster of oak trees in an expanse of flat land, they stopped. Ronan positioned himself behind the immense trunk of one of the trees and silently beckoned for Michael to join him, but to do so quietly. Curious, Michael quickly ran next to Ronan without making a sound, anxious to find out why they had come to a place that didn't seem to contain any human life. Smiling proudly like a father on Christmas morning, Ronan turned Michael around so he was standing in front of him and placed an arm around his chest, his hand resting on his shoulder. Ronan's lips brushed against Michael's ear when he whispered, "Look."

Straight ahead, all Michael could see was an old-fashioned extension bridge made of thick rope and a narrow row of rectangular slats of wood that seemed to levitate over an unexpected quarry. The bridge wasn't terribly long, but was necessary since the excavation ran the length of a mile in both directions and was at least five stories deep. Michael couldn't believe he had never seen it before, it was such an extraordinarily beautiful creation, breathtaking. It even made him forget about the hunger pains stabbing at the back of his throat.

The cliffs on both sides were smooth and seemed to angle inward. He imagined it was possible to climb down one side and then up the other but, on second thought, realized it would be challenging for even an expert rock climber. No, the bridge really was the only way to get from one side to the other, though it wasn't what could be called a desirable means of transportation. Even now in the stillness of the predawn air, it was swaying left to right. "Look closer," Ronan said, reading Michael's thoughts. When he did, Michael saw that the bridge wasn't swaying because of the wind, it was swaying because someone was walking across it.

The woman was looking straight ahead, every one of her steps deliberate as she planted her foot squarely in the center of each wooden plank, holding on to the ropes tightly until she reached the center of the bridge and stopped. Squinting, Michael could see her shoulders rise and fall several times as if she were breathing deeply, perhaps to find the courage to walk the rest of the way or turn around and go back. Watching her intently, Michael never expected her to turn to the right, lift the ropes over her head, and stand on the edge of one of the planks with nothing separating her from the open air. It was clear that she had no intention of crossing the bridge. She was poised to jump off of it.

"I took a chance," Ronan explained. "I've followed her

three times this month, but she's never gotten this far before." He threw his other arm around Michael's waist, fully embracing him from behind, and rubbed his cheek against Michael's forehead. "I had a feeling we'd get lucky this morning."

Despite knowing that he was watching a woman on the verge of suicide, Michael felt his heart race, his breathing quicken. He knew he should feel sorry for her, empathize with her situation and the desperate state she must be in, but all he could think about was that his body was practically blood-empty and he needed to replenish.

"Get ready," Ronan commanded.

The woman leaned forward, the bridge bending and dipping as her body extended as far as it could without her hands letting go of the rope. Her movement was met with silence, birds didn't chirp, the wind didn't stir. It was as if the world were giving this woman a few uninterrupted moments to conjure her strength to finally do what she had come here so many times to do. When she looked down, Michael watched her face intently, searching for fear, doubt to creep into her eyes, but none came. Whatever the woman saw, whatever she felt, didn't appear to provoke an expression. Until she looked up. Seeing the sun beginning to rise, a smile slowly grew on her face. Michael was relieved; he understood that she was happy.

Ronan telepathically instructed Michael not to hesitate but to follow him when he moved. Less than a second after the woman let go of the ropes and jumped into the waiting air, Ronan and Michael raced forward, appearing to be as airborne as she was. They were three people suspended, separated, until they were one.

Halfway between the bridge and the jagged rocks, the woman stopped falling. *This wasn't how it was supposed to happen,* she thought. She was supposed to feel freedom and then nothing; she wasn't supposed to be interrupted by two angels. She looked from one face to the other and she couldn't decide which was more beautiful, the black-haired angel or the angel whose hair was the same shade as the rising sun. It didn't matter, they had come for her, just as she hoped they would; they had merely come earlier than expected.

As if in slow motion the three bodies, connected as one, began to descend. Ronan bit into her neck first. Her blood tasted sweet as it rushed past his lips, eager to escape its doomed host, her cry of ecstasy swallowed up by the imposing landscape that surrounded them. When Ronan released his fangs, Michael penetrated the other side of the woman's neck. Again she cried, again the sound was muffled by the stones and rock. As her glorious blood flowed through Michael's body, he felt weightless. He clamped his mouth down harder on her neck as he felt his legs rise behind him until they were almost over his head. He closed his eyes, images of the stranger's life bombarding his brain, and he knew he should stop drinking, but her blood was truly splendid. He stopped only when he felt Ronan's fingers intertwine with his.

Looking over at Ronan's face, Michael saw that the fresh blood was already beginning to have an effect on his boyfriend. Ronan's skin was glowing, his eyes were shining with more intensity than the sun. When Ronan's blood-stained lips smiled, no words formed, but Michael heard him clearly. *Yes, Ronan, let's both take the blood that this woman no longer wants.*

Just as their feet were about to touch the ground, Michael and Ronan pierced the woman's flesh at the same time, causing her to writhe with such pleasure and joy that the three of them were lifted up, up, up into the air. The boys responded to the unexpected jolt by holding on to each other tighter, pressing themselves even closer into the woman, and jamming their fangs even deeper into her neck in order to drain every remaining drop of blood from her body until it went limp. Her role in their monthly ceremony complete, the boys gently placed her on the top of a large boulder, exactly where she had hoped to land.

His temples vibrating, his vision hazy, Michael kissed the woman's forehead and thanked her, not only for her blood but for helping him to understand his mother better. He would never fully comprehend why Grace chose to end her life, but now he knew that there was the possibility, the chance, that her choice was not made out of desperation, not as a means to escape some unimaginable horror, but as a way to find happiness. Until proven otherwise, he was going to believe that his mother's face had looked like this woman's when she gazed into the rising sun. He was going to believe she had, for one final moment, been happy.

Just as happy as he was, in fact, to once again kneel before The Well. Gripping the cool curved stone, Michael felt Ronan's hand cover his and a beam of warm energy flooded his naked body. The vibrations emanating from the stone intensified and soon their hands and feet widened as the webbing grew, their fangs sharpened and extended even further past their lips, their entire bodies seemed to lengthen, and they were no longer two teenagers, they were descendants of an ancient race.

Each boy dipped a webbed hand into the clear liquid within The Well of Atlantis and brought their hands together as one, raising them high over their heads. Speaking in unison, they recited the prayer:

> *Unto The Well I give our life*
> *our bodies' blood that makes us whole.*
> *We vow to honor and protect*
> *and ask The Well to house our souls.*

In response, The Well hummed louder, its vibrations inten-
sifying, the sound embracing both boys until it grew so loud,
there could be only silence. When there was no more sound,
a light grew from beneath the liquid and propelled upward
from the center of The Well, and for a moment Michael was
frightened. He thought yet another one of his dreams was
going to come true and a grotesque face would reveal itself in
the sacred fluid, but he was wrong, The Well was simply
communicating with them. Ronan had told him that while
the ceremony never varied, The Well's response sometimes
could, as it did now.

Sunlight glistened on the walls of the cave, and Michael
was reminded of the first time he had stood before the
stained-glass window of Archangel Cathedral and it had
looked as if tiny rays of light were showering down upon
him. That's how he felt now, bathed in heavenly light, only
now was better because now he was standing next to Ronan.

Bowing their heads, they drank from their hands, drank
The Well's offering and immediately felt it combine with the
blood that was flowing through their bodies. Michael was
amazed that the feeling was even more exquisite than the first
time he'd experienced it. He had thought he would grow
used to the sensation, but that was not the case. Each time he
drank from The Well was like the first, like each time he
looked into Ronan's eyes. Unable to resist the magnetic pull,
Michael grabbed the back of Ronan's neck and pulled him
down until his lips met his. He just needed to feel their
warmth, their tenderness, and Ronan willingly obliged. Even
with their eyes closed, they could feel the burst of yellow
light that suddenly exploded throughout the cave, and it was
definite: The Well truly approved of their union.

His eyes still closed, his lips still pressing against Michael's, Ronan spoke, his voice deep and honest. "I wish we
could stay here all day, love, just like this." Michael couldn't

find the words to respond, so he simply kissed his boyfriend deeper, let his webbed hands caress the strong muscles of his lower back. He didn't want to waste any time talking before they had to get back to school. "But Volman's giving a Latin test first period," Ronan said. "And after this feeding, I'm feeling right jammy."

Michael smiled. Ronan and his Britishisms. "Well, I hope my luck holds out too. Father Fazio expects me to know something about a triangular theorem, and right now all I can think about is you."

Ronan knew exactly how Michael felt, but he also knew that their new power required discipline. "Use The Well's energy to focus on whatever task he throws at you," Ronan advised. "It will never fail you." Michael knew that made logical sense, but why should he have to focus on stupid math problems when all he wanted to do was focus on how good Ronan felt and how delicious he tasted? When the light in the cave receded and the shadows started to cling to the sides of the walls, Michael knew it was time to leave, time to return to reality. When he opened the door to his dorm room, he knew reality had changed.

"Saoirse!" Ronan exclaimed. "What the hell are you doing here?"

Propped up on their bed was one of the most beautiful girls Michael had ever seen. Young but ravishing, with light emanating from her just as it had from The Well. He was so startled by her alluring presence that it wasn't until she spoke that he realized who she was. "Oh, come on! Is that any way to greet your baby sister?"

"Saoirse!" Michael exclaimed. "You're Ronan's sister."

Oh my God, he is so much cuter than Nakano! "And you must be Michael," she responded, jumping off the bed, "Roney's new boyfriend." Stopping in mid-motion Saoirse readjusted her approach. She tossed back her head, which gave her long, straight blond hair a bounce, and a ray of light swept the room. *Wow, his eyes are even greener than mine,* she thought. *I wonder if he noticed too? Oh, stop it, stop staring and say something, do something so you don't come off like a two-year-old.* "It's so good to see you again, Roney!" she squealed. Then forgetting about her previous instructions, she practically leapt into Ronan's arms, surprising them both.

Arms extended, unsure of what to do with them, Ronan could not believe his sister was embracing him, he couldn't believe she was here. This was not good, not good at all. He looked at Michael, who was clearly entertained by his inability to return Saoirse's exuberant display of affection, and Ronan wished he could make him understand just how serious the situation was, how potentially dangerous, even if it looked like nothing more than an awkward reunion between two long-separated siblings. No need to get into all of that now, Ronan reminded himself. *Keep it light, act like the annoyed big brother and maybe she'll leave as suddenly as she appeared.* "What are you doing here?"

"*Merde!*" Saoirse shouted, "Don't repeat yourself; it's *très* boring." *Perfect! The worst way to make them think you're sophisticated is to try to sound sophisticated.*

Ronan didn't even notice her attempt. His focus was on making sure his voice sounded commanding when he spoke and not as unsettled as he truly was. "Answer my question and I won't have to repeat myself."

Still unable to control her nervous energy, Saoirse rolled her eyes and tilted her head from side to side, making herself look like a toddler who couldn't stand still. "Your last letter was so sweet, it made me realize that I hadn't seen you in, like, forever, so I hopped a Chunnel train and here I am."

Dammit! Ronan cursed himself. He should never have

written that letter; he knew it was a mistake, he knew it was a stupid thing to do.

"So you did reach out to her like I suggested," Michael said, beaming with pride. He then looked at Saoirse, his smile growing even wider. "Can I get a hug too?"

He wants what?! Facing Michael, Saoirse felt her normally ruddy cheeks grow warm and knew they were turning a deeper shade of red. She examined him with a more skeptical eye and couldn't hide the fact that she liked what she saw, nor could she stop herself, yet again, from trying to impress him with her foreign language skills, *"Bien sûr,"* she said. "That's French for 'of course'." Since talking was obviously a failure, Saoirse threw herself at Michael and wrapped her delicate arms around him, her light, her energy consuming him. *Ooh, he smells good,* she thought, *like fresh water and something else, something sweet.*

Michael was surprised by the gesture, even if he did misinterpret her girlish excitement for a lack of self-consciousness. To him, not only did Ronan and his sister lack any physical resemblance, their personalities couldn't be any less similar either. Responding to Michael's quizzical stare, Saoirse replied, "As much as I hate to admit it, I really do resemble my mother." She was right, Michael thought, she was just as petite as Edwige. "If it weren't for her black hair, she'd probably try to pass us off as twins." Michael didn't need to see Ronan's expression. He knew the girl's comment meant that mother and daughter hadn't seen each other in quite some time, nor did they confide in each other.

"Actually Mother's a bottle blonde now," Ronan informed her. "And I'm sure she'd love the world to think you two were sisters."

Briefly, Saoirse's wide, round eyes looked as if they were going to cry, as if Ronan's comment conveyed more than just its words, but soon the room was filled with her high-pitched laughter. "Blimey! That's Edwige for ya, always trying to be something she's not!"

Watching his sister fall onto his bed in a fit of giggles, Ronan wished he could laugh along with her, enjoy her homecoming, but he knew that she never did anything without a reason, so he knew that she did not suddenly show up because he wrote a heartfelt letter that made her feel lonely. She was up to something. "I'll ask you one last time: What are you doing here?"

Sighing, Saoirse grabbed a pillow from their bed and covered her face with it. "Stop badgering me, Roney!"

Ripping the pillow out of Saoirse's hands, Ronan flung it across the room. "If you call me Roney one more time, I swear to God!"

"Or what?! You're gonna bite me in the neck and suck out all my blood?!" Stunned, Michael couldn't believe what he just heard. Sure, brothers and sisters fought, knew exactly how to rile each other, but this was so, so blatant. How could she know that Michael was also a vampire? He didn't think that was something Ronan would have communicated in a letter. Impishly shrugging off her outburst, Saoirse turned to Michael and whispered, "Don't worry. Your secret's safe with me."

"What about your secret, Saoirse?" Ronan faced his sister, his tone of voice and his expression further evidence that he was not as thrilled to see Saoirse as she was to see him. Briefly the light around her faded, but she was not yet ready to give up.

"I want to see Ciaran," she pouted. "I want to see my other brother, he's so much nicer to me than you are." By now she was practically skipping in place and when she spoke, it was more like a song. "Probably 'cause we're both human beings."

Furious, Ronan grabbed his sister's shoulders, forcing her

to stop moving. Instead of looking upset, she smiled at him as if she was happy for the attention. "Listen to me, we have to get to class, so we don't have time to babysit," Ronan started. "Tell me the truth right now. Why are you here and what did you do?"

Michael watched Saoirse's expression and once again couldn't tell if she was about to burst into tears or shrieks of laughter. Girls were truly an alien species to him. With great interest he watched her take a deep breath, exhale dramatically, and reach up to clasp her hands around Ronan's neck. "I was going to get expelled from Ecole de *Roaches*, so I decided to perform a preemptive strike and run away."

Ronan grabbed Saoirse's hands fiercely, and Michael thought he might break them in half. "You were going to get expelled?! Why?!" Michael wasn't interested in Saoirse's response. He couldn't believe she wasn't screaming out in pain; Ronan's hands were like two vises around her wrists, his veins protruding, the newly obtained blood pumping down the length of his forearm, and yet Saoirse didn't respond. It was as if she couldn't even feel Ronan's grasp.

"Because my daft guidance counselor thinks I'm going to commit suicide."

When Ronan let go of Saoirse's wrists, Michael thought they looked red. He used his preternatural vision to get a closer look, but he was wrong, they were unscarred. Then her words finally penetrated his mind and he couldn't believe the coincidence. They had just fed on a woman who craved suicide and now here—no, Saoirse was too young; she couldn't have any reason to end her life.

Ronan, however, wasn't convinced she couldn't be telling the truth.

Frightened, he looked at his sister, searching her eyes for something, any kind of proof that she was lying, that this was some sort of cruel joke. "Why?" he whispered. "Why would your counselor think that?"

Whipping out her cell phone, Saoirse began texting and talking at the same time. "Because he's a smarmy git. You know the type, pasty, middle-aged, has nothing else to do but make my life miserable."

Yanking the cell phone from out of her hands, Ronan waved it in front of her face, "I'm not our mother! I'm not going to listen to your lies and accept them as fact! Tell me! Why the bloody hell were you going to get expelled?!"

Once again Saoirse faced off against her brother. "Oh, because I cut myself a few times!" Rolling up her navy blue sweater, she revealed, with more pride than embarrassment, a thin forearm that was decorated with several tiny slashes. Ronan wanted to look away, but couldn't. The marks, deep blue, almost purple, each a few inches long, were mesmerizing. To Michael, however, the image was too painful. The marks looked way too much like the ones on his mother's wrists, he had to close his eyes, lean against the wall to steady himself.

"Saoirse, my God! Why? Why would you do such a thing?" The way Ronan was looking at his sister, his eyes a mixture of fear, concern, and sadness, was almost too much even for the cavalier young girl. She pulled her arm away and roughly pulled down her sweater, covering up the truth. There, no more scars, no more need to talk about them. But Ronan couldn't let it go; he had to know. He refused to be like his mother and allow something so urgent, so vital, to be ignored. "Please, Saoirse, tell me?"

He really is a good guy, Saoirse thought, *he really cares about me, even if, you know, he lets our mother dictate how often he can see me. It would be nice to share everything with him, let him know exactly why I wanted to come back, but no, a girl has to keep some things to herself.* "It's no big deal," she began. "I may not be Miss Immortal, but I am not suicidal."

"But why the cutting?" Ronan sat on the bed next to his sister, letting the cell phone drop to his side. "I've heard about kids doing this, girls mostly, and it's serious."

"It's only serious if you're doing it for attention," Saoirse replied. "Or to, you know, cut yourself really deep that you hurt yourself." She sounded as calm and detached as if she were reading a textbook. Then an idea popped into her head, a lie that would sound like a plausible story. "A lot of kids were doing it," she said matter-of-factly. "You know how stupid girls can be when we have a sleepover. Somebody did it first, wrote her boyfriend's name in her arm and by the end of the night, we all had scars. Of course I was the unlucky prat who got caught." With downcast eyes, she waited to see if Ronan would buy her lie. He was silent. Well, at least he was contemplating her tale; he wasn't refuting it outright. "That's why they were going to expel me. Zero tolerance for self-mutilation," she explained. "But trust me, Roney, I wasn't trying to off myself."

His breathing steadier, Michael decided this wasn't the time to dwell on his past. This moment was about Ronan's present. From behind, he rubbed Ronan's arm softly in the hopes that he would understand that it meant he should respond gently no matter how angry or scared he might be. Ronan appreciated the gesture, loved Michael for it, but he didn't love what he was thinking. "We have to tell Mother," Ronan said, then lied, "She'll be worried sick."

Yeah, right, Saoirse thought, *wouldn't that be nice if it were true?* "Worried about her daughter?" she shrieked. "That'll be a first."

Ronan bit down hard on his lip, he couldn't argue with her there. When Edwige dropped Saoirse off at boarding school in Normandy several years ago, she didn't expect to see her again until graduation. And Ronan didn't expect to have to act like a parent. He had his own problems and didn't need to sort out Saoirse's as well. Anyway, she looked fine, excellent in fact, so maybe this cutting thing was just a phase. She got caught and learned her lesson and that was the end of it. Yes, that worked for him, but something still had to be done, he couldn't just let her bunk here, she was a minor and a runaway. "Well, I hate to say it, but you can't stay here."

Looking at Michael, she teased, "Yeah, like I hadn't already figured that one out, boyo."

Michael hadn't seen Ronan blush in quite a long time. It was cute and helped draw Michael out from his melancholy, from his memories. He was about to make a suggestion, but the room was again filled with sound, not laughter this time but bagpipes. As Saoirse picked up her cell phone, she explained, "It's the Irish national anthem. It makes the French barmy to know I cling to my heritage."

"We need to find you a place to stay."

"It's Ciaran!" Saoirse screamed. "Yay! Now I won't be bored to death anymore!"

Despite the fact that Saoirse had interrupted their morning, almost made them forget their magnificent feeding and their eventful trip to The Well, would probably get them into trouble for being late for class, and might have some serious personal issues, Michael really liked this girl. She was refreshing, different, and she was part of Ronan, so whether she turned out to be exasperating or just plain fun, he wanted to see more of her. Right now, however, the only person Saoirse wanted to see was Ciaran. "He has a free period and he's spending it with St. Albert," she announced, clicking her cell phone shut. "Take me to him." When Ronan glared at her in response, she opened her eyes even wider than they already were and added, "Please."

So that was it, Ronan realized, Ciaran was the one she really wanted to see. Suicide, cutting, it was all a cruel joke. "I've got it!" Saoirse exclaimed. "I can stay with Ciaran for awhile. I know he wouldn't refuse me."

Definitely not. "He already has a roommate," Ronan explained. "And Nakano isn't the accommodating type."

That was an understatement, Michael thought, but he knew who was. "She can stay with Phaedra. She doesn't have a roommate and she could use the company while she's recuperating."

Scrunching up her face, Saoirse asked, "She's not, like, all contagious, is she?"

Michael got the impression that he could explain exactly what Phaedra was and how she had recently come to spend a night in the infirmary but thought, due to their early-morning time constraints, he would leave out any controversial details. "Nope, mere touch of the flu. Contagiousness is over; she's just been a little weak."

Narrowing her eyes, she had one final question. "Do you like her?"

"She's the only girl I've ever felt comfortable with," Michael replied honestly. "Until now."

I'm not sure if you can hear me, Ronan, but I like this one, Saoirse said silently. *I really hope he stays part of the family.* "Okay, then, say hello to Phaedra's new roomie."

In the distance they could hear the school bell ring; the impromptu family reunion had to end. Before leaving, Michael said he would talk to Phaedra, but assured them both she would welcome a new roommate. Outside, Ronan looked around and, when he was convinced they were alone, lifted Saoirse in his arms and raced to St. Albert's. When he placed her down on the floor of the lab, she screamed so loud at the sight of Ciaran that she didn't even hear Ronan say he would see her later during lunch. *Fine, go to him; he's the one you really came to see anyway.* Ronan tried to catch their eyes but was unsuccessful. They were too busy reconnecting with each other, and when he left the room he shook his head dejectedly. Once again the favorite son was the outsider.

Saoirse was so excited to see Ciaran that she didn't ask why he shoved the bloodstained handkerchief with the lilacs on them into his drawer, she had so much more important stuff to tell him. After about ten minutes of prattling on about her horrid French boarding school, the horrid French food they fed them every day, and the horrid French language she was forced to speak with her superiors, Saoirse finally paused and was intrigued to find that she was embarrassed to see Ciaran staring at her arm. She must have absentmindedly pulled up her sleeve. Maybe she did it deliberately, whatever, it didn't matter, the deed was done. "Aren't you going to ask me why I would do such a horrid thing?"

Ciaran didn't have to ask. He understood all too well why people did things that to others seemed inconceivable. "I'm sure when you're ready you'll tell me."

Saoirse touched Ciaran's hand. It was so soft, so simple, it almost made Ciaran weep. "That's why I like you best, Ciar," his half sister said. "You may not look it, but you really are the coolest."

Maybe I really have spent too many hours locked alone in this lab, Ciaran thought. *The tiniest act of kindness makes me feel like I could cry. Wait a second, was that even a kind thing to say?* "Um, thank you ... I think."

For the first time since she'd arrived, Saoirse looked serious. "This room isn't bugged, is it?"

Ciaran had forgotten how infuriating privileged teenage girls could be—one second funny, then sincere, then just a little bit insane. "No, of course not."

"Don't say it like you think I'm crazy! You know these vampire folk cannot be trusted."

For a split second, Ciaran thought about David. But no, he wanted Ciaran to work with him, he wouldn't be spying on him. "No, this room isn't bugged."

Relieved, Saoirse continued. "Okay, here it is. I started cutting myself to do some experiments on my blood to figure out, you know, why I am the way I am. But I'm no good at science. That's why I came here, so you can do some tests on me."

Take that, Ronan. Our sister didn't come to Double A to see you, she came here to see me, because I'm the only one who can answer the riddle of who she is. Wildly excited, Ciaran kept his expression flat; he didn't want to make Saoirse think he wasn't cool, after all. "You don't have to ask me twice," he said. "Of course I'll help you."

This time when Saoirse hugged Ciaran, he hugged her back even harder, crying was the furthest thing from his mind. First David, now her. Finally people were discovering that he had talent, that he was worth talking to, that he was worth hugging. "I only have one stipulation," Saoirse said. "This is our secret. You can't tell anyone. Not Ronan, and definitely not Edwige."

Amazing, just as soon as a feeling of pride and happiness fills you up, a wave of sadness comes to knock it out of your system. "Well, you know, she and I hardly ever speak, so that . . . that really won't be a problem."

If Saoirse could tell that her words hurt her brother, she didn't let on. She had a day of adventure ahead of her, a day filled with freedom to do whatever she wished. She didn't want to waste any more time in a stuffy lab. "Thank you, Ciar!" she cried, hugging her brother again before racing for the door. "I'm going to tour the campus and check out my new home. Let me know when you want to get to work!"

"Make sure nobody sees you," Ciaran cried.

Standing in the doorway, Saoirse turned around. "Don't worry, I may be a scientific curiosity," she replied, "but I ain't stupid!"

Ciaran waited several minutes after she left before moving. Her new home? Oh, how he'd love to see Edwige's response once she heard that news. But since Edwige didn't dwell on him, he wasn't going to dwell on her, he was going to do what he did best—what helped him feel worthwhile and important—he was going to use his mind. Reaching under his desk, he pulled out his notebook, found a clean page, and started to write some words: *Saoirse, experiment, bloodline.*

His sister was back and it was about time he discovered why she defied human nature.

chapter 12

Michael was trying hard to concentrate, he really was. He was trying to understand the difference between mid-segments and perpendicular bisectors of triangles, he was calling upon The Well's strength to focus on what Father Fazio was saying, but his class work held no interest. All he cared about was what was happening in his personal life.

He heard the priest's words, but they made no sense to him, they were just sounds, clusters of vowels and consonants that held no meaning. He saw the diagrams the priest was drawing on the large white Smartboard at the front of the class, but again they meant nothing, they were just a bunch of lines that intersected at various points. It was as if a cloud were descending in front of his eyes, replacing his teacher with an image of Saoirse, then Phaedra, Imogene, his parents, anyone except the person who should have been commanding his attention.

I'm really trying, Ronan, Michael told himself. *I want to do well in school, but there's too much other stuff going on.*

When his mind wandered, as it was doing now, he couldn't believe just how much stuff there really was. So much was happening to him so quickly, he just wanted to make it all stop. Near-death attacks, visions, ghostly apparitions, new questions about his past, old issues about his father, the intensity of his feelings for Ronan—the combination and culmination of all these things were beginning to make Michael wish he had never come here, wish that he was back home, secluded in his bedroom. Well, almost wish, not fully. He wouldn't want to be without Ronan, but all the other things, yes, those other things he could do without. Except maybe the vision of his mother. Learning the truth about her or at least a portion of her truth was remarkable, one of the good things that had happened to him that wouldn't have happened if it weren't for Imogene and, boy, it was nice to see her again even if the circumstances cemented the fact that she was dead. And of course Phaedra, for the most part, was a godsend. Even if she couldn't protect him like she used to, she was still an amazing friend and someone he definitely wanted in his life. On and on and on the thoughts came, circling his brain, pulling his mind away from the classroom until he felt dizzy. Clutching his forehead, Michael didn't even hear himself scream, "Stop it!"

"Dude, I just want to show you my first solo effort."

When the haze lifted from Michael's eyes, he saw Fritz standing in front of his desk, the first post-Penry issue of *Tales of the Double A* in his hands, the rest of the students mostly ignoring him as they hurriedly exited the classroom. *I didn't even hear the bell ring,* Michael realized, *not a good sign.* "Sorry, Fritz, it looks great."

"You didn't even look at it!" Fritz yelled, slamming the comic book on Michael's desk.

Apologizing again, Michael inspected Fritz's latest endeavor much more closely. He was right the first time. The cover was a depiction of Archangel Cathedral during a snowstorm with the self-explanatory title "Archangel Avalanche." "It really does look great."

Convinced that this time Michael was being honest, Fritz beamed. "You really think so, mate?"

The artwork was not as imaginative or as detailed as Penry's, but it was a close-enough imitation, plus Fritz had included some of his own technique, with the edges of the church softer and rounder, the colors just a bit more intense so they popped against the white, snowy landscape. The total look was more primitive than Penry's efforts, different. But that was to be expected. It was, after all, the beginning of a whole new chapter in the series, and some degree of change was necessary. Keeping his eyes on the comic and not on Michael, Fritz asked, "Do you think, um, do you think Penry would approve?"

Without a doubt Michael knew the answer to that question. "Wholeheartedly."

"Are you sure?" Fritz asked again. "I decided not to put Double P, you know Penry, the superhero, on the cover. Thought it might be too sappy."

Michael smiled. "Afraid you're getting too sentimental?"

Scratching his tight curls, Fritz replied, "You know how it is when you, you know, really like someone."

Michael couldn't help teasing his friend. "Phaedra?"

Fritz whacked Michael with the comic book. "Who else, ya git?! Of course Phaedra!" Trying to keep his voice as gruff as possible, he continued, "I was pretty upset when she was sick. I didn't want it to affect my work, you know, detrimentally."

Michael surprised himself by maintaining a straight face, "Oh, of course not, that would've been devastating."

"I know," Fritz replied. "It is, after all, a comic and not some daft romance novel."

Laughing heartily, Michael commented, "No chance of confusing one with the other!"

Good! Relieved, Fritz blew out a breath and then instructed Michael to read the issue tonight and give him a critique in the morning. "But don't let Ronan read it."

"Why not?" Michael asked, surprised by the dictate.

As they walked to the classroom door, Fritz shrugged his shoulders and crinkled up his forehead. "Because he's posh, that one."

"Posh?" Michael asked, stopping in the doorway.

"He's always reading big books, what do you call them?" Fritz replied. "Classics! He's always reading those big, classic novels. I just don't think he's going to get *Tales of the Double A,* you know, not like you and me do."

As they continued on down the hallway, the noise of the crowd forced Michael to raise his voice. "You may have a point there."

"He's a good mate and all, don't get me wrong," Fritz clarified, speaking even louder than Michael. "He's just not like you and me."

"Is that so, Fritzie? Didn't know you were switching teams."

Walking past them was Alexei, the junior who could never make it past the B team in swimming. Despite being a few inches taller and wider than Fritz, he could never intimidate him either. "Say that to my face again, Russkie, and I'll knock you on your arse!"

With a chuckle and a wave of his hand, Alexei disappeared into Father Fazio's classroom. When Fritz turned back to face Michael, he realized an apology might be in order. "Sorry, mate, but, you know, I've got a reputation to uphold."

Far from being angry, Michael knew that Fritz didn't care about his sexual orientation and that his comment wasn't hypocritical or hateful, it was merely Fritz being his boyish, obnoxious self. "No worries, Germany."

Again Fritz's forehead got all crinkly. "What?"

"Germany," Michael repeated, then explained, "You call me Nebraska 'cause that's where I'm from, so I called you Germany 'cause that's where you're from."

Amused, but not willing to show it, Fritz felt the need to put Michael in his place. "Nice try, but that's just not going to work."

"Why not?" Michael said, disappointed that his catchword wasn't accepted.

"Because I said so," Fritz replied. "That's why."

The phrase made Michael's head start to spin again, not because it made him angry but because it reminded him of his father. That's what Vaughan always said whenever he didn't want to explain himself, whenever he didn't want to have a conversation with his son, which was pretty much every time they spoke. The anxiety Michael felt during class rushed back, flooding his body with the same intensity as this morning's feeding, but without any of the exhilaration. It was the same sensation he experienced during his vision, a foreboding, a feeling that while unknown pieces of his mother's life had been revealed to him, more elements of his father's life were being concealed. Right as they were about to leave St. Albert's and dash to their next class, Michael made a decision. "Fritz, could you cover for me?" Michael asked. "Tell Joubert I got sick and went to the infirmary."

Shocked at the implication, Fritz's jaw dropped. When he spoke, his tone of voice was as indignant as his expression. "You want me to lie? In theology?"

"Oh, like it's gonna be the first time," Michael said honestly, destroying any chance Fritz had of keeping up his ruse.

Good-naturedly, Fritz replied, "Can't argue with that, Ne-braska. So why are you ditching class? Afternoon rendezvous with you-know-who?"

I wish. "No, I just have to take care of something and it can't wait any longer."

"Okay, I'll take notes," Fritz said. "That is, if I can stay awake."

Michael started to feel the adrenaline bubble under his skin. He had never cut class before, never been so con-sciously defiant. Maybe he was reacting to the new energy pulsating throughout his body; maybe he just had to quell the nagging doubts he had. Whatever the reason, he had to confront his father, he had to put together a few more pieces of the puzzle before things got too out of control. Feeling al-most as powerful as he did when he knelt before The Well, Michael remembered there was another task he needed to complete. "One more thing, Fritz."

What now? "Seriously, mate, I'm not your personal secre-tary."

"I know, I know," Michael appeased. "Tell Phaedra I need to see her later. It's important."

Fritz nodded and then started to walk down the hallway, but made it only a few steps. "What's so important that you have to talk to my girlfriend?" Fritz asked, spinning around. His question, however, wasn't heard. Michael had vanished and was already in front of St. Joshua's trying to act as if he were rushing to his next class and not rushing toward a long-overdue confrontation.

Even though he knew it wouldn't be easy—talking to his father never was—it felt right, his bones tingled, and he felt his spirit lift. This is why Imogene had come to him; this is why she allowed him to see his mother, hear what she had really said. It was all so he could make his father admit the truth, whatever that truth was, no matter how hard it was going to be for him to hear.

Stopping near the oak tree that he and Ronan would sit under during the spring, Michael questioned the rationale of his spontaneous decision. *Maybe the truth is something I really don't want to know, maybe it's something that should stay buried. No, no! I want to move forward, I want to let go of the past, and I can't do that if I keep treating myself like a child, like a scared kid. Whatever my father is hiding, whatever he doesn't want me to know, I'm going to make him tell me. And I'm going to make him tell me a bunch of other things too, like why he never called when I was growing up and why he didn't protest when my mother moved me halfway across the world—and why the heck Brania is walking across campus?*

A few yards away from him on the other side of the tree, Brania looked like a St. Anne's student who was trying awfully hard to get detention. Her red platform shoes were an inch too high, her skirt was hiked up an inch too short, and her bare legs were in violation of dress code policy. Michael had heard Phaedra complain countless times about how uncomfortable their mandatory navy blue stockings were, but the way Brania was walking, almost prancing, each step more of a strut, it was as if she wanted to be noticed instead of trying to blend in. It was so weird. Up close she really did look like a teenager, like someone who belonged here, but from where Michael was standing, she looked very much like an outsider.

Where was she going anyway? She was moving in the direction of St. Martha's, but she had less of a reason to go to the dining hall than he did. Curious, Michael wanted to follow her. There was absolutely no reason for her to be at Double A, so obviously she must be up to no good. She must be in the middle of some plan, some plot, something that was probably against him and the water vamps. But if that were so, why would she be walking in plain sight? She was capable of a stealthier approach; in fact Michael realized she was probably capable of more things than he could imagine. *Maybe if I keep my distance and follow her,* he thought, *I can figure out what she's up to, but no, no, do not stray from your purpose! Concentrate! I do not need to channel Agatha Christie and follow Brania into the woods. I have more important things to do.*

Brania completely agreed. Tucking her hair behind her ear, she tilted her head slightly and cast a sideways glance. Yes, her gut instinct was correct; she was seen by a water vamp. She only saw a swatch of blond hair, but it was enough for her to deduce that her watcher was Michael. Thank God there aren't that many of them, she thought; otherwise they might be harder to keep track of.

Bounding across campus, her arms swinging freely by her sides, she relished the feeling of being observed. It was nice to be the object of someone's attention even if that someone was an enemy of sorts. A hint of danger always put a little lilt in her step, but allowing more than a hint to creep into her world was simply the act of a fool, and Brania was many things, but not foolish.

When she came to a fork in the road she stopped and bent down, acting as if she was tying a shoelace that had come undone. Looking all around her, peering into every crevice, within every shadow, she saw that she was alone. Michael was nowhere to be found. *Good, no need for him to see me visiting Father.* Not that she was even certain that Ronan had informed Michael of their connection; it was just that every once in a while, Brania liked to play it safe.

*   *   *

The safe route, however, was not the road Michael wanted to take today. Banging on the door to his father's hotel suite, he didn't even know if anyone would answer. He had merely called his father's office, said he was a client who needed to see him immediately, and was told by a chatty secretary that he was conducting business out of his hotel in Eden today. He took a chance that the information he was given was correct.

"Michael!" Vaughan exclaimed, then quickly recovered from the unexpected sight of his son. "Shouldn't you be in school?"

Deep breath, Michael, say what you practiced on the way over. "I had some free periods and I wanted to see you," he said quickly. "It's been, you know, a really long time."

Vaughan believed only one part of what Michael said, the part about its being a long time since they saw each other. "Well, isn't that nice, son. Come in." When Michael heard the door close behind him, he had a moment of regret. Maybe this wasn't such a great idea after all.

When Brania saw Nurse Radcliff exit her father's office just as she was about to knock, she had the same thought as Michael. It deepened when she saw her father run out after her, holding the nurse's cardigan sweater, a polyester creation teeming with pink peonies on a bed of overgrown green grass, which he placed gently over her shoulders. "You wouldn't want to misplace such a lovely frock," David told her. Giggling, Nurse Radcliff shuffled out of the room, and there was silence as father and daughter stared at each other until Brania was compelled to speak.

"You've had empresses, virgins, a sea nymph if I recall," she said. "And after all that, you've chosen a frumpy, old-maid nurse."

"She's actually a divorcee," David replied.

Laughing much more heartily than Nurse Radcliff, Brania continued, "I cannot believe you're having an affair with . . . *that!*"

"If you wish to see me, stop laughing."

Another father had a similar thought regarding his child's spontaneous visit. "If you wanted to see me," Vaughan said, "you should've called first."

Michael was pacing the small space between the living room and the dining area, unsure of where he should sit or if he should stand. Maybe standing would make him appear stronger, more adult. "With your schedule, it never seems to matter if we make plans," Michael replied, pleased at how testy and adultlike his voice sounded, "So, you know, I figured I'd be spontaneous."

"Well, I'm glad you did," Vaughan replied warily. "I can take some time out from work. What seems to be on your mind?"

Tired of pacing, Michael finally opted to sit on the couch, slouching into the cushions and clutching a pillow so he wouldn't have to worry about what to do with his hands. Talking was proving difficult enough. "Nothing much," he mumbled. *Say something, Michael. You told him you wanted to see him; you can't just sit here. Ask him about your mother. No, I'm not ready for that.* "I met your new driver. He, uh, seems nice."

"Jean-Paul's wonderful. I'm lucky I found him so quickly after Jeremiah up and left," Vaughan said, sitting on the far end of the couch, leaning forward, his hands clasped, fingers drumming together. "Not that I could fully blame the bloke, family emergency and all."

That's not what Jean-Paul said. "I thought Jeremiah got a new job."

This is why I don't like to talk. Too many loopholes, too many opportunities to say the wrong thing. "No, some sort of family problem back in the States," Vaughan said as he stood up, rubbing his hands on his thighs to dry them. "Jean-Paul must have gotten it wrong." Michael nodded but was more convinced than ever that the real truth was that Jeremiah and Alistair were lovers who ran off together. "Can I get you something to drink?"

"Uh . . . a glass of water would be good."

"Coming right up," Vaughan announced, then retreated to the kitchen. "And then, Michael, why don't you tell me why you're really here."

"Brania, darling, why are you really here?" David stared at his daughter, not expecting her to show any surprise, and he wasn't disappointed. He had raised her well. What he did expect, however, was an honest answer, which is what he got.

"To give you an update," Brania replied, crossing her legs and becoming aware for the first time all day how short her skirt really was. "Vaughan's factory has already produced beta versions of our new implants. I've been advised that these permanent contact lenses will keep out more of the sun's rays than ever before."

She's trying; I can't fault her for that. But she's not trying hard enough. "Yes, I know all of that, dear," David sighed, giving the large wooden globe next to his desk a spin. "I've already instructed Amir to bring me some samples that Vaughan brought back from his factory."

Shifting nervously in her chair, Brania uncrossed her legs and felt her throat tighten. She knew all too well what was happening, her position was being challenged. It was not the first time, but it was easier to handle when her father was thousands of miles away. Now that he was here, ensconced in the heart of her world, the world she had come to love, it was much more difficult to ignore his presence and his insinuations. "I didn't realize that," she said meekly.

A condescending smile formed on his lips. "I know. And you should know that you will need to work harder if you wish to remain my favorite child."

Another vision penetrated Brania's mind, obscuring everything else. It was evening. She was slightly older now, around ten or eleven, dressed in a sumptuous black and green silk dress, much more appropriate for a woman twice her age, but one that shone luxuriantly in the moonlight. Her hair was swept back from her face with a diamond and emerald tiara and cascaded down the middle of her back in a spectacle of ringlets and curls. Even then, holding her father's hand, walking in a piazza in the Vatican, she looked much older than her years.

She remembered her father telling her that he loved to walk among the shadows of piety, loved to feel the edges of moral justice fall at his feet, nipping at him but never infecting him with their self-righteous ethics. Strolling amid such ridiculous religious idolatry, he felt like a god among fools, and Brania, though she didn't understand everything her father said, felt like a goddess. However, it was only when she heard the music that she felt truly divine.

Somewhere from behind one of the gilded doors, just on the other side of an ornate window, floated a voice, a voice that made Brania's heart flutter while it made her body become motionless. She couldn't move, not while the voice was calling to her, calling to her in a beautiful, haunting soprano that she swore belonged to an angel. A mortal being could never touch her soul like that. The only being who ever came close to touching her so deeply, so unforgivingly, was her father, and his mortality had been long removed.

Her mind returned to the present and she had to stop herself from shouting out loud, "I'm also your *only* child."

Reading her mind, David closed his eyes and was transported back to the Vatican with Brania. He heard their heels click on the gold-laden pavement, he heard the gorgeous notes of the angel-soprano, he felt Brania's tiny hand in his, but what he remembered most was the darkness. How he longed to feel the warmth of the sun on his face on land that wasn't consecrated; on land far from Double A, beyond Eden. How he longed to lead his people back into the light.

He was so consumed with his ambitious reverie that he let his guard down and Brania was able to get a glimpse into his thoughts. "Do you really think that day will come?" she asked. "When we can walk in the sun as freely as They can?" She didn't need to call water vamps by their name. David knew who she meant. She also didn't need to elaborate, but she did. "Shouldn't we consider ourselves lucky that we can walk in the sun here, on Archangel Academy ground?"

Lucky? Luck had nothing to do with it and luck will play no part when we are able to walk every inch of the earth in the sun. "Thanks to me."

Or so you say. Maybe it was the close and constant proximity to her father, maybe it was the fact that she has been a child for so many centuries, but Brania was feeling oddly rebellious. It wasn't a feeling she was completely comfortable with, but one that she was starting to embrace. "You've never fully explained how that's possible," she mentioned. "After all I've done for you, I would welcome knowing the truth of our origin."

David was sure that Brania would like to know about their origin, the offering he made to Zachariel, the woman he loved, the same woman whose life he sacrificed in order to give his people a glimpse of the sun. But David didn't want to share any of his secrets, even though he feared he would not always be able to conceal them. Someday their truth, his truth, would be revealed. So he remained silent.

David rubbed his bearded chin with his thumb and forefinger, allowing them to linger over the roughness of the stubble, his eyelids fell slowly closed, and his fingers stopped moving. It looked as if he had fallen asleep. But Brania knew better. When he opened his eyes abruptly, David's voice was as harsh as his words. "There is nothing you have ever done for me that wasn't done for your own gain."

Hardly stunned, it was the response Brania expected. Laughing, she replied, "To quote one of the queens who was smitten with you at one time, I am my father's daughter."

David's face froze. It showed no emotion to betray his feelings. Brania was right: She was like him and it was all his fault because he had raised her in his image.

Vaughan, however, could place the blame elsewhere. *This is not my son,* he thought. *He may look like me, but he wasn't raised by me, he doesn't share my principles, and now he's one of Them. Even if I wanted to bridge the gap, what would it matter?* "So what really brings you here, Michael, in the middle of a school day," Vaughan said, anxious to get back to business that he could handle.

Well, Michael, you came here to get some answers, so you might as well start by asking some questions. "I, um, remembered some things that Mom said, and, well . . ." *Focus, focus on why you're here and what you need to say and just say it.* "Why would Mom say that she was ashamed of you? What did you do to her?" There, that wasn't so difficult. If that was true, why was his heart beating so quickly? For that matter, why was Vaughan's?

A few short strides and Vaughan was back behind his desk, in his comfort zone, confronting business issues, not personal ones. "There are things between a man and a woman, personal things, that you wouldn't understand, Michael."

What?! How can he say something like that? Just because I'm gay, he doesn't think I can understand what goes on between a man and a woman? "I understand about relationships, you know!" Michael shouted. "You may not want to accept it, but I'm in one!"

Breaking the pencil in half that he was twirling between his fingers, Vaughan tossed the pieces across the room, "I don't want to hear about that."

"You know what I am, don't you?!"

Oh, Michael, I know more than you think I know, but I don't want to talk about it. "Don't say it!"

The venom in Vaughan's voice was palpable. Michael could feel it reach out and wrap itself around his throat, tighten and pull, until he could hardly breathe. His father didn't even want to hear the truth about him, didn't even want him to say the words, but Michael refused to remain silent even though it was his father's wish. "I knew one of my parents was ashamed of me because I'm different, because I'm gay!" he said, proud that there were no tears welling up in his eyes. "I just thought it was the wrong one."

Vaughan couldn't look up from his desk, he couldn't look at his son, but he couldn't continue the conversation either. "I think you should go."

"If you have nothing else to say," David declared, "I think it's time for you to go."

Rising from her chair, Brania walked toward the door, looking as obedient and willing as the child she had been so many centuries ago, but she wasn't leaving the room. She was merely locking the door to give her and her father more privacy. "Oh, I do have a few more things on my mind that I'd like to express," Brania said, sauntering along the perimeter of the room until she got to the window behind her father. Once there, she stopped moving, which forced David to turn around in his chair to face her, an act of submission that he was willing to perform if it meant his solitude was once again within reach. "Why do we need Vaughan? And why do you want his relationship with Michael to mend?"

Unused to being questioned so directly, David felt a mixture of pride and hatred as he looked at his daughter, her auburn hair softened by the sunlight. "You know how I loathe manual labor. For that reason alone, Vaughan's factory is vital to our future."

"And how does Michael fit into all of this?"

Ah, Michael, the young man who holds the other key to their future. "I need the boy to feel at ease. I know he and Ronan are a loving couple, but it would be helpful if he had a more harmonious relationship with his father. A child needs a parent, Brania," David said. "You of all people should know that."

Brania knew that, but Michael didn't.

"Remember one thing, Dad," Michael spat, "I survived for years without you. It won't be hard for me to learn to live without you again!"

A few seconds after the front door slammed shut, the closet door opened. Smug, Amir shook his head. "I could've taken him, you know!"

Whirling around, it was all Vaughan could do not to grab the punk and hurl him across the room. "Shut your mouth!" From under his desk he pulled out a box and tossed it to Amir. "All you need to do is take this package to David!"

"I know what's expected of me." *Yell at me all you want, old man,* Amir thought, his skinny arms wrapped around the box protectively. *Headmaster isn't going to be happy to know you still can't get along with your kid.*

*   *   *

"Vaughan will not let me down," David declared. "Once Michael is persuaded that all aspects of his life are moving toward a common, more sanguine goal, he and Ronan will become complacent, stop looking over their shoulders, and unwittingly lead us to The Well."

"And we're certain that thing even exists?" Brania questioned.

Such discouragement from my own offspring, truly disappointing. "Yes, I am certain, and when I find it I will have it destroyed, ending their life force, ridding the planet of their race, and, most important, restoring Archangel Academy to its former glory," David explained calmly. "In fact, I'm planning a celebration to commemorate the event."

Inches from her father, Brania was struck by just how pompous he truly was. "Don't you think that's a bit premature?"

Before this moment, David had never realized how insignificant his daughter truly was. "Broaden your vision. Several months from now, we will celebrate the arrival of the Black Sun, pay homage to the solar eclipse, when darkness conquers light."

Intrigued, Brania wanted to hear more, but when her father swung his chair around and picked up the phone, she knew it was time for her to leave. David, however, had one more thing to say. "When that time comes, I expect you to sit on my left side."

While David dialed, she was compelled to ask, "And who will sit on your right?" More interested in placing his phone call than responding to Brania's question, David ignored her.

Outside, Michael and Brania were each wandering aimlessly across campus, lost in their own thoughts, their own private conversations with the fathers they had just left. Fists clenched, his heels hitting the ground harder with each step, Michael was too angry and furious to notice Brania. All he wanted to do was get home, see Ronan, and forget about the miserable day he had had.

Brania wished she could forget, forget about her conversation, forget about her past, forget about the fear that was growing inside her heart. Something was not right, something was not the way it was supposed to be. But when she heard Imogene singing in the distance, heard that glorious, angelic voice, it was as if all her pain was washed away. Instinctively, hopefully, she reached up to hold her father's hand, but it wasn't there. Standing alone at the edge of The Forest, Brania allowed the voice to comfort her, and for the first time in over a century, she allowed herself to cry.

chapter 13

Michael didn't even feel Ronan's mouth on his neck. The softness of his lips, the tentative sweep of his tongue, all unnoticed. There were just too many thoughts racing through his mind pulling him away from the present, away from Ronan.

"Someone lied to me," Michael announced.

Ronan sighed. He didn't want to talk, he wanted to use his mouth and lips to communicate in a completely different way, silently, but it was clear that Michael had a different objective. He was preoccupied, worried about something, and whatever it was, Ronan knew from experience that it needed to be dealt with or else Michael would never kiss him back. "So who do I have to beat up for lying to my baby?" Ronan asked, moving back to his side of the bed.

"That's the problem," Michael answered. "I'm not sure."

Lying on his side, Ronan cradled his head in the palm of

his hand, aware that it made his bicep bulge even larger.
"Can you narrow down the field of suspects to perhaps a
handful?"

Tossing the heavy flannel covers off of him, Michael sat
crossed-legged on the bed, his right foot dangerously close to
Ronan's mouth. It was all Ronan could do not to bend over
and playfully bite one of his toes. "It's either Jean-Paul or my
father."

"Hmm, that bites," Ronan said with a smirk, but Michael
didn't catch the joke.

"Why do you say that?"

Rolling onto his back, Ronan traced the cleft of his chest
and then the thick outline of his pecs with his index fingers.
Just because Michael wasn't going to touch him didn't mean
he couldn't. "I really don't fancy beating up your dad."

Still oblivious to Ronan's flirting, Michael continued questioning him. "How can you be so sure my father's the liar?"

Moving his fingers down to his taut stomach muscles,
Ronan wondered how long he'd have to multitask before
Michael joined in. "What reason would his driver have to lie
to you? He hardly knows you," he explained. "And what's
this big lie about anyway?"

Shifting his weight, Michael flipped around and lay on his
back. *Well,* Ronan thought, *that's a little progress.* But
Michael still wasn't done talking. "Jeremiah," he replied. "I
don't know why it really bothers me, but Jean-Paul said Jeremiah got a new job, and then my father told me he left because of a family emergency." Swinging his legs up and
raising his hands at the same time, Michael grabbed on to the
soles of his feet. Ronan wasn't sure if he was stretching his
muscles or teasing him. "You know why I think I care so
much?" Michael asked, but spoke again before Ronan could
respond. "It ticks me off that they just can't admit Alistair
and Jeremiah ran off together."

Not that again. "Maybe they don't know about the two of them?"

Letting his arms and legs flop onto the bed, Michael stared up at the ceiling. "Or maybe, since my father's homophobic, he can't admit that two men might fall in love and run away together. Which is something he better get used to," Michael said. "Because newsflash, his kid's a homo too."

Moving suddenly, Ronan rolled over onto his stomach, resting his body on his elbows, his eyes widening like a child's. "You are?"

Laughing, Michael slapped Ronan's shoulder. "Shut up!" The touch and the laughter broke the spell and Michael finally noticed how big Ronan's arms looked.

That's better, Ronan thought. *At last he's looking at me the way he's supposed to.* "And you're a pretty hot homo too."

Feeling bashful and passionate at the same time was such a wonderful feeling. "You think so?" Michael asked, knowing full well how Ronan would reply. This time when he was kissed, Michael felt it, felt the softness, the wanting, and he kissed back, pleasing Ronan immeasurably. How he ached for this connection, how he strived every day to keep it alive. It was the reason his race existed. After a few minutes, he could feel the warmth between them grow, the exchange of kisses become more intense, but Ronan didn't want Michael to think that every kiss needed to lead to sex.

Sitting up, Ronan turned Michael so his back was against his chest. He extended his legs, his toes sliding down Michael's thighs, his calves, until their bare feet were rubbing against each other. Snuggling into Ronan, Michael let his body melt, let his head rest against Ronan's chest and listen to the beat, beat, beat of his heart. Both boys were at peace, amazed at how good it felt to be held. Stroking Ronan's arm, Michael closed his eyes and enjoyed the sensory overload. Ronan's muscles always felt stronger after a feeding, and The

Well's scent still clung to their bodies, fresh, fragrant, like early morning rain. Dreamily he spoke. "I think he's the reason my mother took me to Weeping Water."

Caressing the veins of Michael's hand and in between each finger where only this morning there was webbing, Ronan whispered, "Who?"

"My father," Michael replied, "She wanted to keep us safe. I'm not sure why, but I think she wanted to protect me from him."

Upon hearing that word, Ronan froze, just for a second and not long enough for Michael to notice. "What do you mean *protect* you?"

Michael interlocked his fingers with Ronan's, reveling in the strength of his boyfriend's grip. "I think he was really mean to her, maybe to us even, and she was afraid," Michael quietly admitted, wishing the words weren't true. "She used to say he was evil."

This time Michael did notice that Ronan's hand flinched within his. "Evil?" he asked.

Nodding, Michael was aware that the conversation was getting a bit too solemn, so he tried to lighten the tone. "I thought she was just crazy, which, you know, she was, but still . . ."

Evil, protect, these were Lochlan's words, the same words he used when he was talking about Alistair. *Do something, change the subject.* Ronan kissed Michael's temple, holding his lips there longer than expected. "She was a good mother," he said, his voice hushed. "You should know that." Michael nodded, breathing in slowly, deeply. "Mothers protect children," Ronan added knowingly. "And in turn children protect their mothers."

Facing Ronan to look into his kind, blue eyes, Michael saw that they were also sad. "And where does that leave their fathers?"

Suddenly the room was consumed with flames and the crackling of fire. Ronan could hear voices shouting, chanting, invading his ears. *No, this isn't real, this isn't happening again. Something like that will never happen again.* "That depends on the father, I guess."

Michael could sense there was something upsetting Ronan. His smile had returned, but the look of sadness only deepened. "You okay?"

"Yeah, sure." Ronan forced the pain of the past to lift from his face. "Just thinking about tomorrow, big day and all."

His face brightening, Michael pounced on top of Ronan and exclaimed, "That's right, how could I forget?!"

Looking up at Michael, his blond hair falling into his face, Ronan beamed. "I don't know. How could you forget such an important day?"

"I have my first driving lesson tomorrow," Michael squealed.

That's okay, Ronan thought. It's not a big deal that he didn't remember. "Yes, well, it should be *all that*," he said. "I never bothered going for mine, didn't really see the purpose."

Michael bent his arms and pressed his elbows into Ronan's chest so their faces were mere inches apart. "Don't say another word. Ciaran's already pointed out that I don't need a car to travel, but I don't care, I really want my license."

"And so you should have one," Ronan said, smiling to hide his disappointment. "You should have whatever you want."

Feeling the passion rumble in his stomach, Michael kissed Ronan and spoke at the same time. "You can have whatever you want too you know." Even though Ronan knew that the comment was sincere, right now he knew there was no chance of getting his wish.

* * *

The next day, however, one of Michael's wishes was about to come true. The day had dragged on, class after lecture after pop quiz, and all he could think about was his driving lesson. Yes, it was absurd; yes, for a vampire, human transportation was unnecessary, but yes, he was as excited as any typical mortal sixteen-year-old. And just as confused.

"What the hell are you doing?" Blakeley asked. Car keys in hand, Michael paused in front of the driver's side door of the familiar-looking Honda Civic, realizing too late that in this British model, the driver's side door was on the opposite side. "You're not in the States anymore, Howard," Blakeley informed him. "It's time you learned to drive on the right side of the road."

Shrugging off his mistake, Michael walked around the front of the car to the right side, the driver's side, and got in. And then the excitement he had been feeling all day long seeped out of his pores and was replaced with anxiety. He had been behind the wheel of a car before, but that was back home, and the wheel on his grandfather's truck was on the left side. This was completely different. How could he have been so stupid not to know there was going to be an intercontinental learning curve? At least he wasn't so naïve to think that Blakeley would cut him some slack since he wasn't a native. "Don't think I'm going to be easy on you 'cause you're a Yankee."

"Actually, I'm from the Midwest," Michael corrected him, knowing it was a mistake even before the words came out of his mouth.

"I don't care where the bloody hell you're from! If you want to drive here in the *U.K.*, *you can't* expect leniency!"

The words bounced off the windows and echoed in the car, growing louder and louder until they were replaced by Blakeley's raucous laughter. Michael's first thought was that his gym teacher was insane, possibly manic-depressive. He never laughed. He soon discovered that he never laughed while coaching. Sports were serious. Learning how to drive, that was entertaining. "Get it? U.K., you *can't*," Blakeley asked, laughing so hard at his lame joke that he didn't notice Michael remained silent. "Sorry, Howard, just having a little fun at your expense. Now start her up and let's get going. We've only an hour, you know."

An hour that I'm suddenly dreading, Michael thought. Regardless, there was no way of escaping, so Michael took a deep breath and started the engine. So far so good. Next he put the car into drive and slowly accelerated down the cobblestone road, thankful that the ancient, uneven pathway made it impossible to drive over ten miles per hour. But all that changed when they reached the Archangel Academy gate. Michael slammed on the brakes, making Blakeley lurch forward in his seat, then hurl back. "Don't you have to turn off the electronic fence?"

Impressed, Blakeley eyed his pupil. "Already took care of that," he said. "The fence is shut down on the days I give lessons, but good instincts." Blakeley waved his hand, giving Michael the go-ahead to drive past the gate and onto the main road, but the car stood still. Michael's foot wouldn't move over to the gas pedal. "Don't wimp out on me now," Blakeley said in a voice that was frank without being harsh. "You got a lot more courage than that."

You're right coach, I do. Pressing down on the gas pedal, he made the Civic hesitantly move forward, and they left the cobblestone path for the slightly smoother road that was the only passageway off school grounds. Gripping the steering wheel tightly and cruising at the incredible speed of eighteen miles per hour, Michael realized that driving on the wrong side of the road wasn't that difficult after all. It helped that Blakeley looked so relaxed, leaning back in his seat, humming along to the radio, a vast difference from the few times he drove with his grandfather, who criticized his every move while blowing cigarette smoke in his face. Blakeley was the complete opposite. Far from being critical, he praised Michael. But not for his driving.

"I think it's cool that you and Ronan are so open about your relationship." The heat started in Michael's stomach and quickly spread out to his arms, his hands, his neck, until little beads of sweat formed on his forehead. Glancing quickly at his student, Blakeley grimaced. "Don't be so shocked. Everybody knows about you two."

Parched, the words came out a bit strangled. "They do?"

Nodding his head a few times before speaking, Blakeley smiled. "Back in my day, I would've beaten you up for it, you know, just for the hell of it," he confessed, but then his smile faded. "But now, well, good for you for being true to yourself."

The heat in Michael's body lingered, but now it was mixed with a burst of pride, a much more pleasant feeling. "Thank you, sir," Michael muttered. If only his father could extend him the same encouragement, if only his father could muster up the same empathy, if only Imogene weren't standing in the middle of the road. Imogene!? "What the hell?!"

Swerving to the right, Michael careened into the field that bordered the narrow road. He punched the brakes once, twice, but there wasn't enough traction on the grass, and the car veered from side to side. "Howard! Get control of this bloody car!"

"Can't you see?!" Michael shouted back.

"See what?!" Blakeley asked, looking all around but clearly not seeing the dead student.

Michael couldn't remember what he had read in his driver's education manual about how to control a car when entering into a skid, so he was unable to keep the Honda from spinning on a hidden patch of ice. Without warning, they spun around in a complete circle. The entire time Blakeley yelled and cursed at Michael for his stupidity, but Michael didn't hear him, he was fascinated by Imogene, who was now floating in midair a foot above the hood of the car, spinning in the same direction, and wearing an expression that was so empty, so lost, that Michael took his eyes off of her only when he saw Fritz a second before the car hit him.

"Fritz!" Michael screamed, hitting the brakes even harder.

Jumping out of the car before it came to a complete stop, Blakeley raced over to where Fritz had fallen, but he couldn't immediately find him. "Ulrich! Where are you?!"

"Avalanche!"

Moving in the direction of the voice, Blakeley found Fritz lying on the ground, almost completely concealed by the tall blades of grass. "How bad are you hurt?"

"Avalanche!" Fritz cried out again.

"What the hell are you talking about?!"

"His comic book!" Blakeley whipped around to see Amir Bhatacharjee grabbing at pieces of paper that were swirling around in the wind. " 'Archangel Avalanche.' It's the latest issue!"

As the coach bent down to assess how badly Fritz was hurt, Michael scoured the area for Imogene, left, right, up, down, but she had disappeared. Was she trying to communicate with him again? Was there something else that she needed to tell him, show him? For now, any questions Michael wanted to have answered would have to wait, there were more practical matters to attend to, like getting Fritz to the infirmary.

"Howard!" Blakeley barked, his arms positioned underneath Fritz's armpits. "Grab his feet, but be careful!"

Michael did what he was told, gently taking hold of Fritz's ankles. Following Blakeley's lead, he stood up slowly and walked backward toward the car, all the while studying his friend's face to make sure he wasn't hurting him. But Fritz looked far from incapacitated, on the contrary, he seemed to be enjoying the ride. "I'm so sorry," Michael said. "Are you all right?"

"You could've killed him!" Amir shouted as he scurried alongside them, picking up the last of the pages.

In midair being transported into the car, Fritz disagreed. "I'm fine! You only nicked me."

Greatly relieved that Fritz was conscious and seemed to have only a few minor cuts and bruises, the color started to return to Blakeley's face. However, he wasn't willing to let Michael off the hook. "You know all those things I said about you in the car?" Michael nodded. "I take every one of them back!"

"Hey, coach," Fritz said from the backseat of the car, his legs propped up on Amir's lap. "Seriously, I'm okay."

Closing the driver's side door with a loud thud, Blakeley wheeled around and leaned over the seat, his hand gesticulating wildly, the color in his cheeks now a deep red. "Oh, really?" he asked. "Then do you mind telling me what the hell you two were doing out here? And if you tell me you had permission to be off school property, I'll make you swim a hundred laps every day until the end of term!"

No stranger to run-ins with authority figures, Fritz had learned long ago that it was always best to confess when backed into a corner or when trapped in the backseat of a car. He explained to Blakeley that since he knew the fence would be disengaged, he figured it would be the perfect opportunity to sneak out of school, go into town, and see if the general store would sell his comic books. "The owner let me leave a few copies in the magazine rack, you know, as an experiment to see if they generate any business," Fritz offered.

"Really?" Michael asked. He was going to ask exactly how many issues he was able to leave, but Blakeley threw him a look that made Michael think it was better to remain silent.

"So if you wanted to," Fritz said, "you could look at it as sort of an internship."

"Well, I don't want to!" Blakeley shouted.

"Sorry, coach," Fritz said sincerely. "It really was a successful outing and if you have to reprimand me, go ahead, but Amir was only along for moral support."

He had heard enough. Blakeley turned around and started the car, revving the engine violently, and jerking the transmission stick into drive. "I'll deal with all three of you later," he barked. "Right now I want to see what the doctor has to say about that leg of yours." Speeding back onto the main road toward the entrance gate, Blakeley added, "And so help me God, if he says you need time off from swim practice, I'll break both your legs!"

At the moment, the doctor had nothing scientific to say, nothing that had to do with medicine or logic or reason. All that was on his mind, all he ever found himself thinking about lately, was the fantastical message Alistair had left. Now standing in his office with Ronan, he felt he was finally getting nearer to the bottom of the mystery. "It took you long enough to come around," MacCleery said, wiping his eyeglasses vigorously with his shirttail. "What finally made you realize I'm not just some crazy old man?"

"I never said I didn't think you were daft," Ronan huffed. "I just want to know what you meant when you said there's evil here at Double A."

Lochlan felt tremendous relief. Ronan was trying to be evasive, but the doctor could tell he believed him. Finally he could unburden himself, he couldn't keep the secret any longer; he had spent too many sleepless nights, spent too many days paranoid that he was being watched, scrutinized, singled out. He was desperate for an opportunity to share his information with someone and here it was, it didn't matter that he didn't trust Ronan, it didn't matter that Ronan was a student and one of the people Alistair wanted to protect. He was someone who wanted to know the truth and even if he wasn't the perfect confidant, he would do. "Here," Mac-Cleery said, shoving the crumpled note in his face. Intently he watched Ronan read the words and he could see their effect in his eyes. He believed them, he understood they were real. Whatever secrets this kid was hiding, he knew that evil exists. "Do you still think I'm crazy?"

If I told you everything I know, Ronan thought, *you'd think I was the one who should be put in the loony bin.* "You found this in Hawksbry's office?"

"Yes, after he disappeared."

Killed, you mean, but why quibble over semantics? "And you haven't shown this note to anyone else?" Ronan asked.

"You're the first." *Enough questions,* MacCleery thought, *I need answers.* "Do you think Alistair was talking about Zachary?"

Staring at the doctor, Ronan truly didn't know what to do. He didn't even know why he was here. Joining forces with this man whom he didn't completely trust, who he knew disliked him, might not be a wise move, but he knew what havoc David was capable of creating, and if Michael's father was on David's side, the threat was closer than ever before. He couldn't ignore the issue any longer. He had to take action. He just wasn't sure he should act with MacCleery. Until the doctor convinced him.

"I wish I had never read that blasted note," MacCleery admitted. "But I did and I can't forget Alistair's words. I'm a doctor, and doctors make wrong things right again. That's what I'm trying to do here, but I need your help, Ronan. I can't fight this . . . this *evil* if I don't know where it's coming from." Suddenly the doctor was very tired. Awkwardly he reached behind him to find his chair and slumped into it. "I'm not the type of man to ask for help, but that's what I'm doing now." He struggled to say the words, words he couldn't remember the last time he spoke, but he had no choice. He couldn't continue alone. "Help me."

Ronan felt something for the doctor he never thought he would feel. Respect. "Yes."

Startled, Lochlan wasn't sure he heard him correctly. "Yes . . . yes what?"

"Yes, I think Hawksbry was talking about David Zachary in this note."

Fighting the fatigue that clutched at his body, Lochlan stood up, weary but hopeful. Now maybe he could make sense of Alistair's gibberish, now maybe he could protect the children like he wanted him to. But he couldn't do anything until he first took care of his patient.

Before MacCleery knew who had burst into his office, he ripped the note out of Ronan's hand and shoved it into his pants pocket. He thought that his movement was swift and unseen, but he was wrong. Amir saw his quick action and the wave of fear crest over the doctor's face. Whatever was on that paper was a secret and worthy of protection and definitely something worth mentioning to the headmaster.

"He got hit by a car," Blakeley announced as he and Michael placed Fritz on the examining table.

"It scraped me," Fritz clarified. "I don't even think it broke any skin."

Rushing to Michael's side, Ronan thought he should be the one on the doctor's table. He looked a little pale, weak, guilty. "Were you driving, Michael?"

Nodding his head, Michael wanted to explain what had happened, but this was definitely not the time or the place to discuss surprise visits from the dead. "I'll explain what happened later, but it really wasn't my fault and nobody was seriously hurt." Then Michael realized he wasn't the only one who needed to offer up an explanation. "What are you doing here?" he asked. "Are you all right?"

Lie, tell the truth, Ronan didn't know what to do. However, when he looked around the room and saw Amir staring at him, he knew he shouldn't say anything that he wouldn't want to have repeated. "I'm fine," Ronan replied. "I'll tell you the rest later."

"There's nothing wrong with the patient," MacCleery announced.

"Thank God!" When Phaedra ran into the room and saw Fritz lying on his back, the doctor leaning over him, her heart did something strange, it tightened and along with that came a rush of emotion that she was only beginning to understand. These feelings she was having for Fritz were growing stronger every day, and when she got Michael's text telling her that Fritz was being rushed to the infirmary, her mind immediately filled with despair. She couldn't help but think the worst, and she dropped everything to rush to his side. So this was what it's like to be in love? It might prove to be her most difficult task yet.

"Are you okay? Are you hurt? How is he, doctor? He's going to be fine, isn't he?"

When MacCleery didn't respond, Phaedra started to panic. "Are you going to answer me?!"

"I wasn't sure if you were done asking questions," the doctor replied calmly.

"I'm sorry," Phaedra blushed. "I'm just a little scared, I guess."

Softening at Pheadra's obvious concern, MacCleery told her there was nothing to be worried about. "Your boyfriend's going to be just fine."

Unable to control herself despite the crowd, Phaedra

threw her arms around Fritz and kissed him several times, the last one more tender than the others and right on his lips. Fritz was definitely embarrassed, especially when he saw Blakeley fold his arms and scowl, but he was also ecstatic, he finally found a girl who actually made him get embarrassed. Reaching out to grab Phaedra's hand and make sure everyone saw him do it, Fritz smiled proudly. "Not that I'm complaining," he said, "but how'd you know that I was here?"

"Michael sent me a text."

"Thanks, Nebraska," Fritz said. "I owe you another one."

Smiling sheepishly, Michael stole a glance at Ronan. *No need to thank me, Fritz,* he thought. *Just make her as happy as Ronan has made me.* Unfortunately, the same could not be said for how Michael was about to make Ronan feel.

"Oh, Ronan," Phaedra said, not letting go of Fritz's hand, "Saoirse told me to tell you happy birthday."

Birthday?! Michael felt like he had been punched in the stomach and was being strangled at the same time. He couldn't breathe, he couldn't see clearly. How could he have forgotten Ronan's seventeenth birthday?

"Oh, sorry, mate," Fritz said. "I forgot today was the day. Happy birthday."

Hardly happy. "It's no big deal," Ronan replied. "Just another day."

When they walked into their dorm room, Michael still found it difficult to look at Ronan. He didn't want him to see him cry yet again; he also didn't want to see Ronan's disappointment. But he was his boyfriend, the person he loved more than anyone on the planet. How could he forget something so important, how could he hurt him so deeply? He had to say something; he deserved an apology. "Ronan," Michael started, his tears making it difficult to speak, "I'm sorry."

One look at Michael, and Ronan knew he was sincere. He knew he felt terrible, which only made Ronan want to ease his pain. "It's okay, love," Ronan assured him, hugging him tightly. "Vampires don't really celebrate birthdays anyway."

Pushing Ronan away, Michael said, "But boyfriends do."

He was right, Ronan told himself, *he should have remembered. It doesn't matter that I don't age, that we're not going to grow old; it's still my birthday and it's a special day, a special day that went uncelebrated, forgotten.* But Ronan couldn't bring himself to yell at Michael. He knew that these past few months had been a difficult transition and he knew that it was all because of him. Michael's life was complicated now and sometimes unbearable, so if he forgot his birthday, it wasn't the end of the world or, worse, the end of their relationship. "I'll be honest. I am a wee bit disappointed," Ronan said. "But I'm not going to hold it against you."

Wiping the tears from his eyes as new ones started to fall, Michael stood before Ronan and pledged, "I'll try harder, I promise."

Ronan held Michael's hand, heartbroken that it was trembling, but also encouraged. Michael wasn't like the others, the other boys he had loved. He was different and even though, years earlier, Ronan had thought he'd found his soul mate with someone else, he now knew that was a mistake, it turned out to be a relationship that didn't last. The person he was meant to share his eternity with was standing before him. "You don't have to try harder; just be yourself, Michael," Ronan said quietly, kissing one cheek. "Forever beautiful." Then he kissed the other cheek. "And forever mine."

Overcome with guilt and love and confusion, Michael didn't attempt to speak, he just stood there and let Ronan undress him.

"Now come on, love," Ronan said. "Let's go to bed."

chapter 14

David jumped up and landed on the branch so gently the white-tailed eagle wasn't disturbed. A foot away, he admired the creature's harsh beauty, its yellow, sharply hooked beak; its talons, the same color and shape; and, of course, its feathers, long, interwoven, and various shades of brown. But what he loved most was the unexpected color of its chest and head—pure white, like a virgin snowfall—which gave the eagle a look of innocence. This, however, was no innocent animal, the eagle, like David, was a predator. That's why, when it shifted its gaze, and its large, expressionless eyes took in David's form, it didn't immediately perceive that it had become prey.

David grabbed the eagle by the throat and their eyes met, one inhuman being facing another. Unused to being in a position of vulnerability, the eagle didn't know to struggle. The only part of the bird that moved was its feet as they shuffled slightly in order to grab a more secure hold of the thick branch. The razor-sharp nails of its talons plucked pieces of bark free until it regained its balance and was once again as steady as David. Squeezing tighter, David didn't sway in the slightest, he looked as if he were standing on the ground and not on a branch fifty feet above it. The eagle, confused, could not maintain its position and finally reacted as David had hoped, releasing its hold on the branch and un-furling its wings as if it were in mid-flight.

Outstretched, the eagle's wings looked magnificent, almost eight feet in length from one tip to the other. Oh, to be graced with such beauty, David thought, such majesty, to have the tools to soar, float through the sky. As a centuries-old vampire, David possessed remarkable abilities, more so than most of his kind, but true flight was not one of them, and David longed to know the full scope of an eagle's freedom. Sadly, freedom for this particular bird was about to come to an end.

Twisting his grip to hold the eagle by the back of the neck instead of his throat, David jumped off the branch and used the animal's innate skill against him so together they could soar into the morning sky. With his free hand, David reached out, stretching, grasping toward a freedom that was not yet his, imagining he was the one allowing them to fly because of his power, his ability, his wings.

When he looked at his reflection in the mirror that hung in the anteroom to his office, the eagle in front of him, its wings fluttering, David knew Zachariel would welcome the sacrifice and understand the symbolism behind his gesture. If the eagle understood what David was about to do, it would have used every ounce of strength to fly from the room, not that an attempt to escape would have been successful. David was in complete control. And in no rush.

"Be patient, my friend, your time will come," he said. "But first I must send a message to my children."

The text was intriguing. It wasn't the words that impressed Phaedra, but the power behind them. David was able to cast a spell even when his words were unspoken.

My students, The Carnival for the Black Sun is almost upon us! Come to St. Sebastian's today so we can begin preparations for the festivities. Only together can we make this a memorable event in Archangel Academy's history!

In only a few sentences, David called for unity among his students, pride in the legacy of their school, and service to the common good, and he did so using the students' preferred method of communication. Phaedra would have been even more impressed by his skill had she known that David was born more than three hundred years before the digital age.

"Must be some fascinating text you got there."

Phaedra looked over at the other side of the room, at Saoirse, who was lounging in bed. Michael had been right. Having company these past few weeks did help speed up her recovery. "Our new headmaster has sent us a command."

Jumping off her bed, Saoirse ran over to Phaedra, grabbed the cell phone out of her hand, and collapsed onto the mattress. "Ooh, let's see." David Zachary: Headmaster, Vampire King, Text Meister. How many secret talents does that man have? "Cool, this is as good a reason as any to show my face in public," she said. "I'm tired of hiding out."

"Are you sure that's a wise idea?" Phaedra asked.

"I'm a fifteen-year-old runaway who escaped one boarding school to hide out in another," Saoirse replied, tossing the cell phone back to Phaedra. "I've no idea what's wise."

As always, Phaedra couldn't tell if Saoirse was being serious or sarcastic. She thought living as a teenage girl was difficult; living with one was even trickier. She wouldn't change the arrangement. She enjoyed Saoirse's company, her irreverence and good energy, but that same energy could be exhausting at times. And depressing. Saoirse's presence made Phaedra realize how much she missed Imogene.

Poor Imogene. When her friend was taken from this world, Phaedra thought her learning would cease, but the opposite occurred; her knowledge grew. She understood the grief of losing a friend and now the joy of rediscovering a new one, one who was a bit more complicated than Imogene. "I think you're a lot wiser than you let on," Phaedra said.

I wonder how much she knows about me, Saoirse thought. *As much as I know about her?* "That's 'cause you're anti-human."

More complicated, but just as sassy. "We told you about me in confidence, in case I suddenly got all, you know, foggy and stuff!" Phaedra screamed. "But it's a secret!"

Straight-faced, Saoirse chastised her roommate. "Then why are you shouting so the neighbors can hear?"

Phaedra wasn't an expert, but she thought Saoirse had the "little sister" act down pat. "I'm not shouting!" she replied, playfully flinging a pillow at Saoirse. "And besides I'm not *anti*-human."

Welcoming the pillow fight challenge, Saoirse pelted Phaedra in her shoulder with the cushiony weapon. "You are too!"

Quickly the two girls were kneeling on Phaedra's bed, hitting each other with pillows, shrieking with laughter, each one of Phaedra's *Am not*'s met with an *Are too* from Saoirse until a deeper voice put an end to their shenanigans. "Blimey! I didn't know the match already started!"

The sight of Phaedra bouncing on her bed, her smiling face the center of a mass of curls, gave Fritz some not-so-innocent ideas. She looked so light, so bouncy, like she could fly, like she wasn't born to be attached to the ground or something. All Fritz wanted to do at the moment was take her by her hands and pull her back down onto the bed, show her that being grounded can be just as much fun as being airborne. Saoirse had other ideas. "Pillow fight!" she declared. "Boys against the girls."

Michael saw the looks of terror. Neither Fritz nor Phaedra relished the fact of engaging in close, physical contact with each other while two other people were in the room. "Sorry, I was brought up not to hit girls," Michael announced.

Adorable *and* a gentleman. "Even if the girl hits first?" Saoirse inquired, then threw Phaedra's pillow at Michael's face.

So much for trying to make things less awkward for my friends, Michael thought. *A challenge is a challenge.* "Prepare to be defeated, lassie!" Michael cried, whacking Saoirse's legs with the pillow. Giggling, she returned fire with a wallop to the side of his head, and soon the two were using Phaedra's bed as their own personal arena, laughing, shouting, hurling pillows at each other, while Fritz and Phaedra stood on the sidelines watching them, not brave enough to join in, each secretly hoping that when their time for physical entertainment came, it would also involve pillows, but of a more stationary kind.

Saoirse was laughing so hard that when Michael's pillow hit her in the face, she lost her balance. When she hit the ground, however, she was the only one who continued to laugh. "Saoirse!" Kneeling beside her, Michael brushed her hair from her face, he was sure she hit the side of her head against the bedside dresser, but there wasn't a mark on the girl.

Looking up at Michael, Saoirse couldn't decide if his eyes were green like the meadows near her old school or green like her favorite angora scarf. Didn't matter, they were still gorgeous. "You win!" she wailed. "I dub thee Michael, King of the Pillow Fight!" Close call, but obviously a false alarm. Saoirse was already standing up. "What's next on the agenda? Sword fighting? Russian roulette? I know! Let's have a duel!" When three sets of eyebrows raised at the same time, Saoirse was compelled to amend her statement. "With water pistols if you're all chicken."

"Are you sure you're related to Glynn-Rowley?" Fritz asked.

"Hatched from the same old bird," she confirmed.

Shaking his head, Fritz looked at Michael. "Like night and day, those two."

Running to the other side of the room, Saoirse practically dove underneath the bed to retrieve her sneakers. Sitting on the floor, she shoved one on and then the other. "Speaking of my brother, where is he? I thought the two of you were, you know, joined at the hip."

Michael blushed a little. Even though everyone knew he and Ronan were a couple, when spoken out loud in front of people, it made him feel, not embarrassed exactly, but self-conscious. For all his bravado he wasn't yet completely comfortable declaring his homosexuality, but he was getting there. "Hardly," he replied. "He's at the library."

"Doing some *posh* reading," Fritz added, garnering a huge laugh and a high-five from Michael as well as dumbfounded looks from the girls.

"Boys!" Saoirse shouted, rolling her eyes at Phaedra. Looking at Fritz, Phaedra repeated the sentiment to herself. *Yes, boys, what a wonderful concept.*

Noticing the onset of what could grow into a long, awkward silence, Michael thought it time to explain to the girls why they barged into their room in the first place. "Did you get Zachary's text?"

"You mean his decree?" Phaedra asked, scouring her closet for her coat.

"Yeah," Michael said. "We weren't sure if St. Anne's students got it too."

Zipping up her coat, Phaedra assured them the entire student body got his message. "He sure knows how to amass an army."

"Should be fun, though," Fritz said. "You know, all of us ... *amassed* army recruits decorating for this carnival thing."

Crawling back under her bed to find her jacket, Saoirse whispered dramatically, "The Carnival for the Black Sun. It sounds so mysterious."

"Nothing mysterious about it," Phaedra replied. "It's the solar eclipse in a few months."

"C'mon, missie," Michael said. "It's time to go." Grabbing Saoirse by the back of the neck, Michael led the way out of their room, giving Fritz enough privacy to grab hold of Phaedra's hand. Her grip was soft, but firm, the way Fritz liked it. He liked it almost as much as Saoirse liked having the last word.

"Sure, complete and total darkness in the middle of the day," Saoirse replied sarcastically. "Nothing at all mysterious about that."

When they got to St. Sebastian's, the only mystery concerned David. Somehow he had convinced almost the entire student body of Double A and St. Anne's to volunteer their time on a Saturday morning to start decorating for the upcoming social event of the school season, and yet he was nowhere to be found.

What they didn't realize was that David had no intention of being a participant; he was hoping to become a voyeur.

In one swift movement, David bit the eagle's neck and started sucking out the creature's flavorful blood. Screeching and flapping its wings wildly, the eagle tried desperately to escape the clutches of this thing that was taking its life, but David was too strong, his thirst too great, and soon the eagle's bloodless body grew limp, its head slumping to the side.

David pulled out his fangs slowly and cradled the beast to his chest like a newborn before placing it on the floor, stretching out its wings to their full width. Leaning over the animal, David brushed its eyes closed with his fingers and allowed a few drops of blood to fall onto the eagle's chest, staining the white feathers as a way to claim his victim. And then it was time to, hopefully, claim his reward.

Facing the mirror, David bent over until his bloodstained lips were a breath away from Zachariel's portrait and kissed his namesake, smearing the eagle's blood all over the archangel's likeness until its face glistened red. Then he knelt beside the eagle—reluctant to disturb its eternal slumber, but aware that he must in order to make a proper offering—and ripped the wings from its body. Standing before the mirror, his lips and beard wet with blood, he held the eagle's fully expanded wings in his hands and extended his arms, his elongated reach almost filling up the entire room.

> O Zachariel, archangel of the sun
> Share your power with a child of the night
> As my grasp extends like an eagle on the wind
> Grant your son the gift of omniscient sight.

The room was suddenly plunged into darkness, and David fought the unfamiliar tingle of fear that invaded his body. *No! Zachariel is loving, he cherishes my loyalty, my devotion; he wouldn't cast me into blackness, he wouldn't be so cruel.* And David was right. A white light erupted from the sculpted image of Zachariel, illuminating the room, and then David's request was granted.

He could no longer see his reflection in the mirror, he could no longer see his own image staring back at him. What he did see was something much more exceptional: his subjects. The mirror had transformed into a window, a window that allowed David to see his followers, track their every move, and right now, he saw them working in St. Sebastian's Gym, painting signs, building sets out of wood. He delighted in the images, Amir showing a group of students how to use black velvet to create art, Saoirse having returned to her family in obvious defiance of her mother's wishes.

But not everything he saw made him happy.

With the music playing and the smorgasbord of food, it felt more like a party than an early morning work session, except that Michael didn't have a date. "Ronan still upset that you forgot his birthday?" Phaedra asked as they spread out a roll of white material on the gym floor.

"No, he doesn't seem to be," Michael replied. "But I did screw up, big-time."

Stealing a glance at Fritz, Phaedra said, "I think this relationship thing is pretty hard to master, so you should give yourself a free pass on this one."

Opening a can of black paint, Michael looked at the liquid, so thick, so creamy, he could get lost in the darkness. When he looked out of the windows that overlooked The Forest, he saw a more enticing invitation. "And just how many passes does one bad boyfriend get?"

"One forgotten birthday doesn't make you a bad boyfriend."

Michael wasn't referring to Ronan's birthday, he was alluding to Jean-Paul. Outside, at the edge of The Forest of No Return, Jean-Paul was leaning against his car, arms folded, cap dipped forward, as if he were taking a nap standing up, exactly the way R.J. used to do at the gas station on a warm day. Long legs stretched out, ankles crossed, bored, waiting for someone to rouse him, waiting for a reason to move. Michael could give him a reason.

Looking in Michael's direction, Phaedra knew exactly what was on his mind. "Neither does thinking Frenchie is sexy."

Startled, Michael almost knocked the can of paint onto the floor. "It doesn't?"

"Nope," Phaedra said, dipping a stick into the paint and giving the blackness a swirl. "Just makes you gay."

Startled again, this time Michael laughed. She was right. Just because he thought Jean-Paul was sexy didn't mean he loved Ronan any less. It just meant what she said, that he's gay and finds his father's driver sexy. Damn sexy actually.

Unfortunately, Nakano felt the same way. From across the gym, he watched Michael watch Jean-Paul and he had to fight the urge to let his fangs descend and pounce on his nemesis in front of the entire school. *First he steals Ronan from me, and now he's trying to get his disgusting webbed hands on Jean-Paul.*

"Want me to teach him a lesson?" Amir asked, practically panting at the proposition.

"No," Nakano replied. "I can handle this."

Peering into the mirror, David waited for Nakano to take action. He willed him to, but the boy didn't move, he just watched.

He wasn't the only bastard son who didn't comply with David's wishes.

Standing in front of Jean-Paul was like standing in the past. It was a hot, summer day, the smell of gasoline filled the air, a small bead of sweat traveled down R.J.'s cheek, onto his neck, disappearing underneath his loose-fitting T-shirt, going places Michael only dreamed about going. He was so wrapped up in the memory, he didn't even hear the meadowlark call out to him. *Da-da-DAH-da, da-da-da.* All he heard was Jean-Paul's greeting. "Bonjour."

Swallowing hard to get some moisture into his mouth, Michael replied, "Hi."

Jean-Paul moved as if in slow motion, flicking the brim of his cap with a long, thin finger, uncrossing his legs, placing both hands behind him on the hood of the sedan. When he spoke, his voice was smooth, but slow, like honey dripping off a heated spoon. "Looks like your headmaster has, uh, what's zee phrase? Rallied zee troops." Michael nodded and took a few steps closer, rubbing his bare arms, suddenly aware of the chill. "March weather, she's always unpredictable," Jean-Paul said.

"Yeah, life, she too can be unpredictable," Michael said, cringing at his attempt to be clever.

Jean-Paul nodded, smiling, either oblivious to Michael's nervousness or relishing it. "So how have you been, Michael Howard?"

"Good. I've been good." Glancing to the side because he didn't want to stare too long at his face, the cleft in his chin, Michael focused on the car, the black exterior was shining in the sun. It had the same sheen as Jean-Paul's eyes. "I remember the first time I saw this car," Michael said. "When Jeremiah picked me up at the airport."

"You like to drive?"

"That's weird you should say that. I just started taking lessons."

The dirt crunched underneath Jean-Paul's spotless black boots as he walked toward Michael and opened up the passenger-side door. Jean-Paul climbed in, his leather-clad fingers unbuttoning his suit jacket as he sat. "Then why don't you take me for a spin?"

"Seriously?!"

With a grin, Jean-Paul told Michael to get in the car, then slammed his door shut, making the meadowlark flinch from his perch high above them.

What to do, what to do? Michael looked around, into St. Sebastian's, and saw that he was being watched, his friends were all clumped together in a huddle and from his own private viewing room, David was watching too. They were all waiting to see what he would do next, and whatever he did, Michael was sure Ronan would find out. But really, what was so wrong with what Jean-Paul was asking, well, telling him to do? Michael needed to get experience driving a car, and what better way to learn than from a guy whose job it is to drive?

Walking around the front of the car, an odd feeling started to grow within the pit of his stomach, not good, not bad, apprehension mixed with excitement. It was similar to how he felt when he was kissing Ronan, but not nearly as pleasant. His brain was fighting his body. There was something wrong with what he was about to do and he knew it, but his body won out and soon he was sitting in the driver's seat next to Jean-Paul, sinking into the luxurious heated leather seat and letting the smell of cinnamon envelop him. When Jean-Paul spoke, his full red lips hardly moved. "Isn't it nice to sit up front with zee adults for a change?"

Not everyone would agree. When Nakano raced past Phaedra and Fritz, they both knew where he was going, they both also knew they were thinking the same thing, that Michael was acting inappropriately and Nakano impetuously so there was no to need to speak.

Saoirse, however, couldn't keep silent.

" 'Scuse me," she said, squeezing in between them. "There's been a change in today's schedule, people; the fireworks are about to begin!" How they hoped she was wrong. "And doesn't Kano's hair look better grown out and longer like that?" she added. "He doesn't really have the face for a crew cut."

Or the temperament for remaining calm. *I cannot believe he's sitting in the car next to my boyfriend! I cannot believe the two of them are driving away!* The words raged in Nakano's skull, making the bone hurt, making his heart ache. *Was everything Jean-Paul said to me a lie? I thought he loved me.* Nakano knew for certain that he loved Jean-Paul. No, no, this wasn't Jean-Paul's fault, it wasn't his doing, it was Michael's. Stinking water vamp ruins everything!

He should teach him a lesson once and for all; he should race after them. Damn the spectators. *Let them all see my preternatural speed and chase after the car, overtake it, fling open the doors, and make Michael pay for making a fool out of me.* But something prevented him from taking that first step. He wished he could call it maturity, good sense, but he needed to call it by its proper name: Ronan.

Yes, Michael realized, this was definitely a different feeling from when he was with Ronan. Jean-Paul was sexy, really, really sexy, there was no doubt about that, but what Michael felt had more to do with himself than with Jean-Paul. Being in his presence, knowing this other man's body was so close he could touch it if he wanted to, was liberating. He had taken another step toward not hiding from his true feelings and it felt wonderful.

But he was the only one who felt that way.

* * *

"Doesn't feel so good to watch your boyfriend drive off with another guy, does it?" Nakano asked, the words spitting out of him like rancid blood.

"Nothing wrong with taking a driving lesson from an expert," Ronan replied, convincing neither of them that he believed what he said.

"Yeah, you keep telling yourself that." When Nakano got next to Ronan, he stopped and looked up at his ex. "And when you see that smarmy boyfriend of yours, tell him to keep his hands off of mine!" Shoving Ronan out of the way, Nakano sprinted past him and away from the gym to find a private place where he could cool down. Ronan preferred to stay put, sitting on a tree stump to wait for Michael to return, his only company the meadowlark's comforting melody.

"I should get back," Michael announced. "I'm not really supposed to drive with anyone other than Mr. Blakeley."

"I understand," Jean-Paul said, his dark eyes peering at Michael. "It's fun to break a rule, but only if you don't get caught."

And how incredible is it to break your own rules, he thought. Little by little, Michael was breaking down barriers, breaking down the walls that he built while growing up too scared to reveal his true self to the world. All those walls were starting to crumble, and Michael was beginning to feel what it's like to be a man. For now, though, he would accept being a teenager, one with an incredibly beautiful boyfriend.

"Ronan!" Michael said, delighted to see him.

When Ronan looked up from where he was seated, the way the sun was shining in his eyes, Michael was momentarily unrecognizable. Once he stood up, he realized it was an illusion. Michael looked the same as he did this morning, the same as he did every morning, and yet there was a difference. The meadowlark noticed it too and, disappointed, it flew away in the opposite direction of the car.

As Jean-Paul drove away, Michael confessed, "I can't believe you don't want to learn how to drive. It's really exciting! And that car feels a lot better than the Civic Blakeley's making me use." Michael rambled on a bit more about how Jean-Paul's car handled better, how it had better traction and a smoother flow over the ground, until it was clear that he was the only one doing any talking. "You're mad at me, aren't you?"

Mad? Yeah, a little, but Ronan knew they had an audience and he wasn't about to give them a show. "I'm just hungry."

"Really? Our next feeding isn't for a few more days."

But I want a connection now. I want to feel that we're connected so tightly that no one, no matter how fascinating or sexy or older can break that hold. "The Well allows us some leeway if we need to feed a day or two early," Ronan explained. "It acknowledges that even immortals have weaknesses we can't control."

Michael was young, but he wasn't stupid, he knew Ronan wasn't talking about The Well, he was talking about him. "Nothing happened, Ronan. Nothing is ever going to happen," Michael stated firmly. "You know that, don't you?"

I don't know, Michael. All I know is that I hate feeling jealous, I hate feeling that all this could end, that history could repeat itself. But I trust you and you said nothing happened, so I'm going to choose to believe you. "I do," he said. "But I'm still hungry."

The feelings Ronan stirred within Michael were indeed more powerful than the ones he felt while sitting next to Jean-Peal. Sure it was exciting, gratifying to feel his stare, but this, the magnetic pull between him and Ronan, was unique, and Michael recognized that. He couldn't promise that he wouldn't take Jean-Paul for another spin if he offered, but he could promise that he would never do anything with him except drive. Kissing, feeding, and all that other good stuff was reserved for only one person. "Well, love," Michael said, imitating Ronan's accent, "let's go eat."

As usual, Ronan led the way and while their friends continued to paint banners and glue material onto wood, Michael stood next to Ronan on a ledge six stories high, outside the hospital room of a woman who was closer to death than the ocean is to the horizon. Ronan slid open the window, and a whiff of death floated past them. It was an artificial smell, though, this woman was being kept alive by machines that were interfering with nature. The scent of death should be intoxicating, not manufactured. Maybe this was Ronan's revenge, run off with a handsome man and your reward is an unsatisfactory feed. No, not this time. Before they could enter, Michael heard a noise in the distance and then an intoxicating smell engulfed him, the unmistakable smell of someone who was about to die naturally. "Follow me," Michael ordered.

Ronan watched in shock as Michael jumped off the ledge. He wasn't worried that he would hurt himself, but Michael had never taken charge during a feeding before. Things were definitely changing. Instead of feeling apprehensive or concerned, Ronan found himself feeling proud. And when they stood on the top of the overturned truck, the wind carrying with it the delightful scent of a life about to end, Ronan grabbed Michael's hand and kissed it. It was a small gesture, but hopefully one that communicated a great many emotions. Standing high above the ground, his hair windswept, his chest puffed, Michael truly looked like a young king and Ronan his loyal servant. Michael understood what Ronan was trying to convey and he was grateful, but now he too was ravenously hungry.

The handsome man, sprawled on the grass a few feet from the truck, was barely conscious. He didn't feel the shards of glass sticking in his chest and arms, but he did feel something pierce his neck, something sharp, oddly pleasurable, and then he felt his blood swirl underneath his skin. Crouched over the man, Michael was gripping a handful of his curly brown hair tightly as he sucked the blood from his thick, muscular neck. He was so enraptured by the experience, so absolutely becoming an extension of this man, that he didn't stop feeding until he felt Ronan's hand grip his shoulder. Extending his tongue to flick the stream of blood that dripped from the side of Michael's mouth, Ronan whispered, "He needs to feed both of us."

Not only was their feeding unusual, so too was the ceremony at The Well. They knelt, they drank, they prayed, and then they were plunged into darkness just as Michael's vision prophesied. "Ronan!" The only response was a flash of light. The break in the darkness frightened the boys even more because, when they looked into The Well, a distorted image, a grotesque face, stared back at them before the darkness returned.

At the same time, David's mirror turned to black. "No!" he shouted, the wings he was still holding fluttering in the air. "Zachariel, don't abandon me!" Slowly his reflection returned. Gone were the images from St. Sebastian's, gone was his miraculous vision. Only he remained in the mirror. A rumbling started to grow within the room. The walls vibrated, the floor shook, and David fell to his knees when Zachariel spoke. "As you ask your children to be patient," the angel growled, "I ask the same from mine."

Suddenly, The Well was flooded with light. Ronan was standing next to Michael, where he belonged, and from the cave's ceiling fell the most beautiful white roses, like the ones that grew outside of St. Joshua's. The shower of roses was such a lovely antidote to the grotesque face they had seen that they beamed. The roses clustered together and hovered a few feet above their heads, one giant bouquet, suspended, until the petals separated and fell, their softness gently brushing against their skin like wisps of satin.

The feathers from the eagle's wings began to separate and lift, encircling David, until every last one was sucked into Zachariel's carved image. The archangel had accepted his sacrifice. David heard a crackling and saw that the torso of the eagle had burst into flames, all that remained of the animal was fire, then ash, then nothing. Overjoyed, David realized this was a turning point in his immortal life, his first undeniable communication with Zachariel, the archangel of the sun.

Two separate rituals, two different resolutions. The three of them, however, had no idea how closely they were all connected.

chapter 15

Ronan woke up with a plan. Ever since Saoirse took a risk by going out in public to decorate for the school's upcoming carnival, he knew he would have to take action. He didn't want to, but it was inevitable. So instead of going to first period, he was going to see Edwige.

His mother would not be happy to hear that Saoirse ran away from Ecole des Roches to avoid expulsion; that Phaedra impersonated her to assure the French headmistress that Saoirse was safe, sound, and living with family; and, most disturbingly, that Saoirse had been cutting herself out of peer pressure. But his mother needed to be told, his sister needed guidance, and Ronan no longer wanted to act like her parent. It was time for Edwige to resume that role.

Racing out of his dorm room, he kissed Michael good-bye and wished him luck on his British lit quiz. "Don't forget. Charles Dickens got paid by the word," Ronan reminded him. "That's why he was so long-winded."

"What was Proust's excuse?" Michael asked, feeling oh-so-literary.

"Self-indulgent," Ronan replied. "But don't give that as your answer. McLaren's got a stiffy for the old bugger."

Now Michael felt confused. He thought Ronan was off to confront his mother and yet he was cheerier than he had been in days. Standing in the doorway, he called out, "You're in an awfully good mood this morning."

Climbing back up the stairs two at a time, Ronan almost collided into Michael. "Trying to be more like you, love," he said, throwing his arms around him. "And put a positive spin on something I really don't want to do."

When Ronan looked down, a clump of hair flopped out of place. Michael brushed the loose strands back with his fingers. "You don't have to. You could force Saoirse to call her mother and take responsibility for her own actions."

Ronan's laughter filled the stairwell. "That's one of the reasons I love you," he said. "You've got a cracking sense of humor." One quick kiss on the lips, one more for good luck, and Ronan was once again racing down the steps. Running out of St. Florian's, he shouted, "See ya at practice!" but he didn't pause for Michael's response. He was determined to get to his mother's flat before he lost his courage.

Standing outside Edwige's front door, his hand poised to knock, Ronan almost turned to run all the way back to school. He could already hear her shouting, going off on a tirade, blaming him for not making Saoirse return to school, beg forgiveness, and get herself unexpelled. He knew it was going to be his fault because he should have understood the gravity of the situation and how dangerous it could be to have Saoirse in such close proximity to David, Brania, and the rest of their kind, and that he should have immediately asked Edwige for her help. He was wrong.

"I'm so very proud that you've been taking care of your sister."

"What?! You've known all along she was at Double A?!"

Standing in front of the oval mirror, Edwige secured the gold pin to her chocolate brown crushed velvet poncho, one complete shade darker than her suede knee-high boots. The pin was the silhouette of an ocean wave with two crests, a simple design. But the contrast it made against the brown material made it look as expensive as it was. Underneath the poncho she wore a tight-fitting cream-colored cable knit dress that fell a few inches above the top of her boot. She absolutely loved the look. Swinging around to face Ronan, she caught a glimpse of her movement in the mirror, the poncho flouncing at her waist, and thought what a shame she had never experienced London's Carnaby Street in the sixties. She would have been so popular. "The headmistress called several weeks ago to inform me that Saoirse had run away."

Ronan no longer had to worry that his courage would falter. His anger gave him strength, if not focus. "I can't believe you didn't look for her. Why didn't you say anything? How did you know she was in Eden?!"

Fists on her hips, Edwige was becoming as angry as her son, but for wildly different reasons. "How many questions are you going to hurl at your mum before you ask her where she found this smashing outfit?!"

She's insane! That's another thing I have in common with Michael. Both our mums are absolutely bonkers. "Will you listen to yourself?!" Ronan pleaded. "Your daughter ran away and you didn't even go looking for her! What the hell kind of mother are you?!"

Two long strides and Edwige was standing inches from Ronan. Looking up to him, she forced herself to remember that he was her child, her favorite, the only one who had not caused her pain so she didn't want to inflict pain on him, but he was getting very close to feeling her hand across his face. "The kind of mother who knows that her daughter is being protected by that curly-haired creature," Edwige said slowly. "And the kind of mother who knows that her daughter would like some time on her own before I swoop in to ruin her life."

Ronan raised his chin so his mother had to tilt her head back even further to look him in the eye. So she knew Saoirse was staying with Phaedra. Somehow she knew everything she wasn't supposed to know and yet she never knew how she was supposed to act. Despite her calm rebuttal, despite her logical reasons for not taking action, Ronan didn't believe she had given Saoirse a second thought until just now. The only thing he did believe was that her thoughts were not of a positive nature. "And is that what you plan to do, Mother, ruin her life?"

Yanking open a drawer, she grabbed her brown suede gloves and started to put them on, careful not to catch her nails on the cashmere lining. "I plan to do what a mother does best," Edwige declared. "Give her child an ultimatum."

Unbelievable! She really doesn't get it, does she? "Is that what you think good parenting is? Abandonment and ultimatums!"

Stealing a glance at the mahogany box near the window, Edwige wished that Saxon were still alive. With him by her side, she knew how to be a mother, she knew how to handle her children, but ever since he left her, ever since he was ripped from her life, it had become much more difficult. She was always saying the wrong words, doing the wrong things, and worst of all, she was beginning not to care. "I haven't abandoned my daughter," Edwige said wearily. "I've been waiting for the right time to reach out to her."

"And when exactly would the right time be, Mum?" Ronan asked.

"Now."

Outside Edwige's flat, Ronan scuttled after her, even though she was half his size, he was finding it difficult to keep up. Down the block, around the corner, through an alleyway, Edwige brought them to a deserted part of her neighborhood, not stopping until she reached the train tracks. "Call your sister."

Dutifully, Ronan flipped open his cell phone and started to dial until he realized he had no idea what to say. "What exactly do you want me to tell her?"

Closing her eyes, Edwige lifted her face toward the sun, its warmth pleasing, appreciated, and told Ronan to make sure Saoirse was in her room and to stay there until he arrived. When he was done with the call, Edwige asked, "Is her babysitter with her?"

"No," Ronan replied. "She said Phaedra was in class."

"Pity. I was going to bring her a hot-oil treatment as a thank-you."

Shaking his head in amazement, Ronan marveled at how shallow Edwige could be even during moments of crisis. And how easily she sucked those around her into her superficial musings. "Phaedra really doesn't care about her appearance and such," he said.

Twirling to face her son, allowing her poncho to whip around her for full effect, Edwige commented, "Such idiotic thinking will make her one very lonely efemera."

The train whistle prevented Ronan from explaining that there was no chance Phaedra would be lonely as long as Fritz was around, so instead, he followed her silently as she sprinted down the tracks toward Double A. Less than five minutes later, the train miles behind them, they arrived at St. Anne's, but outside the door to Saoirse's room, Ronan heard something that ticked him off even more than his mother's attitude and made him want to abandon his entire plan. He heard laughter. Saoirse didn't care that he was trying to protect her, all she wanted to do was goof off with Ciaran. "We should go," Ronan announced. "It's not worth the trouble."

"Don't fret, I'll be civil," Edwige replied. When she saw that Saoirse had company, a large part of her wished she had accepted her son's proposal.

"Look, Ciaran!" Saoirse cried. "Mum's finally come to visit!"

Awkward. That was the only way to describe the impromptu family reunion. It was as if Edwige's body had turned to stone, her body, her face, became rigid. Ronan and Ciaran were just as motionless except their eyes grew wide and darted about the room, at each other, their mother, their sister, trying to figure out how they had all wound up in the same space and how it might be possible to leave without being noticed. The only one who seemed to be enjoying the meeting was Saoirse. She bounded off the bed and gave her mother a hug that was barely reciprocated, but when she stepped back to stand between her brothers and spoke, the tone of her voice belied the sincerity of her actions. "Wow! A poncho," she said. "I thought they went out of style. Again."

As Edwige crossed to the other side of the room, as far from her children as she could get, Ronan and Ciaran both bit their lips to stifle a laugh. It was only when they each turned to slap Saoirse in the arm for her comment did they realize they both found their sister's rudeness highly amusing. Edwige pulled out one of the desk chairs and sat. "No, darling, you're mistaken," she replied tersely, taking off her gloves. "Just like you're mistaken that you'll be able to get away with this latest escapade."

Saoirse actually batted her eyes several times before speaking. "Whatever do you mean, Mummie?"

Hunched forward, her hands clasped, Edwige looked at her three children as they formed a tentatively united front, and was comforted. She didn't feel the pangs of maternal affection, but it was good to know her children were bonding.

For Ronan, it was disquieting. One minute he was the outsider, the next included in the inner circle with his siblings. But he had to admit he preferred the latter location even if it meant being on the opposite side of his mother.

So did Edwige. Even though Ronan was her treasure, her hope, he was also a reminder that she was something she no longer wished to be, a mother. But could she really be that cold, that apathetic toward her own flesh and blood? Blood. Maybe that was it. Maybe she had spent so many years feeding alone without a partner, searching for the perfect victim by herself that she had become content in her solitude, resentful of those who relied on her, offended by those who wanted her to do anything more than accept their bodies as a final offering, to be a participant in their death but not in their life. Victims she could handle; children seemed to be beyond her capabilities. But they were her children, shouldn't she try harder to act like their mother? Isn't that what Saxon would have wanted and expected from her? "I mean, dear, that you need an education," Edwige began. "So you have a choice."

Wary, Saoirse glanced at her brothers, both of whom ignored her, more interested in knowing what options Edwige was going to offer the girl. "I'm listening," Saoirse said.

"You can either enroll in St. Anne's," Edwige replied. "Or be homeschooled by me."

Saoirse took all of three seconds to decide. "I'll pick the saint over the sinner."

As she expected, Edwige was overcome with disappointment. Hardly the sign of an emotional breakthrough, she wasn't disappointed because Saoirse didn't want her as her teacher; she simply hated being rejected. Unfortunately, it was something she was getting used to. "Come, then," Edwige said. "I've already scheduled an appointment with Sister Mary Elizabeth."

Ronan almost stopped them from leaving, he wasn't sure enrolling Saoirse in St. Anne's was the best solution. But on second thought, if they couldn't keep her sequestered at a foreign school, keeping her in plain sight might be the smartest thing to do. It would be much more difficult for anyone to harm her if her location was public knowledge. Ronan's plan to force his mother to take action had turned out to be successful. Now that they were alone, he hoped his attempt to have a conversation with his brother would be equally triumphant. "Some screwed-up family we got saddled with," Ronan said.

Thrilled that Ronan spoke first, Ciaran heard the words pour out of him. "That's a bloody understatement! We'd be quite normal, though, if you erased our family history and, of course, gave Edwige a personality transplant."

Usually, Ronan stood up for his mother, but today she revealed a bit more of her true self and he wasn't happy with what he saw. He was, however, quite happy right where he was. "Can you imagine if Saoirse wanted to be home-schooled?" Ronan asked, plopping down on the bed next to Ciaran. "Mum's bloody head would've exploded!"

Roaring with laughter, Ciaran reveled in the possibility. "Would've served her right to have to teach Saoirse algebra and bio; she's even less academic than she is maternal."

God, how long has it been since we've just sat together and laughed, Ronan thought. "I'd have given them three days before they ditched the books and went on a shopping spree."

"Do you know my stepmum homeschools her brats?" Ciaran asked. Ronan shook his head, he didn't know that. He knew very little about Ciaran's other family, except that they were even crazier than most of the adults he knew. "And to them a shopping spree is going into the sewing room to make their own clothes!"

Ciaran fell back onto the bed hysterical. His laughter was infectious, but Ronan didn't just find the statement funny, he found it unusual too. Ciaran never talked about those people; the subject was typically taboo. "I'm, um, surprised to hear you say that."

Sitting up, Ciaran shrugged his shoulders. "It's just the two of us, Rone, why lie? Why make things seem better than they are?" Honest communication between the two half brothers, suddenly Ronan was all for that. "My stepfamily is just as bloody mental as this one, maybe more so," Ciaran professed. "Did you know that when my father took my stepmother and fled London to settle in Devil's Bridge, he thought that name was ironic, not symbolic?"

Mouth open, Ronan didn't know how to respond, but for the first time in a long while, he didn't feel the need to apologize, nor did he think Ciaran was bringing up the subject to make him feel guilty. It was just a fact that the two boys shared. "Maybe it's parenthood," Ronan mused. "Once you have a kid, you lose a wee bit of your mind."

"C'mon, mate, you know it's more than that," Ciaran said flatly. "I was born because my father raped our mother and then he made things worse by murdering your dad. It's no coincidence he wound up in a place called Devil's Bridge."

And that could explain why Ronan rarely hung out with Ciaran, the conversation often stumbled into a dark, unpleasant, and brutally honest place. Forcing himself not to accept the ugly images that were forming in his mind or lash out at his brother for the crimes of his father, Ronan chose to keep his tone light. "That's a right bleak proclamation, mate."

Yes, it was, but Ciaran didn't want to backtrack; he didn't

want to cover up the past with an empty platitude. "It's our truth, Ronan," he said. "Might not be proper to say in mixed company, but between the two of us, there shouldn't be any secrets."

Now, that was an interesting proposition and one that Ronan immediately accepted, but for purely selfish reasons— if he could learn to be completely honest with his brother, perhaps he could learn to be completely honest with his boyfriend. "No, there shouldn't," Ronan agreed. And then he decided to put their new agreement to a test. "Shouldn't you be in your lab right now performing some incredibly difficult, yet boring, experiments?"

"Yes," Ciaran replied. "But trust me, my lab work is hardly boring." Ciaran knew that Ronan wasn't interested in science so there was no chance he would ask what his experiments were about. If he did, he would tell him he was trying to find out why Saoirse was so unique and if Michael's blood contained any information that could help David. He meant what he said, he didn't want there to be any secrets between them. However, he believed that some secrets should be kept hidden for as long as possible. Ignoring the fact that he was splitting hairs with a sharp and very hypocritical knife, Ciaran changed the subject. "So you want to skip class and hang out for a while?"

Why not? Ronan thought. Ciaran was proving to be a lot more interesting and unpredictable than any of his professors. So as two family members grew closer, two others prepared to widen the gap between them.

Edwige appreciated minimalism, but sitting in Sister Mary Elizabeth's office, she felt the nun had taken the esthetic to the extreme. The four walls, painted a dull gray, the color of an overcast sky, were bare except for a small holy water font near the door and one thin, gold cross that hung over the sister's plain, wooden desk. Facing the nun's work space, Edwige and Saoirse sat in two wooden chairs, not decorative or comfortable, and to their right was the only window, unadorned, no curtains, no shutters, no cosmetic treatment whatsoever. Of course cleanliness could be next to godliness, Edwige thought, when there was absolutely nothing to clean.

"Your daughter's academic record is quite good," Sister Mary Elizabeth remarked. "Some disconcerting questions, however, are raised in her personal file."

Before Edwige could put a spin on Saoirse's colorful past, her daughter raised her sleeve to reveal the cuts on her arm. "You mean these, Sister?"

Suddenly, Edwige and the nun had something in common, they were both shocked. "Well, yes, dear," Sister Mary Elizabeth said. "Why would you do such a thing to yourself?"

Saoirse didn't want to lie to the nun; she wasn't that disrespectful, but if she told her the truth, she figured Edwige would kill them both. In this instance, lying was definitely the more honorable route. "Sister, I know it looks bad, but it really was a harmless prank."

"Self-mutilation can hardly be considered harmless or a prank," the nun replied. After a moment of silence, she asked, "Would you consent to counseling?"

If it means not having to be homeschooled by my mum, sign me up. "Yes," Saoirse said. "Not that I need counseling, but, you know, so you can all see that I'm perfectly normal and this was just a dumb joke that got out of hand."

Doubtful that Saoirse was telling the truth, Sister Mary Elizabeth was at least grateful she would accept counseling. The way her mother was sitting, the disinterested aura she was putting forth, it was clear the girl would not be getting any help from her. "Then I see no reason why you shouldn't become the newest student at St. Anne's," the nun declared.

"And may I be the first to welcome you."

The three of them were startled when they heard the voice, but once they realized the voice belonged to David, their surprise waned. They all knew the man differently, but they all knew him to be mysterious and with a penchant for showing up places unannounced.

"David," Edwige purred. "How unexpected."

Looking down at the woman who once shared his bed, David thought she hadn't aged so well for a woman who wasn't supposed to age. "No," he replied. "How opportune."

"David!" Saoirse squealed. "Do you remember me?"

Smiling impishly, David bent down to give the girl a hug. "Of course I do, Saoirse. How could I ever forget you?" Noticing the nun's befuddled expression, David realized an explanation was in order and, to Edwige's relief, he, like Ciaran, understood the importance of keeping some secrets secret. "Ms. Glynn-Rowley and her family are old friends of mine," David confessed. "I've known Saoirse since she was a little girl."

Looking into David's eyes, Saoirse relived one of her earliest memories. Barely five years old, she climbed up David's leg, reached out to grab his arm, and hoisted herself so she could sit on his shoulder. Once secure, she leaned over and let her long, blond hair dangle. It was a game they would play constantly while she was living with him. "Your hair is getting longer every day, Rapunzel," David said.

"Thank you, David the Giant," Saoirse would reply. "Will you let me escape today?"

Despite his benevolent smile, David would never agree. "The outside world is no place for an enchanted princess."

Pouting, Saoirse obstinately pressed on. "But, David the Giant, when will I be able to see the world?"

His eyes twinkled more than the girl's. "When the world discovers why you're so enchanted?"

Folding her hands on her desk, the Sister straightened her

back and released the tension in her shoulders. She didn't understand why, but whenever she was near David, she became tense, on guard; this tête-à-tête only made the feeling stronger. "How did you know I was interviewing an applicant, Headmaster?"

Because my god is more powerful than yours. "I know everything that concerns the children," David said. "And may I say, Saoirse, you've picked quite an exciting time to join us."

Saoirse knew why but decided it best to play dumb. "Why?"

As duplicitous as her mother. "We're preparing to celebrate the upcoming solar eclipse."

"An odd reason for a celebration," Edwige stated.

Only for those who are frightened by the dark. "I can't think of a better reason to be festive," David replied, "than in honor of the enigmatic nature of *Nature.*"

He's as dull and uninspiring as always. The revelation reminded Edwige that she was bored beyond belief. "Are we done here, Sister?"

"No," she said opening her desk drawer and pulling out a navy blue vest and a small metal box. "Saoirse has one final task to complete before she can officially become a St. Anne's student."

"Ah, yes, your little ritual," David said haughtily. "Which is my cue to exit." At the door he turned, knowing all three would be watching him. "Ladies, it has been my pleasure."

After David left, calm was not entirely restored. Saoirse was a bit nervous that her induction into her new school, and therefore her separation from her mother, was not yet complete. "Exactly what kind of task is it?" Saoirse asked.

Sister Mary Elizabeth explained that each new student was required to hand-sew a patch of the Blessed Mother onto her vest, alone and in silence, as a symbolic gesture to their patron saint. "Do I get a few tries if I mess it up?" Saoirse asked.

Laughing at the girl's honesty, the nun reassured her that the Blessed Mother didn't judge any of her children by how well they sewed, she loved them all equally and unconditionally simply because of their effort. Acceptance? Being loved unconditionally? No wonder Edwige was hurrying out of the room. "Thanks, Mum, this is going to work out for the best," Saoirse said, grabbing the vest and sewing kit from the desk. "For all of us."

Edwige wished she could believe her daughter's prediction, but when she glanced at the font of holy water and noticed that the liquid had frozen over in an attempt to protect itself from David's spirit, she knew better. She also knew better than to confront the man, but she needed him to understand a few things.

Standing in the anteroom to his office, the ornate décor already a significant improvement over the nun's quarters, Edwige hated to admit it, but she felt more in her element. She ignored the fact that she was closer to evil than to good and took solace instead that she felt welcomed in the presence of the angels. Well, almost all of them.

Entering David's office without knocking, she caught him on the phone, by the sounds of it on a business call that had nothing to do with academia. Waving Edwige to come closer and sit, David continued his conversation until he noticed she was restless. "Sorry," he said, hanging up the phone. "Even in the more civilized world of education, business never seems to end."

Holding the sides of the armchair firmly, Edwige kept her gaze on David firm. "Is that the only reason you've come here, to conduct business?"

She's nervous, David thought. *That's unusual for her.*

"One of the reasons," he replied. "The other is to be closer to your flesh and blood."

He's lying, Edwige realized. *How typical of him*. "David, old friend, you're as welcome to my flesh as you ever were, but my blood is off-limits."

Laughing like the untrusting ex-lovers they were, David and Edwige parried and sparred, tossed a few double entendres into the air, reminisced about the old times they had shared, ignored the veiled and not-so-veiled barbs they threw at one another, until Edwige could no longer make small talk. "I hope your newfound focus on Archangel Academy doesn't mean you've forgotten our truce."

Remembrance does not equal obligation. "Of course I do," David said. "I have a wonderful memory."

"Our species, while separate, were joined in peace," Edwige stated. "I trust you'll honor that memory."

Examining Edwige closer, David changed his earlier opinion, she didn't look that bad, not for a water vamp anyway, and they had shared some truly passionate moments. It was a shame to have to look into her eyes and lie. Luckily he didn't have to. When the phone rang, David automatically pressed the speaker button so he wouldn't have to answer Edwige's question, they were both surprised when Vaughan's voice filled the office. "David, I have the factory on the line; we may have a problem."

Startled, David ripped the phone from its cradle and noticed the way Edwige's body stiffened; she recognized Vaughan's voice. That's all right, just two men conducting business. "If you'll excuse me, darling," David said. "Duty calls."

Walking as slowly as she could, Edwige froze when she heard David speaking Japanese. Her worst fear was confirmed. Vaughan's factory, their special contact lenses, David's arrival, all part of a plot against her people. They were more than business colleagues; they were two vampires who were working together in order to attack her race. Willing herself forward, she finally made it into the anteroom and shut the door behind her. Disgusted by her reflection, she could hardly look at herself. *Such a stupid woman you've become, such a stupid, pitiful woman! Trusting men, allowing them to lie to you, conceal their despicable motives and turn you into a fool! What in bloody hell have I become? What have I allowed these men, these fiends, to turn me into?! Their actions are unacceptable, unforgiveable!* Edwige didn't need to fully understand the connection between David and Vaughan to want revenge. She needed only to know how to make it happen. Sneering at her image, she decided Vaughan would be the first to pay. Leaving the anteroom, she sped like a missile, like a white-hot burst of furious light until she reached her destination, a secluded cave nestled within the bowels of The Forest of No Return.

Throwing back the coffin lid, she told Imogene to shut up and stop singing. "It's time for you to show Michael the truth about his father."

chapter 16

When she was alive, Imogene thought free will extended to the afterlife. She assumed that as long as you didn't go to hell, you could sort of create your own existence, do what made you happy, do all the things you never got a chance to do on earth. When she died, she realized she was wrong.

She was basically a prisoner. She couldn't roam the world, she couldn't visit deceased relatives or eavesdrop on old friends to find out what they were saying about her, she could only do what Edwige told her to do. It wasn't that bad. Edwige only ordered her to do things with Michael and she liked him, so it could be a lot worse, she could be forced to befriend Nakano, whom she totally despised. It was just that she had hoped in death she would reconnect with Penry. What Imogene didn't realize, what she wasn't yet able to comprehend, was that while she had been killed, she wasn't technically dead.

When she was murdered, there was a witness. Brania had watched—her eyes brimming with a mixture of respect and jealousy—as Edwige drained Imogene of her blood. But after Brania left, having grown tired of seeing her nemesis feeding on the prize she felt should have been hers, Edwige let some of that blood rush back into Imogene's body to keep it from decomposing. She then slashed the palm of her hand with her fangs and allowed some drops of her own preternatural blood to mix in with Imogene's. That's when the confusion began.

The vampire-tainted blood that flowed through Imogene's veins contained some life-altering properties that tricked her body into thinking it was still alive. As long as Imogene's body didn't start to decay, her soul clung to its physical host. And as long as her soul was intact, she would never see heaven. So even though her home was now a coffin, she was still conscious; her mind alert but effectively brainwashed; her body now possessing some incredible powers, yet seemingly unable to make a move on its own; and her soul, innocent, but stuck in limbo. Stuck to do as Edwige commanded, even if Imogene disapproved.

"But he's my friend," the girl said without speaking. "I don't want to hurt him."

"Michael needs to know exactly what his father is capable of," Edwige declared. "Trust me, you'll be doing your friend a favor."

I don't trust you, Imogene thought, *but for whatever reason, I'll just do as you say.* Imogene nodded in agreement, as Edwige knew she would, for as long as Edwige's blood ran through her veins, she believed any attempt by Imogene to refute her wishes would be pointless. "You'll be giving your friend the best gift of all, dear," Edwige said condescendingly. "The gift of knowledge."

"That knowledge will devastate him."

The voice rang through the crypt strong and clear, but neither Edwige nor Imogene saw anyone speak. Until Grace materialized. Her image hung in the air, undulating at the foot of the coffin, soft as a breeze, the voice that emerged from the translucent vision, powerful and bold in contrast. "Don't do this, Edwige," she said. "Don't hurt my son because you want revenge on his father."

Despite loathing interruptions of any kind, Edwige wasn't upset by Grace's intrusion. On the contrary, it made her curious. Maternal concern that transcended mortal life—now, that was radical thinking. Here was a woman, dead for several months and yet still protective of her child. But instead of seeing the beauty within that concept, Edwige saw only its futility. Why not use Michael? she thought. Children shouldn't stand in the way of a parent's happiness.

"I'm asking you as one mother to another," Grace cried. "Don't use my son to get to Vaughan!"

"But I want Vaughan to pay for his actions," Edwige replied. "Certainly, you must want the same thing."

"I do! Vaughan deserves to pay for everything he's done!" Grace shouted. "But please, Edwige, I'm begging you, please don't use Michael to make it happen!"

Grace no longer inspired curiosity in Edwige; she inspired revulsion. *"Please, I'm begging you,"* Edwige mocked, then added pointedly, "Don't ever beg in my presence again."

Turning from the specter, so angry that she missed how the flutter of her poncho resembled the flutter of Grace's image, Edwige looked at Imogene, who was sitting up in her coffin, and telepathically gave her instructions. "Now go!" But Imogene didn't move. She was staring at Grace, her face showing the barest hint of some emotion, empathy, pity, dread. Edwige had no idea which it was, but the connection between one form of the undead and another made her incredibly uneasy. "Do as you are told!"

When Imogene walked through Grace's spirit, she felt the woman's desperation and for the first time, for just a fleeting moment, Imogene's body listened to her mind and she stopped moving. Her rebellion was short-lived, but not unnoticed. Edwige thought Imogene might be different, but she was just like her other children, defiant and disloyal. It disheartened her terribly to have to admit what she had come to suspect, that children were completely overrated. So were overprotective mothers.

"Please, Edwige," Grace said, her voice and her image growing fainter. "Don't do this."

Edwige couldn't take it any longer—Grace's supplication, Imogene's impertinence, Vaughan's betrayal, her children's disrespect—no one was simply listening to what she said and doing exactly what she wanted. No one was treating her the way she wanted to be treated! This was not the life she thought would be hers when she and Saxon offered their souls to The Well, it was not the life that she was promised, and soon, yes, very soon, things would change. But for now, the feeling of disgust that was rumbling in the pit of her stomach lengthened and rose until it reached her throat and needed release. "I SAID MOVE!!" Edwige's shriek was loud enough that it made both Imogene and Grace disappear. Alone, breathing deeply, she clutched the side of the coffin and closed her eyes, waiting to be engulfed by the peace that, thus far today, had eluded her.

Imogene wasn't completely at peace, but she was hopeful. Outside, walking toward The Forest, still unable to resist Edwige's command, she realized her pause had given her hope that maybe her intuition wasn't wrong, maybe someday she would reclaim her free will and have the type of death she had always dreamed about. However, when she remembered what she was setting out to do, the feeling of hope was lost and she felt like the sky that was starting to change from dusk to night. Her dreams might still come true, but right now she had to destroy her friend's.

Michael stopped when he heard the sound, *da-da-DAH-da, da-da-da*. Looking up, he saw the meadowlark perched on a branch that slanted steeply toward the ground, almost as if the weight of the tiny bird was too heavy a load to carry. Michael knew how the branch felt. Sometimes he just wanted to shake his shoulders, force the burdens that clung there to fall, fall, fall and be swallowed up by the earth so he could walk lighter, with more freedom. "Sometimes I just want to stop moving," Michael told his friend. "Sometimes I feel like I'm losing my way."

"And sometimes you feel amazingly happy," the lark added.

Smiling, Michael nodded in agreement and the lark understood. He felt wonderful, not so wonderful, like he would never feel wonderful again, sometimes all in the same minute, as if he had multiple personalities and they were all jockeying for position simultaneously. He felt his head and his heart would explode at any moment, and at any moment it felt either exhilarating or terrifying. "Am I going crazy?" Michael asked.

The bird hopped toward the end of the branch, causing it to bounce slightly, its yellow feathers ruffling, bringing light to the darkening sky as it sang *da-da-DAH-da, da-da-da*. "Just means you're still more human than not."

That was a relief. As much as Michael embraced being a water vamp and reveled in his new powers, he just didn't want to lose sight of what he used to be. Maybe it was simple math. He had been human for much longer than he'd been an immortal creature, so it made sense that he would cling to what was familiar, what was more natural. "If x means that Michael was human for sixteen years and y means he's been a water vamp for six months, how long will it take for him to feel more like y than x?" Michael mused. Father Fazio would surely appreciate that he was giving theoretical principles a practical use. The lark, however, had a more abstract response.

"Sometimes our journeys lead us to unexpected places," the bird said. "Places we don't want to go to, but that we must if we want to grow."

When Michael looked up to question the meadowlark, make him clarify his vague pronouncement, he saw that the branch was empty; his friend was gone. But Michael wasn't alone. Imogene had returned.

As she held out her hand, Michael's first instinct was to tell her that he couldn't go with her because he was on his way to swim practice, but then the lark's comment echoed in his brain. Imogene's arrival was no coincidence, she was here to take him on another journey, to a place that most likely he didn't want to go. He felt like turning around and running to St. Sebastian's, breathe in the familiar scent of chlorine, hear Blakeley's whistle blow, signifying the start of yet another practice meet, but he wanted to grow, as painful as it sometimes was, he wanted to grow up, so he reached out to grab her hand.

And then they disappeared.

Michael wasn't the only one who was skipping practice. Standing on the shores of Inishtrahull Island, Ronan looked out at the ocean, the cold water rippling over his bare feet, reminding him that he was forever connected to the glorious water. It also reminded him that he was forever connected to his inglorious mother.

The morning spent with Edwige haunted him all day, he just couldn't get over how callous she had become. It shouldn't have hit him like a revelation. She was acting no differently from the way she had been for years, but maybe it was because for the first time he stood in solidarity with his siblings, so when he looked at his mother, he was looking at her through their eyes, and the view was enlightening.

It was so obvious that over the years she had changed drastically, become much less of the mother he remembered and more like, well, more like a woman he'd like to forget. But could he do that? Could he banish his own mother from his mind? Could he actually sever all ties with her? Yes, no, why was it so confusing?! Sitting on the beach, clutching his knees close to his chest, Ronan tried to make sense of it. He knew that she loved him and would protect him, but he also had to admit that a very large part of her wanted nothing to do with him. As long as he carried out The Well's mandate and spent his eternity loving Michael—which he had every intention of doing—she would be fine with never seeing him again, and the feeling was doubled where Ciaran and Saoirse were concerned. What had happened to the mother who cradled him in her arms? Who told him bedtime stories of an enchanted land called Atlantis? Who made him want to be just like her when he grew up?

"Don't be a stupid prat, Ronan," he said, chastising himself. "You know exactly when she started to change."

"Burn the devil!"

The growling voice burst into the present from Ronan's memory, bringing along with it a disturbing image of Saxon tied to a stake, half his body consumed by fire, his eyes closed as if he were dreaming. He looks so different from

Mum, Ronan thought. Daddy looks like he's sleeping and Mum's woken up from a bad dream.

On the beach Ronan shuddered, remembering how Edwige looked as she watched her husband's body melt, her eyes containing more fear than he thought possible, her mouth wide, the sounds she made like a wounded animal's, her body twisted, contorted as it tried to break free from the two men who were holding her back. He remembered as a little boy calling out to her, "Sssh, Mum, you'll wake up Daddy."

As a child he had no idea the turmoil Edwige was experiencing or the self-control she was displaying. She looked like a woman who had lost all her inhibitions, but she was actually a water vamp who understood that if she revealed her true self, she would find herself disintegrating alongside her husband. It wasn't the unthinkable pain that she feared, it was knowing that if she died, she would leave her children orphans in a brutal, barbaric world. She kept her truth hidden so her children could at least have one parent.

"We still need you, Mum," Ronan heard himself whisper to the waves.

He heard Edwige reply, "Mummie needs you, Ronan, now more than ever."

But it was a request from the past. Physically exhausted, her eyes swollen and red, Edwige simply couldn't pick up Saxon's ashes all by herself.

Michael picked up the straightjacket and wondered why Imogene had brought him here. He knew exactly where he was and it was not a place he wanted to visit, either in real life or in a vision. Being inside the psychiatric clinic where his mother died was not exactly what he would call appealing. Throwing the jacket on the makeshift bed, Michael silently asked Imogene to take him away from here, but she turned her head. In order for Edwige to have her revenge, it was necessary that he stay.

When Grace entered the room, the first thing Michael noticed was how calm she looked. She wasn't screaming or trying to run away from the orderlies as she was when they took her from the house in Weeping Water. She looked normal. Maybe this vision would be a good thing after all, maybe it would allow him to see that his mother really hadn't lost her mind.

"Should we put her in the jacket?" the younger orderly asked.

"Nope," the gray-haired one replied, grabbing the straightjacket roughly from the bed. "Doc said she's so drugged up, she can't hurt a fly even if she tries."

Michael jumped when the door slammed shut. It was such a small room, nothing in it but a mattress on a cot and a pillow, the padded walls and thickly carpeted flooring making it look even smaller. The only window was an inch from the ceiling, thick glass, horizontal in shape, and covered in bars. A small patch of sky was all that could be seen and Michael imagined it permitted only a thin ray of sunlight to enter the room during the day. It was heartbreaking to think that this is where his mother spent her last moments in life, in such a barren, confined space. But as much as the room seemed to make Michael upset, it seemed to bring Grace comfort.

Kneeling beside the bed, Michael watched his mother sleep. Her face was soft again, as if she had fallen asleep on the couch with the TV on back home, she looked unworried and Michael was relieved to see that the drugs they had given her were working. She wasn't restless, she wasn't anxious, and when Michael saw the envelope that had been stuck underneath the mattress fall to the floor, he understood why. Bending down, his instinct was confirmed. His name was written on the envelope in his mother's handwriting; inside was her suicide note. She was sleeping peacefully because she had already decided to end her life. He couldn't believe that in a few short hours, she would awaken and kill herself. How could that be possible? If only she could remain asleep until the morning, maybe history could be altered and she wouldn't die. But then Vaughan woke her up.

"Grace," Vaughan said, shaking his ex-wife's shoulder gently. "I've come for you just like I promised."

Stunned, Michael crawled backward until his back hit the padded wall and then he scurried into the corner underneath the window. What the hell was his father doing here? Michael glanced over to the door and saw that it was still locked. How in the world did he get in? As bizarre as the scene was to Michael, when Grace opened her eyes, she re-acted as if this was exactly what she was expecting.

"Hello, Vaughan," she said quietly. "I was wondering how long it would take you to come."

She must be dreaming, that has to be it. There's no way she could think this was normal. Yes, she had been dreaming of Vaughan, and his appearance was simply a vision within a vision. He saw Imogene shake her head and heard the words in his mind, "No, Michael, everything you see here actually happened. It's all real, it's all the truth."

How?! This just isn't possible. "I want to go home!" Michael shouted. "Get me out of here!"

Imogene was the only one who heard him and her re-sponse was to turn her back on him and look up toward the window to count the stars. She didn't care about astronomy, all types of science were her least favorite subjects, but watching the stars was better than watching the past unfold.

"It's time for you to go away," Vaughan whispered. "Per-manently."

Michael couldn't see his father's face, but he could see his mother's reaction, and whatever Vaughan did made Grace recoil in horror. She tried to scream, but no sound escaped her throat. She jumped up and stood on the bed, her back pressing into the cushioned wall, her arms spread out wide, her fists banging into the wall as if she were trying to break through the padding.

"Grace, you can no longer fight this," Vaughan said. "I've decided that now is the time."

As terrified as she looked, Grace apparently disagreed. "Not like this!" With her eyes focused on Vaughan's face, she kicked his chest so unexpectedly and with such force that he flew across the room, his back facing Michael, his body inches from his feet. Cowering in the corner, Michael saw his mother run toward the door, but just as her fingertips scraped against the metal handle, Vaughan grabbed her hair and threw her onto the floor.

"NO!" Michael screamed, scurrying on his knees to where his mother had fallen. He tried to grab her hand, help her up, but her body wasn't solid, his hand went right through her. Grace remained on the floor, frozen more by fear than any physical injury she may have incurred. When Michael turned to see Vaughan standing over her, he understood why she was afraid. His father looked grotesque, his handsome face replaced by features Michael knew all too well. "This can't be real," Michael heard himself say out loud.

But it was.

His father was a vampire.

Saliva dripped off of one of the fangs that hung past Vaughan's lower lip, and landed on his chin. His face was sallow, like sun-bleached sand, his cheeks so sunken that the bone looked like it might pierce the flesh. Worst of all were his eyes, completely black, lifeless and hollow as if they could transport you to the depths of hell, which is exactly where Grace believed she was about to be taken.

"Vaughan, no, please, don't do this," Grace pleaded, slowly inching her body across the floor away from him. "I promised you I'd never say a word and I haven't."

She knew? His mother knew his father was a vampire? Michael's head was spinning, he felt dizzy, he had to fight the urge to succumb to the sensation and faint, allow his body to rescue his mind so he didn't have to bear witness to this horror. But he couldn't, he couldn't abandon his mother, not now, not when there was so little time left to save her. He knelt next to her, hoping she would somehow feel his presence, hoping he could find a way to help her fight back.

"Yes," Vaughan responded as he walked toward them. "You've been a very good girl and I thank you."

"Then let me leave by my own hand. I'm ready to do it now, I promise," Grace pleaded.

Vaughan thought for a moment and then said finally, "No, I've been looking forward to this."

Michael looked up and saw Vaughan standing above them, his neck so elongated and curved that his head looked like it was separated from his body, his face almost horizontal as it peered down at them. Vaughan smiled and his mouth grew wider. The drop of saliva became so large that it could no longer hold on to his fang and fell, slowly. Michael winced when it passed through his body, he had never felt such coldness before. "And we both know that unless you're gone, you'll never let me have my son," Vaughan said. "You'll never let Michael be mine."

The sound of her son's name sucked the fear out of Grace, leaving only strength behind. "And you'll never have him!"

The laughter distorted Vaughan's face even more and Michael had to look away, he was hideous. His features, his eyes especially, were just like Nakano's when Michael unwittingly saw his true self. "Gracie, haven't you learned by now that there's nothing you can do to stop me? It's the only way

I can raise Michael the way I've wanted to all these years, in my image, without your interference." So that was it, that was the only reason Vaughan wanted to bring Michael to Eden, to enroll him in Archangel Academy, so he could be one of Them. That's why he so ridiculously suggested he should marry Brania. Well, too late, Dad. None of that's ever going to happen!

Grace felt the same way. Standing up, she looked directly at her ex-husband, his misshapen face not frightening her any longer, and the fury that she had kept locked away inside her for years was unleashed. "No matter what you do, our son will never be yours! He will never become something as disgusting and vile as you!" she seethed. She took another step closer to him and looked directly into his blackened eyes. "Haven't you learned that yet, Vaughan?"

For a moment, his father found it hard to breathe, his chest rising, expanding, his nostrils flaring wide. Michael watched his father's face, and beyond the monstrous features, he recognized the emotion behind his expression. It was doubt. But Vaughan hadn't come here to talk or discuss or negotiate Michael's future, he had come here to end Grace's.

Baring his fangs, he reached out for Grace, who made one last attempt to reach the door. This time she wasn't even close. Vaughan grabbed both her arms at the same time and lifted her off the ground. Squirming, Grace tried to break free, her legs flailing, kicking, hitting Vaughan, but he didn't feel her. The only sensation he felt was the sweet taste of her blood as his fangs bit through the bandages and tore open the flesh at her wrists.

A low, guttural moan seeped out of Grace, bled out of her every pore. Her body was weeping not because her blood was being taken from her, but because her child was. Looking out the window, up into the heavens, she began to whisper, "Dear God, please protect Michael from this man, please protect his soul and keep it safe." She kept on praying, pleading as Vaughan kept on feeding, feeding, feeding, one wrist, then the next. All the while he was gulping, devouring her, Grace prayed, even when her legs no longer moved, when her eyesight was almost completely gone, she kept begging God to take action. "Do with me what you will, but please, *please*, send someone to protect my son."

Raising Grace's near-dead body high over his head, Vaughan screamed, "My son doesn't need protection from his father!"

By the time Grace's body hit the floor, Vaughan was gone, his deed done. He made it look like the unstable woman had finally succeeded at the task she'd attempted so many times before. He cleverly made it look like she slit her wrists and committed suicide, when she simply became another one of his victims.

Paralyzed, Michael realized his mother hadn't abandoned him. Even facing death, she had tried to protect him, as Phaedra had said. That's all she had ever done. And now all Michael could do was watch her gasp for breath. He knew that if he shouted, no one would hear him. He couldn't alter the past, he could only become its witness. No! No, there had to be something he could do; he couldn't just watch. Crawling to his mother, he tried to press on her wounds, but again his hand moved through hers. He was flesh while she was spirit. But she was also his mother; he couldn't just leave her to die. "Imogene!" The girl still remained more interested in the stars. "Imogene! Please let me hold her," Michael pleaded. "Let me hold my mother!"

Turning away from the night sky, Imogene looked at Michael and Grace, and she remembered how she felt when she died by herself and how Penry must have felt when he experienced the same fate. She understood the need for physical connection and the absolute horror of its absence. She understood what Michael was asking; she couldn't deny the request and it seemed that neither could Edwige. After all, she got what she wanted, Michael saw the truth. What did she care what happened next?

This time when Michael reached out for his mother, he felt her flesh, cold and scared, and he let out a cry. This was not the way it was supposed to be. A son was not supposed to cradle his mother in his arms; it was supposed to be the other way around. And yet it felt right. Grace looked up at him, and Michael saw the love and pride in her eyes and he knew that she recognized him, she knew she was being held by her son, and they were both grateful. Because when Grace died a second time, she wasn't alone.

chapter 17

The End of the Beginning

Outside, the earth was different. Inside, so was Michael.

"Michael." No answer. "Mr. Howard," Professor Willows clarified in a much louder voice. "Would you mind answering the question?"

Looking up from the blank page of his notebook, Michael saw his professor staring at him and was startled. He had actually forgotten he was in class. Glancing to the left, he saw some students looking in his direction as well. One of them was Fritz, his head leaning forward, eyebrows raised. Clearly, they were all waiting for him to speak.

"Shall I rephrase the question?" Willows asked. "Translate it into German? Perhaps Swahili?"

Michael's surly growl of a response cut right through the students' laughter. "I don't know."

Willows's right hand moved with a mind of its own. His middle finger tapped against his thumb, quickly, repeatedly, his ring finger bouncing along with it, his pinky, not moving, but thrust outward. His nervous twitch didn't reveal itself only when he was nervous, it also manifested when he was faced with an uncooperative pupil. He expected certain students to act like boors; Michael wasn't one of them. Nevertheless, he had been a professor long enough to know that even the most scholarly teenager could sometimes act like his more loutish counterparts.

His lips clamped tightly, Willows exhaled slowly through his nose and clutched the edge of his desk to stop his hand from shaking. If the professor thought Michael was merely cranky because he didn't study and couldn't answer the simple question about the United States confederacy, he would have pressed the issue with him, but he recognized the look in his eyes. He was angry, and when a teenager was angry, Willows believed it was often best to ignore them until the feeling abated. "Amir," Willows called out. "Name the three Southern states that stayed neutral and didn't join the confederacy in an attempt to secede from the Union."

"Kentucky, Missouri, and Maryland," Amir said, failing to restrain himself from tossing a smug smile Michael's way, which everyone except Michael noticed. With his mind overcrowded with images of his parents, there really was little space for anything else to penetrate.

When the bell rang, Michael got to the door so quickly Fritz had to push another kid out of the way to catch up with him so he wouldn't lose him in the crowd. "Hey, isn't Nebraska, like, right next to Missouri?"

"Just 'cause I'm from the States doesn't mean I know

everything about them." Michael hoped his comment would shut Fritz up, but quite the opposite.

"I know what'll sweeten your pissy mood," Fritz said. "Help me write the latest issue."

Again with that stupid comic book, Michael thought. Why doesn't he just let it die like Penry did.

"I got this great idea that all the profs get food poisoning at some special banquet honoring a former headmaster who's now a zombie," Fritz said, his voice brimming over with excitement. "But it's not really food poisoning, the food's been cooked in zombie blood, so now all the profs are zombies just like the headmaster." When Michael didn't respond, Fritz continued. "Picture it, mate. There are zombies everywhere and all the students lock themselves into St. Sebastian's to hide out and then the profs break through the windows and then there's this right gory war on the gym floor. Brilliant, I know. I just don't know how to kill them all off, which is why I need your help." Suddenly, Fritz looked very serious. "Have we established if Double P can kill a horde of zombies?"

If Michael had been listening, he still wouldn't have been able to help his friend. He was completely focused on figuring out how to deal with the new information he'd acquired thanks to Imogene. "Sorry, Fritz, I can't help you."

When Fritz finally stopped talking and looked at Michael's face, he noticed what Willows had recognized earlier. "Hey, what's up with you?"

I just found out my father's a vampire and he killed my mother to make it look like a suicide. "Nothing."

Again Fritz's eyebrows raised. "Mate, a blind codger could see something's bothering you."

A very tiny part of Michael's brain understood that Fritz was trying to be kind, trying to get him to talk, open up, but the rest of Michael's mind resisted. He didn't want to talk, he just wanted to be left alone. "Really it's nothing, I'm fine." When Michael felt Fritz's hand on his shoulder, he reacted harshly, raising his arm, his elbow coming dangerously close to Fritz's face. "Sod off, will ya!"

Fritz didn't stop stumbling backward until he hit the wall. "What the bloody hell's gotten into you?"

Without breaking his stride, Michael turned around to shout, "Just leave me alone!"

For the rest of the school day, Michael felt like one of the zombies Fritz wanted to write about, as if he were sleep-walking through every class, every lecture. The second the school bell rang signaling the end of class, Michael ran. He wandered through The Forest aimlessly, pausing a few times when he thought he heard the meadowlark's song, but kept walking when he realized it was some other bird's tune, some melody that was far less soothing. He walked into areas he had never explored before, pieces of The Forest he never knew existed, and was stunned to see just how expansive it was. He always thought The Forest of No Return was a name that contained more mystery than meaning, but after ambling for almost two hours in foreign territory, he began to think you really could find yourself forever lost within this uncultivated terrain.

Sitting on the ground, leaning against the enormously thick stump of a fallen oak tree, Michael stared at his cell phone, his father's number staring back at him. For the third time that day, his thumb hovered over the SEND button, and for the third time he snapped his cell phone shut without making the call. He wanted to call his father, scream at him, tell him exactly how foul and disgusting he thought he was, ask him how he could live with himself after what he'd done, but while the words, the questions, churned inside his head, pressed against the back of his eyes, filled his throat until he choked, they never escaped his lips. He couldn't give them freedom because freedom meant truth and as long as he could remain silent, maybe he could convince himself that what his father did never really happened.

Unfortunately, it proved to be an impossible task. Even when he stood at the edge of The Forest and looked into St. Sebastian's to watch Ronan during swim practice, he didn't notice how marvelous he looked in his Speedo, how his body was just one muscle that flowed into another, how he dove off the platform and entered the water with such grace and fluidity, his body, his movement more at home in the water than on land. He could only think of his father devouring his mother's flesh. Just as Ronan emerged from the pool, Michael turned and ran back into The Forest, preferring to lose himself within the unfamiliar than stay close to the world and the people he had come to know so well.

"Did you see that?" Ciaran shook his head, unsure of what Ronan was talking about. "I thought I saw Michael run into the woods."

That didn't surprise Ciaran. Michael had been acting strangely the past few days and when Fritz filled him in about his outburst earlier today, Ciaran assumed he and Ronan had a fight. Michael was good-natured most of the time, unless he had a real strong reason not to be, a reason that typically had something to do with Ronan. "Is he, um, mad at you for something?"

Drying his arms and chest with a towel, but looking out into The Forest, Ronan couldn't think of anything that happened between them recently that would get Michael angry, not that Ronan was always aware that he had done something that ticked Michael off. He had noticed that he was quieter than usual yesterday, but he was studying for a few big tests coming up, so Ronan didn't think much of it. Maybe he misinterpreted the silent treatment. "I don't think so," Ronan replied, now quite confused. "Did he mention anything to you?"

Grabbing one end of Ronan's towel, Ciaran bent over and used it to dry his hair. "No, but he threw a wobbler and bit Fritz's head off this morning."

After hearing about the incident, Ronan grew more concerned. "That's not like him."

"No, mate, it isn't," Ciaran agreed. "Nakano's got the monopoly on angry, and quiet and depressed, well, that's more my thing. Your Michael's the fun-loving, happy-go-lucky type bloke."

Ronan smiled. Lately, Ciaran was sounding more and more like a real brother. "Well, then I have to find out what's troubling my Michael."

Standing in front of the bathroom mirror, Michael knew exactly what was troubling him. His problem was he didn't know how to deal with it. When he saw Ronan standing behind him, his eyes soft but worried, the answer was simple. "I saw Imogene again," Michael, said looking at their reflections. "She showed me some things, some really horrible things."

"Come here." Michael wrapped his arms around Ronan and felt the coolness of his skin lower the temperature of his own. He felt the heat, the anger, lift off of him, and when he breathed in, he could no longer smell his mother's blood, but only the pool water that clung to Ronan's body.

Resting his cheek against Ronan's chest, Michael described what he had seen, how he had witnessed his mother's death at his father's hands, and only when he was finishing his story, explaining how Imogene let him hold Grace and give her some comfort as she died, did he realize Ronan wasn't surprised to hear that Vaughan was a vampire. He didn't say anything, his body didn't flinch, his heart rate didn't increase. It was as if Michael had told him something unimportant, or worse, something that he already knew. Stepping back, he asked, "How long, Ronan?"

Ronan wasn't sure what he was more afraid to look at: his reflection or Michael's challenging stare. As a result he didn't look at either, instead focusing on the bathroom floor, and as he expected, Michael didn't allow him to get away with not answering for very long. "How long have you known that my father is a vampire?"

Look him in the eye, Ronan. He deserves that, as well as the truth. "For a while. My mother told me."

Suddenly the bathroom felt claustrophobic, as if the walls had moved in a few feet on all sides, leaving precious little room for oxygen. Entering the bedroom, Michael kept walking until he reached the far side of the room, but still he couldn't stop moving and started walking in a small circle around and around and around, continuing his path even when he spoke. "And you never thought this was something I might want to know?"

Ronan was getting dizzy watching Michael, but he wouldn't allow himself to take his eyes off of him. "We . . . I was trying to protect you." And finally Michael stopped.

"I don't need your protection!" Michael shouted. "I'm not your little brother or . . . or your dog, I'm your boyfriend!"

"That's why I wanted to spare you this," Ronan said, his voice starting to shake. "So you never had to find out that someone you love is one of Them."

"I don't love my father!"

"Yes, you do!" Inching closer to Michael, Ronan felt the tears slide down his face, but he didn't know if he was crying for Michael's loss or for his own. "He may not be perfect, he may be a bloody ass, but he's your father, Michael."

Standing his ground, not stepping closer toward Ronan or

moving out of the way, Michael heard himself scream, "He's a murderer!"

The thunder of Michael's voice stunned Ronan. He was right, what *was* he saying? Maybe he had spent too many years around vampires; maybe he was starting to take life and death for granted. Vaughan did a heinous thing, he committed a vile act against Grace, against Michael, and Ronan's silence made him an accessory. It didn't matter that he didn't know what kind of secrets Vaughan was keeping, he knew he was one of Them, he knew what types of evil those kind are capable of, he shouldn't have listened to Edwige when she told him not to tell Michael, he should have said something. "I'm sorry," Ronan said quietly. "I should've warned you about your father instead of trying to shield you from the truth. I . . . I was just trying to prevent you from being hurt."

"Because you love me so much," Michael replied in a voice drenched in sarcasm.

"Yes, Michael, I do love you," Ronan said, his hands automatically reaching out to hold his hands, but Michael leapt over the bed and away from him.

"Then why do you keep lying to me?!"

Because I'm scared. Because I'm scared that you're going to leave me like everyone else in my life. "I don't know."

Furious, Michael kicked the bathroom door, ripping it from its hinges. "Not good enough, Ronan!"

"Calm down, Michael, please!" Ronan cried, rushing toward him, grabbing his arm.

When Michael turned around, Ronan saw that he was beyond consoling. His fangs were fully descended, his face elongated, his eyes narrow, and his voice seething with so much rage, it was almost unrecognizable. "*LET GO OF ME!!*"

*   *   *

Those were the same words Vaughan shouted when he opened his door and Michael attacked him. Without warning, Michael lunged at his father, grabbing his arms and pushing him to the floor. Caught up in the speed and momentum of his actions, Michael flipped over, his back landing squarely on the hardwood floor, and even though the crowns of their heads were touching, Michael still held on to his father's arms. "Why did you kill my mother?!" Michael shrieked, his voice bouncing off the ceiling and plunging down onto Vaughan.

So Michael found out, Vaughan thought, *somehow he uncovered the truth. Well, if he knows that I killed Grace, he must know my other secret; no sense hiding that from him any longer.* Flinging his arms to the side, Vaughan broke free from Michael's hold and used the preternatural strength in his legs and thighs to jump up to a standing position. He whirled around to face his son, but Michael was nowhere to be found. Because Michael was now behind him.

When Michael's fist slammed into the side of Vaughan's head, he realized that his son was much quicker and stronger than he presumed. He might be a water vamp, on the wrong side of eternity, but he was still incredibly powerful. And inquisitive.

"Tell me!" Michael demanded.

Shaking away the fog that threatened to take hold of his body and mind, Vaughan leaned his hand against the living room wall. "If I hadn't killed your mother, she would never have allowed you to leave that godforsaken Weeping Water and live with me," Vaughan explained breathlessly. "If I hadn't intervened, your life would have continued on in the same endless, horrible cycle as before."

"You didn't *intervene*. You killed her!"

His balance regained, Vaughan remembered he wasn't

talking to another immortal creature but to his son. "And you should be thankful for that."

"Thankful?! You killed the only person who ever loved me!"

Far from an immortal creature, Vaughan realized, his boy was still very much a product of his human upbringing. "Grow up, Michael. I loved you more than your mother ever did. I'm the one who freed you! I'm the one who set you on the path toward your destiny!"

Michael couldn't believe what he was hearing. This was the man who was always breaking promises and flying off to Tokyo or some other foreign country; the man who wanted him to be a lowly, repulsive vampire like him; the man who couldn't stand him because he was gay. This man didn't know the meaning of the word love. "Fine. Do you want to see how thankful I am, Dad?" With one hand, he lifted the sofa by its leg and held it in the air. Instinctively, Vaughan raised his arms to defend himself, thinking Michael was going to throw it at him, but instead Michael flung it into the dining room, not flinching when it broke through the window and he was showered with shards of glass. "Do you love me now, Dad, because I'm big and strong?!"

Without the couch to use as a barrier between himself and Michael, Vaughan slowly started to walk backward. "I did love you . . . *I do*, I do love you . . . in my own way," Vaughan stammered. "It's just . . . it's been a long time since I've been a father."

Watching his father try to slink out of the room, Michael couldn't believe he was actually this coward's son. "It's been an even longer time since you've been a man."

Before Vaughan could escape into the bedroom, Michael caught him by the shoulders and hurled him back into the living room, his body not stopping until it skidded into the wall. Rushing toward his father, Michael allowed the hatred he had been feeling for days to take control of his body. Turning Vaughan over, Michael punched him in the face, the chest, he watched the blood spill from his nose; he was no longer aiming, he simply allowed his fists to land wherever they could. Michael was so enraged, he didn't notice that Vaughan wasn't fighting back. Vaughan might be a coward, but Michael was still his son and despite everything, he did love him. There was no way he could bring himself to assault his own child. All Michael cared about was making his father suffer as much as his mother had, but when he raised Vaughan's wrist to his fangs to make him feel her pain, he stopped.

Looking at his father's bloodied face, he saw himself. He knew that if he pierced his father's flesh, if he took his blood from him, he would be no better than he was, and worse, he would make his father proud by becoming just like him. Horrified, he let go of his arm and let it fall clumsily at his side. He forced his mouth and his hands to return to their original shape so he could look more like his mother, and fled from the room. He had to get out of there, he had to get away from that thing that was his father.

Exhausted, Michael stumbled outside. The wind was starting to pick up and the crisp breeze felt refreshing, almost medicinal. It took Michael a moment to notice how beautifully it lifted Jean-Paul's hair so it could float around his face. The driver was sitting on the hood of the sedan, holding his hat in his hands and smiling at him, his long legs dangling, a few strands of hair getting caught between his lips. Michael thought dark brown on red was a perfect combination. He felt his stomach start to flip, no longer with anger, but with something else. The sensation grew as Jean-Paul hopped off the car and opened the passenger side of the car. "Looks like you could use a quiet place to . . . how do you say? Oui, chill out."

Yes, that's exactly what Michael needed to do, chill out, relax, erase all the images of his parents, all the blood, all the screaming, and replace them with the smiling face of this handsome Frenchman. Just sit next to him for a bit, nothing more, just sit, let the smell of spicy cinnamon envelop him, sink into the warm leather seats, close his eyes and listen to Jean-Paul's sexy accent. Yes, that's exactly what he needed.

"We need some music," Jean-Paul announced. Instead of turning on the radio, however, he leaned across Michael to reach for a CD that was in the slot on the passenger-side door. He twisted his head so his hair fell on Michael's hand, the loose tresses caressing his bruised, reddened knuckles that had just punched his father's face. Seconds after he popped in the CD, the soft wail of a saxophone glided through the car. Jazz wasn't Michael's favorite, but he thought he'd give it a try, thinking it might be a sign that it was time to experience new things. "You're very strong."

Opening his eyes, Michael turned to Jean-Paul, his body immediately tensing up. "What?"

Jean-Paul's fingertips felt even nicer grazing across Michael's hand. "I saw what you did in there. You have a solid right hook."

Staring at Jean-Paul's face, searching for a sign that he was more than just handsome, Michael couldn't tell, he looked human, but until a few days ago, he never suspected that his father was a vampire either. Then he realized most people would look at him and never imagine he was anything more than a teenager and once again, he heard his mother's words echo in his ears: *Not everything is what it seems.* "Thank you," Michael whispered. "How did you see us?"

Ignoring him, Jean-Paul looked up at Vaughan's living room window and then into Michael's eyes. "You are a much better man than your father."

Shifting his weight, Jean-Paul reached his arm over Michael's head and placed it on the back of the seat. A whiff of leather and some cologne, something musky, hit Michael hard in the face and he couldn't tell if the smell was gross or enticing. Regardless, he breathed it in and held the smell for a moment before letting it escape his mouth. "Lean your head back and close your eyes," Jean-Paul instructed. "That's the only way to really hear this music."

Michael did as he was told and leaned his head back against Jean-Paul's arm. It was lean and strong underneath the leather jacket, the way he imagined R.J.'s would feel if he had ever been so lucky to lean back and feel R.J.'s body pressing against his. He heard the sound of metal clinking against metal, and his eyes fluttered but didn't open. He didn't want to disobey orders. There was the sound again and he assumed Jean-Paul was crossing his legs and accidentally hit the car keys that were hanging from the ignition. He was certain of it when he felt bone press into the flesh just above his own knee, not quite touching his thigh, but very close.

What a feeling this was. The knot in his stomach had finally subsided, his muscles were relaxed, his eyes felt as if they were floating in their sockets, and he was drifting deeper and deeper within his body. His heart started to race only when something tickled his lips. Michael couldn't stop himself from opening his eyes and he was glad he did. Jean-Paul's face was an inch away, his hair falling forward, and each time Jean-Paul breathed, his hair danced across Michael's lips. After Michael closed his eyes, he felt more breath than hair linger over his mouth and then he heard Jean-Paul whisper, "You have the face of an angel."

That's because I'm a young king, Ronan. This time when he opened his eyes, Michael was horrified. What the hell was he doing? Why was he about to let someone else, someone other than Ronan, kiss him? Recoiling, Michael felt the door handle jab him in the side. He hit the door a few times in a feeble attempt to unlock it.

"What are you doing?" Jean-Paul asked. "We're supposed to be relaxing."

"I'm sorry . . . I can't do this."

Finally, Michael unlocked the door, pushed it open, and stumbled onto the pavement. The chilly breeze acted like a tonic, washing away the spell Jean-Paul had cast, and allowing him to run, to get farther and farther away from doing something stupid, something that would stain everything that he and Ronan shared. Yes, Michael was angry with Ronan, furious, but he didn't want to hurt him out of spite. He just knew it wasn't something a real man would do.

Standing in the back of Archangel Academy, Michael had newfound respect for the angels, the immortal men, who adorned the stained-glass windows that decorated the walls of the church. Michael used to think that angels had it easy, an immortal life must be nothing but fun and adventure. He had no idea that immortality, like a more temporary life, didn't automatically give you good judgment or the ability to resist temptation. You still had to make choices. Today, Michael was lucky; he had ultimately made the right choice. But what about tomorrow? What about when he came face-to-face with the next temptation? What about the next time he had to look into Ronan's eyes? When he genuflected by the side of the last pew, he was relieved. Maybe what he really needed to do was stop asking so many questions and sit next to a friend.

Ciaran saw Michael and smiled. By the time Michael sat next to him, he had stopped writing in his journal, relocked it, and tucked it back into his bag. For a few minutes, the boys sat next to each other quietly, looking at the cross that hung over the tabernacle, empty except for blots of blood on each of the four points of the cross, until Ciaran, sensing that Michael couldn't find the right words to open a conversation, spoke. "After the lab, this is my favorite place on campus."

Michael didn't know that, probably because he never asked. "I guess they're both kind of peaceful," Michael stated. "You know, in completely different ways."

Not so different actually, Ciaran thought. Science and religion were a lot more intertwined and reliant upon each other than most people imagined. But noticing Michael's sullen expression, Ciaran didn't think he'd come here for intellectual discussion. "You haven't been yourself lately."

That's because I don't really know who I am. "Sometimes I wonder if I should ever have come to Double A," Michael said. "Maybe it was all a big mistake."

Ciaran knew he wasn't talking about school because two other things that were intertwined and reliant upon each other were Michael and Ronan. "Do you have any idea how much my brother loves you?"

Michael wasn't surprised by this comment. Ciaran was quite perceptive. He nodded his head several times but still found himself saying, "That doesn't stop him from lying to me."

Love doesn't stop people from lying to each other, Michael. "That veneer of invulnerability my brother likes to wear is all an act," Ciaran said, then chose his words carefully. "He's been, um, terribly hurt by guys that he's loved."

I know, he's alluded to that a few times, but I'm not just another guy, Michael thought, *I'm supposed to be his soul mate, I'm supposed to spend eternity with him. What if those other guys were supposed to do the same thing, though? Maybe lying and keeping secrets is Ronan's way of protecting himself more than it is to protect me?* Michael sighed. Coming to church was supposed to instill a sense of peace, not conjure up more questions than answers.

"Look, I know my brother can be stubborn and pompous, but I have never known him to love another person as much as he loves you," Ciaran said. "That should be reason enough to convince you that you're right where you belong, Michael."

Finally, an answer. "Sounds like something my mother would say."

"I don't know about that, but, dude, I'm starving," Ciaran said. "I know you don't eat, but want to come to St. Martha's with me?"

His head cocked to the side. Michael asked, "Did you just call me dude?"

"Too American?"

"Just not your style," Michael replied, smiling.

"Ah, well," Ciaran said, grabbing his coat and bag then pausing in the aisle. "You coming?"

Michael remained seated. "Thanks, but I can't. I need to go home."

An hour later, Michael felt he was on the verge of finding some peace because despite his time away, Weeping Water looked exactly the same.

chapter 18

The graveyard appeared to be alive. Michael looked around and saw tall, lush elm trees, their leaves large, deep green, the cool breeze that floated in between the drooping, twisted branches causing the leaves to flap up and down, making them look as if they were greeting Michael, welcoming him home.

Short spider bushes populated the sides of several dirt paths, some of their spindly leaves so long and overgrown they scraped against Michael's leg as he walked by. He leaned over to breathe in the scent of dogwood, tugged on the branches of larkspur, disrupting a few butterflies from their perch, and smiled as they encircled him several times before fluttering away. He heard a rustling and saw that the butterflies were off to follow some friends. A stream of six or seven birds emerged from within the belly of a particularly leafy tree, a ray of orange and black flying up and into the blue morning sky until birds and butterflies united into one cluster and disappeared out of view. Ironically, much of Weeping Water was barren and dry, but here in the place where death reigned, the landscape was alive and fertile.

It's even more beautiful than I remembered, Michael thought. That's because he chose to forget how desolate it really looked and was glorifying the past, remembering it not for what it was, but for what he had hoped it would be. When he turned the corner of the path, however, he was reminded of what he really did leave behind.

GRACE ANN HOWARD, AT PEACE. Michael knew that the words carved into the gray speckled stone told the truth. After years of anxiety, worry, fear that his father would return to reclaim his son, his mother was resting peacefully. At least the harrowing vision Imogene showed him brought him that knowledge. He knew that his mother's body, her bones, still lay under the ground here on earth, but her spirit and her soul were definitely in heaven.

Next to her grave was her parents' tombstone. On the bottom, the name CONSTANCE JENNINGS HOWARD was etched into the stone, followed by the dates of her birth and death. On top was carved THOMAS MICHAEL HOWARD, with only the date of his birth under his name. Nothing else. No epitaph, no confirmation that his grandmother was at peace or had been beloved or was remembered. Sadly, Michael thought it was fitting because his grandmother really had no identity other than being connected to her husband.

It seemed so long ago that he saw his grandparents, heard his grandfather's grumpy voice, sat within his grandmother's silence. He didn't always miss them; their company wasn't always comforting. But they did share their home with him and his mother, that was something, wasn't it? Maybe they acted aloof and distant because they always knew Michael wanted to get as far away from them as possible. Like Ronan, maybe they were just protecting themselves.

So tell me, do you guys miss me too? Come on, Constance, Thomas, fess up. Michael laughed. It was weird thinking of his grandparents as real people with real names. It was weirder still watching his grandfather walk toward him, head down, carrying a bouquet of daisies.

Before he was seen, Michael ran behind a marble sepulcher that stood opposite the graves and was almost as large as the toolshed his grandfather had back home. On the roof was a stone carving of a gargoyle, ghastly-looking, its half-opened eyes watching for intruders, its mouth barely concealing thick, square teeth, and the arches of its wings rising high over its head, giving the creature a powerfully compact look. Even though he knew his mother and grandmother weren't really housed in the graves across the path, he couldn't help thinking what a terrible neighbor this was for them to be saddled with. Surprisingly, his grandfather felt the same way.

"I told you to stop staring at my girls, you goddamned eyesore."

You tell 'em Grandpa. The voice was as harsh and grouchy as always, but knowing that he wasn't on the receiving end of his grandfather's tirade made Michael think the tone sounded more comical than mean.

He waited a minute and then quietly walked around the edge of the mausoleum until he saw his grandfather kneeling between the two graves. As he hunched over and the thin material of his jacket stretched across his back, Michael could see the man's bones protruding, pressing against the cloth, and when he reached forward to brush away some rocks and twigs that had fallen on the graves, Michael saw that the bone in his wrist was more pronounced than ever before. Even from behind, he could tell that his grandfather had lost weight.

The old man placed the flowers gently between the head-stones, the white and yellow daisies a burst of color amid the gray rocks, and then sat back, his thin body resting on his haunches. He was still for a moment, his hands clasped in his lap as if he didn't know what else to do. Or perhaps this is what he always did. Michael couldn't tell. But then he made the sign of the cross and when he bowed his head, Michael did the same. He didn't pray along with his grandfather, he simply wanted to give him some privacy.

Finished with his prayer, his grandfather looked at one headstone and then the other. "Hello, girls, did you miss me?"

Never had Michael heard his grandfather speak so softly, so reverentially. There was sadness in his voice, and Michael had to fight the urge to come out of hiding and throw his arms around him to ease his pain.

"Well, I'll tell ya girls something, I miss you," he said. "I miss you more than I can bear." A rabbit scrambled through the thrush in the distance, and Michael's grandfather abruptly turned in the direction of the noise. Flattening him-self against the sepulcher to avoid being seen, Michael was amazed at how delightful the smooth marble felt. Should a house of death really feel so wonderful? Should it really be this inviting? Maybe it was built this way to augment the feelings of misery that consumed the air around it. If so, it was fortunate that it was so close to his family's gravesites because, as Michael's grandfather continued to talk, it was obvious he was teeming with hopelessness.

"I just don't know how much longer I can go on without ya both," his grandfather said, his voice even thinner than before. "I got nothing, I got no more reason to live now that I don't got you two."

You have me, Grandpa, Michael thought. *I've come home.* It didn't matter that the first time around wasn't sensational. It didn't matter that it was much less than that. At the moment Michael wasn't remembering how the past really was; all he was thinking about was that he wanted his family back, whatever tattered fragments of it were left. Michael took a step forward, still careful not to make any noise, which unfortunately meant he was able to hear what his grandfather said next when the gruffness returned to his voice. "The only good thing that's come from all of this is it got me rid of that grandson of mine."

No, that can't be what he said. Michael leaned in a bit closer. He must have misheard his grandfather, that had to be it. He's changed, he's different, he's bringing flowers to a cemetery, for God's sake. The grandfather Michael grew up with would never do something so thoughtful. And this man here would never say something so cruel. Unfortunately, the two men were one and the same.

Pointing to his daughter's headstone, Michael's grandfather rattled on, his voice now as strong and loud as ever. "Sorry, Gracie, but that sissy punk of yours was never any good and you know it." Michael heard the hateful words and even though his mind refused to believe them, his body reacted as if it had just been assaulted. He leaned back against the wall to steady himself, no longer experiencing delight at how it felt. He wished he could be like Phaedra, dematerialize and vanish within the marble so he could block out his grandfather's voice, his vile words. But he only had himself to blame; he had wanted to come home, so he had to hear what home had to say. "If I had to lose the two of you to get that useless grandson out of my life for good, then so be it!"

I knew my grandfather didn't love me like my mother did, but I didn't think he hated me. Then, unexpectedly, Michael found himself starting to laugh. He clasped his hand to his mouth so he wouldn't be heard. How absurd this all was! First he had to watch his father kill his mother because he wanted him back in his life, and now he had to listen to his grandfather express absolutely no remorse for the deaths of his mother and grandmother simply because it meant Michael was out of his life forever. He wasn't a son, he wasn't a grandson. He was a pawn, a plaything, something that could be thrown out with the trash when it was no longer wanted.

When he heard his grandfather curse, he was pulled away from his thoughts. When he saw that he had fallen and was struggling to get up, he stopped laughing. The old man pressed his bony hand into the ground, and Michael watched as it shook, watched the tremor grow and slowly consume his whole arm. Leaning on the headstone for support, his grandfather pushed himself up only to lurch forward, his foot stomping hard on the daisies.

"Goddammit!" the old man hollered. His shout became a watery cough, and still using the headstone as a crutch, he spit onto someone else's grave.

Michael felt his chest tighten, watching his grandfather falter, because he knew there was nothing he could do to help. Finally the old man was able to stand, but it took a few more moments for his body to become completely upright. Once he caught his breath, he grumbled, "You see girls, I still need ya." Then mumbling mostly to himself he added, "It's no good on my own."

Watching his grandfather hobble down the path toward his beloved Bronco, Michael realized with regret that he pitied the man, and you shouldn't pity your grandfather, you should respect him, aspire to be like him. But he was broken, physically and emotionally, because that's what he chose. He chose to fill himself up with hate, he chose to ignore his wife and daughter until it was too late, and he chose to disown his grandson.

"You're just like my father," Michael whispered. "Pathetic."

Long after the Bronco was out of sight, Michael kept staring in the direction where he last saw his grandfather, feeling strange because he didn't feel angry. But how could he be angry with a man who had nothing? It would just be a waste of time, no matter what Michael said or did, the man wasn't going to change. "Good-bye, Grandpa," Michael said out loud. "Guess there really isn't anything left here for me after all."

"Then why don't you come back home."

Spinning around, Michael saw Ronan standing before him, the sun glowing behind him, creating a haze around his face, and Michael thought it might be just another vision, a mirage. But no, Ronan was really there, his presence not the result of magic but friendship.

"Ciaran told me you were going home," Ronan explained. "And I knew what that meant."

Michael took a step closer so he could see Ronan more clearly, without the sun gleaming in his eyes. "Looks like I owe Ciaran a thank-you," he said. "And you an apology."

Sheepishly, Ronan looked away. "No, I'm the one who should apologize."

Michael touched Ronan's chin and turned his face until their eyes met once again. "My hometown, so that means I get to go first."

Ronan nodded his agreement and followed Michael's lead as he slid down the side of the mausoleum to sit on the ground. "I'm sorry I took off like that and, you know, for the things I said," Michael began. "There's nothing left for me here. I was a jerk to think there would be."

"You're hardly a jerk, Michael," Ronan said.

"What would you call me, then? Stupid? A fool?" Michael asked.

"I'd call you bloody amazing," Ronan said proudly.

Incredulous, Michael turned his attention to a worm he spotted burrowing into the dirt. "Is that some sort of vampire joke?"

Laughing, Ronan grabbed Michael's hand and was thrilled that he didn't pull away. "I heard the things your grandfather said. I heard the hate in his voice," Ronan admitted. "If you were some dumb git, you would've lashed out, gotten into a huge row with him. You were the victim, but you didn't act like one, you acted like the adult."

Rubbing Ronan's forearms, Michael shrugged his shoulders. "Guess I didn't have any energy left after beating up my father."

Even though Michael's fingers felt so good tracing the veins in Ronan's arms, he still felt uncomfortable. "I'm sorry I didn't tell you about that."

Michael didn't think his blue eyes ever looked more sincere. "I know why you did; I get it. You wanted to protect me."

"Funny thing is, you don't need my protection," Ronan whispered. "Which doesn't mean I won't always have your back."

Facing his boyfriend, Michael wrapped his hand around Ronan's neck, ran his fingers through his hair. "Tell you what, you can be Harold and I'll be Kumar."

"What?"

"The buddy movie," Michael explained. "The one me and Saoirse were watching."

"Oh, that one," Ronan said, rolling his eyes. "You were laughing so hard you couldn't even hear what they were saying."

Shaking his head, Michael realized there was a lot Ronan

still needed to learn. "That, Mr. Fuddy Duddy, is how you watch Harold and Kumar. Maybe if you're lucky, one night me and the kid'll teach you."

Even in a cemetery, among shadowy relics of the past, Ronan was struck by how Michael's lighthearted nature shone through. *I want to be more like that,* he thought. But a shift in personality would have to wait. Right now, Ronan had to make amends. Brushing Michael's cheek softly with his thumb, Ronan said, "I may take you and the kid up on that, but first I need to show you something."

Smiling devilishly, Michael leaned in close. "Come on, Rone, I've already seen you naked."

Delightfully shocked, Ronan didn't have a good comeback, so he just grabbed Michael's hand and seconds later, they were standing in the middle of a different past. Graves and tombstones were replaced with books and portraits; they were in the anteroom of St. Joshua's Library. "What are we doing here?" Michael asked.

Ronan started to speak and then realized the anteroom and the library proper were filled with students studying, reading, lounging, eavesdropping. Any one of them could overhear what Ronan might say, and these days, during these uncertain times, he knew it was better to err on the side of caution. He sat on the velvet couch and telepathically instructed Michael to sit next to him. But Michael's mind was so confused, he didn't hear him.

Forced to use more pedestrian means of communication, Ronan patted the cushion next to him and Michael finally got the hint. Sitting next to Ronan, Michael felt a bit dizzy having traveled so fast from Weeping Water and he had to blink several times so the brown and gold paisley pattern of the sofa would stop swirling, stop threatening to come alive and suffocate him. If he knew what was coming up next, he probably would've gotten up from the couch and fled the room.

"I need you to listen." This time when Ronan spoke to Michael telepathically, he was heard. *"I want you to look at the portrait."*

Michael looked up over the fireplace to the portrait of Brother Dahey, the monk who was one of the founders of Archangel Academy. "Why?" Michael responded quietly. "We look at it practically every day."

"Telepathically!"

"Sorry," Michael said. *"I mean, sorry."*

"I need you to look at it differently," Ronan replied. *"I need you to look at it with a vampire's eyes."*

Glancing around the room to make sure that no one was close enough to see his face, Michael allowed his eyes to narrow, to become truly vampiric so he could receive the full benefit of his preternatural vision. Adjusting himself on the couch so he was looking directly at the painting, Michael looked at the monk and tried to see beyond the brushstrokes, past the drab colors and patina, but all he saw was a fifteenth-century face with a really bad haircut, staring back at him. *"All I see is the same old picture,"* Michael said, his frustration resonating loudly even though his words were silent.

Staring at the portrait, Ronan said, *"Look into the eyes, look at the mouth."*

This time when Michael stared at the monk's face, he remembered waking up right here on this couch a while ago and sensing that the monk was staring at him. It had been only for a fleeting moment, but he knew there was something strange about the way the eyes in the painting were glowering, how they were fixated upon him, and now he knew why. The face didn't belong to a monk, it didn't belong to a student of religion or a defender of Christ. It did, however, have everything to do with eternal life.

"He's a vampire!" Michael said out loud.

Ronan's eyes bulged out and he put a finger up to his lips to remind Michael that they needed to be quiet. *"Keep looking."*

Straining to push himself further into the portrait, to the truth that lay behind the canvas, Michael started to get lightheaded. He was still a novice at these vampire skills, but he could tell by Ronan's attitude that it was imperative that he keep trying. With his eyes acting like laser beams, he saw that the monk's teeth were actually fangs, his eyes pools of blackness, the rest of his features malformed and distorted. This was definitely the portrait of a vampire. But then the colors of the painting started to shift, brighten, the fangs receded, the eyes turned more human, and another image appeared on the canvas. At one time, Brother Dahey may have been a monk, but today he was a headmaster. "Oh my God! David Zachary is Brother Dahey?"

Whipping his head around, Ronan didn't think anyone heard Michael, but he couldn't be sure. He understood this news was shocking, but he needed Michael to understand how important it was to keep this information a secret. *"Not out loud,"* Ronan shushed.

"I'm sorry," Michael replied, then continued on in silence. *"This is crazy! How is it possible?"*

Shrugging his shoulders, Ronan told Michael the truth, which was that he didn't really know. *"I know I've been a vampire a little longer than you, but there's a lot about them that I don't know,"* Ronan explained. *"And I know even less about Them, you know, the ones with the capital T."*

As wild as it sounded, it all made sense. David and Brother Dahey both had red hair, a commanding stare, and a link to Double A. It also explained why David so effortlessly and immediately gained the respect and admiration of the entire student body. Hawksbry was beloved, sure, but he had been there for years, he'd earned the trust of the students one term after the other. Zachary used his vampire skills to cast a spell and hypnotize them into thinking he was some sort of academic god, which, Michael surmised, in a way he was. *"But what's he doing here?"* Michael asked. *"A powerful vampire like that has got to have better things to do than spend his days cooped up in a boarding school."*

"Well, I have a feeling it might have something to do with the fact that David is also Brania's father."

Seriously?! Michael did some quick genealogy in his head. *Brania is David's daughter, David once lived with Edwige, Edwige is Ronan's mother, which could only mean one thing:* "David is, like, your stepfather!"

"Michael!" Ronan shouted, then corrected himself and told Michael telepathically that he had to stop talking out loud.

"I'm sorry, you know I'm not used to this mental thing," Michael responded silently. *"And FYI this news is really blowing my mind!"*

Ronan couldn't argue with that. Learning he had a familial connection to David was indeed mind-blowing. Nevertheless, it needed to remain secret. *"You're right. But David was never officially my stepfather,"* Ronan said. *"We didn't live with him and Brania for very long and he never married my mother. In fact, the day she got her inheritance, we left. I never saw David again until he walked into St. Sebastian's announcing that he was our new headmaster."*

Michael sank back into the cushion and shook his head. The more truth he uncovered, the more confused he got. *"So you really think he's taken this position just to be close to Brania?"* Michael asked. *"She, um, isn't all that pleasant to be around, you know."*

Phaedra is right; Michael really does find humor in most every situation. *"I don't know why he's here,"* Ronan replied. *"But I know he never does anything without a self-serving reason."*

Suddenly, Michael got very excited and started waving his hands and pointing first to the portrait and then to his chest. If anyone was watching them, they would have thought they were playing a game of charades. *"I think I know why he's come back,"* Michael said. *"He wants to separate us."* Ronan's forehead wrinkled. He wasn't following Michael's logic. *"It's like my dream, Ronan, and when we were at The Well and separated by darkness. The face I saw in The Well must have been David's."*

As tidy an explanation as that might be, Ronan knew it wasn't plausible. Only water vamps could connect with The Well physically or spiritually. It was impossible for David or any of his kind to infiltrate such a holy place. The Well and the cave where it existed were impenetrable to outsiders. *"I don't think that's possible, Michael,"* Ronan said. *"But it doesn't matter anyway, because we'll never be separated. Remember, you're forever mine."*

Even though he continued to speak telepathically, Michael still leaned in close to Ronan, just because he felt like it. *"And please remember that I'm also forever beautiful."*

Laughing out loud, Ronan no longer cared who heard them. "I want to do something for you, for both of us really," he said. "I want to bring you to your real home tonight."

That works for me. "I wasn't planning on going anywhere other than our room."

"No, love," Ronan said. "I don't want to sound like some bloke in those cheesy movies you and Phaedra cry over . . ."

"We do not cry!" Michael protested.

"Right! And I understand the bloomin' appeal of Henry and Kumar," Ronan cried.

"Harold," Michael corrected.

"Whatever," Ronan said. "Home isn't just a place, it's

where your family is. And like it or not, my family is now yours."

Thinking about all the members of Ronan's family, Michael realized there were more good than bad. "I would really like that."

"Smashing!" Ronan exclaimed. "I think it's about time that Edwige acted like the mum she is and had us all over for dinner." Michael tried not to crack up but couldn't stop himself. "I know, I know, Mum's hardly a domestic, but that's okay 'cause most of us don't eat anyway."

Michael kept on smiling because he no longer wanted to cry. "Thank you."

After they left, Lochlan MacCleery was still in shock. Sitting in the high-backed chair behind the couch, he had heard every spoken word Michael and Ronan shared. David Zachary a fifteenth-century monk? And a vampire? It was insane, illogical, and yet the doctor believed it completely. Alistair's note finally made sense. Evil *had* come to Archangel Academy, but it didn't come as some abstract concept; it came in the form of a new headmaster.

If there was any doubt left in Lochlan's mind, he got all the confirmation he needed when he looked up at the portrait of David Zachary disguised as Brother Dahey. The eyes had turned completely black and at both sides of the mouth hung two very sharp fangs.

chapter 19

Edwige did not like playing hostess; she did not like entertaining people in her flat, even if those people consisted mainly of her children. That's why when Ronan asked her, as the Glynn-Rowley matriarch, to throw a dinner party, a family gathering, she immediately said no.

But then Ronan pleaded, confessing that he wanted the party to unofficially welcome Michael into the family since he had effectively become an orphan, and Edwige felt guilty. Ordinarily she ignored feelings of guilt, but Michael was Ronan's chosen life partner, and the recent revelation of his father's duplicity and evil nature were the result of her own orchestrations, which is why she relented. Giving into guilt and her son didn't change the fact that she didn't like company, however, so when she heard Ronan and the others stampede into her home from behind her locked bedroom door, she made them wait.

Hearing her silent order, Roan told the others—Michael, Ciaran, Saoirse, and her dorm mate and new best friend, Phaedra—that Edwige was running late and they should wait for her in the living room. He ad-libbed, saying she wanted them to make themselves comfortable, not realizing how difficult a task that would be. Edwige's living room, while eliciting admiration from visitors for its tasteful decoration, didn't provide comfort.

When Ciaran sat in the brown leather side chair, he was surprised to find the seat's soft cushion didn't extend to the back of the chair, it was like leaning against plywood. And when he propped his feet up on the small hassock, he realized that the embroidered surface—depicting a scene of a Christopher Columbus Era sailing vessel coming face-to-face with a heretofore unexplored tropical paradise—merely covered a similar hard surface, its purpose ornamental, not utilitarian.

Ronan and Michael were tucked on opposite sides of the cornflower blue velvet settee, sitting hunched forward, their elbows resting on their knees so Saoirse could squeeze in between them while Phaedra sat at the mirrored desk in the clear acrylic Ghost chair, gorgeous to look at, its seamless construction a marvel, but every time she shifted her weight, the back of her thighs stuck to the seat of the chair, making a sucking noise as if someone were peeling an adhesive bandage off of a wound. It made the girl, already nervous being in Edwige's flat for the first time, even more anxious.

Not that she was the only one who felt uncomfortable. Ronan might not be the host, but he was the ringleader, the reason they were all gathered here, and he was completely aware that it felt more like a group detention than a party. *Maybe I jumped the gun,* he thought, *maybe I pushed too hard? Too late now, you prat, this whole mess is your fault. Wait, maybe if I look like I'm enjoying myself and at ease, it'll catch on?* Smiling at Michael, Ronan was glad to see that his look of happiness was contagious. Too bad Michael was only being polite.

Smile. Don't let Ronan see that you're freaking out inside. Michael liked Edwige, but after their unexpected meeting on campus a while ago that left him feeling as if she would become a more hands-on mother-in-law, he hadn't seen her again. He knew she accepted that her son had a boyfriend; he was just no longer convinced that she believed he was the ideal choice for that role. He hoped this get-together would dispel his fears, but the evening was not getting off to a rousing start.

Meanwhile, Ciaran was shocked that he even got an invitation. "Are you sure she said she wants me to come?" he had asked Ronan when told of the impromptu event.

"Of course," Ronan assured him. "It's a family party and you're family."

In name only, Ciaran thought. But if Edwige was making an effort, why not attend? It wasn't like he'd be walking into the lioness's den alone. He would have backup, right? Glancing at the tense, wary faces around the room, Ciaran had the urge to flee for the more comforting silence of the lab.

Thankfully, Saoirse was able to put an end to the awkward silence. Biting into a piece of a raw baby carrot, she crunched so loudly, everyone thought she'd broken a tooth. "Careful," Ronan chided. "The tooth fairy doesn't visit teenagers."

Dipping the rest of the carrot into the small silver tureen filled with what looked like ranch dressing, Saoirse snipped, "Like you wouldn't fancy the chance to put on a tutu and slip a few pounds underneath my pillow." Her comeback was just what the so-called party needed—a reason to laugh.

Ronan, however, was too shocked to join in. "A *few* pounds for one bloody tooth?"

Spitting the carrot into her hand when she tasted the unexpected flavor of curry, Saoirse replied, "Notice how my brother doesn't balk at the idea of wearing a tutu." She grabbed a napkin, wrapping the half-eaten curried carrot in it. "P.S. Food-eating people, the dip is gross."

"Not as gross as Ronan in a tutu," Ciaran joked.

Laughing along with the rest of them, Michael felt the need to defend his boyfriend. "I think Ronan's got the perfect legs for a tutu."

Saoirse opened her mouth to respond, but before she could utter a sound, Ronan warned her, "Another peep out of you and I'll make you scarf down that whole bowl."

Unable to allow her brother to have the last word, Saoirse squealed, "Ooh, I'm scared!" Running behind Ciaran's chair, she continued her mock cry for help. "Save me, somebody, the big bad vampire's gonna force-feed me an appetizer!"

This time when the rest of the group cracked up, Ronan joined them, laughing heartily, thrilled to be the brunt of a joke. His laughter grew louder along with that of the others, the cheerful noise drowning out the sound of the string quartet that filled the air, and stopped only when Edwige entered the room from the hallway. "Blimey, Mum!" Saoirse shrieked. "What've you gone and done to yourself?"

Smiling stiffly, Edwige sauntered into the center of the room. She knew her daughter wasn't commenting on her ensemble; the look she spent the last hour crafting was stunning. She wore impeccably tailored cream-colored leather pants, cropped at the ankle to show off, to maximum effect, her matching colored patent leather pumps with four-inch heels, and topped off with a long-sleeved, hand-knit, fuschia sweater made of Scottish mohair. The sweater came high across her neck, but in the back swooped low to reveal taut muscles and to create several layers of draped material that bounced every time she moved. It was magazine-perfect. No, her daughter was commenting on her hair.

"Saoirse's right, Mum," Ronan said. "Why'd you go and switch colors again?"

Posing beneath the oversize painting of the two male swimmers she so adored, Edwige tried to think of Ronan as one of the idealized figures in the artwork and not as the son who was questioning her appearance. "I woke up this morning and realized I was bored with being a blonde," she said. "So I rang up Marcel, and he restored my natural beauty."

"I think it looks beautiful, Ms. Glynn-Rowley," Phaedra said. "It's almost like you're standing underneath the moon in the painting, it's so shiny."

Edwige had no idea how to respond to a style comment from a girl who, to her eye, never used a hair-care product in her life, so she simply smiled and then, of course, instructed her to call her Edwige. Unlike Phaedra, Saoirse wasn't as kind. "Come off it, Mum, you dyed your hair black again because you couldn't stand the competition," she said, twirling around so her own long blond hair swung like a yellow pinwheel.

This is only good-natured teasing, harmless, normal, Edwige thought. *Then why do I wish they would all shut up and disappear?*

Noticing Edwige's discomfort, Michael interjected, "Are you looking at the same woman? Your mother doesn't need to worry about competition from anyone."

That's lovely. The outsiders compliment me, my own flesh and blood don't even have the decency. Clearly, Ronan has chosen well this time. "Thank you, Michael," she said. "You are indeed a welcome addition to the family."

Beaming, Ronan led a round of applause that only turned into another chorus of laughter when Saoirse, plopping onto Ciaran's lap, asked her mother why she couldn't pay as much attention to food preparation as she did to her wardrobe. "I still can't get this disgusting taste of curry out of my mouth!"

Shaking his head, Ronan couldn't believe how effortlessly sassy his sister could be. Whatever she thought just rolled off her tongue. It was a trait he mostly admired but, in the presence of his mother, made him nervous. The combination of his sister's sass and his mother's quick temper could be volatile. So far, Edwige seemed to be in a pleasant mood.

"Sorry, dear," she said. "I attempted to make some homemade dishes, but after that one failure, I decided it was best to cater."

"If you knew the dip was goppin'," Saoirse said, "why'd you leave it out for us to eat?"

A smile formed on Edwige's lips that made Ronan reconsider her pleasant mood was just a façade. "Darling, you know how I hate to waste food."

After dinner, it was clear there was no risk of that. The dishes of those who had eaten were wiped clean. "That was delicious," Phaedra remarked.

"Yeah, you sure picked a great caterer," Ciaran added.

Lifting up his glass, Michael toasted the hostess. "And this is the best water I've ever tasted."

And you, Michael Howard, are the best boyfriend ever. Ronan telepathically welcomed Michael to his nonconventional family and thanked him for his compliments to Edwige. They seemed to be keeping her calm, which in turn helped Ronan relax. After he'd convinced his mother to throw a family gathering, he wondered if it was a smart thing to do. Maybe a family should be left alone to coast and exist within its framework, each playing the part they've come to portray so well instead of being forced to acknowledge that the framework could use some reinforcement and that their roles needed to be reexamined. Maybe Ronan's own personal desire for growth had made him think the rest of his family wanted the same. Well, things did seem to be going smoother than expected, but they still had to get through dessert.

"Be honest, Michael," Saoirse said, stabbing the middle of a cream puff with her finger. "You can't tell me you don't miss eating dessert."

Watching Saoirse devour the filling, Michael replied, "I never really had a sweet tooth."

Ciaran stuffed the rest of his second cream puff into his mouth and swallowed hard before adding, "C'mon, mate, there's got to be something you still crave."

He thought a moment and then replied, "French fries."

"Really?" Ronan asked. "You fancied chips that much?"

"Yeah," Michael replied. "That's the only food that I really miss eating."

Her eyes bulging, Phaedra understood. "I love French fries! Just the other day at St. Martha's, Fritz made me a plate smothered in cheese and brown gravy. I told him I could eat them every day."

Edwige rose from the table. "Not a wise idea, darling, if, of course, you want to maintain your figure," she stated. "Excuse me."

After she left the room, Saoirse told Phaedra not to mind her mother and whispered, "She's just jealous 'cause she's old and doesn't have our metabolism."

A minute or so later when Edwige hadn't returned from the kitchen, Ronan thought he should check on her. Before he entered the room, Edwige peered out into the hallway and said, "Go on back to our guests. I'm preparing a little surprise."

A surprise? The idea should have filled Ronan with joy, but instead he was filled with terror. A surprise from Edwige had the potential to be a disaster. When Ronan informed the others what Edwige was up to in the kitchen, his opinion was shared.

"Maybe she's planning on poisoning us all," Ciaran whispered.

Hysterical, Saoirse grabbed her two brothers by the hand and dragged them onto the sofa. "Before she makes us drink the Kool-Aid, let's have some sibling bonding time." Squashed in between Ronan and Ciaran, she called out, "You guys don't mind, do you?"

From across the room Michael shook his head. "Not at all." In fact it was perfect. He had been dying to talk to Phaedra privately all night. Since the evening started, he had been trying to figure out what was different about Phaedra, when she stood under the crystal chandelier that hung near the minibar and was illuminated by the harsh light, he thought he had his answer. "Riddle me this, efemera," Michael whispered. "How'd you manage to get a tan in April in England?"

Glancing in the mirror, Phaedra touched her cheek. It was true, her usually pale complexion had a darker undertone, not quite brown, more reddish. "You've noticed too."

Michael looked at Phaedra's reflection, then at the girl herself examining her skin tone. "You're not as fair, all right, even your arms," Michael said. "Oh my God, do not tell me you found a tanning salon in Eden? I know those things are deadly, but I could use a jump start on my summer tan." Phaedra tried to interject, but Michael kept rambling, "Wait a sec, what am I talking about? A few ultraviolet rays can't hurt me now. I'm no longer human!"

"I think they could hurt me," Phaedra said quietly.

It took Michael a few moments for Phaedra's comment to penetrate his laughter. "What exactly are you trying to say?"

She had to tell someone. She couldn't keep it to herself any longer. "I'm changing," Phaedra replied, looking over her shoulder to make sure no one could overhear. "I think I'm turning human."

Stunned, Michael wanted to say that was impossible, but he knew better. Double A had taught him many things, mainly that anything was possible and he was about to learn something new. "When an efemera falls in love, she has to make a choice," Phaedra explained. "Return that love and become human or deny it and remain as God intended."

Bypassing all the metaphysical implications, Michael cut to the crux of the situation. "So you *are* in love with Fritz."

When Phaedra blushed, the color of her skin grew even darker. She thought of a line from an old Greek play she just read in class, the character with the same name as hers asks, What do people mean when they speak of love? She had no idea. "I must be," she said. "Otherwise this wouldn't be happening."

Michael was excited for his friend. "Well, that should make your decision pretty simple, shouldn't it?"

This is far from simple. "No matter what I feel for Fritz, I don't think I can turn my back on my heritage, on you," Phaedra admitted. "I was put on this earth to protect you; that's all my race understands."

Michael wanted to reach out and hug his friend, comfort her, but he didn't want to draw attention, make the others think they were having as serious a conversation as they were, so he grabbed her hand tightly. "Don't worry about me. I don't need your protection any longer, I'm getting stronger every day," Michael declared. "Plus I have Ronan." Whispering into her ear he added, "He really gets off on being my protector."

Looking into the eyes of the child whose mother had called her gave her purpose to rise from the fog, to carry out the will of her God, Phaedra wasn't sure she could forsake her legacy, no matter how strong her feelings for Fritz were, especially since she sensed Michael's good spirits were a cover-up. "I'm not the only one who looks different, you know," she said. "There's something wrong that you're not telling me."

Michael knew exactly what Phaedra was talking about. This morning he noticed there were dark circles under his eyes, thanks to a series of sleepless nights. Even vampires need a good night's rest before it starts to show. "Well... let's just say this immortality thing doesn't mean all your problems disappear overnight," Michael said, then decided to be candid. "I guess it's been a rough couple of weeks."

"That solves it," Phaedra replied. "You still need me."

How to make her understand? "Look, I can't tell you what to do, Phaedra, but I know what I have to do," Michael started. "Stand on my own two feet." Suddenly, he felt very wise. "Hey! Maybe your destiny is to become mortal, just like mine was to become immortal."

And suddenly Phaedra felt very calm. "I never thought of it that way."

She wouldn't be able to think about it at all because Ronan and Ciaran's spirited debate over the merits of the upcoming Carnival for the Black Sun carried over to their side of the room. "Bollocks! It's hardly a ruse to conceal some wicked plot," Ciaran cried. "It's a school outing."

Could he actually be that mental? "Do you seriously believe that?" Ronan asked. "You know what David's capable of."

"Mate, the guy's not all bad just because he's one of Them."

Jumping off the couch, Ronan turned to the rest of the party gobsmacked, arms widespread, hoping for support. "He's not *one* of Them, he's their bloody leader!"

Ciaran wasn't about to bad-mouth the only adult who'd ever shown an interest in him, in his abilities, and treated him with respect. "Which doesn't automatically make him evil."

"Yes, it does!" Ronan cried. "And I'm telling you right now, he's up to no good with this bloody carnival!"

Standing between her brothers like a very petite referee, Saoirse stuck two fingers in her mouth and whistled. "This is supposed to be festive!"

Right on cue, Edwige entered the living room, her singing drowning out the arguing. By the time she finished the last line of her song—*Happy birthday, dear Saoirse, happy birthday to you!*—they were all dumbfounded, not because of Edwige's poor singing ability, but because of her poor timing.

"My birthday isn't until the end of next month!" Saoirse declared.

"Why wait until then when we're all here now?" Edwige replied, placing the chocolate frosted cupcake in front of her daughter. "Now make a wish and blow out the candle."

Never one to give up a chance to be the center of attention or to make a wish, Saoirse leaned over to extinguish the flame. "Now this is more like it, people," she said. "Roney, take notes. A party should have singing, not shouting." After both Ciaran and Phaedra declined a bite, she shoved half the cupcake into her mouth, but before she was finished chewing, she just had to share with everyone what she considered to be a brilliant idea. "Let's make this a real family celebration!" she exclaimed. "Somebody get the daddy-in-the-box!"

Now who needs a class in party etiquette?! It took Ronan about a minute and a half of telepathic begging to convince Edwige not to slap Saoirse's face and that she wasn't trying to be disrespectful. She didn't witness Saxon's death, she didn't live through the horror. All she believed was that her father was cremated and his ashes were kept in a beautiful mahogany box on a side table. "I think Dad prefers his place by the window," Ronan said nervously. "He was never one for big social gatherings anyway. Isn't that right, Mum?"

Looking at her eldest son, then her middle child, then her youngest, Edwige slumped into the chair next to the box that contained her husband's ashes and nodded her head.

* * *

"Will you look at the way she's sitting there?"

Brania was complaining about Nurse Radcliff. Standing next to her father in the anteroom to his office, she was looking in the mirror, watching the nurse sitting at her desk as Lochlan tottered in and out of the room. "She's an absolute pig!" Brania cried out. "Slumped over, hair a mess, and I have no idea how she's done it, but she's actually *gained* weight since you had a lapse in judgment and brought her into the fold."

Crossing his arms, David's black eyes narrowed. "I think she looks lovely, like the women immortalized by Raphael in his oil paintings."

"Which is the sophisticate's way of saying she's fat," Brania corrected. Unable to gaze into the mirror any longer, she turned away and started to pace around the room. She noticed a few marks on the walls where the green paint had chipped away, a few places where the plaster peeked through the dark brown crown molding. Her father was getting careless, his typically fastidious nature pushed to the side while he continued on with his plot to restore Double A to its former glory. Brania wasn't sure if she was impressed or disappointed. When she looked back at the mirror, she was merely disgusted. "She is slovenly, Father! A fat slovenly hog!"

Nurse Radcliff, still a newly converted vampire incapable of controlling her cravings, was holding her finger over her head and squeezing it so her own blood dripped onto her tongue, thanks to the paper cut she had given herself moments earlier.

"It's quite resourceful really," David said. "It will keep her satiated until she can properly feed."

She knew her father was trying to be stubborn, but his attitude still infuriated her. *Why is he constantly taking someone else's side? Why is he defending this heifer instead of agreeing with me, his own daughter? Why can't he just leave here so things can return to normal?!* When Brania realized how she had let her mind wander in her father's presence, unguarded and without caution, she was surprised that he didn't react to her silent tirade. Was he not listening? Did he no longer care? *Could he actually find this abominable excuse for a woman more interesting than me?* she thought. "I cannot believe you slept with that hausfrau," Brania spat.

Chuckling at his daughter's envy, David thought one unwarranted comment deserved another. "She's an educated woman, dear," he said. "Maybe if you had spent more time in school as a child, you would know the difference."

Staring at her father's profile, Brania thought she could lash out and rip the flesh off his cheeks, slash her nails against his throat and expose the muscle and veins underneath. Not caring if he heard or ignored her, she let her mind react with all the fury she felt in her heart. *How dare you?! How could I go to school when I was constantly doing your dirty work?! When I was acting like your henchman instead of your little girl!*

"No!!"

Too bad if you can't accept the truth!

But David wasn't responding to Brania's accusations, he hadn't even been listening, he was calling out to his fledgling creation. "No, Margaret, I have bigger plans for the good doctor; he's to be the centerpiece of the carnival."

Confused, Brania looked into the mirror and saw Nurse Radcliff, her back to Dr. MacCleery, her fangs beared, her fingers in her mouth, and a look of ecstasy consuming her face. What Brania didn't witness was the nurse giving herself another paper cut, this one much more severe, so when the blood oozed out of her finger, it overwhelmed her. She couldn't stop her fangs from descending, she couldn't stop herself from sucking the red liquid from her own finger even as the doctor watched. When she saw his horrified face, she knew it was too late. She knew he had uncovered her secret, and like any creature who wants to remain hidden in the shadows, she prepared to attack. Until David's command prevented her from taking action.

"Leave the room, Margaret," David ordered. "Leave now and come here so we can feed together."

Together!? Now he's going to feed side by side with this, this . . . *thing*! Brania couldn't remember the last time she fed alongside her father, and as a result, she couldn't remember why she was wasting her time standing next to him now.

When Nurse Radcliff left the doctor's office, and the mirror returned to its natural state, David wasn't surprised to see only his reflection staring back at him, Brania no longer by his side. "Oh, Zachariel," he said. "Why must our children always disappoint us?"

Someone not disappointed this evening was Lochlan. One eye pressed against the microscope, he didn't know exactly what he was looking at, but he hadn't expected to either. When he took the piece of paper Nurse Radcliff had left behind, the one on which she deliberately cut herself, and placed it underneath the microscope's lens, he instinctively knew the bloodstain wouldn't be human. "Could it be?" he mumbled, the very thought that was infecting his mind making his hand tremble, making the paper shake. "Could this be vampire's blood?"

The second the words were spoken, the doctor felt very cold. If what he had just stumbled upon was true, if what he overheard Michael and Ronan talking about was fact and not just the product of uncensored teenage imagination, he was in danger. He ran toward the door and slowly opened it, just a crack, to see if anyone was lurking in the darkness. No one, at least no one he could see. Slamming the door shut, he locked it and then closed and locked both windows, his panic not allowing him to peek through the blinds to check one more time for inhuman loiters. *This is insane!* Standing in the middle of his office, he marveled, "Could my mind be playing tricks on me? Did I really see fangs? Could all the legends be true?"

No! No, Lochlan, you're a doctor, you don't believe in supernatural nonsense! Ripping his glasses off his face and wiping them furiously with his shirttail, he repeated. *You don't believe in myth, you don't believe in fantasy.* And yet somehow, *somehow* he knew this was the truth. Vampires existed and they were living right here beside him, among the sculpted archangels, stalking the innocent students. But not all the students were innocent. Some of them understood, some of them knew exactly what type of evil had taken up residence at their school. It was time they understood their secret was out.

Ronan was perplexed when he looked at his cell phone. Why was Dr. MacCleery texting him? The message was straightforward—*I need to see you in my office*—but before he could respond, Saoirse yanked the phone out of his hand, turned it off, and shoved it in the back pocket of her jeans. "No texting at my birthday bash," she informed.

"Fine," Ronan said. "Just give me back my phone."

Waving her pinky in his face, she said, "Do you vampire-swear that you won't text or take a call?"

"Or make any more daft comments about our headmaster," Ciaran added.

"That man is evil and you know it!" Ronan shot back.

Edwige knew her eldest son was right, but she didn't have the strength or desire to support him. Just as David didn't have the strength or desire to chase after Brania. History, being repetitive by nature, had taught them both that children, after a certain age, could no longer be controlled, so it was a waste of their time to try. While her children and their friends continued to shout and dispute the real purpose behind David's brainchild, Edwige finally came to a decision. Her real purpose was not to be a mother, a guardian, a woman alone leading a brood. She didn't know what her destiny was, but she knew it had nothing to do with her children, and so it was time to set them free. Starting with the most recent addition to her family.

The voices continuing to rise and fall around her, Edwige telepathically informed Imogene that she was being released from her power. She was now free to go wherever she wanted, do whatever she longed to do. But like an infant who cries for her favorite toy only to realize when she's holding it that it wasn't the reason she was crying in the first place, Imogene didn't know what to do with her free will. Now that she had her freedom, she didn't know where to go, so for the time being, until she could think of something else to do, some more exciting place to visit, she would simply sit in her coffin and sing.

Edwige got up and, unnoticed, retreated into her bedroom. Let them get used to being without her, she thought. It was only a matter of time before they would all find themselves completely on their own anyway.

chapter 20

One drop, two drops, three drops, four. Archangel Cathedral was quiet. Even though it was Sunday morning, everyone, including the priests in residence, were preparing for the day's carnival instead of attending mass. It wasn't typical, but it's what David wanted.

Initially, there had been reluctance, concern that such a celebration would disrupt tradition. Early morning Sunday mass was a Double A custom, not embraced by every student, but deemed a part of school culture. Those who took the tradition—and religious service itself—more seriously were especially worried. They thought the observance of the so-called Black Sun could be viewed as inappropriate, pagan. However, when the most senior priest and Sister Mary Elizabeth met with the headmaster, they realized their concerns were unjustified. Apologizing for questioning his judgment, they left David's office wondering how they ever could have misinterpreted the integrity of an innocent school activity.

Since that meeting, the religious faculty worked alongside the teachers and students to transform St. Sebastian's and the campus near The Forest into a mini fair complete with makeshift booths housing a gypsy fortuneteller, wheels of chance, and even a dunking chamber in which the professors would take turns sitting on a rickety board while eager students threw sandbags at an attached target in the hopes of dunking their favorite or not-so-favorite teacher into a pool of ice-cold water. Interspersed among the amusements were food stands serving cotton candy, popcorn, and Fritz's contribution, apples dipped in dark chocolate to resemble the eclipsed sun. And built right on the edge of The Forest was an attraction that made David chuckle: a mazelike structure with walls adorned with fun-house mirrors that distorted everyone's reflections, humans and vampires alike.

When the building process was complete, the adults couldn't agree as to what was more shocking: the professionalism of the construction or the willingness of the students to participate. Not one student balked at having to help out, not one feigned an illness to get out of doing their share of hard labor. For the first time in years, the student body was in complete support of a headmaster's wishes and worked as a unified team to see those wishes fulfilled. It was a wonderful surprise and yet, to some, disturbing. It just wasn't right, just like it wasn't right not to hold mass on Sunday morning.

As a compromise, David suggested that a twilight service be held at midnight on Saturday so religious obligations could be met and everyone could have Sunday free to worship the Black Sun. When he first proposed the change to Sister Mary Elizabeth, she readily agreed, but as time went on, she realized it didn't make sense. Why couldn't they have both, church in the morning and the carnival in the afternoon? Why did she always give in so easily to David in his presence and then experience doubts later on when she was alone? Why didn't she voice her opinions to him? She wasn't confrontational, but she was hardly submissive, particularly when it came to her beliefs. If she knew what David had planned, what he had already set in motion, she would have done more than question herself. She would have begged God to intervene.

Water is mixed with blood once more. No one was in the church, so no one heard the sound. Plop, plop, plop. The holy water rippled within the insides of the font each time its smooth surface was broken, each time something fell from above to splice into the consecrated liquid. If anyone was in the church, all they had to do was look up to see what was creating the sound. The cross that was usually bare now held a body.

Mimicking the crucifixions from the Bible, the man was nailed to the cross, one piercing in each outstretched palm, one through both feet, which were placed one on top of the other. Unlike typical religious iconography, there were two more piercings in the body, these two created not with the aid of nails but with fangs. Two holes, more like gashes, were visible on the left side of Lochlan's neck, both large enough so that whatever blood was left in the doctor's body could spill out and contaminate the blessed water below. Sister Mary Elizabeth was right. Canceling mass had nothing to do with keeping the students' schedule free. David merely wanted to put the church to better use.

And Ronan merely wanted to know what the hell happened to Dr. MacCleery. Standing in the middle of his office was like standing in the aftermath of an explosion. The desks were overturned, cabinets were leaning on their sides, their contents spilled out and strewn throughout the room. There were huge dents in the walls created by fists or thrown bodies, and splattered all over the floor in a random pattern was blood. It was not what Ronan expected to find when he raced over to the doctor's office after seeing that he had sent him several texts last night and early this morning. He thought he would find the doctor waiting for him, eager to explain what his puzzling messages meant. He didn't think he would find more mystery.

Instinctively he kept the truth about his rendezvous from Michael. Even after his promise to be honest, he still felt the need to protect him, still couldn't fight his innate reflex to conceal. "I'll meet you at St. Sebastian's in an hour or so," Ronan shouted as he left their dorm. "I forgot something." He didn't see Michael peek out of the bathroom, expecting a good-bye kiss. He was already racing across campus. All the way he kept wondering if he had made the right decision, the feeling only got stronger when he saw the doctor's ransacked office. Then he looked into the corner of the room and saw two things that made him forget all about Michael and made him realize the doctor was in grave danger.

Jutting out from behind a fallen lamp were the doctor's eyeglasses, one lens shattered, and a crumbled piece of paper. Ronan didn't have to squint to see the word "evil" written on the page and he didn't have to think twice to know the paper was Alistair's note. MacCleery might rush out without his glasses, but he would never leave the note behind. He had been taken by force. Angry and frightened, Ronan didn't know who attacked Lochlan, but he knew whoever it was, only did so because they were following orders.

"Headmaster, I'm sorry I'm late! Please forgive me!" All heads turned when Amir burst into David's office, the door slamming behind him. He was greatly relieved, however, when he saw that David wasn't in the room.

"Amir!" Nurse Radcliff chastised. "You should be ashamed of yourself."

"Why don't you get stuffed?" Amir shouted. "I was carrying out Headmaster's orders."

Which doesn't make you special, you dumb twit! Of course, Nakano didn't speak that comment out loud, he didn't want Jean-Paul to think he was immature or anything. "Hey, mate," Nakano said. "She's just talking about the blood that's dripping off your face."

Extending his tongue so it glided across his chin, Amir tasted the doctor's surprisingly sweet blood as he wiped his face clean. Sitting next to Nakano he quipped, "Guess I didn't have time to freshen me face."

Seated directly behind him, Nurse Radcliff muttered under her breath, "Sloppy."

"Like you should talk, *Margaret*." The nurse's given name hissed out of Brania's mouth like acid, turning the already rancid air toxic. As David's daughter, Brania knew that she should be immune to the unattractive human traits that characterized the group of dysfunctional immortals and not sink to their level, but she couldn't help herself. She despised them, the nurse most of all. The feeling, predictably, was mutual.

Pulling her cardigan tighter across her ample bosom, Nurse Radcliff looked in Brania's direction and lifted her chin. "This from someone who dresses so disrespectfully in her father's presence." Seething, Brania felt her back stiffen and her fangs tingle as she tried to inconspicuously pull down her black leather skirt so it would at least reach the middle of her thighs. Satisfied at putting her master's spoiled child in her place, Nurse Radcliff beamed. "And don't think He hasn't noticed."

"That's because I notice everything."

Before the door closed behind David, everyone had stood up to greet their leader, everyone except Brania. As his only child, she didn't feel the need to rise in his presence. She felt that, over the centuries, she had proven her loyalty enough to remain seated. David didn't agree. "Lethargic, darling?"

The ticking of the seven-foot oak and gold grandfather clock, hand-made by one of David's many admirers, a now-deceased master carpenter from the Lower Rhine region of Germany, was the only sound that could be heard as everyone waited for Brania's response. "No, Father," she replied. "Bored."

David didn't hear Nakano snicker or Jean-Paul slap him in the arm to caution him. He was too busy listening to Zachariel. "She may be your child, but she *is* a girl," the wise voice counseled. "She is not created in my image and therefore she is worthless."

Spoken like a true father. Before David spoke out loud, he paused to stand behind his desk, his black eyes shimmering, his red hair aflame, every muscle of his body hard and expanded, pressing against the tight-fitting black silk material of his imported suit, to allow his subjects to see what a true leader looked like. Then it was time for them to hear what a true leader sounded like. "Brania, please take your place with the others."

What?! Brania couldn't believe that her father was relegating her to take position with, with . . . *them*, those inferior beings. How dare he? Oh, how she wished he had never returned! Again, silence permeated the room, and the ticking of the clock was deafening. But when the thin second hand, made of twenty-four-carat gold, had traveled more than halfway around the clock's face, Brania realized her father was serious; he expected her to sit among his subjects and not by his side. Things were changing. Brania could feel it, changing to her, around her, within. Maybe her father was testing her loyalty? Possibly, but hadn't she proven herself so many times before? Still she had her pride. She wasn't about to let these nothings see how hurt she was, how utterly disappointed. When she got up to walk toward the empty seat next to Nurse Radcliff, she didn't care that her skirt had ridden up her thighs and was exposing most of her legs. When she saw the older woman eyeing her exposed flesh, Brania pulled her skirt up an inch higher. Why not let the pig see what she would never, ever have?

"Now that you have all taken your rightful places," David said, "the Carnival for the Black Sun may officially begin!"

After the cheers and hoots died down, David sat in his chair, leaning back into the leather upholstery, and folded his hands in his lap. He looked like a kindly professor about to tell an anecdote instead of a man about to lead his subjects to war. "This is the end of the beginning, my friends," David said softly. "My purpose in returning here was not to be Ruler of Academia but to reclaim our dominance. Today is the first step in a battle that I have longed to wage, a battle against those vile half-breeds who call themselves water vamps and who threaten our position as leaders of the immortal world."

"We are the true leaders!" Amir shouted.

Proud, David let Amir's words and fury wash over him. "Yes, we are! And today's carnival is step one in uncovering the location of their precious Well, their life force."

"So we can destroy it?" Nurse Radcliff said, clutching her cardigan so tightly her knuckles turned white.

"Precisely!"

Brania listened to the applause. She heard the roar of approval, the craving for victory, but she felt numb and had no idea why. She hated the water vamps and their arrogance as much as anyone else in the room. Perhaps it was because her father was the one leading the charge? Perhaps she had stood behind no man for so long, she didn't know how to step back in line? Or perhaps she just felt like being defiant? "Do you really think destruction is an attainable goal?"

David's face turned as gray as the shadows bleeding through the windows. Sometimes children were so spiteful. And stupid. "Have you been listening, dear?" David queried. "Destruction of The Well is not on today's agenda, merely its location." The others in the room looked positively gleeful by David's tongue-lashing. Most believed Brania too haughty for her own good anyway. "Does that strategy make sense to you now?" David asked condescendingly.

Breathing deeply, Brania ran her fingers through her thick auburn hair, making it bounce freely, and gave her father the answer he wanted to hear. "Yes."

Triumphant, David declared, "Let the festivities begin!"

Shadows and light. The sun was not yet covered in darkness, but the mid-morning sky was starting to look like dusk. St. Sebastian's was filled with students eating, laughing, not at all understanding the magnitude of the Black Sun or even caring about its arrival, merely thankful not to have to spend hours in the library or the cathedral or hovered over their desks doing homework. To them the day was a respite from the endless study and pressure that was common at the end of the school year. To Dr. MacCleery, it was much more significant.

On a crimson stain. A pall crept through the stained-glass windows of Archangel Cathedral, turning the hopeful yellow color somber, like the sound of prayer when spoken by someone who doesn't believe in its power. Lochlan opened his eyes and looked down. His vision was blurred, fading, but he could see the drop of blood that had fallen from his neck foul the holy water below. He felt the last few breaths that his body clung to quicken as the blood drop exploded and swirled so there was now more blood than water in the font. He was not a religious man. He wasn't going to spend the last few moments he had on earth begging forgiveness for a lifetime of cynicism, nor was he going to become a hypocrite and plead for mercy. He was, however, a practical man and, if there was a God, he assumed he would be listening, which is why he began to pray for the safety of the children he could no longer protect. When he finished his prayer he started another, this one for the child who had taken his life.

"Amir," David called out as everyone was leaving his office. "Thank you."

Flushed with humility, Amir had to resist the urge to genuflect in front of David. Instead he bowed his head and clasped his hand over his heart, unable to find the proper words to convey what lay there. He didn't reply.

"You have proven your loyalty today," David continued. "And once you succeed in your next assignment, you will be legendary."

I can't believe he's entrusting me with such an important task, I can't believe he thinks I'm so special. When Amir finally found the words, they raced out of his mouth in a strangled whisper. "There isn't anything I wouldn't do for you, sir."

Placing his massive hand on Amir's bony shoulder, David looked at the boy, making sure his eyes shone with a father's pride. "And that's why I have complete faith in you."

This time Amir couldn't resist. He clutched David's hand and bent low on one knee, his eyes cast downward, not worthy of looking into his master's face. From across the room, near the door, David caught Jean-Paul's stare, and the two men had to look away from each other to stop themselves from laughing at the spectacle. When Amir finally stood up and found the courage to once again look David in the face, the headmaster's countenance had resumed its serious nature. "You have a busy day ahead of you," David remarked. "Go make me proud."

"I will." After a few moments, Amir was able to pry himself away from David's presence and leave the room. When Jean-Paul closed the door, they could no longer retain their composure and burst out laughing, David's deep baritone intertwining with Jean-Paul's higher-pitched voice, the new sound echoing off the walls loudly.

"You do know thees eez a suicide mission?" Jean-Paul asked, catching his breath.

Pulling out a crisp white handkerchief from his jacket pocket to wipe away the tears his laughter created, David replied, "That's why I'm not sending you, my love."

When he heard those last words, Nakano's hand froze on the doorknob. He wasn't eavesdropping, he wasn't being an immature git, he was just looking for his boyfriend. He never expected to overhear his headmaster call him *love*. He also never expected the two of them to embrace.

What the bloody hell is going on?! What are they doing? When he felt his hand start to shake he let go of the doorknob so he wouldn't jiggle it, so he wouldn't make any sound and interrupt the two of them from doing what seemed to come so naturally. He didn't want to bear witness to the scene; he wanted to pounce on them or flee. Instead, he watched. He felt his stomach lurch when he saw David hold Jean-Paul's chin between his thumb and forefinger and stare into his eyes. He felt something cold and painful squeeze his heart when he saw David tenderly kiss Jean-Paul's left cheek, then turn his face to kiss the other. *No, not again! Am I that ugly? Am I that stupid that I can't even keep a boyfriend?! What is wrong with me?! Put one foot be-*

hind you, Nakano, so you can get the hell out of here before
they see you, before they make you look like an even bigger
fool! One foot, that's it, then the other, yes, go, leave! He
stumbled out of the anteroom, but just as he turned to run,
he bumped into Brania.

"Watch where you're going, you fool!" she exclaimed.

Nakano stared at her. He wanted to scream back, tell her
how disgusting her father was, but he felt that if he opened
his mouth he would cry.

Watching him run off toward campus, into the burgeoning
darkness, Brania couldn't get over how much younger
Nakano looked. It could be the longer hair; it softened his
appearance, made him look more vulnerable, more like the
child he really was. It wasn't so much his physicality, though,
as his demeanor. Nakano ran toward a fight, not from it,
something must have happened to change him. Studying
Jean-Paul, his arms wrapped around her father, she had her
answer. "You're sleeping with the old nurse *and* the hot
Frenchman," Brania denounced. "My word, Father, how
varied are your tastes?"

"It seems that you've lived among these humans far too
long," David remarked. "Their primitive instincts have permeated your brain."

"I'm the one being primitive?!" Brania shouted. "You're
so primal, you can't even limit yourself to one gender."

Outraged, Jean-Paul took a step toward Brania, but David
grabbed him by the elbow, preventing him from getting any
closer. "You should not speak to your papa that way."

It was bad enough she had to deal with her father's scorn.
She refused to be preached at by his latest concubine. Side-
swiping a chair with a brush of her hand, sending it flying
across the room, she screamed, "I will speak to my *papa* any
way I choose to!"

"But you will not raise your voice to your brother!"

Her knees buckled, just slightly, but enough to warn her that she needed to hold on to something or else she might fall. Brania clutched at the back of one of the leather chairs, pressing her nails so hard she broke through the fabric. "My *what*?"

This was not the way David had planned to hold the family reunion. He wanted to wait until the location of The Well was discovered to proclaim that he and both his children would lead His people to victory, Brania seated on his left, and Jean-Paul, a smidge closer, seated on his right. Ah, well, what was that colloquialism? No time like the present. "Brania," David said, "I'd like you to meet your baby brother, Jean-Paul Germaine."

This is ridiculous, this cannot be happening. It's a joke, yes, my father's attempt at a cruel, a very cruel joke. "That's impossible."

"I assure you it is possible and it is fact," David declared. "I remember every second of Chantal's labor, thirty-six long, but ultimately extremely rewarding, hours."

Smiling, Jean-Paul touched his father's shoulder affectionately. "She still blames me for zee pain."

Joining in the laughter, David kissed Jean-Paul's hand. "Oh, she has no one to blame but herself, my son."

Son?! How in the world can he have a son? Her entire life she was the only one, no one else. That wasn't going to change now; she wouldn't let it. "I'm your only child! That's what you always told me!"

Growing weary, David was beginning to regret his disclosure. "I said you were my only daughter, I never said you were my only child. Maybe if you would stop listening with human ears, you would hear the truth."

It was as if Brania stepped through time, as if she tumbled through a tunnel and landed two centuries earlier. She felt like Nakano looked, young, vulnerable, like the child she had been and, unfortunately, still was. The tears were so un-expected, so unfamiliar, that they stung, they blinded her so she couldn't see her father's face; she could only focus on the memory of him. "I have dedicated my life to you! I . . . have . . . *compromised* myself and done things that were *abhorrent* only to carry out your whims and earn your love." She wanted to continue; she had so much more she wanted to say. But she couldn't breathe properly, she was gasping, her chest heaving. Her father's harsh summation made it unnecessary for her to speak another word.

"As it should be."

Brania felt her body fold in half; she reached out to grab another chair, but there wasn't one and she stumbled forward, causing David to take a step backward or else feel her touch. Hunched over, she looked up into the face of her father, then her newly discovered brother. She was surrounded by more family than ever before and yet she felt more alone than she had ever felt in her entire life.

Lochlan felt the same way. He wished he didn't, he wished he could feel some pain, but that stopped quite a while ago, and without the pain as a distraction, all he could do was think. He thought about how he had spent his life, the wife whom he lost years ago, the children they never had, and he acknowledged, ruefully, that there was no one on earth that he wanted to spend his final moments with. This was not the way he assumed he would die, but he had to admit it was better than dying in a hospital after a long illness, the medical staff expecting family to gather round and, when none showed, feeling sorry for him, not because he was about to die but because he was about to die alone.

Which is what he thought would happen until he saw Ronan.

*   *   *

After he left the doctor's office, Ronan scoured the campus for a trace, a clue as to the doctor's whereabouts. When he smelled the blood coming from the cathedral, he knew his search had ended. He had no idea, however, that he would find something so ghastly.

Looking up at MacCleery, Ronan realized he had been crucified for his sin, the sin of being human. All he wanted to do was protect him, protect all the children at Double A, carry out Alistair's wishes, do what the former headmaster had been incapable of doing, and this is how he was repaid. It wasn't fair, but it proved what Ronan always believed: David and his kind were truly evil and he was right in keeping the truth from Michael and trying to shield him. Mac-Cleery's impaled body was evidence—when you uncovered the truth, this was what happened.

Will the sun prevail. Ronan was only a child when his father died, so there was nothing he could do to make his death easier, this time was different. Ronan narrowed his eyes and shot beams of light to disintegrate the nails. Untethered, the doctor fell into his waiting arms. Placing Lochlan gently on the altar, Ronan could barely hear him breathe, in a matter of seconds, the man would be dead. He wished he could think of something to say to him to lessen his fear, but what did an immortal creature, someone who took death from the living as a means of survival, know about alleviating a dying man's fears? Fortunately, it was the doctor's turn to make things easier for Ronan.

"It's up to you now," MacCleery sighed.

Or will darkness reign. As a deep shadow passed over Lochlan's body, he spoke once more. "You have to protect them from David."

And then with Ronan as his only witness, he died.

chapter 21

Ronan's shadow fell at Brania's feet and they both stopped. When she couldn't smell any human blood, she knew the body Ronan was carrying was dead and for a fleeting moment, no more than a second, she wished she could trade places with the corpse. So did Ronan.

"This is because of you!" Ronan's words were silent, but they still smashed into Brania with such force that she clutched her stomach. *"Innocent blood! Spilled because of you and your father!"*

Holding MacCleery's body close, protecting him even in death from the enemy, Ronan asked, "Are you proud?!"

While his eyes bore into Brania, Ronan tried again to mentally contact Edwige and Michael. Once again, neither one responded. Sometimes Michael couldn't hear him, but Edwige always did. Where was she? Ronan needed help. He needed to give the doctor's body a proper burial and find Michael and the others to warn them that they could be in danger. Obviously the doctor had been right. It was up to him, up to him to do everything.

As Brania watched Ronan run off toward where there was still some sun, where darkness was not yet king, she felt the sound begin to rise from her toes. It consumed her, ravaged her entire body until she could no longer physically contain it and had no other choice but to give it release. "NOOOO!!!!" Again and again she shouted, disrupting her surroundings, making the birds squawk, flee, making her body shake, screaming until her voice was sore, screaming so her feelings and thoughts would leave her.

She looked at Archangel Cathedral, the yellow stained glass pale and hushed, the fading sunlight and shadow in a duel for supremacy, and she wondered if those who worshiped that other god were also disappointed. She had put all her faith in her father only to find out he was a false prophet, a liar, someone whom she couldn't trust and someone not worthy of her love. Could this place be different? Could all the stories she heard be true and not just the desperate hopes of those who were sadly mortal?

One stubborn ray of light shone from the window and traveled through the premature dusk in a line that landed a foot from Brania's face. She gazed into it and although she knew she was acting like one of those desperate fools, she walked toward it. When her body touched the light, she was amazed how quickly the throbbing in her mind, the rage, ceased. The only thing that prevented her from entering the church was the music.

The soft soprano voice floated through the air, a melody that existed purely on its own. It wasn't seeking an audience, but it had found one. Brania listened preternaturally and finally surmised that the voice she had heard so many times before was coming from near St. Sebastian's, but as far as she could tell, it had nothing to do with the celebration for the Black Sun, nothing to do with her father's people. This was a voice that was on its own.

Crisscrossing through the trees within The Forest, Brania's eyes narrowed and blackened. She needed her full vampire vision to maneuver inside the darkness that had overtaken the woods. The voice acted as radar, calling out to her, bringing her home. Her pace accelerated and she ran through the brush, sidestepping boulders and tree stumps, her memory returning to when she was a young girl, the folds of her long satin dress clumped in one hand, her other hand outstretched so the blood that dripped off her fingers wouldn't soil the fabric. She had to get to the lake to wash before Daddy saw her. He always got mad when she made a mess. He wanted His little girl to be perfect, not remind Him that He was not.

When she reached the entrance of the crypt, she was startled to see that her hand was blood-free. She still felt stained, but when she moved farther into the cave and saw Imogene sitting in her coffin, she no longer felt like a little girl.

The purity of Imogene's sound, the effortless notes, swirled around and through Brania as if they were cleansing her soul, and she found it difficult not to cry. But a parent isn't supposed to cry in front of her child; a parent is supposed to instill her child with a sense of comfort and security, love and compassion, and that's what Brania planned to do. Stepping into the coffin, she sat facing Imogene and felt for the first time in centuries that she had found her true purpose.

Standing in the doorway of Ciaran's lab, prepared to satisfy the second part of David's command, Amir felt the same way. He knew long before he was plucked from a slum in Calcutta to study at Double A that he was special. He dreamed about immortality long before David approached him one afternoon and asked him if he wanted to live forever, and he understood that dealing with this human was just another step closer to holding the keys of eternity in his hands. Those keys were meant to be his and no stupid, prissy science geek was going to stand in his way. "I knew I'd find you here," Amir informed Ciaran. "You're not the festive sort and you really don't have any mates, do ya?"

Ciaran was not afraid of vampires. He grew up aware of their existence, he coexisted with them, a part of him wanted to be one, but when he saw Amir, his top lip twitching uncontrollably, he gasped. "You shouldn't startle a bloke holding a test tube," Ciaran replied, struggling to keep his voice calm. "It could have dangerous results."

The sound of Amir's heels against the tiled floor was steady. Ciaran maintained eye contact with him so he wouldn't notice that he closed his journal and snapped it shut just as Amir's heel made one final click. When he placed his spindly fingers on the table, Ciaran's journal was covered by a pile of notes. "Spill it, science boy," Amir barked. "David wants to know what you've discovered for us."

Us? If Amir actually thought his name could be mentioned in the same breath as David's, he was not only delusional, but dangerous as well. Best to give him what he came here for and get rid of him. "Take a look," Ciaran said, spinning the microscope around so the lens faced Amir.

Peering through the lens, Amir saw a blob of colors, red, white, yellow, interswirled like an abstract painting, pretty but with no meaning. "We don't have time for flippin' games, Eaves," Amir shouted. "What is this?"

Ciaran pulled the microscope back to his side of the table and explained that what Amir saw was a chromosome unique to water vamps. "I was able to isolate a cell in Michael's blood and test it against elements found in the sun," Ciaran said. "I thought I was right barmy to try something so basic, but it worked. Looks like water vamps' blood, unlike yours and mine, contains some of the same elements."

"Oh, sod off with your bloody science talk, will ya!" Amir bellowed. "What's it mean for us? David wants a final report."

He gave Amir information. Now it was time to get rid of him. "I'm working on a transfusion of water vamp blood, but it will take time." Gathering his books, Ciaran stood up. "Vampires weren't created in a day, you know."

"What about the human child?"

Keep walking, Ciaran. Don't let this prat think you know what he's talking about. "Pardon?"

Stepping in front of Ciaran, Amir blocked the exit, his wiry body so rigid he looked like he'd grown another foot. "I'm talking about your sister! The bitch hiding underneath the table."

"I am not..."

"Saoirse!" Ciaran was having difficulty controlling Amir; he couldn't handle two wild cards at once. Trying to block Saoirse from Amir's line of vision, Ciaran forced himself to laugh. "Absobloodylootely, mate. Saoirse's human just like me."

"She may be human, but she's nothing like you!"

Shrugging his shoulders, Ciaran took a step closer toward Amir. "I'm not sure what you've heard, but you know how these stories get twisted, one part truth, twelve parts fiction."

"Bugger off, Ciaran!" Amir screamed. "We all know the stories are true, no matter how hard your kind try to keep it a secret!"

Before the last word spat out of Amir's mouth, he disappeared. Ciaran whirled around and was terrified to see that he didn't go too far, he was on the other side of the room, holding Saoirse by the back of the neck, lifting her two feet off the ground. "Tell me why this one's so special!" Amir cried.

"Let go of me!" Saoirse shrieked.

Ciaran had never seen his sister so frightened, he had never worked harder to remain unruffled. "Amir, mate, what's it matter?" he asked. "She's different, that's all."

Shaking Saoirse like a rag doll, Amir bellowed, "It matters because we want to know!"

"Ciaran, help me!" Saoirse shouted, her feet treading air.

His patience gone, replaced with an uncomfortable combination of fear and frustration, Ciaran yelled back, "We all want to know, but none of us can figure it out!"

"Ciaran," Saoirse said, her voice now choked as Amir pressed harder on her neck, "make him put me down."

Outside, there was an explosion of firecrackers, the carnival was under way. That's where he should be, Ciaran thought, with his friends, enjoying himself, not in here trying to reason with a madman, trying to save his sister's life, not watching Amir's face distort and lengthen, his fangs descend, pure white, as thin as the rest of his body. "C'mon, mate, just put her down!"

Amir grinned devilishly. "Make me."

Without thinking, Ciaran tossed his books at Amir and sprang forward, lunging not at Amir, but Saoirse, hoping he could wrestle her away and give her a chance to run free. No such luck. Amir's reflexes were too quick and he was able to jump out of the way, Saoirse's flailing body securely tucked under his arm, and make it to the doorway with enough time to watch Ciaran fall to the floor and crash into the base of the lab table. Scrambling to his knees, Ciaran turned around just in time to see Saoirse reaching her arms out to him. "Help me!"

"We'll be where the sun is blackest," Amir said. "Ronan'll know where that is."

Ciaran understood the cryptic remark, but before he could respond, Amir and Saoirse disappeared from his view. Running to St. Sebastian's, he couldn't stop blaming himself. He knew he was no match for Amir physically, but he should have been able to outsmart him, make him realize nothing could be gained by kidnapping his sister. No one understood why she was so different, and people had been trying to figure it out since she was born. An act of unprovoked violence wasn't going to bring forth an answer; it was only going to elicit more violence.

"Ronan!" Ciaran shouted into his cell phone, his feet smashing into the grass as he ran. "Call me, it's urgent."

Once inside St. Sebastian's, Ciaran had to close his eyes. There was way too much going on around him. The carnival was in full swing, music thumping, lights flashing, kids screaming. There was a loud crash, then a splash, and Fritz yelling, "Blakeley down!" Where was Ronan in this swirl of activity? Ciaran couldn't find him, but he found the next best thing. "Michael!"

"Hey you," Michael said, holding a cloud of pink cotton candy on a stick. "Here, have this. I only grabbed it 'cause I like the smell."

"No, thanks," Ciaran said, waving his hand. "Have you seen Ronan?"

Shaking his head, Michael replied, "No, I was going to ask you the same thing."

Dammit! Why is my brother never around when I need him? "Any idea where he is?"

"He said he would meet me here, but I can't find him," Michael said, looking into the crowd. Then he leaned in closer to Ciaran. "He's probably trying to send me a telepathic message right now, but you know, I just can't get the hang of that." When Ciaran didn't laugh or make a snippy comment, Michael realized he was definitely not wearing a happy carnival face and out of all of them, he was the one most looking forward to the day's outing. "What's going on?"

"We have a problem." Ciaran hesitated. He knew Ronan wouldn't want Michael to be involved, but he didn't have a choice, he couldn't waste any more time trying to find him. The second after Ciaran explained that Amir was waiting at Inishtrahull Island, the northernmost part of Ireland, where the sun would be the blackest during the eclipse, and with Saoirse as his hostage, Michael started to run out of the gym.

"Where are you going?" Ciaran asked.

Ciaran really could be so dimwitted at times. "To help Saoirse, where do you think?"

Michael really could be so ignorant at times. "Stop! There are things about her you don't understand."

Tossing the cotton candy into Ciaran's hands, Michael informed his friend that there were no more secrets between him and Ronan and raced off into the crowd. If only that were true. There was much more that Ciaran wanted to tell Michael, much more that he himself didn't understand, not that it was his place. Ronan should be the one to inform Michael of the riddles that confounded their family, but where the hell was he? For that matter, where was David or Nakano or even that French guy Nakano was going out with? As far as Ciaran could tell, there wasn't one vampire inside of St. Sebastian's and, at Double A, the odds of that happening were pretty slim. *What an idiot I've been. Ronan was right after all.*

Scouring the gym for an inhuman face, Ciaran found none. He ran up to the windows and peered outside. The looming shadows from the half-covered sun made it difficult to see, yet he only saw mortals. *I'm sure there are a lot more that I don't know about, there's got to be.* Even though that was true, it didn't make Ciaran feel any better. He had been duped into believing the carnival was nothing more than a school function when clearly it was another one of David's tactics. Ciaran had the distinct impression that he had fallen right into his trap, and Michael had no idea that he was headed in the same direction.

Just as he was about to enter The Forest so he could sprint unseen to the other side of campus before heading to Inishtrahull Island, Michael saw Phaedra enter the maze. A second later he was standing by her side. "I need you."

Startled, Phaedra jumped. "What do you mean?"

Talking quickly, Michael tried to explain the situation as succinctly as possible. "Everything I said the other night about not needing you—erase it, delete it, I need your help."

Phaedra was silent. She knew this would happen, she knew the moment she admitted to herself what she truly wanted, how she honestly wanted to spend the rest of her future, no matter if she had a day left or an eternity, something would happen to force her to change her plans. Something like this. "I thought you said Ronan had your back?"

"I can't find him," Michael explained. "I have to save Saoirse. It could be dangerous and I need your protection!"

It should all be so simple and yet Phaedra couldn't decide. Somewhere close by was Fritz and he was the one she wanted to be with. She didn't want to transform into fog, she didn't want to let go of the lovely feelings that were becoming so strong, so much a part of who she was, she didn't want to . . . she could hardly say the words to herself: She didn't want to be an efemera any longer. She wanted to be human. "I . . . I don't know if I can."

Michael was stunned. He shouldn't have been, but he was. After all, he was the one who had told Phaedra to embrace her mortality as he embraced eternal life, but things had changed. He wasn't sure if he had the strength to save Saoirse by himself, he didn't know if he would just find Amir on the beach or if there would be a pack of vampires waiting for him. He was trying to be practical, realistic, but he needed Phaedra to do the same. "One last time, Phaedra," Michael begged. "Please!"

You've become a dear friend to me, Michael, probably the best friend I've ever had, but right now I hate you. "One last time."

Michael felt Phaedra stiffen when he hugged her, but he figured she was just ticked off at him for making her choose to do something that in her heart she didn't want to do. He had no idea that she was reacting to his reflection. The image she saw in the mirror was alarming. It wasn't the result of a fun-house trick, it was Michael's true spirit and it was grotesque.

"Meet me at the island," Michael shouted as he ran out of the maze.

Following him, Phaedra made it as far as the edge of The Forest before stopping. She knew she had to keep her promise, but she was conflicted. What was happening to Michael; why did he look so different? She knew he was a vampire and no matter how good or gentle he might be, he was still part of a dangerous species. Oh, none of that mattered! Her purpose in life was to protect him regardless of whether he was a vampire, immortal, a creature who preyed on the living. It was that simple. When she saw Fritz staring at her from inside the gym, things once again got complicated.

All the sweet possibilities, all the magic she had hoped to share with him, this rough-edged but tenderhearted boy, all of that would never be. She would never know what it means to be completely human and completely in love.

She lifted her hand to Fritz, a quiet gesture. She wanted to say so much to him, touch him, kiss him, feel his hands embrace her, but no, that was meant for teenage girls, and no matter how much she looked the part, no matter how much she convinced herself that that's what she was, that she was human, she wasn't. And she feared she never would be.

What the bloomin' hell was that? Where'd Phaedra go? Fritz pressed his nose closer to the window. He knew he saw Phaedra, she was right there at the entrance to the maze; she waved to him. But when he looked closer, all he could see was a puff of smoke, like she actually disappeared into thin air. Fritz swatted his forehead with his rolled-up comic book. *It's the mist rolling in, you stupid prat; nature's all wonky from the eclipse. Nobody disappears just like that. But wait a second, maybe that's just what she did, maybe instead of waving hello, she was waving good-bye.*

No! Don't make it over before it even gets started, before we even get to all the good stuff! Despite his protests and his hopes, Fritz had a bad feeling that the latest issue of *Tales of The Double A—The Day Darkness Took Over* was starting to come true.

"It's starting, my son, the darkness has returned." With Jean-Paul by his side, David was peering into the mirror watching Amir race through the shadows, Saoirse clutched in his arms. "It's the dawn of a new age," David whispered, "when darkness can roam freely in the sun."

Jean-Paul smiled at his father. He made sure David could see that his eyes were filled with admiration, but he worked hard to conceal his thoughts. He didn't want him to pick up on the doubts circulating within his mind. The strategy was sound, but his father was also zealous and often underestimated his opponents. Jean-Paul had been observing water vamps for years and he knew they were a formidable lot. As he had gotten to know Michael better, he discovered his theories were astute. "How marvelous to be a part of it, Father," Jean-Paul said. "But I think I can be of greater assistance."

Jean-Paul explained that even the most loyal and ambitious of his flock needed help, so he volunteered to assist Amir. "He's getting preoccupied with zee girl," Jean-Paul explained. "When all he needs to do ees get Ronan to follow him into zee ocean so he can find zee Well."

David was reluctant to let his son leave his side, but quickly saw the sense of his suggestion. "All right, go," David allowed. "But remember, if you must choose between saving yourself and saving that boy, know that I will not honor your death."

I have no intention of dying for such a foolish child. "I understand your ways, Father," Jean-Paul replied. "Remember I am not like my sister."

In the open air, Jean-Paul heard a noise and stopped. He instinctively thought he was being watched and narrowed his eyes to cut through the shadowlight. Nothing. Racing north toward the island, he didn't look back. If he had, he would have seen Nakano following him. But the chase was witnessed by David. "Oh, Zachariel, how heartening to see all my servants working together."

On the shores of Inishtrahull Island, however, one of David's servants was still on his own. Saoirse wisely stopped trying to break free from Amir's hold. She wasn't strong enough and it merely wasted her energy, she had a feeling she was going to need to conserve her resources. She also knew that she needed her brother, the first thing she asked Michael when he showed up was why Ronan wasn't with him.

"He's right behind me," Michael lied.

"Well, he better hurry up," Amir ordered. "Because I'm losing my patience."

In the unnatural darkness, it was difficult to see. Michael figured it had more to do with his fear than his vision. He had to concentrate, he had to focus on keeping Saoirse safe until Ronan and Phaedra showed up. If it was just him and Amir, he would strike first and think later, but his fangs were too close to Saoirse's neck, there was no way Michael could reach Amir in time before he plunged them into her flesh. He had to be cunning.

"I'll make you a trade, Amir," Michael suggested. "Me for Saoirse."

"I don't want you!" Amir spat.

Michael inched forward, hoping his movement would be concealed in the growing blackness. "C'mon, David's much more interested in water vamps than he is in humans."

Watching the scene with growing interest, David nodded his head. He tried to reach out to Amir telepathically, tell him to release the girl and find The Well, but the distance and the boy's own ego were getting in the way. Amir was not only loyal, he was also ambitious.

"The only trade I'll make is if you show me The Well," Amir declared.

Impressive, David thought, the boy might be too anxious for prestige, but he was shrewd.

Ronan was right all along. They are up to something; they want to locate The Well. "That's impossible," Michael said. "You can't get near it, you can't see it, you're not a water vamp."

"And I thank Zachariel every day for that!" Amir screamed. "Show me The Well or I'm killing your boyfriend's sister!"

Dammit, where was Ronan?! Where was Phaedra? *This guy isn't just a vampire, he's insane. He thinks he can defy nature and find out where The Well is without having his soul be connected to it.* There was no way that was going to happen and there was no way Michael was going to be able to save Saoirse. *No, no, don't think that way, think of everything you've accomplished. Yeah, right, and think of everything that's been taken away from you—your mother, your grandmother, your entire family, your mortality!*

"What's it gonna be, Michael?!"

"Shut up!" *Concentrate, Michael, try! You're not that weak little boy any longer. You're a water vamp!* The first thing Michael felt was the webbing grow between his fingers, then his toes. His face elongated, his eyes narrowed, and when his fangs grew past his lips, they felt sharper than ever. Even though he transformed, even though he was equipped with his preternatural armor, he wasn't fast enough. Amir wasn't here to play fair.

When the fangs sunk into her flesh, Saoirse howled. Michael watched in horror as Amir took his hands off her and was only holding on to her by his teeth, digging in deeper, shaking her violently. Michael lunged forward, wrapping his arms around Amir's waist and tackling him to the ground. He saw Saoirse fall to the side—at least she was free. When he turned back to face Amir, he saw him already up and running toward her. Springing forward, Michael slashed his hand through the air blindly. He felt his nails dig into Amir's face, ripping away pieces of skin to expose the muscle and bone underneath. His cries of agony were cut short, however, when Saoirse started to glow.

Shrouded in the darkness of the near-eclipse, Michael and Amir watched, fascinated, as Saoirse's body emitted a bright light, a strong white glow like the one Michael had seen once before in The Well. It radiated her body and lifted her off the beach as if to separate her from the world around her. She was part of the earth, yet detached from it at the same time.

The light was so strong, it hurt his eyes and he had to raise his arm to shield them, but even with compromised vision, he and Amir both were able to see her body levitate. As Saoirse floated in the air, the light that emanated from her body rose above her until it was nothing more than a speck of white amid the darkness. When it had almost fully disappeared, it collapsed onto Saoirse's neck, at the site of her ripped flesh, burrowed back within her body, and as it did, the wounds healed themselves, the ripped, torn flesh, the blood, all gone. Her skin was as clear and smooth as before.

When Saoirse's eyes opened, they were her own. When she spoke, the voice was not. "She is not what you think she is."

chapter 22

"It's a girl!"

When Edwige heard Saxon speak those words, she was thrilled. After having two boys, she desperately wanted a girl. She wanted a daughter whom she could dress in frilly clothes, play house with, who would cherish her own treasured collection of dolls and stuffed animals. She simply wanted to enjoy an eternity of mother-daughter experiences. The moment Saoirse let out her first cry while being held in her father's arms on the same sacred ground that housed The Well, Edwige knew her child was a blessing. The moment The Well spoke to her, she knew her child was, in fact, a curse.

"Because you broke your bond of love with your soul mate, because you have defiled the sanctity of The Well and of all the descendants of Atlantis," the deep, richly textured voice began, "this child is your punishment."

There were only two points of light in the cave, one rising from the mouth of The Well, the other shrouding Edwige's face, which was wet with salt water and sweat. The rest of the space was draped in darkness, so Edwige knew Saxon and her daughter were spared the admonition. It was meant only for her to hear. "Your daughter will never belong to you in the purest sense. She will never become a water vampire like her parents," the voice instructed, "until you atone for your sin."

Edwige knew exactly what her sin was, but instinct, panic, made her proclaim her innocence. "No! I've done nothing wrong!"

The only response was a rippling sound, as if the water within the stone encasement sighed, heaved, causing a small wave to rise and fall against the curved walls. Leaning on her elbows, her legs still bent in the same position as when Saoirse was born, Edwige's eyes narrowed and emitted a preternatural light that she hoped would break through the darkness and connect directly with her life force. "She is my daughter, created for you, created out of love!"

The ground underneath Edwige shook and she fell backward, clawing her webbed hands into the dirt for support. A wave crashed loudly against the inside of The Well, and the light that shone from it flickered. Edwige tried to find Saxon and their child within the blackness, amid the rumbling, but she couldn't. She was alone. "I didn't sin!" she cried out. "I was raped!"

"LIAR!!"

Violently, the earth rumbled and Edwige felt its angry vibrations assault her weary body. The light from The Well intensified, became dazzlingly bright, and grew until it grabbed hold of the light that illuminated her face. Edwige was never closer to The Well and she never wanted to be farther away. "This rape never took place," the voice bellowed, each word carrying with it wrath and wind. "How dare you claim such a travesty occurred? How dare you compound your sin?"

Blinded by the light, frightened by the severity and the truth of the words, Edwige was frozen, unable to move. She could only repeat the lies she had uttered so many times before, the lies she convinced Saxon and all those who loved her were the truth. "Ciaran's father raped me," she declared, her whisper trembling. "He . . . he took me against my will." Edwige waited for a response, she waited for The Well to reply, to forgive, condemn, anything. But there was only silence. Like a cornered animal staring into the expressionless face of its hunter, Edwige did the only thing she could, she fought back. "I did not break our covenant!!"

It was a wasted attempt. Once again the stream of light uniting Edwige to The Well was broken, the ground stopped shaking, the wind calmed. As the light from The Well receded, the voice was no longer enraged, but quiet, indifferent. "Edwige Glynn-Rowley, you are not what you think you are." When the cave resumed its normal appearance and the natural light returned, Edwige could see Saxon holding Saoirse, her dimpled legs wiggling in her father's arms, her blond curls like a flaxen crown, and she was relieved they had safely returned to her side. She was even more relieved that she was still the only one who could hear The Well's voice when it spoke one final time. "And this child is not what you think she is."

"Then what the bloody hell are you?!" Amir insisted.

Saoirse was no longer floating. The spell that enabled her to hover in midair had broken and she was standing on the beach, acting as if nothing remarkable had happened, as if she hadn't just been possessed by a powerful, supernatural force. She acted as if her memory was concealed by the same shadow from the half-dark sun that cloaked her body. Brushing off sand from the back of her jeans, she replied matter-of-factly, "A human born of two vampires."

A what?! Michael digested this information, this incredible news. He didn't understand Ronan's family history completely, and he acknowledged it was complicated, but he didn't realize Saoirse's parents were both vampires when she was born. If that was true, how could she be human? He had never heard of such a thing, never imagined such a thing could be true. It just didn't make sense. If Saoirse's parents were vampires, shouldn't she be some sort of a vampire too? "Does Ronan know about this?" Michael asked.

What a stupid question, Saoirse thought. "Of course he does." Then she realized how stupid her answer was. Obviously Ronan didn't fill Michael in on why she was considered to be the special member of not just their family, but of their entire race. "But you know, it's really not a big deal," Saoirse lied, trying to backtrack from her initial snide comment.

"Sounds like a pretty big deal to me," Michael replied, feeling even dumber than before.

Sometimes she wanted to strangle Ronan. He could be an absolute twit when he wanted to be. Couldn't he see how perfect Michael was? Gorgeous and funny and loyal and exactly the type of boyfriend she hoped she'd find for herself one day, without, you know, being gay, of course. If Michael were her boyfriend, she'd treat him right. She wouldn't keep any secrets from him, she wouldn't turn their entire relationship into something shambolic! "I guess it all depends how you look at it," Saoirse said, shrugging her shoulders. "But I am certain of one thing, I owe you a big fat thank-you."

"What do you have to thank me for?" Michael asked.

"Not you, silly. Amir."

Saoirse was so wrapped up in her own daydreams, her own concerns, she didn't notice the glare that accompanied Amir's response. "Me?"

"Yes, you," Saoirse confirmed. "You helped me find out something I never knew about myself."

His sneer made the shadowlight appear darker. "What would that be?"

"Well, I always knew a water vamp couldn't transform me," she explained, fixing the barrette that had come loose in her hair. "Now we all know I'm impervious to the bites of regular vampires as well." Watching Michael and Amir stare at her as if she were a three-headed alien, Saoirse thought she may have screwed up her vocabulary words. "Impervious does mean resistant, right? Can't hurt me, can't make me one of you."

The questions grew inside Michael's brain like building blocks, first one, then another. *Why didn't Ronan tell me this? Didn't he trust me enough? Didn't he think I should know something so important?* It was difficult to think, difficult to stop the confusion, the anger, from distorting his face, difficult to not want to leave Saoirse here on the island by herself and find Ronan to confront him. But he couldn't do that, not while Amir was still here looking like that, his fangs cutting into his flesh.

Amir had had enough. He couldn't stand listening to this girl tell him he couldn't do something, he couldn't stand seeing her look so nonchalant, as if she weren't in the presence of a member of a superior race. He knew he had more important things to do, but there was always time to teach a freak a lesson. "If I can't turn you into a vampire," Amir fumed, "maybe I can kill you."

Instinctively, Michael stepped in front of Saoirse. He reached back and felt her hands latch on to his shoulder and arm, she might always try to appear unfazed by danger, blasé, but he knew Amir's threats, his unpredictable nature, made her afraid. Unfortunately, it didn't make her quiet.

"Kill me?" she cried. "You can't even clean up your own beastly face!"

Amir felt the warmth spread up from his neck to his forehead. *Just who the hell does this arsehole think she's talking to like that?* A breeze erupted around him and he felt the wind sweep by his torn cheek, the one Michael had slashed open, and realized that was what she was talking about. *Fine, you want to see me clean up? Watch this.*

Extending his tongue, he flicked it to the side and lapped up the gash on his face, delighted to discover that his blood tasted even sweeter than the doctor's. A few more licks and he felt the wound bubble, felt a tickling where the skin was being reborn. Less than a minute later, his cheek was fully repaired, as bronze-colored and smooth as before Michael attacked him. If the transformation hadn't been so disgusting, Saoirse would've been impressed.

"That is goppin' foul, Amir!"

His fangs may have been fully extended, but they didn't prevent Amir from laughing hysterically. "When I'm done with you, I'll show you what foul really looks like!"

"I seriously doubt that's something you can do on your own," Michael declared.

A freak and a fool. Amir smirked. "What if I have backup?"

Whipping around, his arm still protecting Saoirse, Michael was stunned to see Jean-Paul staring at them, his fangs as long and straight as the hair that fell in front of his jet-black eyes. He looked different, he looked menacing, wicked, like Amir. How in the world did Michael ever think he looked sexy?

Gripping Michael's arm tighter, Saoirse whispered, "Where's Ronan?"

"I don't think he's coming," Michael whispered in response, praying that no one else could hear him. They couldn't. They were too busy listening to David.

"Be careful, my son," David warned. "You only need to lure the child and the water vamp away from the ocean." Jean-Paul didn't respond but followed his father's orders, walking in a circle, clockwise, until he was in front of Amir, at which point he started walking toward Michael, making him and Saoirse react by inching backward and away from him.

Staring into Jean-Paul's eyes, Michael tried to keep his face a blank mask. He was trying to determine, without giving away his growing sense of apprehension, if he would attack. He had been so nice, no, he had been more than nice. He had acted as if he wanted to be much more than Michael's friend. Why was he coming at them like this, looking hostile, menacing, like he wanted to harm them, like he wanted to help Amir find out if he could kill Saoirse?

Because he is one of Them, you idiot! It's like Ronan always said, their kind cannot be trusted, no matter how good-looking, no matter how friendly and understanding they might be. Michael didn't have time to berate himself. He had to be prepared, be ready for anything. Dammit, where was Ronan?! It would be so much easier if he was by his side where he was supposed to be. And Phaedra, where was she? She had promised to follow him, help him. There was no way he could protect Saoirse *and* fight off both Jean-Paul and Amir if it came to that. Luckily, David had other plans.

"Remember your instructions, Amir," David seethed. "Forget about the girl and find The Well."

Reluctantly, Amir obeyed, but just as he was about to turn and run into the ocean, he saw two blurred images approach the island, one swoosh of darkness coming from the inland, and a swirl of gray smoke flying in from the sea. When Nakano landed on the beach, Amir wasn't terribly surprised. Wherever Jean-Paul was, his daft, lovesick boyfriend was never far behind, but when the cloud of smoke hovered over

Michael and Saoirse, he was amazed. This wasn't a natural phenomenon like the eclipse, this was something else, something preternatural, unreal. Amir just had no idea if it was something good or something like him.

As the fog began to twist and descend, Saoirse grabbed Michael even tighter, but Jean-Paul could tell by their expressions that this wasn't something harmful. They weren't afraid of what was happening; it was something they expected. "Go!" Jean-Paul shouted. Stunned, Nakano didn't realize that Jean-Paul was ordering Amir to get on with his mission and find The Well. He thought his boyfriend was screaming at him to leave.

"No!" Kano shouted back. "I'm not going anywhere without you!" What happened next would make that proclamation a difficult one for Nakano to carry out.

When Michael and Saoirse were almost completely enclosed within the fog, Jean-Paul leapt forward and into the mist. On reflex, Nakano imitated his boyfriend's actions and sprang toward the gray mass, reaching out his hand to try and latch on to Jean-Paul's arm. His target, however, proved to be as elusive as the tendrils of smoke that wisped about his face. Using his free hand, Jean-Paul effortlessly pushed Nakano away and saw him fall onto the hard sand a moment before he disappeared completely into the fog. Astonished, Nakano watched the gray cage start to rise off the ground, his eyes averting from the apparition only when he noticed Ronan looking down at him, his fangs bared, his expression filled with contempt. But Nakano didn't care. Nothing his one-time boyfriend could say or do mattered to him. He had to deal with someone else. And so did Ronan.

Jumping up, Nakano grabbed hold of the fog that was now as hard as stone. Using every ounce of strength he had, he punched, punched, punched at the gray rock, chipping away at its surface, determined to burrow a hole inside.

Phaedra had other ideas. Spinning around, slowly at first, the hardened fog soon became a twister and Nakano spun with it, his body horizontal, his grunts, his cries, cutting through the cyclone's wind. One by one Kano's fingers slipped and separated from the rock. He tried to dig his fingernails into stone to maintain his hold, but it was no use. Soon he was flying wildly into the almost complete darkness to crash-land about a mile from the shoreline. Ronan would have tried to catch him to break his fall if he hadn't seen Amir run into the ocean. He didn't want Nakano to get hurt, but he had to protect The Well. That was, after all, why it had called him here.

"Listen to me carefully, my child," The Well had said. "Enemies are drawing near and I need your help."

My help? Ronan felt he had been lifted from a nightmare and placed within the center of a miracle. He had just buried Dr. MacCleery in a clearing in The Forest, buried a man who died simply because he was trying to be a guardian to the students at Double A, and now The Well was seeking his assistance. It was unprecedented and even though he had never heard The Well's beautiful voice speak to him directly before, he immediately knew that it belonged to his life force. "Anything," Ronan replied, his voice hushed and filled with humility. "I will do anything to protect you and our people."

When The Well replied, Ronan could hear the pride in its voice. "I knew I could count on you, Ronan. All of Atlantis can count on your devotion."

Ronan didn't need to speak. The Well knew what he was thinking. "Don't worry, child. Your sister and Michael will be protected."

Greatly relieved that his commitment to preserve The Well would not result in any harm coming to Michael or Saoirse, Ronan was ready to do whatever was asked of him. After hearing his instructions, he had been confident he would succeed. Now watching Amir swim toward the horizon, he wasn't so sure.

Sprinting barefooted down the beach, the sand spewing out at his sides, Ronan entered the sea, not even noticing the ice-cold temperature of the water. Without breaking his stride, he dove into the air, his body one long, muscular line, and he remained suspended for a few moments before plunging into the ocean after Amir.

It was then that the moon overtook the sun and the world was plunged into an unnatural darkness.

chapter 23

Michael thought he heard Ronan's voice. He listened harder. Nothing, no update as to his whereabouts, no reassurance that he was all right, no apology. All he heard was Saoirse's nervous, rapid breathing behind him and Jean-Paul slowly inhaling, then exhaling, in front. Every few seconds he could feel a hot stream of air float over his face. Several days ago the sensation would have been enticing, tempting, like the desire to reach out and pluck a piece of forbidden fruit from the vine. Now it merely filled him with disgust and disappointment. It was exactly how he felt about Ronan.

Why did he lie to me again? Why does he constantly make me feel like an idiot? Michael wanted answers; he wanted to know why he wasn't here with him in the blackness of the fog so he could scream at him. Pound his fists into him. Throw his arms around him so Ronan would know how thankful he was that he was safe.

Stop it! Stop thinking about Ronan and concentrate on shielding Saoirse from Jean-Paul in case he attacks in this confined space. He hasn't made a move, but he simply can't be trusted. That's what Michael told himself because as long as he and Saoirse were locked in the fog with Jean-Paul, they couldn't waste time hoping that Ronan would rescue them. They would have to rely on themselves.

As he swam deeper into the ocean, Ronan forced himself to push thoughts of Michael and Saoirse out of his mind. The Well had sworn that they would be safe and he had no choice but to believe that. He knew The Well could do many things; lie was not one of them. It was just so hard being separated from those he loved, he wanted to be with them, especially Michael, just for a moment, just so he would know that Ronan was doing something wonderful, something important, and that he had not abandoned him, he would never, ever abandon him. But in the darkness, it was hard not to have doubts. Surrounded by the black, impenetrable water, it was hard not to feel scared.

Imogene stopped singing when everything turned black. She was afraid that her world was changing again, that she was dying and maybe this time she would be dragged into hell. She reached out and was grateful to feel Brania hold her shaking hand, put her arm around her shoulder, and promise that everything would be all right. She wasn't sure she believed it, but it was comforting to hear nonetheless. "There's nothing to worry about now," Brania said softly to her newfound ward. "It's only the moon playing a trick on the sun."

Using her vampiric vision, Brania could see that her words

were calming Imogene. She was still nervous, wary, but she was accepting the fact that she had a new guardian, a new mentor who would treat her with kindness and compassion, like a parent should. She could sense that Imogene knew she wouldn't use her as a pawn, collateral, a way to make sure her unpleasant tasks were completed without Brania having to get her hands dirty. Unlike her father and Edwige, and, for the most part, Vaughan, Brania was used to getting her hands filthy, which is why she wasn't afraid when Nurse Radcliff burst into the crypt, begging for blood.

"Give me the child!" the nurse screamed through the darkness. "I need to feed while the sun is black!"

Rubbing Imogene's shoulder reassuringly, Brania slowly stood up in the coffin and watched the slovenly nurse practically hyperventilate as she followed the curious scent of Imogene's blood, a unique mixture, half life and half death. She bent down, took Imogene's still-shaking hand and kissed it. "Mother will be right back."

Nurse Radcliff was so delirious from the intoxicating and unusual smell of Imogene's blood that she actually thought Brania was stepping out of the way to give her a wide berth to feed. When she saw Brania's face more clearly, she understood her mistake. The girl was unrecognizable, her fangs as sharp as stilettos and her outrage as black as the sun.

The first slap against her face took the nurse by surprise; the second made her realize Brania was not going to make it easy for her to feed; after the third, she decided she needed to fight back. Scurrying on the floor, Nurse Radcliff grabbed Brania's ankle and swung her body into the cold, notched wall. For a fledgling vampire, she was surprisingly powerful and had learned how to corral her new strength faster than most. However, she lacked experience and that's why Brania was able to quickly get the upper hand.

Wiping away some rock dust that clung to her chin, Brania grabbed the nurse by her throat, cringing when she felt her sharp nails penetrate the clammy skin near her shoulder. She hurled the nurse forward and heard a sucking noise as her nails withdrew from her plump flesh. When the ground shook, she knew the nurse's back had rammed into the other side of the crypt. With one eye watching Imogene cowering inside the coffin, Brania swiftly ran to Nurse Radcliff's side before she could get up. Unfortunately, it was what the nurse was expecting her to do.

When Brania hunched over to grab the nurse's shoulders and hoist her up so she could finish her off, she was only partially successful. On her knees, Nurse Radcliff took the rock that was concealed in her hand and swung her arm overhead, bashing it into Brania's temple with such force that Brania spun around, arms wide, free, useless, and slammed onto the stone floor. Breathing hard, Nurse Radcliff watched Brania's motionless body for several moments, remembering what David had said about the importance of reveling in each victory. Eager for another celebration, the nurse cocked her head to the side so her eyes could fall on the young girl too afraid to leave her coffin.

Even though she was protected by the darkness, Nurse Radcliff crouched low to the ground and moved toward Imogene stealthily. Imogene couldn't see, but she sensed a presence coming toward her and she knew it wasn't Brania, it smelled sickly, sour. When she felt a hand grab her knee, she kicked her leg out and scrambled into a corner of the coffin. She knew she was no longer safe, but she didn't have the courage to leave. She would simply have to pray that Brania would protect her, that she would be true to her word. She was.

"Don't touch my child!!"

The force of the words was nothing compared to the force of Brania's fist striking the side of Nurse Radcliff's face, so strong that her cheekbone splintered underneath the skin, fragments of bone pierced her flesh, causing her to howl in agony. Brania ignored the nurse's pleas for mercy. Any feelings of empathy, compassion, were lost in the confusing rage that swirled around her brain and her heart, the rage against her father, his injustice, his duplicity. Killing the nurse wouldn't be as satisfying as killing her father, but it would be a start.

Lifting the nurse like an overstuffed rag doll, Brania held her up high so she could get a good look at her victim. She wanted to see her fear, she wanted her to be fully aware that there was no escaping the horror that was about to befall her. Nurse Radcliff understood. She also understood the ramifications of Brania's impending actions. "You'll burn in hell for killing your own kind!"

"Where do you think I've lived for the past two centuries?!"

Those were the last words Nurse Radcliff heard before her body was hurled into the air, stopping only when a long, jagged rock pierced her back, splicing through her heart, and she erupted in flames.

Stepping into the coffin, Brania sat behind Imogene and wrapped her arms around her as the crackling fire warmed their skin. Thankful that her fierce protector brought comforting light back to the crypt, Imogene began to sing. Brania was so content, so joyful, that she hummed along.

Fritz wasn't joyful, but the two glasses of spiked punch he gulped down were making him feel much less despondent. He and Phaedra had planned on spending the denouement of the carnival together. When the sun was completely black, Fritz had planned on caressing the soft skin on the back of her neck, twirling his fingers through her falling curls, and kissing her more deeply than usual, but all those plans were shattered now that Phaedra had decided not to show up, now that she had chosen not to be with him.

Stuck in between Ciaran and Alexei, a part of the crowd of students and faculty watching the eclipse from within St. Sebastian's, Fritz felt like a complete loser. The only way he knew how to shake that feeling was to have another drink. And to make sure he didn't drink alone.

Fritz poured some whiskey from his flask into Ciaran's plastic cup. "Now taste that."

"What is it?" Ciaran asked.

"Don't worry, mate," Fritz advised. "It's Irish, you'll like it."

Ciaran could smell the alcohol before he lifted the glass to his mouth and hesitated. He had no idea what was happening to his sister or to Michael or where Ronan was, he attempted to contact Edwige, but she was nowhere to be found either. He tried not to think about what could be taking place because he had no power to stop it. He was the human, the limited one; they were the ones with unnatural gifts. The pungent smell of the whiskey made him wince, but that first whiff grew more tempting. Besides, there was nothing he could do to help them; there was nothing he could do to make their lives better or safer, and it was time he understood that. Maybe he would continue with his experiments, then again maybe not. He decided right then and there that he would only resume his research if it's what he wanted to do, not at the behest of some lying headmaster or some troublesome sister. From now on, he wanted to put himself first, think about his own happiness, and what better way to commemorate that resolution than with a drink.

Coughing, Ciaran felt the rough liquid erupt in his stomach and gurgle up into his throat like a volcano. Even so, he took another drink until his cup was empty. Fritz smiled approvingly and he smiled back. His head felt like it was on fire, his lips weirdly numb and burning at the same time, and his mind slowly pushing thoughts of his family aside so he could join in with the rest of his mates and sing. Fritz, as always, led the group in a rousing version of the alternative lyrics to Double A's alma mater, written long ago by some student who believed that not all aspects of education needed to be revered.

> *O weathered kings that rot below this prison*
> *we call home*
> *Immoral creatures, wankers' foes, protect us*
> *as we roam*
> *O'er four long years 'n more for some, with*
> *soddin' saints from A to Z*
> *Guide us so we don't return, 'til each bloomin'*
> *one is free*
> *From this shafted ground, this bloody place,*
> *Archangel Academy.*

Laughing uncontrollably, Ciaran and Fritz were happy to forget their problems if only for a little while. They knew they shouldn't be drinking, they knew it didn't solve anything, they knew it wasn't right, but it was only a little after twelve noon and the sky looked blacker than midnight. Really, who knew what was right and wrong any longer?

Ronan did. He knew that if Amir went any farther into the blue-black water, it would be the wrong move and he would never return. When Amir paused, Ronan made one last attempt to go after him and bring him back to the water's surface and away from places he had no right to be.

Like a missile with only one purpose, Ronan lowered his head, bent his legs, and pushed back to propel himself deeper into the ocean. His webbed feet flipped rapidly, helping him to gain even more speed, so in no time, he was able to see Amir clearly only a few feet in front of him. Amir may have felt the rush of water swoop past him, but he was too fascinated by The Well that shimmered at him in the distance to see or hear Ronan approach him from behind. All he heard was David.

"You found it!" David shrieked, watching the action alone in his anteroom. "You've found their damned Well!"

David's triumphant cries rang in his ears. He was so close, he just had to get a little bit closer, he had to prove to Headmaster that he was worthy, he had to solidify his place in his people's history, so that for all eternity the name Amir Bhattacharjee would be synonymous with victory, heroism, and the dawning of the destruction of the water vamps. Unfortunately, Ronan was not about to let that happen.

Before Amir could even move his arms, they were thrown up over his head as Ronan grabbed him in an old-fashioned wrestling hold, his arms underneath Amir's shoulders, his webbed hands pressing against the back of his head. Startled, Amir began to twist and turn his body to free himself, but Ronan was too strong. Amir felt himself being pulled away from The Well, being forced to rise, and he pressed his arms against Ronan's, but his lean arms were no match for Ronan's muscled frame.

"Let go of him!" David roared.

Encouraged by David's voice, Amir sunk his fangs into Ronan's forearm, biting at his flesh like a rabid dog. Crying out in pain, his scream swallowed up by the ocean, Ronan ripped his arm from Amir's mouth, a trail of blood the only thing that now connected the two boys.

Free, Amir swam with renewed energy toward The Well, David's passionate voice pushing him forward. He was going to do it, he was going to ensure his place in history, when suddenly he felt something like a riptide engulf him, toss him to the side. He thought it was Ronan, but one quick glance behind him and he saw that he was alone.

Undaunted, he started to swim again, but felt another surge crash into him, this time into his chest, harder, with more force, and for the first time, he thought he wasn't going to reach his destiny. Even if he thought he would die, Amir still would have agreed to this mission to ensure his legacy, but he was immortal, he couldn't die, anyway. David would never put such a loyal, obedient follower in harm's way. When the water started to churn at his feet, he didn't realize that's exactly where he had been placed.

The same voice that told Ronan to come to The Well now ordered him to stay back, to come no farther or risk death. He had done his job; he had made sure the enemy entered the hallowed ground alone, and now The Well would make sure the vampire understood he was trespassing and would have to pay the price.

Ronan watched in awe as The Well began to coil and bend in shape. It wasn't the real Well at all, but a hallucination, a decoy, a mirage that led Amir farther into the depths of the ocean to make him think that he had found their life force. How fitting that during David's phony Carnival for the Black Sun, it was The Well that had performed the most amazing trick, the most cunning act of deception. Yes, it was cruel; yes, Amir was about to lose his life, but first and foremost The Well and all its descendants, all the creatures of Atlantis, would be protected. Forcing himself to swim toward the surface of the water, Ronan had never felt more proud of his race.

As he was being sucked lower and lower into the belly of the ocean, spinning wildly within the grip of the whirlpool, Amir felt the sting of salt water on his tongue and soon became aware that the air in his lungs was being replaced with water. *Now, David, take me out of this now, he silently shouted.* He had no idea if David could hear him, the rush of the water whirling around him was so loud, he couldn't even hear himself, but David had to hear him. He was the headmaster, their leader, he could hear everything, he could *do* anything. Then why wasn't he swooping in to pull him out? Why wasn't he freeing him and placing him where he belonged, next to David on his very own throne? Why was he letting the darkness win?!

"Because sometimes the darkness is too powerful."

That's what Edwige told herself. That was the response she heard in her mind when she asked why she was here in the darkness instead of at her children's side. She wasn't feeling guilty, she was merely curious. She knew that her place was next to her children, to try and keep them safe, help them fight whatever game David was playing, and not in a strange bed making love. But that's where she was and she only assumed it was because the darkness had finally proven too strong to resist.

She didn't realize it, but she physically felt just as Amir did. She felt as if she was being pulled against her will deeper and deeper into an unknown realm that she didn't want to enter, that she didn't want to witness, and yet it was her fate, it was a place where she was destined to go. She, however, was determined not to go there alone. If she concentrated very hard, if she narrowed her eyes a little bit more, Vaughan looked just like Saxon.

Shielding his face from the alarming vision, Ronan shot through the surface of the water. Below, Amir's body was shredded into a million tiny pieces, each one jutting into the darkened sea like a ray of light. The explosion was so strong that it rose from the bowels of the ocean and nipped at Ronan's feet, so strong that it reached out to everything that was connected to Amir, including David. With no warning and an unmerciful roar, his mirror, his window into the lives of his followers, shattered along with Amir.

Splinters of glass showered down upon David like rain, cutting into his exposed flesh, his hands, ripping open his suit. One pointed piece of glass fell slowly, almost deliberately, slicing the side of his face through the center of his eye down his cheek to the curve of his jaw. As the blood began to trickle from his open wounds, into his eyes, he fell to his knees blindly, the remnants of the mirror crunching underneath him, and prayed to Zachariel for leniency. "Heal me, heavenly Father," David begged. "Restore my vision. Allow me to serve in your holy image until you have been avenged, until our purpose has been achieved!"

David shivered as he felt the hand of Zachariel touch the crown of his head and he felt his wounds ebb into his skin, felt the two disjointed pieces of his eye fuse back together, felt the blood lift and disappear. Such a wonderful, charitable god, David thought, but Zachariel was not through bestowing gifts upon his most loyal disciple. If David was to win this war, he needed every advantage. He felt Zachariel's touch travel from his head to the middle of his spine and then he knew what Amir felt like just before his body exploded.

"Ahhhh!!!!" The pain that ripped through David's body was agonizing. It was as if two jackhammers were placed on opposite sides of his back and were drilling holes through his skin, past his muscle, into his bone, until they emerged through his chest. "Ahhhhh!!!" David's scream flooded the room. He wanted to form words, but his mind wasn't functioning, it was only processing the arrival of a beautiful, breathtaking pain.

When he felt the first wing rip out from his shoulder blade, he lurched forward, palms crashing into the floor, splintering the wooden slats, he barely had enough strength not to collapse entirely. The second was even worse, and the excruciating pain sent him flying forward, facedown onto the floor. He stayed there, fists clenched, eyes shut tight, as he felt the wings lengthen and grow until they took up almost the entire space of the anteroom. By the time his wings started to flap gently, stirring a cooling breeze in the room, the pain was a memory and David realized the transformation was complete.

Standing up, he saw that Zachariel had restored the mirror. He no longer saw Amir or the rest of his subjects, but he could see his new glorious self. David smiled as he saw two magnificent, powerful black wings flutter behind his massive shoulders. Finally he looked exactly like the archangel he so devoutly worshipped.

Inside, darkness was given more power to reign even as the first rays of light returned to resurrect the outside world.

chapter 24

Whether light returns after an evening of darkness or after an hour of unnatural shadow, it is welcomed. It's a reminder that no matter how bleak, no matter how disheartening the world might look, there's always hope. Standing on the shore of Inishtrahull Island, wet and exhausted, Ronan had to remind himself of that when he saw the fog evaporate completely to reveal Michael standing in front of Saoirse, but dangerously close to Jean-Paul.

"Get away from them!"

Jean-Paul turned his head so quickly, the long strands of his hair whipped out and brushed against Michael's cheek, causing him to flinch, reel his head back so it looked to Ronan as if he had been struck. Without warning, Ronan sprang toward them, his face contorted into a warrior's scowl, fangs bared, only one thought raging through his mind: Kill Jean-Paul before he can hurt the two people he loved the most. Michael had other ideas.

"No!"

Stepping in front of Jean-Paul, Michael caught Ronan's arm at the wrist and held it tightly. Ronan tried to break free, but couldn't. Michael's grip was too strong, stronger than ever before, and more than just his increased physical strength, there was something going on in his mind, something that was not going to allow Ronan to get past him.

Confused, Ronan stared into Michael's eyes, the only thing he recognized was the color. He was here to save Michael from whatever this French git was planning to do to him and Saoirse, and this is his reaction? This is how he expresses his gratitude? *What the bloody hell happened up there in that fog?* Ronan thought.

"Nothing happened!" Michael shouted.

So you can read my mind when it suits you? "That's not what it looks like to me!"

Michael couldn't believe this. Ronan was the one who up and disappeared, leaving him alone to keep Saoirse safe, and instead of thanking him, he was jealous, he was accusing him of cheating on him while trapped in Phaedra's fog with Saoirse clutching his hand the entire time. It was absurd! "Are you calling me a liar?!"

Yes! No! I don't know!! Ronan didn't know what to think; all he knew was that Michael found Jean-Paul attractive and that he had been alone with him before and now the jerk was here inches from Michael's face. He couldn't imagine he would've done anything, especially not with his sister so close, but still, why did he have to be here? Why did anyone else have to be here? Why couldn't everyone just leave them alone!?

Ronan yanked his arm away so suddenly and with such

force that Michael stumbled back a few steps. If Jean-Paul hadn't grabbed him by the waist to steady him, he would've fallen onto the beach. "Don't touch him!!" Ronan ordered.

"You should not treat him like you own him!" Jean-Paul yelled back.

"I don't *own* him!" Ronan cried. "I love him!"

"Eef that's zee way you water vamps express your love," Jean-Paul said quietly, "I am so very happy I am not one of you."

"Trust me, Frenchie, so are we!" Ronan shouted.

For a few moments no one spoke, but no one let their fangs recede either. Jean-Paul, Ronan, and even Michael were still ready for battle if it came to that. By the way Michael was glaring at Ronan, it was unclear if they would be fighting as a team or against each other. *Why is he mad at me? What the hell have I done now?* Ronan couldn't figure it out and he knew he wouldn't get any answers until he and Michael were alone. Unfortunately, Inishtrahull Island was about to get a little more crowded.

"Jean-Paul!"

The sun had returned with such strength, such vigor that they had to squint in order to see Nakano run toward them. He was running so quickly, they could hear him panting like a wild dog from fifty yards away, the sand flying out at his feet mixing with the sunlight to surround him and almost make it look like Kano was floating toward them. They just didn't know if he was so eager to reach them to fight or to re-unite with his boyfriend. Once he arrived, Nakano didn't know either.

He looked at Jean-Paul, beautiful as ever, and Jean-Paul was staring back at him, but his expression was unreadable, practically stoic. He didn't know what was going on under-neath those breathtaking features. Was he happy to see him? Was he happy to see that he was alive after he jumped into the fog and left him alone? Or would he prefer that he curl up on the beach somewhere and die so he could be alone with David?

He turned to look at Ronan and he felt like a merciless hand was squeezing his heart, squeezing until it burst and it was useless, dead, he was so overwhelmed with feelings of jealousy. He looked so smug, so condescending with his boyfriend at his side, the boyfriend he chose over him, and that freak of a sister behind him. Why did Ronan have everything? Why did he have a loving boyfriend, a family, friends who would fight alongside him, and why did Nakano have nothing? Why was everything that Nakano ever had, ever wanted, taken away from him?

The scream roared in his head, but Nakano didn't allow it to seep out of his mouth. He kept it contained, kept it to himself so no one would know how distraught he was, how lost. He wanted to destroy, he wanted to unclench his fists and rip the flesh from their bodies. First Michael, then the girl, then sink his fangs into Ronan's neck, his thick, muscular neck, and suck out every last drop of his blood. He wanted to connect to something, he wanted to latch on to someone, to as many people as possible, and destroy them, make them feel the pain that he was feeling, the absolute anguish that was living and breathing just underneath his flesh. But instead he did nothing.

When he turned back to Jean-Paul, he was ecstatic that he was still looking at him. He was interested; he hadn't turned away. He had so many questions that he wanted to ask him. He heard the words in his head, the sentences were formed, they were ready to be spoken, but as usual, he was afraid, so he remained silent. He didn't want to upset Jean-Paul, he didn't want to destroy the best relationship that he had ever had. *That's right, Ronan, what you and I had was nothing compared to this, this is the best!* It didn't matter about David, none of that mattered, nothing mattered as long as Jean-Paul kept looking at him, looking in his direction. And reaching out his hand to him.

"Eet eez time for us to go," Jean-Paul said.

Nakano put his hand into Jean-Paul's, and his instinct was to pull back, let go. He felt no warmth, no comfort, only a hand, but he stomped on his intuition and held on to Jean-Paul anyway. Out of the corner of his eye he saw Ronan and Michael standing so close to each other they were practically one person, and his crushed heart felt another sting. Ignore it, Nakano told himself, ignore the questions, ignore the doubts, and squeeze Jean-Paul's hand harder. *All that matters is the connection, all that matters is that I'm not alone.*

And physically he wasn't. But when they started to leave, Jean-Paul turned back to get one last glimpse of Michael, one last look at the boy's innocent face. Michael wasn't looking back at him, but he also wasn't looking at Ronan. Jean-Paul smiled as he pulled Nakano closer to him and they sped off, practically flying over the dunes. The lingering thought as he departed was that maybe Michael's connection to his supposed soul mate wasn't as strong as it appeared to be either.

Playing the role of the strong, silent type was not in Saoirse's nature. She had remained silent for as long as she could, longer than she thought possible, but she had finally had enough. Being kidnapped by Amir, not knowing if she was going to be killed or turned into something vile like those other types of vampires, learning firsthand how incredible Phaedra's powers were, it had all been too much. Saoirse didn't like to take life seriously; she preferred to ignore ugly truths and remain blissfully ignorant, but she suddenly realized there were moments when you had to grow up, act like an adult, and take responsibility for your own actions. At least her version of taking responsibility. "This is all your fault!"

Ronan stared at his sister in disbelief. "My fault!? How the bloody hell did you come to that conclusion?"

Saoirse didn't have to explain herself. Michael did it for her. "You should've told me, Ronan. You should've told me about your sister."

So that was it, that's the look that's been in his eyes, the look Ronan couldn't decipher. It was anger. "No one fully understands," Ronan explained. "I just . . . I didn't think it was important, I was trying . . ."

"Yeah, I know," Michael interrupted. "You were trying to protect me."

"Yes! That's exactly what I was trying to do!" Ronan screamed, louder than he had intended. He was tired of being judged for trying to shield the people he loved from danger. After seeing MacCleery's dead, mutilated body and now Amir, destroyed beyond recognition, his soul God knows where, he knew he was right, and he was not going to apologize. "If you had listened to me, maybe none of this would've happened! If you had just accepted the fact that this whole carnival was a bleedin' farce, you would've been on your guard, Michael, and you, Saoirse, wouldn't have allowed yourself to get kidnapped!"

Rolling her eyes, Saoirse waved a hand in her brother's face. "I didn't *allow* that twit to kidnap me."

"That twit is dead, Saorise!" Ronan shouted, grabbing his sister by the shoulders. "And so is Dr. MacLeery!"

"What?!" Michael cried. "How?!"

"Because they killed him!"

"Oh my God, no!" Michael cried.

Ronan answered Michael before turning back to his sister. "This isn't a game! This is why I didn't want you to come here in the first place!" A mixture of fear and anger flooded Ronan's body and he started to shake, Saoirse along with him. "They want to find The Well and destroy it, destroy us, and you being what you are makes you an easy target, don't you understand that?!"

Ronan didn't stop shaking his sister because her face had turned white or because he realized he might be hurting her, he stopped because he felt Michael's hand on his shoulder. His touch was soft, but undeniable, they were still connected, they were still linked. It was exactly the confirmation he needed to allow the anger to escape his body.

He looked at his sister and hugged her gently. He didn't understand what he was feeling, he was scared and proud and relieved all at the same time. Maybe it's because whatever he did helped keep her safe. By his following The Well's orders, she was unharmed at least for today. He knew there would be another attempt on her life, he knew that she didn't fully grasp what was happening around her, but that didn't matter right now. Right now all that mattered was getting her home safely. "Where's Phaedra?" he asked.

"I'm right here."

The voice materialized before the body did. When they turned around, they saw Phaedra walking down the coastline lazily as if she were daydreaming, letting the waves trip over her bare feet, her curls floating in the breeze. She looked like she was enjoying the return of the sun, soaking in the moment, instead of having just saved two people from uncertain danger, having just done an efemera's job.

When she got closer, Michael was the first to notice that her features were once again hazy, soft, not as defined as they had become, not as permanent. She had made a choice with this last transformation, a choice because of him, a choice that he knew might cost her a chance at experiencing love.

"I'm sorry," Michael said.

"Don't be," Phaedra replied, a tender smile on her lips. "I'm just like you. I am what I was born to be."

Understanding didn't make it any easier, and Michael still felt guilty. He wished there was a way that Phaedra could remain an efemera *and* fall in love with Fritz, to have the best of both worlds, but he knew that was impossible. The universe held lots of mystery, yet very little compromise. "If it's any consolation, I'm grateful," Michael said. "I don't know what would've happened if you hadn't shown up today."

Phaedra was feeling the same way. "I'm grateful to you too."

"Me?" Michael asked. "Why?"

Taking hold of his hands, her touch light as a feather, Phaedra replied, "If I hadn't shown up here, I would never have known real love." Her cheeks started to shimmer with the most beautiful, translucent tears, almost like silver rain. "If Fritz ever asks, if he ever wonders," she said, "please tell him that I did love him, I loved him with a full almost-human heart."

Saoirse's jaw dropped. Could this day possibly get any worse? "You're leaving?"

Although she smiled at the young girl with deep affection, there was a hint of envy in her eyes. Saoirse very shortly would get to experience all the emotions Phaedra never would, all the joy, the love, and even the heartache. "Yes, I'm being called back home."

Michael felt his own tears threaten to fall. This couldn't be happening, this shouldn't be happening, not after everything they'd been through, not after everything Phaedra had given to him. "You can't leave!" Michael protested. "Please, I still need you, we all do."

She touched his cheek and it felt like breath. "No, you don't," Phaedra replied. "You have each other and you have your own strength, that's all you need." When Phaedra wrapped her arms around Michael, he knew he was being enveloped by more than just his friend's touch; he felt his mother's love. "I've fulfilled your mother's wishes and now I must go. I must return to the Holding Place and wait until I hear someone else's prayers."

Once again, understanding didn't make it any easier. In fact it made it even harder, and Michael didn't want to let go of his friend. Phaedra's place in his life, on this earth, was temporary. He only hoped she understood how grateful he was that their paths, however briefly, intertwined. "Thank you" was all Michael could say through his tears. The only reason he was able to let go of Phaedra's embrace was because now he felt Ronan's hand on his shoulder.

Looking at Ronan, Phaedra knew she was leaving Michael in good hands. They would always squabble, they wouldn't always agree, and it might take them some time to completely understand how important their coupling was, how important it was that The First and The Other be united for all eternity, but she knew their love was strong enough to overcome any obstacle and accept their destiny. Just as she had come to accept hers.

"There's only one thing left for me to do before I go," Phaedra announced. "And that's make sure you, little lady, get home safely."

Before Ronan let go of Saoirse's hand, he instructed, "Leave her with Ciaran. She'll be safe with him."

Phaedra nodded. "Yes, she will."

Another ending, another person leaving his life for good. Michael wasn't sure he could take it. He wasn't sure he could watch her leave without trying one last time to make her stay, but the choice wasn't his. Phaedra had made her decision.

"Good-bye, my friends."

Her final words hung in the air even as her body lost its

shape and dematerialized into swirling wisps of fog that encircled Saoirse, gray ribbons that spun round and round, in-
terconnecting and growing in size until they encased the girl
completely and she disappeared from view. Together, Michael
and Ronan watched as the gray mass hardened and then rose
high above the beach, into the sunlight, and then toward the
horizon to return to Double A. Michael found it incredible
that this was the last time he would ever see Phaedra. When
he looked over at Ronan, he found it even more incredible
that his boyfriend had lied to him yet again.

"I thought you said there weren't going to be any more secrets between us?" Michael asked.

Staring at the sand, Ronan blew out a long breath and
replied, "Isn't that what you're doing to me?"

*What's he talking about? What's he trying to do, turn this
around, make it like it's my fault?* "I don't have any secrets
from you, Ronan, and you know that."

Smiling wistfully, Ronan looked at Michael and asked,
"What about the face in The Well?"

A grotesque image filled Michael's mind, distorted, disturbed, the image that he saw in his dream and when they
fed. "I told you I don't know what that face is," Michael explained. "I . . . I think it has something to do with David. He's
up to no good, you know that. I don't know, maybe part of
his plan is to separate us." Ronan didn't say anything, but
Michael could tell by the look on his face that he didn't agree
with him. "Then maybe it's my father. He's proven that he's
evil, or Jean-Paul! Maybe he didn't hurt us, but he's still one
of Them, he's still against us!"

Ronan fought the urge to reach out and grab Michael's
hand, feel his tender skin. "Haven't you figured out yet that
the face in The Well is yours?"

Horrified, Michael stepped back. "You think that disgusting face is mine?!"

"It's a part of you," Ronan replied. "A part that you're keeping hidden from me and from yourself."

Waving his arms wildly, pacing this way, then that, Michael couldn't believe what he was hearing. His boyfriend thought he was repulsive; he thought he was revolting! This is what Phaedra left him with, a boyfriend who thought the absolute worst of him! Ronan was also a boyfriend who wouldn't be pushed away.

"Do you trust me?" Ronan asked.

Frowning, Michael didn't trust himself, how in the world could he trust anyone else?

Holding out his hand, Ronan asked another question. "Will you let me show you the truth?"

Tentatively, Michael touched his hand and it felt the way it always did, like cool water over rock-hard stone. Ronan hadn't changed, so maybe Michael had. "Yes."

Seconds later they were kneeling before The Well. Michael peered over the ledge into the still water and held Ronan's hand tighter for reassurance. He didn't have to, Ronan was never going to let go. Suddenly darkness flooded the cave. Michael couldn't see Ronan, but he could still feel his hand securely holding his own. The water shimmered until an image appeared on the surface, the same image Michael saw here before, the same image he saw in his bedroom window so many months ago, in his visions and in his dreams, the same one Phaedra saw in the fun-house mirror, the image of a distorted face, the physical personification of some emotional struggle. Softly, a wave rose and fell within The Well and when the water's surface was once again smooth, Michael saw that that image was his own reflection.

Terrified, he stepped away from The Well and the light returned. There was nothing left for him to see. "That's me!" Michael cried. "That disgusting thing is me!"

"No, love," Ronan corrected, grabbing Michael's other

hand. "It's only a part of you, a part you need to face so you can set it free."

Michael wanted to run; he wanted to get the hell away from the cave and The Well and even Ronan, but Ronan wasn't letting go, he wasn't giving up. When Michael saw the determination in Ronan's eyes, he knew he couldn't give up either, not on them or himself. He simply had to tell the truth, confess what had been on his mind for months. "I love you, Ronan, I do. I love what I've become, but . . . but it all happened so quickly, so much has happened so quickly!" Gasping for breath, Michael squeezed Ronan's hands tighter. "My mother dying, my grandmother, my grandfather wishing that I was the one who died, learning what my father did to my mother!" There were no tears now, only strength, conviction, honesty. "Moving halfway around the world, becoming a vampire, falling in love with you!"

Their hands slipped away from each other and even though there was very little space between them, it felt huge. "Do you still love me, Michael?"

Without a moment's hesitation, Michael answered, "Yes."

"Do you have any regrets?"

Again, Michael answered instantly, his mind finally understanding what had always been in his heart and his mind. "No, none. But like I said, it all happened so fast, I gave myself over to you before I gave myself a chance to get to know the new me."

Turning away, Ronan murmured the last line of the short story that reminded him so much of Michael. "But no man dared look upon his face, for it was like the face of an angel."

When Michael turned Ronan's face back to him, he saw the fear in his eyes. "The problem is, Ronan, I'm not an angel."

Ronan no longer cared if he made a fool of himself. He had to make Michael understand, he had to make him feel what was in his heart. Holding the sides of Michael's face, his words drenched with emotion. "You're an angel to me, love; you are forever beautiful and forever mine." Ronan had to stop to swallow hard before he could continue. "That is, if you still want to be."

Never had Michael felt so loved, never had he felt so conflicted. "Yes, yes, Ronan, I do want to be forever yours, but I also want you to be forever mine." Ronan was nodding in agreement, but Michael wasn't sure he understood. "I want to live an eternity not in your shadow, not looking up at you. I want to live alongside you, right next to you as your equal."

This time when Ronan nodded, he did understand. "You *are* my equal, Michael. I'm sorry if I made you doubt that or if I acted as if you weren't." Wrapping Michael up in his arms, Ronan confessed, "For all my experience, I guess this is new to me too."

Their kiss was passionate, filled with apology, expectation, desire, and continued long after they were sitting, side by side, on the beach. Michael and Ronan weren't the only ones to emerge from the darkness with a different, clearer perspective. All across Double A and even throughout Eden, people were looking into the sunlight and saw change.

In St. Sebastian's, Fritz somehow knew he had lost his first love. He felt the pain and the confusion of his loss, but as he put his arm around Ciaran's shoulders, a crowd of students laughing and singing around them, they each knew that they had made a new friend.

In the crypt near The Forest, strands of sunlight filtered into the space, commingling with the dying embers of Nurse Radcliff's flames. Brania put her arm around Imogene and they both knew they had found purpose, two members of the undead had found a reason to go on living.

In a sun-drenched bedroom in a hotel in Eden, Vaughan

put his arm around Edwige's bare shoulder, and they knew they hadn't found love, hardly, but they had at least found companionship.

And in the apartment over their secret meeting room, Jean-Paul put his arms around Nakano, and they both knew their relationship was over, but until they chose to face the truth, until they each found something better, they still had a connection.

When the first raindrops started to fall, Michael stopped only to look out at the ocean, watch water meet water like soul had met soul, and took it as a sign of confirmation. He and Ronan first met in the rain, it was only fitting that their love should be renewed during a rain shower. "You know, Jean-Paul once told me that I was a better man than my father," Michael said. "He was wrong. I'm only half a man without you."

Grinning mischievously, Ronan added, "That's 'cause Frenchie's a right daft bloke."

"Oh really," Michael replied, twisting his voice into a bad British accent. "Can Frenchmen be blokes?"

"If I say so, love," Ronan said with a laugh that quickly turned serious. "I have to ask again, did anything ever happen between you and..."

"Never, nothing," Michael assured him. "Yeah, I found him pretty hot, but even at my lowest, I would never betray you or The Well. I'm aware of the consequences." Ronan responded by kissing the palm of Michael's hand and held it to his cheek. "Plus, have you looked at your own reflection lately, Mister? You are smokin', Ronan. And I've finally found you a nickname! Smokin' Ronan, 'cause you know you're hot."

Laughing and kissing Michael at the same time, Ronan said, "And you're daft, but I love you."

Michael watched the rain caress Ronan's face, making him

look exactly like he did the night he first fell in love with him. "I love you too."

"I didn't want to admit it to myself," Ronan whispered, "but I was afraid this might be the end for us."

It was Michael's turn to kiss Ronan. "There'll never be an end for us," he answered, his voice unmarred by doubt. "This is just a new beginning."

They looked up when they heard the meadowlark's song, *da-da-DAH-da, da-da-da*, and smiled, agreeing that the familiar melody was a benediction, approval that they were both exactly where they were supposed to be. They had no idea the lark was trying to warn them that they were being watched by a man with an archangel's wings who was flying through the clouds high above them. But even though they couldn't see David, they were no longer children. They knew that danger lurked just on the other side of the rain.

As it continued to shower, quietly, tenderly, Ronan held on to Michael's hand that was draped over his shoulder. "You know, there will be other attacks, probably more dangerous ones," he advised. "Now that David's made his wishes known, he won't stop just because he failed the first time out."

"With you by my side, love," Michael said, pulling Ronan closer into him, "I welcome the challenge."